TIES OF AFFECTION

*A contemporary romance
from this masterful storyteller*

Olivia Fletcher runs an eco-friendly house-cleaning firm in leafy Surrey. Olivia soon realizes why none of her employees want to clean for the eccentric Moorfield family: they are impossibly spoilt and demanding. Olivia, against her own advice, finds herself becoming emotionally attached to the family and soon her life as a single mother is further complicated by the role she begins to play within the Moorfield family.

TIES OF AFFECTION

Tessa Barclay

Severn House Large Print
London & New York

This first large print edition published 2009
in Great Britain and the USA by
SEVERN HOUSE PUBLISHERS LTD of
9-15 High Street, Sutton, Surrey, SM1 1DF.
First world regular print edition published 2008 by
Severn House Publishers Ltd., London and New York.

British Library Cataloguing in Publication Data

Barclay, Tessa, 1925-
  Ties of affection
  1. Love stories. 2. Large type books.
  I. Title
  823.9'14-dc22

ISBN-13: 978-0-7278-7788-8

Printed and bound in Great Britain by
MPG Books Ltd, Bodmin, Cornwall.

One

The crashing of brakes and the angry slamming of the car door foretold trouble. Olivia Fletcher sighed. The quiet afternoon, designed for dealing with tax and other unpleasant documents, was about to be lost.

From the parking area behind the row of shops came the sound of rapid footsteps. The back door opened, and Amy Gaines stormed in.

'That's it! An impossible family!' Amy's voice was high and strained. 'That tyrannical old woman was ordering me about as if I was a slave. I'm never setting foot in the house again!'

Her employer nodded in understanding. No use arguing. She'd have to find someone else willing to go as a house-help to Ashgrove, but the list of possibilities was growing thin. Amy was the fourth of her staff to be sent to the Moorfields' home, and the fourth to declare she was never going back.

'I know they're a difficult bunch—'

'Difficult? Libby, they're impossible! The old girl parades around as if she's Queen of the May, and the son, who does stage designs or whatever, slopes into the kitchen looking for breakfast after I just get it tidied up from their cookery attempts of the night before! Never says a word

5

you can call conversation, just grunts and groans. And the "spiritual" one – the one you sometimes see in the New Age shop in the High Street – she leaves seeds and stuff soaking – to make sprouts or something – and then she forgets them and they go horrid and make the place smell awful!'

'I know, I know. I'm sorry.' Libby had heard it all before. 'They just don't seem to live like other people—'

'You can say that again! I've spent four days trying to work so as to be as little in their way as I can, and then this dreadful old female tells me I ought to know my place!'

'Which one is that?'

'I think she's grandmother to the rest of them. "Grandee", they seem to call her. And that's what she is – a grandee! She actually ordered me to bring up her breakfast tray. I'm there to clean the house, not make her meals for her.' Amy thumped the desk with her fist. 'I'm not going back!

'No, I understand.'

Libby had sensed that what she called 'the Moorfield problem' was really going to come to a head one day soon. She should have found out more about them before she took them on as clients, she now realized. Alas, too late.

Libby ran a small house-cleaning firm from what had formerly been a shop in a side street of Weybridge. Her neat little office with its long-term planning chart and its blackboard with daily work schedules were on the ground floor, along with storage for the cleaning supplies and equipment. She and her little boy Frederick lived in the flat above. She'd been there a little over three years now, busy, sometimes anxious but, on the whole, happy enough.

It had never been her intention to get into the house-cleaning business. At college she'd studied Applied Arts, and had hoped to make a career in restoring antique furniture and perhaps becoming curator at a stately home. But falling in love rather too early and then deciding to have a baby too soon had meant postponing all that. Of course she'd given it up willingly. *In the future*, she'd kept saying to herself. *In the future I'll get back to doing what I really love.*

She still had hopes of doing it, one day. But the death of her life partner, Hugo, had changed all her plans.

Hugo – bright, generous, fun-loving Hugo – had been going much too fast, as usual, on his motorbike. Even before he was taken to hospital, it was too late to save him.

At first she'd been too broken to think about anything. She'd lived from day to day for a while, on social benefits, on little part-time jobs in local shops where they didn't mind her having the baby with her in the back room.

But a natural instinct to be up and doing something had asserted itself. Because she was still interested in the care of furniture, she'd answered an advertisement for full-time work as an office cleaner.

That had turned out to be night work – gruelling stuff. At first she'd hesitated because of the unsociable hours, but then she thought it might suit her. She wanted to be with her little son during the day time. So various reliable baby-sitters had taken care of Freddie while she was at work during the night: neighbours, women she'd come to know while serving in the small local shops.

It was hard and demanding work. She found the work routine in the deserted offices made her very tired, but she had a sturdy body – rather tall, strong-boned, with fair skin and light brown hair from some Viking ancestor perhaps. She found her new life a challenge, and met it with vigour and enthusiasm.

Soon it became clear to the firm supplying the office cleaners that not only was she a good worker, she also had organizing ability. She was promoted to lead a team and, later, several teams. Her wages increased, but it began to dawn on her that she could make more money by running a firm of her own.

After much debating with herself and worry about the financial risk, she launched her little enterprise. One or two of the kind-hearted souls who had been her babysitters formed the nucleus of her cleaning staff. She ran the business at first from her cramped flat in a terraced house, but as her services became more in demand she'd taken a lease on an empty shop with living accommodation above – not ideal, but when she compared it with her life just after Hugo's death, it was luxury.

Now her firm was fairly well known. House-care Helpers flourished because the area was full of rather fine old houses owned by rather well-off people, most of them anxious to be as 'green' as possible. Libby guaranteed that her firm would use organic cleaning materials as much as possible, and would be environmentally friendly in everything they did. They would also be reliable, discreet, and not intrusive. As she looked around her trim, efficient little office, she thought she'd kept her promises to her clients – until now.

Amy was still ranting on about the ill-mannered tribe at Ashgrove. 'And how many of them are there, that's what I want to know. Who are we supposed to take orders from? First bad-tempered old Grandee tells me to do something, then the dreamy one says, "No, no, you're interrupting my meditation," and next some tall bloke comes barging out of his office and says to be quiet, he's trying to work.'

'It's difficult, I know,' soothed Libby. When she had first been contacted by telephone, she'd received rather a favourable impression of the Moorfield family. Rosanne Moorfield, the woman Amy now called 'the dreamy one', was soft-spoken and hesitant. She'd broached the ecological aspect of housework at once.

'I understand from your advertisement that you ... I gather you don't use any harsh stuff ... chemicals, that sort of thing.'

'No, we're devoted to doing as little harm as possible to the health of our clients in their home and to the environment in general, Mrs Moorfield. Our aim is to—'

'You have to care for the background harmony in everyone's life,' said Rosanne Moorfield, taking up Libby's assurance without letting her finish. 'You *will* ensure that peace and serenity are preserved while you're at work, won't you?'

'Certainly. My helpers are trained to be unobtrusive—'

'And of course there's the garden to consider. The person you send – the gardener – must be in tune with nature, you know. I like the garden to be rather relaxed, not too much pruning or mowing, so that things can flourish there – butterflies, the blue-tits, and there's a heron that comes sometimes. He's really more interested in fishing in the canal, you know. Still, he likes our garden and I want him to keep visiting.'

'Of course. We have a man who undertakes most of the outdoor work. I can vouch for Jacob's considerate—'

'Good, well, I think that sounds all right. I think we should go ahead with this.'

On her visit of inspection, to get some idea of the extent of the work, Mrs Moorfield had not been present. Instead she met Philip Moorfield, who was by no means dreamy. He had accompanied her around the house with ill-concealed impatience, and at the end had spoken rather tersely.

'So how much is this specialized care going to cost us?'

Libby had already sent a price list for the firm's services. She produced another and pointed to the relevant paragraphs. He nodded as she went through them. It was a substantial list of domestic functions, but Libby had evolved special packages for clients who had big houses, extensive grounds, or a large household – in other words, those who needed a lot of help all the time.

Philip Moorfield's keen eye had lighted on the special offer that Libby was now heartily regretting: full house-care and gardening service as required at a reduced price so long as the client would sign a contract for a full year.

'I mentioned this to your wife on the tele-phone—'

'Who?'

'Mrs Moorfield.'

'That was my mother.' He shrugged and tapped the advertising leaflet. 'My mother isn't concerned with costs – it's all this gimmickry about the environment that interests her.'

'It isn't "gimmickry", Mr Moorfield,' Libby retorted. 'I fully believe in my use of non-harm-ful ingredients—'

'And I suppose you use a dustpan and brush instead of a vacuum cleaner, to save harmful electricity.'

She took a firm hold on her temper. She didn't want to lose this contract, because it meant a big increase in income. 'It would please me if you had a solar panel on the roof, of course, but until that becomes common practice I make do with what the power companies supply. Of course, where non-electric equipment would be appro-priate, my employees use that. The house will be well looked after.'

So Mr Moorfield, who seemed to be the finan-cial head of the household, agreed the contract and Housecare Helpers took on the Moorfields.

11

It soon became only too clear that Libby's staff didn't like them. From the outset the family members had been reported as uncivil, demanding, careless of their own property, and in the case of old Mrs Moorfield, high-handed. 'Old Mrs Moorfield' wasn't the woman of the diffident voice who had first contacted Libby; it soon emerged that there was another, older one – tall, good-looking and self-important, who from the outset made life difficult for Libby's workers. Various members of the team had been sent to Ashgrove but it always ended with the employee demanding to be relieved of duty.

'They're hateful,' said Gracie, a kindly, plump pensioner who had hitherto proved a hit with every employer.

'They just don't give a hang about anything except themselves,' sighed Elizabeth, an earnest do-gooder who had been shocked at the family's self-centred ways.

So Libby had tried out four reliable helpers. And now, following Amy's departure, she was going to have to find yet one more shield-bearer for the battle with this ill-natured bunch.

For the rest of the afternoon, with only a short interval while she fetched Freddie home from school, she was on the telephone to the various members of her team. There were about twenty of them in all, some of them part-timers who'd step in when they could. No one would take Ashgrove on.

She started again after Freddie was in bed, but was interrupted by a call from the Moorfield household on the office phone. When she picked

12

up, it was Philip Moorfield, very irate.

'I've just got home to find my grandmother complaining about the manners of that woman who was doing the housework today—'

'Complaining?' Libby interrupted, determined not to be browbeaten by the angry tone. 'My employee was very hurt at the way she was spoken to by Mrs Moorfield Senior. She—'

'She was given instructions and refused to obey them! If she's told to do something, that's what she's paid for.'

'My staff are not required to put up with bad manners.'

'What? Look here, when I hire a cleaner I don't expect to get a prima-donna—'

'And when I offer a service I don't expect my employee to be treated like a skivvy!'

'You mean they won't take instructions? That's no way to—'

'They won't take orders to do things that are outside their domain. They are there to look after the house, not act as personal maid to your grandmother!'

There was a sudden silence. After a moment he resumed, in a voice in which there was something like amusement. 'Mrs Fletcher, I will allow that there may be some misunderstanding here. Grandee can sometimes ... Well, let's take that as read. You'll have to send someone else tomorrow.'

'I'm sorry, Mr Moorfield, but I think I have to say that Housecare Helpers wishes to end its commitment to look after your home.'

'What?'

'You've had four members of my staff trying to handle the situation already, and I feel it would be unfair to go on exposing them to the kind of treatment they meet at your house.'

There was a stifled exclamation which might have been bad language. Then Philip Moorfield said in steely tones, 'You can't do that. We have a contract.'

'I would prefer to withdraw from that.'

'Oh, would you? That was a year's contract and it's still got about nine months to run. I should expect a refund of my money and some compensation for the inconvenience.'

It was Libby's turn to fall silent. There was no doubt that Philip Moorfield was in the right. But quite a substantial sum was involved, and she simply couldn't afford to let the money go. It was in the bank, funding daily expenses and some ideas of extending the service. She couldn't part with it, let alone any 'compensation' he might claim.

'Well?' said the impatient voice at the other end of the phone.

'I agree that we have a contract. I hope we can come to some mutual agreement about cancellation—'

'Not a chance. I don't have time to go through all that staff-finding process yet again. I want someone here tomorrow morning as usual, according to our agreement. Otherwise it's money back and a substantial sum in reparation.'

That was a scary word. He sounded like a very hard-headed businessman so 'reparation' might even mean going to court. She found herself

14

saying, 'Very well. I'll see to it.'

'Thank you, Mrs Fletcher. Nice doing business with you.'

'Can't say the same about you,' she muttered after she'd put down the phone.

As she went to bed that night, Libby was angry but resigned. She'd have to go to Ashgrove herself. Nobody else would take it on.

Two

It was just before eight thirty the next morning when she arrived at Ashgrove. She'd left Freddie at home with Amy, to be delivered to school – an idea to which he was quite accustomed, for most of Libby's staff were like an extended family to him.

She had driven west out of the town, along some shady lanes, until she came to the River Wey Navigation Canal, the canal Rosanne Moorfield had named as the heron's fishing ground. The house, as she already knew, was in a secluded turning so that it backed on to the canal, with lawns running down to a towpath bordering the water. The front of the house was grey stone, with a circular gravelled drive in front shaded by ash trees. She parked there, pulling off neatly to one side, and sat for a moment looking around.

At this time of year the leaves were still in

15

tight buds and the frontage lacked something in the way of sparkle. She surveyed it with a shake of the head: a few tubs of spring flowers would have been an improvement.

The building was irregular in appearance. The Victorians had built on extensions and annexes to what had been at first a modest enough late-Georgian house. But it wasn't particularly imposing; it looked what it was, a house that had seen families come and go for well over a century.

Libby had keys for all the locks in the house, given to her when she first accepted the contract and handed over to her yesterday by Amy. She put the keys in the locks of the front door and went in.

And there on the hall floor lay a teenage girl, fast asleep and snoring.

Stifling a gasp, Libby leaned over her. Was she all right? Well, judging by the gusto of her snores, she had plenty of lung power and her breathing was steady. To Libby's eye she looked a mess – tinted hair in a tangle, stains which she took to be wine on the front of her skimpy dress, one shoe missing. And only about seventeen years old, by the look of her.

Libby took the girl by a shoulder and shook her. 'Hey!' she said. No response. 'Wake up!' Still no response. 'Come on, wake up, you can't just lie here!' A more vigorous shake was rewarded with a mutter of protest and a curling-up into a more protective position.

Libby straightened and glanced about. The staircase at the far end of the hall rose up to the

16

bedroom floor, but who was to say there was anyone awake up there? And what would be the reaction if she knocked on a door and said 'Come down and help me, there's somebody dead drunk in your hall'?

A faint chink of crockery and a hint of coffee brewing led her to a door on the far left of the hall. She knocked and went in. A young man in jeans and a sweatshirt was pouring cornflakes into a bowl on a pine table already well endowed with used plates, wine glasses and mugs. She was in the kitchen of the Moorfields' house.

'Excuse me,' she said.

The young man looked at her with casual interest. He looked about twenty-four, with a fashionable stubble growth around his lips and chin, hair cut very short and standing straight up, and splotches of paint or dye on his clothes.

'Eh?' he said. 'Oh, you're the replacement. Morning.'

'Good morning. Excuse me, but there's a young woman lying on the floor of the hall.'

'Oh, yes, I saw her when I came in for breakfast. That's Angela.'

'She's rather the worse for wear. Would you help me get her upstairs and show me her room?'

He turned away to deal with the coffee, which had steeped sufficiently in its cafetière. 'I shouldn't bother, if I were you.'

'I beg your pardon?'

'Leave her where she is and let her sleep it off. She'll take herself upstairs when she's ready, I imagine.'

'But – but we can't just leave her there!'

'Why not? She's OK there, isn't she? Lost in dreamland? It's less trouble that way.'

Libby drew in a breath. 'It's happened before?'

He nodded, his attention on pouring his coffee. He sat down at the table to add milk to his cornflakes. Libby wanted to ask, 'Doesn't anyone do anything about it?' but decided not to. Instead she introduced herself. 'I'm Libby Fletcher.'

'Great. There's a lot of stuff waiting to be washed up. We had a few people in last night.'

Couldn't you have loaded it into the dishwasher? she asked him mentally. 'Are you a member of the Moorfield family?' she said aloud.

'Oh, introductions, you feel we need that?' He shrugged. 'I'm Brenton Moorfield. Angela's my sister.'

'I see. Thank you.' She went to hang her coat up on a rack just inside the kitchen door, bound her hair up in a bandanna, put on her apron, and began to load the dishwasher.

While she was doing so Brenton Moorfield finished his breakfast, went out without a word and, as far as she could tell, walked past his recumbent sister as he opened the front door and left.

She shook her head. Then she gave her attention to tidying the kitchen and wiping the surfaces. The floor she would leave for the moment.

In the drawing-room, she found the ashes of a wood fire in the grate. She left that until she'd collected up discarded newspapers, a plate of

18

very tired-looking sandwiches, and a few wine glasses. She dealt with the ashes using a brush and a handy container that closed on them. She then found the vacuum cleaner in a cupboard in the hall. She was using it to clean traces of ash from the hearth rug when the door of the room opened and an early-middle-aged woman in a pretty shimmering silk kimono came in.

'Oh dear! You didn't know any better, I suppose ... No vacuuming until ten o'clock at the earliest.'

'I'm sorry. Mrs Moorfield, is it?' She recognized the gentle, diffident voice from that first telephone conversation.

'Yes, and I meditate until ten, so ... you know ... the noise level has to be kept down.'

'I'm sorry.'

'You're not the one that was here yesterday.' It was something between a query and a reproach.

'No, that was Amy. I'm Libby.'

'Well, then ... good.' Rosanne Moorfield made a little turning movement, as if surveying the room. 'So you'll just do quiet things now, won't you?'

'Certainly.'

'And Prim's awake, so she'll be down pretty soon.'

'Er ... Prim?'

'Brent's little girl. She'll probably want her breakfast so you won't mind reaching down packets and things for her, I suppose?'

'Of course not. Is there anything she shouldn't have?' As a mother, Libby knew how odd the choices of children could be.

'No, no, she's a good little soul. She almost always has cereal, I think, and orange juice to drink.'

'Who generally gets it for her?'

'What? Oh, well, you see, she's very self-reliant. She gets it for herself if Angela isn't here.'

'But if she can't reach things in the cupboards...?'

'Oh, then, I think she has fruit ... perhaps a banana or something. But Angela sees to it usually.'

Libby decided to be blunt. 'I found Angela asleep on the hall floor when I arrived,' she said in a tone that emerged as accusing.

'Oh, no, she's gone upstairs now,' Rosanne said placidly. 'She's in the shower. I don't know whether that means she's getting ready to start the day or perhaps going to bed.'

'But is she supposed to be looking after the little girl?'

'Well ... I suppose you could say that. But you see, everyone has their own path to follow, and Angela's ... Perhaps she's at a crossroads, you know?' With that she drifted out, apparently unperturbed by the fact that a young member of the family was upstairs trying to sober herself up to start the day.

Libby left the vacuum cleaner switched off and instead began on the dusting. She went out into the hall to decide which room to do next when her attention was drawn to a little figure coming down the stairs very carefully, one at a time. A little girl, about three years old, dressed in jeans and a sweater and fluffy-bunny slippers.

'Hello,' said Libby. 'You must be Prim.'

'It's Primrose really. Primrose Moorfield, Ashgrove, Riverside Lane, Weybridge,' the child recited, in a tone that was clearly learned from a well-spoken adult. She took the few remaining steps of the staircase then toddled round the newel post towards the kitchen. 'I'm going to have my breakfast now.'

'So I hear. Can I help?' She followed the child into the kitchen and watched her open a cupboard next to the sink. Here were arranged plastic cups, plates, and other implements within easy reach.

Prim took a bright blue bowl and a red spoon, then looked upwards at the higher cupboards. 'May I have Puffy Pops? It's the big sunny packet, please.' She was scrambling on to a chair as she spoke, setting the bowl and spoon crookedly by her place.

Libby found the cereal packet. She wondered whether this self-sufficient child would pour her own portion but Prim looked at her expectantly so she shook out half a bowlful for her. 'More please.' She filled the bowl. 'And milk.'

'Right,' said Libby, obediently fetching it from the fridge. It was still in the plastic carton which Brenton had opened. Why wasn't it in a proper jug, she asked herself, but as Prim was apparently expecting her to pour from the container, she did so, 'Juice?' she inquired. Once provided with food and drink, the little girl began to spoon up the cereal. She seemed to have forgotten Libby was there. 'Anything else I can do?' Libby

21

asked.

'No, thank you.' Prim spoke her words very sedately, yet the soft little voice emphasized how young she was. Her grasp of language, however, was quite a lot more advanced than that of Libby's seven-year-old son.

'What do you do after breakfast?' Libby inquired.

'Play group.'

'And how do you get there?'

'And'la takes me.'

Not this morning, thought Libby, unless Angela's condition had greatly improved.

The toddler seemed engrossed in her breakfast, so Libby went back to her chores.

The dining room had a beautiful walnut table that she immediately recognized as Hepplewhite. It was littered with wine bottles and dessert plates, meaning that the host or hostess had invited the guests into another room for coffee. She sighed to see the table treated like this. There were place mats but on the unprotected surface there were spills, and signs of earlier spills. The four chairs drawn up to the table were a variety of nineteenth- and twentieth-century designs but still fine of their type.

She'd already noticed that in the drawing-room there were examples of fine furniture. The sofa, although covered in worn linen, had the lines of some good maker of the 1930s, and opposite the window she'd seen what she took to be a Dutch marquetry bureau dating from about 1800.

It was an interesting house. Someone at some

time had spent money on the furnishings. But her role was to clean it, not evaluate it. She found a tray, loaded it with empty wine bottles and plates, and took it to the kitchen.

Prim Moorfield had got down from the table and was now gazing out of the window. The window was on the east side of the house. The morning sun was shining over a slender tract of lawn and a selection of evergreen bushes. 'Want to go out?' Libby asked.

Prim shook her head. 'I'm waiting for And'la.'

'If Angela can't take you to play group, who does?'

'Nana, p'raps.'

Angela was semi-conscious and Nana – presumably Rosanne Moorfield – was meditating. Libby wondered whether she should go upstairs and try knocking on doors. She retreated from the thought. She was here to do the cleaning, not help in the routine of a little girl. But motherly instinct prompted her to engage the child in activity while she waited. 'Do you usually clear up your breakfast things?' she asked.

Prim looked at her in puzzlement.

'Your bowl and beaker – they should go in the sink. And the Puffy Pops should go back in their cupboard.'

'Oh.' Prim thought about it. 'I can't reach the tall cupboard.'

'Shall I help you to reach it?'

'Mm...' She clearly didn't quite understand the offer.

'I could pick you up and you could open the cupboard and put in the packet.'

23

'Oh.' A slight pause. 'I would be tall, then, wouldn't I? OK.' She reached up her arms. Libby picked her up, stooped so she could get hold of the cereal packet, then took her to the cupboard. Prim opened it after a slight hesitation with the catch, put in the packet, and gave a little crow of delight. 'It's good being tall,' she cried.

'Now for the bowl and beaker,' Libby suggested. She set the child down. Prim took bowl and beaker, one in each hand, and approached the kitchen sink. She was just tall enough to let them fall over the rim with a satisfying clatter of plastic against stainless steel. She gave a little laugh. 'I was clearing up,' she said, using a phrase which seemed new to her.

'Yes, and you did it well. And now *I've* got to do some clearing up in the dining room.'

'I'll help you,' said Prim, and padded along behind her in her fluffy-bunny slippers.

The fine table was now clear of equipment except for a silver candelabrum at its centre. Libby ignored that for the moment, instead fetching from the hall the bag of equipment she'd brought with her. She began to wipe down the surface of the table.

'I want to do that,' demanded Prim.

'You want to do some dusting?'

'I can do dusting.' She made dusting movements with her hand along the table top, but it was rather a stretch.

'You can do the chairs,' Libby suggested. 'I'll get you a duster.' She selected a bright red square, cut from the remains of a T-shirt of last summer. All the dusters that Libby supplied to her staff were brightly coloured, so that they could never be left carelessly in other people's rooms.

Prim held out a hand for it at once, but Libby knelt by one of the chairs and showed the little girl how to do it, wiping the leather-covered seat, covering one of the legs with the cloth and running it over the tapering lines. The chair back she left untouched, because Prim might find it hard to reach the top of it.

So the little girl was occupied in rubbing a bright red cloth over a chair when her grandmother came downstairs. The movements in the dining room drew her there. The shimmering kimono had been replaced by a skirt of rough wool, vertically striped in green and brown, and a long-sleeved cotton top of sunshine yellow. Her greying fair hair was tied with red ribbon into a topknot, leaving her features on show in their mild contours and soft colouring.

'Hello, Primmy,' she said, smiling at the little girl. 'Why aren't you at play group?'

'And'la didn't take me.'

'Oh, of course.' Rosanne Moorfield sighed. 'She's not too well this morning, dear. I'll take you, shall I?'

The child looked uncertain, divided between the joys of housework and the fun of play group. 'I'm dusting,' she said.

'I see you are, dear. But I'm sure Libby would rather be left to get on with her work.'

Prim looked at Libby. Libby's first instinct was to say, 'I don't mind having her here.' But of course the child was better off with other child-

25

ren. She smiled and said, 'Off you go, then.'

Prim straightened from the chair whose legs she'd been polishing. She offered the duster to its owner with evident reluctance. It was a lovely scarlet cloth, soft cotton, pleasing to the touch.

'My dusting,' she said, holding it in two hands clasped together.

'Yes, it's yours, and it's a duster.'

'Can I take it to play group?'

'By all means.'

'By all means,' repeated Prim, pleased with the sound of the words. She looked at her grandmother for approval, but Rosanne was leading the way out to the hall, so Prim followed. Libby heard the front door opening. She went into the hall.

'Shouldn't you change out of your slippers?' she said to Prim. She was thinking that if play group included games with outdoor equipment, footwear of pink felt and imitation fur were hardly suitable.

Prim looked at her feet. She giggled. 'Bunnies like being in the grass,' she said. But she obediently began the long climb upstairs to change into shoes.

Rosanne came back into the hall. 'Where are you going, Prim?' she asked in surprise.

'To change into trainies.'

'All right.' She sat down on a chair in the hall, unhurried and unfussed. She glanced at Libby, smiled, then transferred her abstracted gaze to the view out of the open door.

Libby went back to her work. So far, she thought to herself, Prim is the most responsive person I've met in this family.

Later, she was upstairs in what was clearly Prim's bedroom when she heard stirrings from a room at the back of the house. A door opened, and someone emerged. Libby edged to the doorway and peeped out. A tall, white-haired lady had reached the top of the staircase and was going down in a rather stately manner, head held high and almost as if wearing a crown.

Libby edged back into the child's room. That must be Mrs Moorfield Senior, or Grandee as she was called. Libby had no desire to encounter her. She finished the chores in Prim's room. Next door was a bathroom. She then tapped on the door of the next room, received no reply and glanced in. Angela, wrapped in a towelling bathrobe, was fast asleep on top of the covers.

The next room might perhaps be that of Philip Moorfield or of Brenton. On receiving no response to her knock, she opened the door. This was clearly a man's room, the owner very tidy and organized. The bed, although unmade, had been neatly opened up by folding back the covers. The towels in the adjoining bathroom had been returned folded to the towel rail, and the cap was on the shower gel and on the toothpaste.

This can't be Brenton's room, she thought to herself. She made the bed, did all the chores, then went next door. This was something of a forlorn place; it had men's clothes in the wardrobe but there were almost no personal possessions. A photograph of a pretty girl stood on the bureau, holding a shawl-wrapped baby in her

27

arms. Primrose and her mother? So this might be Brenton's room. The other must belong to Philip, who seemed to be the family's business manager.

The next door led into a suite, beautifully furnished with a canopied bed, a dressing-table of unique design, curtains of heavy silk with swagged pelmets and tie-backs of rope threaded with some gleaming metal. Beyond the bedroom was a boudoir with a chaise longue upholstered in the same silk as the curtains. A portrait hung on the wall opposite the window. It showed a slender, beautiful girl in a dark red dress holding back her hair with two long-fingered white hands. It was stunning.

This is Grandee, thought Libby. Grandee as a young girl. She went close enough to read the signature of the artist: Graham Sutherland. 'My word,' she said to herself, 'if this is Grandee, she certainly moved in very revered circles.'

That might account for her imperious manner. If once you'd been somebody that a famous artist wanted to paint, you might have a right to think you were very special. Indeed, everything in the suite of rooms was special. Even the bathroom, when Libby came to clean it, had tiling of superb quality and the best of modern equipment from Italy.

She stood for a moment gazing out of the window of Grandee's bedroom. It gave a splendid view of the lawn, the trees and shrubs, and beyond them the shimmer of water which must be the canal. Everything was the best, thought Libby.

She completed her work upstairs by cleaning the stairs, which were oaken treads with a fine patterned carpet down the centre, old-fashioned but just right for the setting. This house had some wonderful things in it, was Libby's verdict. It deserved good care.

It was noon, so Libby decided to have her lunch. Members of the family might be coming home for the midday meal and she would have to clear up after them, but she wanted to stay out of their way. She got her sandwich and a bottle of mineral water out of her holdall, put on her jacket, then went outside by a door off the kitchen. She wanted to survey the grounds, which were in the care of Jacob Grover, her employee who took on the outside work.

She followed the path along the back of the house to the narrow lawn at the side. The grass was still unmown; spring hadn't yet brought on enough growth. Some of the bushes had been pruned, and the gravel had been swept clean and level. She went on round to the front of the house, only to encounter Brenton Moorfield as he was about to put a key in the front door.

He gave her a surprised glance. 'What are you doing out here?'

'Having a check over the outdoor work and looking for a place to eat my lunch.'

A puzzled frown drew his dark brows together. 'Why don't you have it in the kitchen? That's what the help usually does.'

She didn't say that she wanted to avoid any members of the Moorfield family. She simply shrugged and made as if to walk past him to the other side of the house. She wanted to check whether the windows were receiving good treatment.

'Aren't you coming in?' asked Brenton, who by now had the door open.

'No thank you. I'm just getting the feel of the place.'

'But it's quite cool out here.'

'Oh, I'm tough,' she said.

He grinned. It made a vast difference to his appearance. He had a dark complexion, not helped by the stubble. His clothes were, to say the least, undistinguished. But his smile brought some lightness into his facade of streetwise kid. She thought him perhaps not as sure of himself as he would like to be.

'I was talking to your little girl earlier on,' she said, since he seemed inclined for conversation. 'Sweet little thing.'

'I suppose so,' he agreed. He glanced about as if expecting to see her. 'She's at play group now, I think.'

You think? Libby was shocked. 'Mrs Moorfield took her.' She hesitated. 'Will she bring her back?'

'Mama? No, Angela generally does that.'

'Angela is lying on her bed with a hangover,' Libby said inwardly. Aloud she said, 'I don't think Angela's up to it. If you remember, she was in the hall this morning?'

'Oh ... yeah.' He thought about it. 'I'll do it then.'

'What time does play group end?'

'Two o'clock. Oh, gee, I'd better have something to eat and then get going.'

Without another word he went in, closed the door behind him and left Libby to continue her inspection.

She went round the western end of the house. It had the addition of a large brick and glass conservatory, built probably in the Victorian era but now adapted as some sort of studio. One corner had the glass obscured by dark blue paint, the reason being, as Libby was to discover later, was that it housed a little living area for Brenton.

She reached the back of the building. Here were former stabling for horses and a carriage house big enough for two carriages. These had been adapted as garage space for the family cars but at present held only two: a Mini, which Libby thought would be Angela's, and an old estate car which was perhaps Brenton's. The motor-mower was there too, and a lock-up metal chest for the gardening tools.

A path took her between some shrubs to the lawn, which sloped down almost majestically to the Weybridge Navigation Canal. A thick hedge of pruned hawthorn edged the property, with a gate to allow access to the towpath. One of the keys on the ring in her apron pocket probably unlocked the gate but she felt that lunch time was nearly over. She found a stone bench by a camellia bush and ate her snack.

She let herself back in by a back door. Glancing in at the kitchen as she went by, she saw that Brenton was sitting at the table eating a very thick home-made sandwich. There was no sign of Grandee having made herself any breakfast or

31

even a cup of tea. A glance into the other down-stairs rooms made it clear that she'd gone out.

She was searching in her holdall for polish when she heard Brenton coming along the hall. He paused as he came close. He said, rather awkwardly, 'I'm just going to fetch Prim now.' There was a hint of self-justification in his tone, as if he felt she had been critical at the lack of proper arrangements.

Libby got up from her kneeling position beside the holdall. 'She helped me do some dusting this morning,' she said so as to open a conversation. She wanted to know where Prim's mother was, and that was her next ploy. 'Her mother's away?'

'In Tokyo.'

'Tokyo!'

He shrugged. 'Jackie's in fashion. She was offered an absolutely great job with Satukuo.'

She'd heard of Satukuo, in fact had seen the shop in Sloane Street on a recent trip to London. Wispy clothes for teenagers, very expensive.

A hundred questions crowded to be asked. Why didn't she take Prim with her? How long has she been gone? When is she coming back? But she asked none of them, because one of the rules of being a good home-help was not to get involved too much in the affairs of the family. Instead she remarked, 'I suppose play group is over soon.'

'Yes, two o'clock. They get a snack lunch at twelve, I think, then a nap, and then a sort of sing-song before they get collected.'

Libby glanced at the handsome grandfather

clock in the hall. He took the hint, produced car keys, and went out quickly.

She was cleaning the patterned tiles of the hall floor with a damp mop when Rosanne Moorfield came home. Rosanne stopped on the doormat, like a castaway on an island.

'It's all right,' Libby said. 'I can mop away your footprints.'

Rosanne came in gingerly. 'I thought you'd be finished by now.'

'Nearly. I have to collect my little boy from school in a bit.'

'Oh, you have a little boy?' But it was said merely in politeness. Libby nodded, and Rosanne went on into the drawing-room.

A moment later another car drew up and from outside Libby could hear Prim's voice. The little girl came in carefully carrying a shallow tray made of thin cardboard. She was saying to her father, 'So we're going to make nanimals to stand inside the farmyard tomorrow.' She was a few steps into the house when she saw and recognized the mop-wielder. 'Libby? Libby, look at my farmyard.'

Libby leaned the mop against the wall and came to examine the handiwork. It had been made by simply snipping the corner of a rectangle and folding them up, and palings had been painted on both the inside and the outside, by an unsteady but eager hand.

'That's very good. What kind of animals live there?'

'I'm going to make cut-out cows and piggies. They're on a page in a book, you push them and they come all out. I'll make the cows black and white.' She thought a moment. 'I don't know what colour piggies are.'

'Pink, I think.'

Prim laughed at the rhyme of the words. 'Pink-I-think! I'll show you tomorrow.'

'Oh, I'm afraid I won't be here tomorrow.'

Prim's face fell. 'Why *not*?' she asked, pouting.

'I'll have to send someone else to do the work, you see.'

Against the unanswerable logic of grown-ups, the little girl was silent. A thought seemed to strike her. She felt in the pocket of her jeans. 'Here's your dusting, then.' There was reluctance in the way she held out the bright red cloth.

'You can keep that if you like, Prim.'

'Can I really?' She put the duster, carefully folded, back in her pocket. 'Thank you very much.'

Her father urged her on into the house. She moved a few steps then paused. Turning to Libby, she asked, 'Shall I be able to do dusting if you're not here?'

'Of course, my love, if you want to.'

Prim gave a great sigh. 'It would be better if you were here,' she said, the ends of her mouth turning down. 'Couldn't you be here instead of someone else?'

'Well, perhaps I could.'

Although this was only said in order to slip out of a little awkwardness, Libby did in fact turn up at Ashgrove the next day. She couldn't persuade anyone else to go.

Three

Brent Moorfield allowed Libby into his studio on sufferance. 'You're only allowed to clean the cubbyhole. You mustn't touch anything else.'

I wouldn't dare, she thought. She could see four assorted computers, about half a dozen video-cameras, lights hanging above a podium and on tripods here and there, all amid a tangle of cables and wires impossible to manoeuvre with a vacuum cleaner. Although this had been a conservatory and was therefore made almost entirely of glass, there were blinds everywhere so that the artist could manage the amount of light that entered. At the moment, the place was dim and seemed to her very uninviting.

The living area took her about ten minutes to clean. There were a shower and toilet in the corner with a folding door, a futon on the floor with a duvet, and a small refrigerator on a table which, when she came to clean it, proved to contain bottles of imported beer.

As she came out at the side of the house, a Mercedes drew into the drive. She waited it for it to pass her en route to the garages. Philip Moorfield rolled down his window to speak to her. 'When I asked for a replacement I didn't expect to get the managing director of the firm,' he said with some amusement. 'Staff shortage?'

'You might say so.'

Something in her voice made him pause. She wondered if he had any idea how unpopular his household was.

'Anybody home at present?' he inquired.

'I don't think so. The two Mrs Moorfields went out about an hour ago, Primrose is at play group, and Brenton drove off just before you arrived.'

He shrugged. 'Do you know if there's any food in the fridge?'

She'd cleaned that while she had the place to herself first thing, and knew it to be empty. But a delivery van had brought a big carton, which she'd placed in the centre of the kitchen table for the attention of somebody – whom, she couldn't tell as yet. 'I think there's food in the cardboard box.'

'That'll be Mama's vegetarian stuff. I think I'd better just turn around and get a bite to eat in the town.' He hesitated, as if he felt he ought to say something more. 'I've just driven down from Glasgow,' he explained.

'Oh, you must have started before dawn!'

'Avoided the traffic. I was there looking for a derelict factory.'

'What?'

'It's what I do. I find locations for film companies. I'm away a lot.'

'I see.'

'That's why I have to make sure there's somebody looking after the house and so on.'

She nodded. She had a feeling that this was

36

some sort of apology for holding her to their contract but couldn't tell what response he expected. She merely smiled, waiting to see if he had any instructions for her. Not at all. He rolled up his window, drove on round the semicircular drive, and was gone.

I should have offered to make him a snack, she thought. And then she told herself, No you shouldn't. Don't offer any services except those you're being paid for.

She encountered Mrs Moorfield Senior for the first time about an hour later. Libby was on her knees examining the narrow strips of decoration on the dressing-table in the lady's bedroom – it was clearly metal, but not silver, and in fact not a material Libby had seen before on furniture. She was wondering how best to revive it, because it had been blotched, either by neglect or some effects of furniture polish.

'What are you doing here?' demanded a haughty voice.

Libby turned, and got to her feet. 'Wondering how best to clean that banding,' she explained.

Mrs Moorfield considered the explanation. She shrugged it off. 'I expect my rooms to be attended to and left in good condition by this time of the day.'

'Do you happen to know what kind of metal that is?'

A reprimand seemed to hover on the thin lips, but after a pause she said dismissively, 'It's chromium.'

'Chromium! I never heard of it being used for decoration before.'

Once again there was a hesitation, as if the lady of the house was unaccustomed to being quizzed. But then the hint of a proud smile lightened her severe expression.

'It so happens the furniture in these rooms was made for me by a close friend – it's hardly likely you would know of him, of course, but Dennis Aggerton was famous in his day.' She looked about her with satisfaction. The room was very handsomely furnished, and she herself was a very suitable occupant. A picture of perfection in her own way, she wore her white hair pulled up and back from an oval face, and her slender figure was shown to advantage in a trim trouser suit of black silk. A trace of perfumed lotions implied that she had just come back from a beauty salon.

Libby estimated she was well into her seventies, yet she could have held her own with any young celebrity.

'Did he design the curtain fabric too?' she asked.

'Of course. He wanted this to be a total work of art. He did the curtains and the bed canopy and so on. Why do you ask?'

'I was thinking that the swagged pelmet is suffering from too much sunlight. Your windows face north-west, don't they?'

Grandee walked on into the boudoir, ignoring the inquiry.

Taking that as dismissal, Libby headed for the door with her basket of cleaning materials. She was worried about those curtains; they were being damaged by exposure to light. She needed a ladder to examine them properly but signs of wear along the scalloped edges could be glimpsed even by just looking up. She didn't care to attack them with the extension from the vacuum cleaner.

She was about to enter Prim's room when Grandee appeared in the doorway of her suite. 'How dare you walk out while I was talking to you!' she protested.

Libby had thought it was exactly the other way about: Grandee had walked out as Libby asked her a question. But she wanted above all things not to be on bad terms with the doyenne of the household, so she said, 'I'm sorry, I misunderstood.'

Grandee frowned and shrugged. 'I suppose I shouldn't expect too much from an employee.' She gestured to the room behind her. 'What were you saying about the curtains?'

'Just that I thought they ought to be taken down and—'

'Cleaned? Good gracious, they're much too precious to be entrusted to a dry-cleaner! I just told you, they were made to a design by Dennis Aggerton. I suppose that means nothing to you, but he was very famous fifty years ago and still has a place in the art galleries.'

'There are specialist cleaners,' Libby said, carefully avoiding any remarks on Aggerton, who was in fact unknown to her. The applied arts had been her subjects at college, not painting or sculpture. She added, 'There's a certain amount of fraying. They may need repairs.'

'And I suppose the firm that sends you here

would ask extra for dealing with that.'

'No, madam. Jake Grover does the garden work and would come indoors to take the curtains down. That comes under the existing contract, but of course the curtain-cleaning firm would be extra to the house contract. They would make a charge for doing the cleaning and repairs and it might be substantial.'

'Humph,' said Grandee, and went back into her domain, closing the door firmly behind her.

With a sigh Libby went back to her tasks. She found Angela downstairs in the drawing-room. It was her first sight of the girl fully awake and in daytime clothes. 'Good morning,' she said. 'I'm the home help from Housecare.'

Angela, stretched out on the sofa with a magazine and with her iPod playing, didn't hear Libby's introduction. Her blue eyes were fixed on the fashion magazine, there was a slight frown between the light brown brows, and though she was pretty she seemed much too pale to Libby.

The girl was too taken up by her music and her magazine to notice someone had come in. For some reason, Libby was determined to have a conversation with this member of the household. After all this was the person who seemed to have charge of Prim. She picked up a collection of newspapers from a nearby side table and thumped them down again with some vigour. There was just enough reverberation to attract Angela's attention. She sat up, taking the earpieces out of her ear.

'You're not going to start cleaning in here, are

40

you?' she asked in a complaining voice.

'Oh no, I've finished in here for today.' Libby glanced about at the gleaming surfaces and polished fire grate. Couldn't she see the room had been cleaned? 'I just thought I'd introduce myself. My name's Libby.'

'Oh yes. Well ... You finished upstairs? Because I want to get into my room and start on my hair.' Stereo sound was leaking from the earphones. She prepared to put them back in her ears.

'It's just the stairs and the landing to do now,' Libby said.

'Good.'

In a minute she'd be absorbed in her music again. 'Going to a party?'

Angela paused. 'Later. The wine bar, probably. But I want to try a few different streaks.'

Libby busied herself with straightening items in the magazine rack. The girl was tugging at strands of her hair, as if trying to picture what the new look would be.

'Does it wash out, the colour you use?'

'More or less.'

'What's the new colour going to be?'

'Mauve, I think. I might mix in a bit of blue.'

'Quite an art, then.' This was said in hopes of raising a smile.

Angela shrugged. 'Makes a change.'

'This whole place seems to be concerned with art in a way. There's Mr Moorfield in his studio, and the other Mr Moorfield doing something with films, and Mrs Moorfield Senior up in that suite with all the special furniture...'

'In Grandee's room? Lord, yes.' Angela sat up, setting aside the iPod. Clearly this was a subject on which she had something to say. 'That's by the *famous* Dennis Aggerton, just one of the *many* who were in love with Grandee when she was young.' Then, with sarcasm, 'I think all that stuff in her room is terribly passé myself, but *she* thinks it's marvellous.'

'The pieces were made especially for her?'

'Oh yes. He used to come here to paint her, you know. She was quite a "celeb" in her day.' She made quotation marks in the air with her fingers. 'Vivienne Ritchie?' She waited to see if Libby would recognize the name and when she shook her head, went on with a noticeable lack of respect. 'Oh, *everybody* painted her – there's the *famous* portrait up in her room by Sutherland, and David Jacobson did one, and I know there were others but who can remember their names.'

'That would be ... when? Back in the Fifties?'

'When life was *so hard* and she was lucky to be so *beautiful* that she was in demand even though they couldn't pay her much – that's the yarn.' Angela blew out a breath that expressed both irritation and disbelief. 'Then you know she married Charles Moorfield, who had oodles of money from the stock market or something, and he bought this house so she could have a studio.'

'So she painted as well as being a model?'

'No, no, she had no talent except as a model, if *that* needs talent. But ever so stunning, if you believe all that, and artists came here after she got married and they'd stay for days sometimes, using the studio to do paintings of her – the studio is that bit on the corner of the house where Brent does his scenery.'

'Scenery? Is that what all the electrical stuff is for?'

'Well ... yeah ... it's not scenery in the usual sense. He does this electronic and laser stuff for the Tyrants – you know?'

Libby had never heard of the Tyrants. But she was having a real and very informative conversation with a member of the family, so to keep it going she said, 'They're in the Top Ten?'

'No, not yet, but they will be before long, and Brent makes all these special effects for their show – it's not just the music, people go just to see the dazzle.'

'I just met Mr Philip Moorfield earlier on. That's ... er ... your brother?'

'Yes, Phil's the eldest, then it's Brent, and then me.' Her lips tightened. 'I'm Mama's little afterthought.'

'And the Mrs Moorfield that was the subject of the paintings, that's your grandmother?'

'Head of the household, and don't you ever forget it!' Angela laughed without much amusement. 'Mama doesn't pay too much attention to Grandee's orders because, of course, she's more or less in a dream all the time. But the rest of us have to mind our manners, even Phil, and he's the money man of the family.'

'I thought you said your grandmother married a very rich man.'

'Yeah, yeah, Grandpa Moorfield, who left her a fortune but she spent all that, didn't she? Still owns the house, so she could throw us all out any time she liked, but then who'd pay her bills at the Beauty Retreat and the health spa if she got rid of Phil?'

Libby felt she couldn't extend the conversation any further. She was uncomfortable enough as it was, to hear this youngster pour out her ill will against her own family. And she was scolding herself for having initiated it. Why should she want to know anything about this tribe, beyond which rooms to clean?

Well, knowing a little bit about them helped to negotiate the difficult spots. For instance, Mrs Moorfield Senior – Grandee – now Libby understood her arrogance to some extent. To have been a beauty once, to be sought after by the artists of her day, to marry a rich man and hold what sounded like a salon for the art world ... And now to be more or less a nobody, tucked away in her old house in a corner where the roads ended at a quiet waterway...

Sighing, she straightened a cushion or two, dusted an already clean surface, and drifted towards the door.

'You do this cleaning lark for a living?' Angela inquired as she was about to go out.

'I do.'

'Can't be much fun.'

'It has its ups and downs.'

'*I'm* in a bit of a down at the moment. Brent talked me into looking after Prim for the time being, but it's not my kind of thing, now is it?'

'Have you had any training for it?'

'Lord, no! Me, train to be a nanny?' Her tone

expressed how idiotic she thought that idea. 'No, I'm just filling in until we can find another one. The last one packed it in about a month ago – Betty, I think her name was. No, perhaps it was Margaret.' She reached the point she'd been heading for. 'You're in this sort of business; you know how to find domestic staff. I suppose you don't know of anybody that'd take on the nanny thing?'

Libby felt a stab of pity on hearing those words. Poor little mite! A succession of nurse-maids, some of whom might have been good at their job, because the little girl was well-trained in the basics – she could clearly wash and dress by herself, knew how to get her own breakfast, and she spoke well.

But when one nursemaid after another went away, she was left in these uncaring hands. Her mother was off in Tokyo, her father was cooped up all day in a workshop where everyone else was forbidden to set foot.

It's not my business, she reminded herself as she denied knowing anything about finding nannies and made her escape. A little later, think-ing over Angela's indifferent attitude, she won-dered if she should remind her that she had to fetch Prim home from play group. But there was no need, because Prim came running in rather early, followed by her father.

'Daddy says Mummy will be on any minute,' she explained to Libby as she ran by.

On where? The answer turned out to be on a video-link, via a computer in the room Philip Moorfield used as an office.

The door was left slightly ajar as they hurried in. The sound of laughter and eager chatter reached her as she finished tidying up in the hall. The conversation lasted about twenty minutes, and the little girl came dancing out when it was over.

'Mummy says she's sended me a *Nihon tokei*. She told me that means a Jap'nese watch in Jap'nese. She says it's got bunnies on it, and a pink strap. She says it's coming tomorrow, she showed me a picture of it and it's pretty.'

'Well, that's lovely.'

'She sended me my bunny slippers. I'm going to put them on now,' she said, heading for the stairs.

Brenton was watching her clamber up as Angela came out of the drawing-room to join him. 'Another addition to the bunny tribe, I gather,' she said to her brother with a shrug. 'She'll need an extension to her room if Jackie goes on like this.'

He looked rueful. 'She keeps saying she's coming home for a holiday but it never quite gels.'

'Oh, come on, Brent. She wants you and Prim-mie to make the trip to Tokyo.'

'Yeah...' He slouched out of the front door, back to his dark secluded studio.

Angela shook her head as the door closed behind him. 'Never gonna happen. *He's* always tied up, and *she's* always busy trying to get something sensational ready for the next fashion show.' She stretched, yawned, and wandered off towards the kitchen. 'Cup of coffee to wake me up before I start on my hair, I think.'

Offer me one, Libby urged her mentally. Then she checked the thought. No, no, she wasn't going to tempt Angela into a discussion about the marriage of Brent and Jackie. She'd had enough of that for one day.

As she was driving home with Freddie later, she remarked jokingly, 'The little girl at Ashgrove was speaking Japanese today.'

Freddie, a seven-year-old cynic, took this with a pinch of salt. 'What, something about Ninja Turtles?'

Libby laughed. 'She's not got as far Ninja Turtles in her TV programmes, I would think. She's more the Teletubbies stage.'

'Oh, a little kid.'

Yes, a little kid, thought Libby. But maybe not as neglected as I was imagining. It seems her mother keeps in touch even from the other side of the world.

The package containing the watch arrived as promised the next day. Libby opened the door to sign for it and noted that it came not from Tokyo, but from an importer of Japanese goods in North London. Well, never mind; it was made in Japan originally.

She placed it in full view on an oak chest in the hall. When Prim came running in the door a few minutes after two, the packet was the first thing she saw. 'My Jap'nese watch!'

She grabbed up the padded envelope to pull it open, but it was an unsuccessful struggle. Angela, coming in behind her, walked past and went nonchalantly upstairs.

47

'I can't open it,' cried Prim.

'Can I help?' Libby offered.

The little girl eagerly handed her the packet. Libby used the handle of a toothbrush, used for cleaning in tight corners, to slit the seal. She pulled it apart, and out came a little rectangular parcel beautifully wrapped in glistening paper and decorated with an exquisite silk rosebud.

The child seized the parcel and pulled off the paper. A plastic box was revealed, painted with cartoon rabbits. Prim prised it open. There was the watch, with a strap of bright pink leather. She took it out, exclaiming in delight. But then a moment later she was wailing in distress. 'There's no bunnies!'

Libby leaned down to look over the girl's shoulder. Held by the pink strap, an oblong surface framed in pink plastic stared up. But it was blank. This was a digital watch, and it needed a battery.

Libby spotted something wrapped in polythene in the case. 'I think this will make the bunnies come,' she said, unfolding the wrapping.

Prim thrust the watch at her, anxious and breathless. Libby slid the cover open, inserted the battery, closed it up and turned it over. The child took it. There was an anguished moment while nothing happened. Then the face of the watch blinked a couple of times and pink cartoon rabbits appeared at either side of the oblong face, followed by the four zeroes that indicated it needed to be set to the right time.

'My bunnies!' Prim was beaming with delight. The zeroes flashed patiently, waiting to be changed. 'It blinks,' she cried, and tried to put it on her wrist. Libby helped fasten the strap, which had a tiny buckle that might prove to be a problem to a toddler.

There was no need to talk about getting the right time on the watch. For the moment Prim was entirely happy with her present. While she helped Libby clean – which seemed to be her favourite game since she was shown how to dust – she kept glancing at the magic watch that winked at her.

By and by it was time for Libby to leave, but there was no one about with whom to leave Prim. 'Let's go upstairs and find Angela,' she suggested.

'And'la's doing her toes,' Prim said in a rather anxious tone. 'It's hard to do.'

This seemed to mean Angela didn't want to be disturbed, because she looked up in irritation when Libby knocked and walked in with her little niece. She was in an armchair with her bare foot propped up on the stool of her dressing-table, with nail polish bottles arrayed along it.

'Prim wants to show you her watch,' Libby said, letting go of Prim's hand but giving her a little forward impetus as she did so.

Prim toddled over with her left wrist held out. 'It winks,' she informed Angela.

Her aunt looked as if she wished it would go and wink elsewhere. 'Very clever,' she remarked. Then, having looked at it, she said, 'It needs to be set at the right time.'

'What time? Playgroup time? Home time?'

Angela, dipping the little brush back into the

nail polish bottle, said, 'No, numbskull, the time it is now.'

'What time is it now, And'la?'

'Twenty past two. Now buzz off, I'm busy.'

Libby repressed a strong desire to hit her. 'I'm leaving now, Angela,' she said. 'Prim had better stay with you, all right?'

She went out quickly before Angela could refuse, but as she went downstairs she was wondering what fun it could be for the little girl to watch her aunt paint her toenails.

Yesterday Libby had thought that the family had some concern for Prim after all. The child had been truly happy at the video-link with her mother. But today there had been no one there to help her open the package, to help her start the watch and find the bunnies, no one to share her delight in them.

Don't get involved, she warned herself as she drove to Freddie's school. You're only there to clean the house.

All right, she would obey her own rules. She would steer clear of these momentary involvements in future. She would be dispassionate about their way of life.

Utterly dispassionate.

But to herself she admitted that she hated them all, except Prim.

Four

At Housecare Helpers, Friday was the day all the staff reported back on the week's work. From about five in the evening until an unspecified hour, staff would saunter in, at first looking up the next week's schedule on the chalkboard, but often wandering upstairs to have a cup of tea or coffee. They would sit about, comparing notes, offering suggestions, bemoaning problems.

Freddie loved these evenings. He could delay going to bed almost indefinitely. Moreover, he could sit beside Jake Grover for a long chat about boats.

Jake was a former merchant seaman, who had reached the position of first mate but then resigned on health grounds after an injury due to mismanaged cargo. He told stories to Freddie, suitably expurgated, about life at sea.

Freddie adored all this because it was his ambition to go abroad one day, to join Grandfather Fletcher in the Bahamas. Grandfather and Grandmother Fletcher had gone to live in the Bahamas about ten years ago, because the climate would be good for Grandmother Fletcher's bronchitis. Grandmother had died before Freddie was even born, however, and that was terribly sad.

But Freddie had been taken when he was really small to visit Grandfather Fletcher and, wonderful to relate, Grandfather was working for a boat-repairing firm on Deadman's Cay. Deadman's Cay! Who could resist that as a travel destination?

It was inevitable that Jake Grover's tales should enchant the little boy. He sat cross-legged on the sofa beside him, drinking in every word.

'So the bo'sun told me the anchor was fouled, and a man'd have to go down to inspect it, and who should that be, me boy, eh?'

'You went down, Jake, didn't you?'

'I did an'all, Freddie, and what d'you think I found?'

'An octopus? A shark?'

'Naw, what would be interesting about them? No, Freddie man, I found a mermaid.'

Passing by with the refilled coffee pot, Libby smiled to herself. One day, when she'd saved up enough, she might take Freddie out there again on holiday. But that was still a long way off. She paused beside them.

'Come on now, Fred. It's time you were in the bath.'

'Oh, just another few minutes...'

'Off you go. I'll be in in a minute to see if you've hung up your bath towel.'

Freddie gave in, with a hug for Jake before leaving. 'He's a great kid,' said Jake, holding out his coffee mug for a top-up. He generally wore short-sleeved T-shirts, whatever the weather, so that there was a reassuring display of strong bronzed arms when he was coping with hammers and saws and mowing equipment.

He was now in his seventies, still erect and vigorous despite occasional back pain, with hair thinning from his forehead to give him what he called 'a noble brow'. No one had ever seen Jake in a bad humour. He was smiling now in recollection of the yarn he'd been spinning to Freddie.

'How're the Miserable Moorfields?' he inquired, patting the sofa beside him to invite Libby to sit.

'Well, they're not a load of laughs. Listen, Jake, you know a bit about metalwork, don't you?'

'Well, I should. Had to help repair a good few busted bits of machinery in my time. Something broken at Ashgrove?'

'No, it's about the furniture in Grandee's room.'

'Grandee? Is that the name for the old lady with the good looks?'

She nodded. 'She's got this suite of furniture, and some of the pieces have got metal banding as decoration, and she says it's chromium.'

'Chromium?' He shook his head. 'Nah, she's got that wrong, maidie. Chromium's that shiny metal that's used just for plating things.'

'That's what I was trying to remember!' cried Libby. 'Chromium plating! Of course. As a finish on things like – well – the decor on old cinema entrance halls, or on things like towel rails.'

'But not on furniture. You mean furniture made of wood, do you?'

'Yes. She says it's chromium, Jake. And she's not the type that gets things wrong.'

'Well...' He sipped his coffee and considered. 'It's possible, I suppose. If the chromium was plated on to, let's say, tin, or steel, and then the steel was cut in narrow strips and embedded with just the chromium showing out – how about that?'

'Narrow strips of some other metal, say steel. Then set into the wood. Yes, and then when the plating began to flake – as it does, doesn't it? – you'd get blotches of darkness.' She was picturing the marks on the decorative stringing she'd tried to clean. If that was chromium, any attempt to clean those dark marks was a waste of time. The only way to cure them was taking out the strips and replacing them. And who on earth would be able to do that nowadays?

'I don't think I'll hand on this information to Grandee,' she remarked. 'Her reaction to the idea of taking down her curtains was warning enough.'

'Scary, is she?'

'They're all a bit daunting. And none of them seem to pay proper attention to the little girl. It's pitiful, Jake. I've had the feeling more than once that I'd like to knock their heads together!'

'Don't let it turn your hair grey, Libby. They're just customers, now aren't they? We go to one after another and they all have their little foibles. Like the old lady – she goes by with her pretty nose in the air if she happens upon me in the garden.' He grinned. 'But all we want from them is their money, not their good opinion.'

'You're right.'

'Remember your own rules. Don't get involved. Do the job you're paid for and nothing more.'

Few of Libby's clients wanted any weekend house care because they themselves were likely to be home for the weekend and wanted the place to themselves. The Moorfields were different, and Libby should have been there on Saturday morning to do the bare essentials.

Jake, however, relieved her of this task. He volunteered to go and give the place what he called 'a rub with a stoker's rag' so that Libby could take Freddie out for the day.

Freddie loved all kinds of ships, and Libby was taking him on a trip to the Royal Naval Museum in Greenwich. Then of course they had to go on a river boat to Canary Wharf, and from there by Dockland Light Railway back to the centre of London. He fell asleep on the train journey home and was put to bed mumbling blissfully about the model ships in the museum.

Jake telephoned to ask if they'd had a good day. 'A huge success,' she told him. 'And how about you at Ashgrove?'

'No problem. Hardly saw a soul. They'd all gone out by about ten. The young Mrs Moorfield was the only one I really came across. She said she was going to her candles and joss-sticks shop in the town – Saturday's a busy day, she said.'

'And what about Primrose? There's no play group on Saturday, I imagine.'

'Yes, there is, but a different one, not the one

she goes to on weekdays. And then I gathered the bigger girl was going to take her shopping.'

'Shopping!' Libby was dismayed. What fun could it possibly be for a toddler to be taken shopping by someone like Angela? Department stores, fashion shops, handbags, shoes, CDs...

'Well, there you are. I left everything fit for inspection and was back home in good time to see *Match of the Day Live*.'

'Thank you, Jake. Freddie bought you some pictures of ships at the museum. Tall-masted sailing ships – he's sure you sailed in those.'

On Sunday Libby caught up with some desk work while Freddie went to a friend's house to play. Unfortunately, an evening spent with her address book failed to yield anyone else she could appeal to as house-help for the Moor-fields, and so on Monday morning she was at Ashgrove again at eight thirty. And so it went on for the next week or two, her colleagues being willing to help care for Freddie but determined not to get roped in to work at Ashgrove.

One day in late April, she had seen Prim leave with Angela for play group, otherwise the house was almost empty. Rosanne had gone for a day's meditation at an ashram, Brenton was in Copen-hagen setting up the stage effects for a special performance by the Tyrants, his pop group, and Grandee was having a session at the Beauty Retreat.

Perhaps because of the lack of any other grown-up, Prim had been more than usually clingy with Libby earlier that morning. She had clambered upstairs with her to dust in the empty bedrooms, had played with the taps in Grandee's super-elegant bathroom, and had peeked guardedly at her father's studio from the safety of the little sleeping area.

Libby didn't mind that the child wanted to be in her company. What had troubled her was Prim's reaction when, yawning, Angela came downstairs to take her off to play group. Prim had been really reluctant to go. That was wrong. A little girl should want to be with other little girls and boys of her own age. It made Libby uneasy that Prim was unwilling to go. It was almost as if she found Libby to be the only dependable element in her routine.

Philip Moorfield was shut up in his office, and had been since before Libby's arrival. She heard him speaking on the telephone now and then. At about eleven o'clock he came out, heading for the kitchen. She saw him go in, heard the sound of a kettle being filled, and guessed he was making himself a cup of coffee.

She came out of the living room and stood hesitantly in the hall. She peeped in at the open door of the kitchen, to see him sitting at the kitchen table with a newspaper. She steeled herself for what she was going to do. Tapping on the door to alert him, she stepped inside. He looked up from his paper.

'Could I have a word, Mr Moorfield?'

He looked a little surprised at the request, or rather at the tone in which it was made. 'Something wrong?'

'In a way. I wanted to speak to you ... that is, I

thought I might just mention...'

'If you're still thinking of getting out of the housework contract,' he said tartly, 'don't bother. It's still got seven months to run.'

'It isn't that. In fact, it's not about work. It's about...'

'Well, what?'

'It's about Primrose.'

'What?' He put down his newspaper, surveying her with astonishment.

'Primrose. She likes to help me do the cleaning – she has a go at dusting, she pushes the vacuum cleaner for a while, she wants to load the dishwasher and so on.'

He was clearly baffled. 'She wants to do housework? That sounds odd.'

'It *is* odd. But she does it because there's no one here for her to play with.'

He was trying to take in this unexpected item of news. He pushed himself away from the table so as to turn and look squarely at her.

'She goes to a play group,' he said. 'She has children to play with there.'

'That's a few hours every day – except Sunday, I gather. Otherwise she's here almost completely on her own.'

'Well ... yes, I suppose so. She ... er ... could have some of her little friends come here to play, couldn't she?'

'She could, if someone would arrange it.'

'Oh, Angela would do that.'

'Only if someone tells her to.'

Now he looked irritated. 'That's Brent's responsibility. She's his kid.'

'But he doesn't see to it,' Libby said desperately. 'Nobody does anything for her. Everybody's always out—'

'Brent works in his studio—'

'Where he shuts himself up doing experiments with fireworks or laser beams or other dangerous things. Primrose is forbidden to go in there. If he leaves the studio it's to go off for days at a time, setting up scenic screens in Amsterdam or wherever that band of his is going to play. I don't think he ever leaves any instructions about Prim.'

'But Angela knows what's expected—'

'Angela is seventeen years old and knows as much as a Barbie doll about caring for a child.'

He almost drew back in alarm at the anger in her words. Then his rather angular features creased into concern. 'My word. It seems you take this seriously.'

Libby made a great effort to regain her cool. 'I'm worried about her...'

'That's hardly part of your job, though, is it?'

'No. I suppose you're going to say it's not my place.' How could she stay cool when this steely business type was being so obtuse? 'Primrose is at a stage where she ought to be learning new things every day, experiencing new ideas and coming to terms with the fact that there's a big world out there. Mostly all she sees is the kids at play group, the women who run it, Angela and ... well ... me.'

'That's nonsense. There's a houseful of people here...'

'Really? *You* are the only other person here in

59

the house at this moment.'

'Well, that's ... that's just today. Normally there's...' He was thinking about it. 'Brent's usually here...'

'He's the Invisible Man, as a rule.'

'Well, Grandee is here—'

'In her suite, most of the time, or else out with friends from the old days. And if you're going to say your mother fills some role in Prim's life, don't bother. Mrs Moorfield is clearly a good and gentle person, but her mind is almost always on something else.'

Something like a smile of agreement flickered for a moment in Philip Moorfield's face but he banished it at once. He said very coldly, 'What exactly is your point?'

'My point is that your little niece is being neglected. She lives in a very nice old house with lots of fine furniture and a room of her own with a little collection of toys and things from her mother, but nobody is really looking after her.'

'But Angela—'

'Don't say Angela is looking after her. I don't want to seem like a telltale, but Angela has as little to do with Prim as she can possibly manage.'

He rose to his feet, stared past her out of the window for a moment or two, then said, 'So what do you suggest'

'Good heavens, it's not up to *me* to suggest anything!' Didn't anybody in this family look outside their own concerns? 'Failing anybody else bothering, I'm saying someone ought to tell

Angela to get a grip. If she's supposed to care for Prim, she should be told to do it properly.' She hesitated, then rushed on. 'It's been on the tip of my tongue to say this to her myself half a dozen times, but she's not going to pay any attention to me. I'm just the hired help.'

He frowned, sighed, and gave something like a nod of agreement. 'She won't listen to me if I try to give her orders either – I'm well known as the bossy big brother.' He was rueful as he went on. 'My mother would just say that each of us has to find their own path through life.'

Libby waited. She hadn't nerved herself to this only to listen to excuses.

'I think you'll have to speak to my grand-mother about it. She's the head of the house-hold,'

Libby was about to demand why this should devolve upon her, but a long ring at the back doorbell prevented her. When she opened it she found a delivery van drawn up alongside, and a man with a list of items for her to check and accept. They were addressed to Brent, so they were clearly equipment for his studio. In his absence, they'd have to go in the garage.

By the time she had dealt with this, Philip had retreated to his office. She sighed inwardly. This family was totally incapable of communicating. The only one who talked at any length was Angela – and she talked mostly about her sense of injury.

Prim came home from play group at the usual time. Angela deposited her in the hall then went back out to her Mini and drove off without a word. Prim rushed to greet Libby. 'Look at my church! It's got a steetle, and inside it's got a norgan, though you can't see it or hear it.'

'If you can't see it or hear it, how do you know it's there?' Libby asked, laughing.

'Cos Bridget at play group says it's there. She says it plays big tunes.' Prim proceeded to la-la something approximate to 'Land of Hope and Glory'.

'That's a really big tune.' Libby examined the cardboard church. 'What's it called, this church?'

'It hasn't got a name,' Prim said, at a loss. 'It's a *church*.'

'But churches have names. The one you pass on your way here from play group is called St James.'

'That's a man's name.'

'Well, churches are called after saints, important people, and they can be men or women. So what's your church called?'

Prim thought for a long moment, then said, 'St Jackie.'

Libby drew in a sharp breath. That was the name of her absent mother. She wondered whether to say anything to that, but she didn't know how to handle the matter of Jackie's absence. Instead she suggested that Prim take the church upstairs to join her farmyard. The child blithely obeyed, saying as she went, 'Can I do dusting afterwards?'

It was the memory of this conversation that drove Libby to take Philip's advice and confront

Grandee the next day. There had to be something more in the child's life than these tiny pleasures, strange and in themselves indicative of the kind of life she was leading.

Grandee came downstairs and went out while Libby was busy in the morning-room, the room farthest from the staircase. 'She's got a posh lunch engagement,' Angela informed her when she inquired. 'Some art organization that's doing something in memory of some old bohemian she used to know.' She added, 'If you're thinking of asking her about that idea of cleaning the curtains in her kingdom, don't bother. She was very hoity-toity when she mentioned that a while ago.'

Libby nodded then hesitated. Should she speak to Angela about Prim instead of trying to approach Grandee? But before she could frame an opening to that conversation, Angela was on her mobile, arranging the evening's amusements.

Grandee came home a little after three o'clock. At that hour Libby was finishing up her chores, preparing to collect Freddie. She had Prim installed at the kitchen table playing with some pastry out of the freezer. It wasn't an ideal moment, but on the other hand, it meant she had to make it a short encounter so as to be at Freddie's school on time.

'Excuse me, Mrs Moorfield,' she said, coming out into the hall to meet her as she entered. 'Can I speak to you for a moment?'

Grandee paused on her way to the drawing room. 'What about? You're not going to raise the matter of—'

'No, no, it's not about the curtains. It's something more important. It's about Prim.'

'Prim?' Grandee echoed, as if she'd hardly
heard of the word. Then, with raised eyebrows,
'Brenton's child?'

'Yes, your great-granddaughter.'

'What on earth can you possibly have to say to
me about my great-granddaughter?'

'I think she's suffering from lack of compan-
ionship and consideration...'

Grandee gave an exclamation of astonishment.
She drew back from Libby as if she were a mani-
festation of life from some other planet. This
was enough to put Libby off her stroke. In the
moment of silence that followed, Grandee found
her voice. 'That is quite enough. You had better
think about what and who you are before you
dare to interfere in family matters, Mrs ... what-
ever-your-name-is.'

'My name is Mrs Fletcher, and by now most of
your family are calling me Libby—'

'Huh!'

'Especially Prim – she's calling me Libby, and
talking to me and following me about, because
there's nobody else in this house for her to relate
to.'

'What on earth do you mean?'

'There's no one else in this house at the
moment except Mr Philip Moorfield, myself,
Prim – and you. You've just come in, and Mr
Moorfield is busy with work in his office. If the
poor child doesn't talk to me, she's got no one to
talk to.'

'I can't imagine that she wants to talk to the

cleaner...'

'Perhaps she doesn't. But for her it's a case of better me than no one.'

'I hardly think so. She has Angela as her companion.'

'She does? Tell me, at this moment, where is Angela?'

This caused Grandee a moment's hesitation. 'I have no idea,' she said with hauteur, 'and I can't imagine that it's any of your business.'

'Then whose is it? I asked Mr Moorfield yesterday if something could be done about it, and in the end he said I should speak to you, because you're the head of the house.'

'Indeed I am. And it's not my view that I should discuss anything with *you*.'

'Then who *will* you discuss it with?'

'That is absolutely none of your concern.'

'I've made it my concern. I can't allow the welfare of a child to be ignored in this way.'

'Child welfare is not what you're here for. You are supposed to clean and tidy up and that's all. And since you seem to be unable to stick to your proper job, I want you out of my house this minute!'

'Oh, so that's how you deal with it, is it? Turn a blind eye and order me out?'

'Will you leave my house, or must I have you thrown out?' Grandee's voice had risen to a screech of fury, and her normally pale face was suffused with high colour.

Alarmed that she might cause her to faint or have a seizure, Libby drew back. 'All right, all right, I'm going. But you ought to think about

65

what I—'

'Get out!' cried Grandee.

Libby went to the bench in the hall where she always left her holdall. There was a patter of footsteps behind her, a cry of anguish, then Prim was clinging on to her skirt with sticky hands. 'Don't go, Libby!' she wailed.

Libby half-turned to calm her, and in doing so upset the holdall. Half its contents cascaded on to the tiles of the hall, making an enormous clatter. Canisters of polish and bottles of cleaning fluid rolled about. Under the high ceilings the sound was enormous.

The door of Philip's office opened. 'What the devil's going on?' he demanded.

Prim, on her knees retrieving cleaning equipment, looked up in appeal. 'Tell her to *stay*!' she begged. 'I want her to *stay*!'

'Be quiet, Prim,' commanded Grandee. To Philip she remarked, 'This impossible woman is leaving.'

'No, no!' cried Prim. 'Not leaving. She's *staying*.'

'Of course she's staying,' Philip said. 'I hired her to do the housework.'

'You might think so, but she's set herself up as a child expert. The impertinence of it!'

'Libby, what happened?'

'I followed your suggestion and spoke to your grandmother about the lack of care Prim's getting—'

'And if you did give her that idea, you show a wonderful lack of judgement, Philip,' Grandee pronounced.

'It seemed a reasonable idea at the time...'

'Good heavens, to listen to the notions of a cleaning woman?'

'Just tone it down, Grandee. This cleaning woman is the best we've had in months and, let me tell you, the last chance we seem to have of getting anyone here to do the work. You can't just sack her because you're having a tantrum.'

'A tantrum?' She straightened herself to her full slender height and faced him with indignant accusation. 'I object when she tries to tell me how to run my family and you call it a tantrum?'

'Well, you're not showing much coolness at the moment—'

'And with good reason! I want this woman out of my house this instant.'

He gave a loud, audible sigh, then said, 'Grandee, I hired Mrs Fletcher. If anyone is going to fire her, it's going to be me. And I say she stays.'

'You're saying you disregard my wishes?' There was utter amazement in her words.

'I'm disregarding your tendency to order everybody about like dogsbodies. We've had a succession of cleaners over the past six months and this firm is the only one that's provided someone suitable. If you're prepared to take on the cleaning and dusting, we might dismiss Mrs Fletcher. But as I can't see you wielding a mop, I think we'll take it as settled that she stays.'

'Yes, stay!' begged Prim. 'Libby, I want you to stay.'

Grandee looked staggered at being defied by both the eldest and the youngest of her tribe. She was trying to gather her forces when the front door opened and Rosanne Moorfield came in with a bag full of fresh vegetables and Angela with a carrier bearing the name of a high-street fashion store.

Prim ran to greet them. 'Nana, tell Grandee Libby's got to stay,' she commanded, pulling at her grandmother's elbow.

'What, dear?'

'She's not to leave. I want her to come every day.'

'Of course, Primmie, she comes every day.'

'She has been extremely disrespectful to me,' Grandee intervened forcibly. 'I have dismissed her.'

'And I've just told you that you can't do that,' Philip said.

Rosanne's face registered total amazement at his tone. No one ever spoke to Grandee like that.

'I don't *want* her to *go*,' Prim wailed. And then, holding back tears and trying to sound grown-up, 'You don't want her to go, now do you, Nana?'

'Sweetie, your hands are all tacky...'

'Libby gave me pastry to play with. So you see, you mustn't tell her to go.'

'No, I won't,' agreed Rosanne. 'And why was she told to go, anyhow?'

'She was giving me unwanted advice on how to bring up Prim,' said Grandee. 'And what makes *her* such a great expert on child-rearing, I wonder?'

'I've got a six-year-old son of my own,' Libby said at once, 'so I think I know a little about it.'

'Indeed? And who's looking after him while

you're out sweeping and dusting for a living?' She smiled around at what she clearly felt was a winning shaft in the argument.

'A colleague of mine takes him to school and I collect him at going-home time. One of my team will always stand in for me if I can't make it. Let me tell you,' Libby said with indignation, 'everyone that works for me is a friend of mine, and I know they can be *trusted.*' At this last word, she couldn't help a glance at Angela, who, still hugging her recently bought evening-top, glared at her, barged past them all, stormed into the drawing-room and slammed the door.

Even Grandee was taken aback at this reaction. She was frowning at her daughter-in-law as she said, 'You know, Rosanne, I don't think Angela's education gave her much idea of good manners.'

This rebuke caused Rosanne to bend her head as if to examine the vegetable fronds sticking out of her carrier. 'But manners are evoked by the atmosphere through which we pass, Grandee. Angela is still at the beginning of her journey through life.'

Philip was trying to hold on to the main issue. 'So it's understood, isn't it, Grandee, that Mrs Fletcher will continue to take care of the house for us?'

The head of the house had calmed down a little since the beginning of the row. Angela's bad manners had proved a distraction, and to Libby it seemed that some faint echo of Philip's common sense was having an effect.

'If the supply of domestic staff is as scarce as

you say, Philip, I suppose we have no alternative. However, I hope I have made my point about impertinence.' Her tone was icy as she directed a withering glance at Libby. 'You and I will speak as little as possible. Is that understood?'

Libby made a slight motion of the head, which might have been taken for agreement. Grandee took that for submission, turned, and went upstairs with her head held high and a straight spine.

Rosanne, watching her go, said in her soft voice, 'Her radiant lumen is always lowered when she gives in to these little tempests. I do wish I could persuade her to take up meditation.'

'But excuse me,' Libby said, 'my main point was about Prim.'

Prim was sitting on the floor among the contents of the holdall, obviously baffled by the behaviour of the grown-ups in her family. Her grandmother stooped to take her by the hand. 'Come along, Primmie, let's put away my shopping in the larder.'

Obediently getting up, the child went with her. Philip watched the pair of them go into the kitchen, then shrugged and sighed. 'I'll try to speak to Angela,' he said, 'though whether it'll have any effect, I don't know. Brent's paying her an allowance for looking after the kid, and if things are really as bad as you make out—'

'Make out! Are you saying I was exaggerating? Let me tell you, I could make out a good case with the local authorities over how Prim is being neglected!'

70

'Hey, hey, get off your high horse. I'm on your side, if you just stop to think about it.'

'We-ell ... yes...' She was apologetic. 'I'm sorry. But really, you've got to take this seriously. Prim can be damaged by what's happening to her in these early years.'

'Let's sit down and talk about this.'

'No, sorry, I have to collect Freddie and it takes me ten minutes to get there.'

'Freddie? That's your little boy?'

Her attention was on gathering up her belongings and getting to her car for the drive to the school. He went on, as if trying to establish some sort of relationship, 'And you're Mrs Fletcher, otherwise known as Libby.'

'Yes.'

'And perhaps you could think of me as Philip.'

'Certainly.'

'Well, perhaps we could have a chat some time tomorrow, could we?'

'Any time you like,' she said, making for the door. She gave him a cursory wave as she went out.

So she was to think of him as Philip, was she? And perhaps she should be a little grateful that he had taken her part against the dreaded Grandee. There was some satisfaction in that.

One thought did not occur to her. By coming out as winner in that controversy, she'd made two enemies: now Grandee and Angela both had reason to detest her.

Five

When Libby arrived at Ashgrove next morning, Angela was in the kitchen making breakfast. Prim was sitting at the kitchen table looking unusually neat, her hair tied on top of her head with red ribbon, and a red kerchief knotted at the neck of her T-shirt.

'Good morning,' said Libby.

'Good morning,' piped Prim.

Angela ignored the greeting. She was buttering toast. Prim was finishing her cereal, into which sultanas had been scattered.

'This is like moosli. And'la says it's better than just Brekkiflakes. See my suntanas?'

'That's a nice change.'

'And toast. And'la's going to put strawb'ry jam on it. You think I'd hate mammalade, don't you, And'la?'

Angela grunted. She put the plate of toast beside the child and swished away the cereal dish.

Prim was chatting rather nervously. She seemed to sense the strain in the atmosphere. Thinking it best to stay out of Angela's way, Libby went to start work on the drawing-room.

Later she had the satisfaction of seeing the little girl being taken into the morning-room to

72

play with a small selection of toys. It was a start, at least, she told herself. But really Prim should be out in the garden now that the weather was warmer. No, that was too much to ask as yet.

When she glanced in on them on her way to do the bedrooms, she saw that Prim was playing at putting her doll to bed in a wicker armchair. 'Now you be good an' go to sleep at once,' she was saying. Angela was listening to something on her iPod, her head bopping to the rhythm she could hear and her feet moving in time.

Libby went in, duster in evidence as a reason for being there. 'What's your dolly's name?' she asked Prim.

'It's Mitzi. That's short for something Jap'nese. Mummy sent her all the way from Tokyo.'

Angela stopped her dance, snatching the earphones out of her ears. She seemed quite taken aback at Libby's entrance, so it took her a moment to find her voice. 'Are you going to start cleaning in here?'

'Not if you and Prim are playing.'

Prim looked from one to the other. 'I'm settling Mitzi down for a nap,' she ventured, her gaze fixing on Libby in uncertainty.

The doll had Japanese features and straight black hair, but was wearing western clothes. 'Doesn't she get undressed if she goes to bed?' Libby asked, in the voice of mother-to-mother.

'She should take her shoes off, but I can't undo the things.'

The shoes fastened with little straps across the instep and had metal buckles.

'Angela will help you,' Libby suggested, and went out.

When she came downstairs a little later she peeped in at the morning room. The doll's clothes had all been removed and were neatly laid out on the table. A tea-cloth from the kitchen had been brought in to serve as coverlet for the sleeper. Angela was sitting in a corner of the wicker settee. Her expression was bored, but the iPod was no longer in evidence and it might be said she was taking some sort of interest in Prim.

Libby went on to the next part of her work. Had she improved matters by interfering?

Philip had suggested they should have a chat that day, but it never came about. He went out soon after she started the chores at Ashgrove; she supposed it was something important to do with film companies.

Brenton returned from abroad the next morning, half an hour after his little daughter had left for play group. He came into the kitchen and to Libby's surprise spoke rather respectfully. 'Phil rang me yesterday and put me in the picture about what happened. He ... er ... suggested that we should have a bit of a conference some time later today, if that's OK with you.'

'About...?' she queried.

'Well, about Prim and Angie and all that. If you could fit it in.'

Libby wanted to declare in loud tones, 'Prim is more important than the housework!' but she knew it would only alarm him. So instead she said, 'I usually break for a bite to eat soon after midday. Would that be about right?'

'Certainly. And ... I remember ... Didn't I see you once, wandering round looking for somewhere to eat a sandwich?'

She shrugged.

'Well, look ... I'll ring for some snacks to be delivered ... And we could sit at the dining table and be ... you know, sort of civilized. Let's say twelve thirty?'

'Very well.'

She left out some of the less important tasks so as to leave ample time for the 'conference'. She had a feeling it might run over the period she usually allowed herself at lunchtime. At twelve, she was summoned to the back door by the delivery of a large tray covered in plastic film under which she could see all sorts of manly snacks – substantial Cornish pasties, meaty sandwiches, all decked out with little scraps of lettuce. Ah well, just for once she'd forget her diet.

She made coffee in the largest of the cafetières. She'd already set out plates and cutlery and coffee mugs, but no wine glasses. She wanted them all to keep a clear head.

Brenton was first to arrive. He'd changed out of the decent suit and tie in which he'd travelled, into jeans and a scruffy sweatshirt. Philip was clad for the business world, albeit without his suit jacket.

Libby busied herself with pouring the coffee. Brenton heaped sugar into his cup, stirred with unnecessary vigour, then said, 'I gather from Phil that you have some worries about ... sort of how Prim is faring ... That's it, isn't it?'

'Basically, I suppose that's it. I explained to your brother that I thought she wasn't getting proper attention.' She turned to Philip. 'You said you'd speak to Angela, and clearly you have. Yesterday and today she gave most of her time to Prim.'

'So that's sorted then, is it?' Brenton asked.

Libby didn't know how to answer that.

Philip said, 'You're hesitating. You've got reservations?'

'I'm not an expert. Your grandmother pointed that out, if you recall.'

'I'm afraid she did. But you replied that you had a little boy of your own, so...' He paused, searching for the right words. 'I mean, Libby, what do Brent and I know about bringing up kids?'

She decided to come at the problem from another angle. 'What did Angela say when you spoke to her on the subject?'

'Oh, she wasn't very responsive.'

Brenton was munching at one of the thick sandwiches. He set it down with irritation. 'She was perfectly agreeable when I suggested our arrangement. She's just got to sort of act as a stand-in, you know, until we can get someone who's qualified. She knows that. Why is she being so difficult about it?'

It was Philip who answered that question. 'Angie's got problems, Brent. You can't have forgotten how she played up while she was at school, and then refusing to take her GCSEs...'

'Oh, I'm sick of having to deal with this sort of stuff!' Brenton burst out. 'Why can't Angie just behave, and do what I'm paying her for? But mostly she just seems to moon about, looking like something from *Apocalypse Now* or getting sozzled with her pals.'

'Good lord, if you felt like that about her, how on earth could you let her take charge of Prim?' Libby cried.

Brenton stared in shock at her tone. He shifted uncomfortably in his chair.

Libby felt herself colour up, and reminded herself she had to keep her cool. There was an awkward silence.

'Mama thinks it's just a phase she's going through,' said Philip eventually, his manner apologetic towards Libby. But Brenton took it as a reproach directed at him.

'It's a phase that's been going on for years! And why? Just because she doesn't know who her dear Daddy was!' The last words were a mimicry of Angela's manner.

'I beg your pardon?' Libby said, taken aback.

'Some bloke from Canada or somewhere. You can imagine – Mama met him at an ashram and never saw him again.'

Libby's mind was trying to catch up with this unexpected information. 'You mean she's only your half-sister?'

'Yes, and twice the trouble to the family. Mama of course explains she's in a "dim lumen phase" or some such thing, and as for Grandee, she just thinks she's badly brought up, and says so every chance she gets.' Brenton looked in appeal at his brother. 'You and I went through progressive education and all that rubbish, Phil, and we don't go around like Doom and Despondency, now do we?'

'You don't exactly radiate a zest for life yourself, kiddo,' Philip replied, but with a smile that robbed the words of harm. 'But what we need to know is, how are you getting on with finding a new nanny for Prim?'

Among the dark stubble round his mouth, it was possible to see Brenton's lips turn down at the corners. 'It's not easy. And I don't have all that much time to spend on telephoning around.'

'I could get up an inquiry letter that could be sent out to half a dozen of the firms at the same time – how about that?'

'I think we've tried most of the established firms in the past. And two of them supplied fully trained nannies. But, you know, when their staff went back to them, complaining about how things are run here, word got round among the other firms and we're on a sort of blacklist – or grey, at any rate.'

'How about trying the au pair network?'

Libby could see it was becoming a practical discussion about hiring new staff. She rose, saying, 'If you don't mind, then, I'll just get back to work.' And with that she left them to it.

Brenton came in search of her later. He hovered about in the doorway of the kitchen as she was taking laundry out of the drier, until she paused for him to speak.

'I don't want you to get the wrong idea,' he began. 'I think the world of Primmie, but I'm not really, you know, a "kiddie person". The pop music world is sort of ... Well, it's different and it takes up a lot of my time. You know?'

'But Prim must get proper attention, Brent.'

'Yes, and I've *tried*, I really have. The last one I hired had all sorts of qualifications but it turned out she smoked like a chimney so I *had* to give her the push.' He gazed at her for her understanding and approval.

'I know it must be difficult,' she agreed. She knew from her own insider knowledge that staff were not willing to come to Ashgrove, and she also knew that word got round among the agencies. 'I could ask around,' she suggested. 'I don't have any contact with the big firms, but I'll keep an eye open for anyone that might fit the bill.'

'It's very good of you,' he said. 'It's not very usual, you know, to find someone who cares so much about somebody's kid that they'd make a fuss.' He studied her with interest, as if she were a new species.

She returned to her task, avoiding any further discussion. She was telling herself she'd gone much too far. Don't get involved; do the job you're paid for. That was the rule.

The following weekend, she had booked into a seminar at a conference centre on the subject of care and restoration of antique furniture. It was something she hoped to return to one day, as a career move. Jake had volunteered once more to take her place on Saturday morning at Ashgrove.

'And you'll get a chance to have a good look at Grandee,' Libby told him, teasing. She was giving final instructions – warnings, perhaps, was more appropriate. 'She gave me a telling-off this morning when she realized I wasn't going to be there. She's got friends coming to dinner tomorrow evening so she'll probably want to oversee your cleaning and dusting.'

'I'll see everything's shining bright for her, bless her hoity-toity little heart.'

'You've really got a soft spot for her, haven't you, Jake?'

'Oh, you know what they say about sailors,' he said. 'A girl in every port.'

'Never got tempted into marriage by any of your collection?'

'Never wanted to settle down when I was fit and less than forty. Now I'm getting on a bit, I wouldn't mind a sweet smile and a soft voice to come home to.'

'Don't set your hopes on Grandee, then! She doesn't seem to smile often, and her voice can get quite shrill.'

'That's because you don't known how to treat her,' Jake laughed. 'If I ever get close to her, I'll melt the icicles.'

Libby took Freddie with her to the conference centre, which provided a play leader for the children of their clients. He enjoyed himself hugely, and in the auction after lunch on Sunday, Libby sold a chaise longue she'd been working on in her spare time. Devoted attention to the wood and careful choice of upholstery fabric resulted in a sale price of £2,000. Delighted at this proof that her skills hadn't deserted her, she bought her son a model boat on the drive home.

They were late back at the flat. Freddie practically fell into bed, still clutching his model frigate. Libby made herself a snack, read some mail that had arrived after she left on Friday evening, and was thinking about a long relaxing bath when her phone rang at about ten o'clock.

'Jake! Why are you ringing so late? Something wrong?'

'There's been a fire at Ashgrove, maidie. Had the brigade there most of the morning.'

'Oh, good lord! Whereabouts? The kitchen?'

'No, 'twas the studio of that lad with the stubbly chin—'

'Brenton!'

'Aye, seems he went off for the weekend on Saturday leaving some of his equipment switched on, and it overheated or faulted or summat. Not much flame but a lot of nasty smoke.'

'How did you hear about it?'

'They called me in, wouldn't you know! They needed to get into the studio when they first smelt the fumes, and nobody knew where the keys were. A hopeless band, they are! So they rang Housecare's emergency line to get keys, and I took 'em to the house. Firemen in breathing equipment everywhere!'

'Did anybody breathe the smoke? It might be harmful. What about Prim?'

'OK, s'far as I know.'

'That's a relief. So did the fire spread?'

'Nah, only smoke drifting. It didn't rise into the air, so the bedrooms should be all right. But you might have a problem or two with cleaning the ground-floor rooms tomorrow.'

She groaned. What a miserable outlook, after such a glorious weekend.

Next day she made an especially early start. One of her staff would take Freddie to school, with no objection from him when he heard his mother was going to something as exciting as the scene of a fire.

The drive at Ashgrove showed damage from the wheels of emergency vehicles. The gravel on the semicircular drive looked as if it had been ploughed, the bushes were somewhat crushed and the trunks of one or two of the ash trees were bruised. A strange, almost chemical odour hung in the air.

When she let herself into the house, she could smell it even more strongly. There was a stickiness on the bench where she always left her holdall. She grumbled inwardly. It would probably be days before she got rid of this after-effect.

She decided she would have to call in extra help, for the studio, in particular – but she would not dare even look in at the damage. Everything was best left undisturbed until the insurance assessor had looked at it. In the house itself, smoke had created a film over much of the ground-floor furniture, and this she could start on herself once she had established priorities. She would have to call in extra help, she felt sure. And the great old tapestry curtains in the drawing-room and the dining room would have to come down for special cleaning.

It struck her as ironic that after her warning to Grandee about sun damage to the curtains in her suite, the first thing to be removed should be the Victorian hangings in the downstairs rooms.

Prim came to join her much earlier than usual. It was clear she had dressed herself this morning, without Angela's help.

'I heard you when you droved up,' she said, coming to stand close to her. 'Did you know we had a *fire* yesterday?'

'Yes, Jake telephoned to let me know.'

'Jake? Was he one of the firemen?'

'No, he came to bring the keys to your daddy's studio.'

'There was lots of big men with *faces*! And'la said they were wearing *breeding* masks, but we make masks at play group and they're not like those, Libby.'

Libby picked her up and set her on a chair at the kitchen table. Then she leaned against the table, casually but so as to be almost touching. 'The masks you make at play group are cardboard, Prim. The masks the firemen were wearing were made of special stuff, to protect them.'

'They all had a *big eye*!'

'Oh yes, a big eye, so they could see what was causing the smoke.'

'But they had *one* eye – they should've had two!'

'Oh no, no, it was made specially like that – like a little window to look out of. Like when you're riding in the car, Prim, you look out of a window, don't you? And you can see other cars, and the shops, and trees...'

Prim received this in puzzled silence. Then she said, 'And'la said the smoke was nasty. It was a fire but there was no flames or anything, only nasty smoke.'

83

'Yes, it's made some of the furniture sticky and horrid. I'm going to have to do more than just dust it today, Prim.'

A pause. 'What are you going to do, then?'

'I might have to wipe things with a cloth that will have special cleaning stuff on it.'

'But I wanted to do dusting for you, Libby.'

'No, today we'll find you another job to do.' She racked her brains. 'I'll tell you what. Grandee did some pretty flowers for the dinner party, didn't she?'

'Yes. Froral arrainments.'

'Yes, rather special. But now the poor flowers have been spoiled, so how about if you take them out of their vases and wrap them in some old newspaper so we can put them away?'

'Grandee doesn't like anyone to touch her arrainments.'

'Not usually. But this is different, isn't it? The flowers aren't going to be happy so we'll let them lie down and rest wrapped up in newspaper.'

Prim leaned towards her so that her head rested against her arm. 'We'll put them in a safe place. Where the big firemen won't harm them.'

'Yes, we will. We'll put them aside. But the firemen wouldn't harm them, Prim. Firemen come to help, not to harm.'

'But they don't have proper faces, Libby.' She whimpered and pressed close against her.

In instinctive reaction Libby put her arm around the child. 'It's all right, sweetie,' she soothed. 'They wear masks so they can breathe and put out the fire. They want to help.'

84

'Ye-es.' It was very uncertain agreement. 'But they won't come back, will they?'

'No, love, they won't come back.'

They stayed in that quiet embrace for about a minute. Then Libby said, 'Ready for breakfast?'

The little girl shook her head without looking up.

'How about cereal with fruit salad?'

'I'm not hungry.'

'Fruit salad with orange and plum and banana? And you can help me make it.'

'We-ell...'

While Prim ate the specially prepared breakfast, Libby collected the flower vases from the ground-floor rooms. It would have been untrue to say the flowers were much damaged, but they had been made ready on Saturday morning for a gathering that same evening, so by now they were a little tired.

She arranged the vases in a row on the kitchen floor. There, if Prim tipped one over, there would be little harm. By and by little newspaper packages were lying in a row alongside the kneeling child, each containing two or three flowers. Prim was delighted with the work. When all the vases were emptied, Libby led her out to the garden. There the packages were solemnly laid on the compost heap.

'Goodbye,' Prim said to them. Then to Libby, 'They'll be all right now, won't they?'

'Yes, they'll have a nice sleep, and then in a while they'll mix up with other things and perhaps in a year—'

'When I'm four—'

'Yes, when you're four, they'll be helping to make other flowers grow.'

Satisfied, Prim allowed herself to be led back to the kitchen. Here Angela had put in an appearance, and looked vexed when she saw her small charge coming in at the back door.

'Where on earth did you get to?' she demanded with irritation.

'I was here, And'la. Eating fruit salad with my Brekkiflakes. And then I wrapped up the flowers and put them to sleep.'

'But why did you get dressed so early?'

'I was awake and Libby droved up so I came down and she made me fruit salad.'

'Well, we'll just have to go upstairs again. You look a mess...'

'Angela,' Libby interrupted, 'Prim's been helping me by tidying up the flower vases.' She nodded towards them, ranged in a row against one wall. 'I'm going to wash them now, and put them away for next time.'

'Huh! Grandee will have something to say about that. Flowers for the house are a special fad with her.' Diverted from scolding Prim, she poured herself coffee from the vacuum jug, glancing out of the window at the paved area leading to the garages. 'You missed all the fun,' she said. 'Hosepipes and dirty water everywhere.'

'Is the damage very bad?'

'Who knows? Only Brent can say. He's on his way back at this moment, I imagine. But he's insured.' She shrugged. 'Good opportunity, eh? Re-stock with brand new stuff after he brings in a crew of big guys to clear up the rubble.'

'Big men with masks?' Prim asked, her voice shaking.

'No, no, just men who'll do the cleaning, Prim.' Libby directed a warning glance at Angela, but Angela was gulping down her coffee in preparation for starting her day.

'Come on, Prim, upstairs for proper washing and dressing. Did you clean your teeth? Yes? Well, better do it all again, just to be sure. Come on.'

She took the little girl by the back of her T-shirt and shepherded her out of the room. Libby grabbed at the bandanna that covered her hair and yanked it off. She wanted to throw it at something. But next moment good sense had returned. She put it back on, sighing and shaking her head.

Rosanne was next to appear. She came downstairs in outdoor clothes. 'Good morning,' she murmured. 'I'll get out of your way, Libby. You'll have a lot to do and anyway that odd chemical sort of smell is harmful to my etheric shield.'

'Prim and Angela will be going to play group soon. Is there anyone else in the house?'

'No, no, Grandee left last night for the Haven, and I don't think she'll come home until the house is back to normal. Philip was here over the weekend but he had to leave for London first thing this morning. Brenton, of course, he was in Copenhagen. He'll be back soon, I imagine. Poor Brenton, he'll be so upset.' She drifted across the hall to the front door. 'You can get in touch with me at the shop. But just hire any help you need, Libby. Philip left word that he had confidence in you.'

Alone in the house, Libby stood a moment in thought. Should she have asked Rosanne about Prim's welfare? There had been dangerous fumes entering the house yesterday – had the little girl breathed in anything that might harm her? If this had happened to Libby's little boy, she'd have taken him at once to the doctor for a check-up.

But no. The toddler was upset enough. A visit to the doctor might only make her more edgy. And certainly Angela wasn't the kind of escort who would give much comfort to Prim if she cried on being examined.

She dismissed the idea from her mind. She made a tour through the ground-floor rooms, assessing what needed to be done. It was no use opening windows in hopes of fresh air. The 'odd chemical smell' would only come in stronger. She made lists of what needed doing in each room. Specialists would be needed to clear Brenton's studio and carry away the spoiled, reeking equipment before she could even think about cleaning that.

The insurance assessor arrived mid-morning, and Libby conducted him to the scene of the fire. He was walking around with a palmtop computer recording his verdicts when the studio's owner turned up.

Brenton Moorfield took one look. He made a stifled sound then hurried off, looking as if he were about to be sick. The man from the insurance company gazed after him with some sympathy. 'Means a lot to him, does it?'

Libby nodded agreement. After allowing a few moments for Brenton to recover himself, she went in search of him. The assessor would need him to supply proof of purchase of the equipment, and other information.

She found him sitting on an old wrought-iron bench in the garden, his face clay-coloured.

'You can replace it all,' she murmured gently. 'It will look better in a day or two when it's all been cleaned up.' She sat down beside him on the bench and put a friendly hand on his arm.

He turned wordlessly towards her and hid his face against her shoulder.

Six

Libby had been quick to comfort Prim, but Prim's father was a different matter. She sat for about ten seconds, making no move. Then she said, very quietly, 'The man from the insurance company will want to check things with you. Won't he?'

He straightened, sighed, and rose from the bench. 'I can't bear to look at it. But you're right.' And off he went, apparently unaware that he'd let his emotions carry him away for a moment.

Libby went back to the house. Brenton never

reappeared. Libby consulted her list then took out her mobile phone to summon the extra help she was going to need. Jake was one of those she called: she needed him to take down the heavy curtains and pelmets, and to shift the furniture off the great old carpets in the downstairs rooms so that they too could be taken for professional cleaning.

'Got the place to yourself,' he remarked when he came in.

'Yes, and if that's a way of asking if you'll get a glimpse of Grandee, you're out of luck. She's off in some health farm or something, until the house is tidied up.'

'That makes sense. What about the stuff in the studio?'

'That's not my affair.' She explained the need for expert technical help.

He went to find a stepladder so he could reach the pelmets. Libby thought about replacements, and decided Rosanne was the likeliest person to know where they were kept. She used the land line in the drawing-room to telephone her at her shop.

'Oh, yes, in the attic,' Rosanne replied to her inquiry. 'I don't go up there – it's not restful to my deep-kenning. But we had a housekeeper for a time who used to bring down loose covers and things like that. She said the soft furnishings were in a cedar chest, I think.'

True enough, there was a large cedar chest in the attic, labelled in copperplate writing: Cloths and Covers. Inside she found flat cardboard boxes of the kind that might have been used for delivering dresses in Edwardian times, each one again labelled with its contents. She took out curtain sets and soft covers for the drawing-room and dining room. The morning-room had old-fashioned wood shutters, and Philip's office had rattan blinds that she thought she could clean in situ.

Her extra helpers arrived in the early after-noon. By that time she'd worked out a routine for them, and so the task of cleaning and clearing up began.

Brenton went off to the Midlands to choose replacements for his machines. He stayed away, as did Grandee at her beauty clinic. Rosanne went out every day, sometimes to her shop, sometimes to some healing centre or seminar. Philip was in London, but kept in touch by tele-phone.

The only people who used the house during the day were Angela and Prim. They of course went out to playgroup, but after that was over, they returned.

'The poor kid doesn't know where to put her-self,' Libby sighed to Jake. 'She wants to help me with the cleaning, but it's not really the best thing for her to be around stuff like borax or washing soda. I cleaned up the morning room first, so she could play in there, but Angela just sits there listening to music or reading maga-zines.'

'And she couldn't have her little friends to play with her while the house is in such a state.' He pulled at his chin with a leathery hand. 'Why can't she be out in the garden?'

'Well, the awful thing is, she doesn't have any toys for playing outdoors. I suppose her mother went off to work in Japan before Prim got to the stage of wanting – for instance – a toddler's tricycle.'

'Tell you what: I could fix her a swing.'

'Oh, Jake, that could be dangerous...'

'No, no, a little kiddy swing, from a low branch on the cedar tree. And if she should happen to fall off, it'd only be on to the grass.' He began making designs in the air. 'Just a little seat with holes bored for ropes with stays on them at the tree branch, so she can't swing too high. And I could make a back to the seat so she can't fall of that way. What d'you think?'

'It could be just what she needs. I'll ask her grandmother next chance I get.'

Rosanne, queried about it, smiled acceptance. 'A swing is such a *natural* thing, isn't it?' She gazed at some inner picture. 'Grass sways in the wind; waves come and go on the shore ... Oh, yes, I think it would be lovely if Prim had such an organic plaything.'

So Jake made the swing and put it up, and Prim was led out one morning to make friends with it. At first she wasn't impressed. 'The swing at play group is red and blue,' she remarked, pushing out her lower lip in disdain.

'But what does it hang from?' Libby asked, guessing the answer was a metal frame or something of that kind.

Prim gestured over her head. 'A big thing. It goes across.'

'Like a big towel rail.'

'Yes.'

'Well, this swing hangs from a tree. When you sit on it, you can look up, and you'll see leaves, and maybe even a bird.'

'A bird?'

'A blackbird. You've got them in your picture books, haven't you?'

'Yes, and hens, and cheeky sparrows. Bridget says sparrows come and eat crumbs, but I've never seen that. Will a blackbird eat crumbs?'

'I'm not sure. But it might sing for you.' She'd heard a blackbird singing quite often from somewhere in the grounds.

Prim approached the swing, her pale features wearing an expression of wariness. She set her doll Mitzi on it, and in doing so caused it to move gently. Mitzi lay quietly on the seat, her eyes closed as if she were dozing.

'Mitzi likes it,' Libby encouraged.

So for the first encounter Prim sat on the grass by the swing, sending Mitzi gently to and fro. Angela, who had witnessed the first meeting in silence, walked indoors and left her to it. Until they left for play group, Libby kept an eye on the child from various windows as she went about her work.

By day three Prim was swinging herself lazily back and forth with Mitzi in her lap. Then came a spell of rainy weather. However, the house was getting back to something like normal, so Prim produced her duster and trotted around helping with the housework. But she still wasn't her old self, Libby thought. She seemed very clingy and easily moved to tears. Always a rather plain child, her expression now was often doleful.

At the beginning of the next week Libby had what she thought was a good idea. Driving her son Freddie to school, she asked, 'How about inviting Prim to your birthday party?'

'Who?'

'Prim. I've told you about her – the little girl at Ashgrove.'

'Oh, a *little kid!*'

Freddie was going to be seven. He let it be known that in the first place, he had no time for girls in general, and in the second place, he didn't want little girls at his birthday party. 'She'd only be a nuisance.'

'She likes ice cream.'

'So what if she does?'

'We could get some extra-nice ice cream if she were coming.' She saw out of the corner of her eye that he was considering this. 'The chocolate chunky one from that shop in the High Street,' she prompted.

'*And* the one with bits of pineapple?'

So that was the deal: two lots of expensive ice cream in return for Prim's invitation to the party.

Freddie's school friends, ten in all, were being taken to a children's bouncy playground on Saturday afternoon as the opening to the party, but Libby felt that six- and seven-year-olds in action would be too much for the little girl. So her invitation was for the party in Libby's flat, due to begin at four, where there would be simple games, ice cream, and a magician.

Prim was delighted at first to be asked to a party, but then she became rather scared. 'Will there be big boys?' she asked in anxiety.

'Yes, and some big girls too. But they're very nice, Prim.' Big, of course, meant anyone too old for play group.

'I don't know them.'

'No, but you'll soon make friends.'

It turned out that Prim didn't have a party frock. For the occasional birthday celebrations held at play group, she'd been sent in her ordinary clothes.

Angela had been amazed when Libby asked her take Prim out and buy her a party frock, but at least it was shopping, which was something she enjoyed. So the little girl was taken straight from play group on Thursday to the shopping mall, and returned with a silk organza dress and matching slippers. Pink, of course.

'You look lovely,' Libby said when Prim tried the outfit on for her benefit.

'And'la says I have to buy something for Freddie's birfday. What kind of thing would he like?'

'Things to draw with. He likes to draw boats.'

So the present was bought and wrapped on Friday, and Libby left Ashgrove that afternoon with the feeling that at last Prim would have a new, happy experience.

Not so. Prim was delivered to Libby's flat at the appointed time by her father, as it seemed Angela had a Saturday date with one of her friends and had refused to take on this chore. Brenton wasn't in a good mood. He handed over the little girl as quickly as he could to Amy, one of the Housecare staff who had volunteered to help run the party.

'He had to get back,' she reported to Libby. 'He says the techies are at the house, settling in the new equipment for his studio.'

Prim ventured into Libby's sitting room looking apprehensive. There Freddie and his friends were in the midst of a game of pass the parcel, too busy to take any notice of her. The room was full of noise and excitement.

Amy gently urged her forward and conducted her as far as Libby, who paused in monitoring the rumpus long enough to give the little girl a hug and a place to sit. Once the winner had been declared, she announced an interlude, during which ice cream and birthday cake would be served.

The blinds were pulled down, the lights were put out, and the birthday cake was brought in with its seven candles alight. It was in the shape of a steamboat, with birthday wishes on a flag and the name 'Frederick' on the prow. There were 'Oohs' and 'Aahs' of appreciation, and applause when Freddie blew out the candles.

The lights were switched on again so that party hats could be tried on and little goodies could be found at each place setting. Freddie cut the cake to the traditional tune, in which Prim joined in a trembling little soprano.

She was led to the birthday boy and proffered her gift. He unwrapped it quickly, said, 'Oh, brill!' at sight of the rows of coloured pencils in their neat case, and then, as previously instructed, said, 'Thank you very much for a very useful present.'

Prim was abashed at what, to her, seemed a

lengthy speech. But her spirits seemed to revive when she was settled at the table and offered a slice from the home-made cake, and then a choice of the rich ice creams. To drink there was fruit juice mixed with sparkling mineral water to make it fizzy.

After a lengthy session at table, the entertainment was introduced and a magician appeared in a suit of dark blue velvet and tall hat dotted with sequins.

His tricks at first were of the simplest kind. Some of them drew both laughter and taunts from the seven-year-olds – 'My dad can do that!' – but then he began to make things appear from the shirt pockets of the boys and the party hats of the girls – strange things like big bunches of flowers, endless silk scarves, an eel that wriggled up the magician's arm to disappear under his collar.

The next set of tricks was intended especially for the boys. They all seemed to involve a loud crack of some kind, or a flash of fireworks.

Prim began to cry.

In the laughter and applause, no one noticed at first. Then Libby saw her get down from her chair and crouch behind it. She was heading towards her when Freddie, sitting a few seats along, noticed her.

He left his place. Libby saw him kneel beside Prim and murmur to her. Prim hung her head, crouching into herself. Freddie pulled her to her feet, spoke to her with childlike authority, and shepherded her from the room while the rest of the magician's audience laughed and cheered.

His mother went to the door to see what was happening. He was explaining to Prim that the magician was only playing a game.

'I don't like it,' whimpered Prim.

'It's for my party. But you don't have to watch him if you don't want to.'

She nodded vigorously. Then she looked at this saviour, wondering what he would say next.

'Would you like to see my boat? Mum bought it for me a couple of weeks ago.'

Prim said neither yes nor no. She was at a loss.

'It's in my room.'

There was a sharp report from the sitting room and a cheer from the audience. Prim gave a little shriek.

'Come on,' said Freddie, 'I'll show you how to sail to the Bahamas.'

Off they went. Libby peeped in at them a moment later, to see her son carefully unpacking his model ship from its box and pointing out its wonders to his guest. 'It's a frigate. That means it's next in line to an admiral's warship and it's got square sails, see? If you pull on this little thread here, the sails get set – how good is that!'

'Does it go in the pond where the ducks are?' Prim asked, enthralled at the sight of the little linen sails spreading on the yardarms.

'No, no, you don't put it in water, it's a model, but I sail it across the floor – you can go to India, that's a really long voyage.'

Libby withdrew quietly. Prim had wiped away her tears and was watching the model ship as Freddie pushed it along on the carpet.

In the sitting room the magician was producing

his finale, an arrangement of little coloured windmills set in motion when he switched on a hidden electric fan, to the accompaniment of the theme music to the Magic Roundabout. It was after six o'clock, time for all the seven-year-olds to be given their goodie bags and collected by their appreciative parents.

Prim was the last to be collected at nearly seven o'clock. Libby went along the passage to Freddie's room, to reassure the little girl that someone was coming for her. She found her kneeling on the floor behind a row of plastic building blocks, which Freddie announced to be Jamaica.

'I'm sailing *Powerful* to chase away the pirates,' he explained. 'Prim's the mayor of Jamaica, waiting to welcome me.'

Prim nodded solemn agreement, waving a miniature Union Jack to demonstrate how glad she was to be rescued from pirates.

'Well, perhaps you'd like to come and get your goodie bag, Miss Mayor,' Libby suggested.

'No, I'm waiting to tell Freddie "Glad to see you".'

At that moment the bell rang at the downstairs door. 'That will be someone for you, Primmie. Perhaps you could sail into harbour, Freddie, so she could say "Glad to see you and goodnight".'

Freddie hastily sailed the frigate across the few yards of carpet. Prim waved her flag, said in an important voice, 'Welcome to Jamaica, Captain Freddie Fletcher,' and collapsed in giggles.

It was the first time Libby had ever heard the child laugh. Astounded at the thought, she went down the steep stairs to the door alongside her office-shop. Brenton Moorfield was there, about to ask for his daughter. But the words seemed to evaporate on an indrawn breath of surprise, and he just stared at Libby.

She was a little taken aback at the mute stare. Then she said, hostess-like, 'Prim is playing with my little boy. This way.' She led him up to her flat and along to Freddie's room, where Prim was gathering up the fortifications of Jamaica and helping Freddie to put them away.

'I've been sailed to Jamaica, Daddy,' she announced in glee. 'Freddie sailed me. I was the mayor and I have a flag, and Freddie says I can keep it.'

'That's ... that's great.' Brenton had gathered himself together. 'Have you had a good time, pet?'

'Lovely,' sighed Prim.

They went to the sitting room to get Prim's going-home present. She took the little pink carrier bag with eagerness, glanced inside, then tucked in the flag from the defence of Jamaica.

Freddie, watching her, said in the superior tones of a big boy to a little girl, 'When you're bigger I'll take you sailing all the way to where my Grandpa works, in what's called a marina. It's a boat place, in the Bahamas.'

'I'll be four soon,' said Prim.

'Say thank you to Libby for the party,' prompted her father.

'Thank you for the party, Libby.'

'Yes, thank you for that, and for ... taking an interest in Prim,' Brenton said hesitantly.

'No problem.'

There was a pause. 'You look quite different from usual,' he ventured.

'Oh? Well ... party clothes, you know.'

Very modified party clothes, as Libby had learned that children, especially little boys, don't like their mothers to look too stylish. But instead of her usual jeans or cotton skirt, shirt, and apron, Libby tonight was wearing a blue poplin dress with a scooped neckline. Her light brown hair, usually tied out of the way in a bandanna, was ruffled about her head. Moreover, she was flushed with the exertions of running the party and looking after ten little guests and a timid child.

'Very nice,' he said. He seemed uncertain. 'It was good of you to invite Prim.' He rubbed his stubbled chin. Libby hid a smile at the sound this made, and wished him away. She was tired; it had been a long and very active day.

'Well, goodnight then,' she said.

'Yes ... Goodnight. And thank you again. Come along, Primmie.'

She took them downstairs and waved goodbye as they drove away from the front of the shop.

The coming week was half-term holiday at Freddie's school. Libby had been troubled about it, because this was usually an opportunity to spend time with her son, but now she would have to work at Ashgrove instead. The problem had been solved for Monday: a teacher at Freddie's school had arranged a field trip, which would take him pond-dipping until mid-afternoon. For Tuesday, the fire at Ashgrove had to some extent simplified matters. Libby planned to leave Jake in charge. The freshly cleaned carpets would be returning to the house, so he would oversee their installation. That made sweeping and dusting in the downstairs rooms well-nigh impossible, so she planned to take Freddie to a children's zoo, then leave him at a school friend's house for tea when she would visit Ashgrove for a quick round of the bedrooms and bathrooms.

Once Freddie was delivered to the gathering point for the Monday field trip, she went, rather later than usual, to Ashgrove. To her dismay, a large contingent of Moorfields was awaiting her, including Vivienne, the domineering doyenne of the house.

'What time of day do you call this?' she inquired, coming to the doorway of the drawing-room.

'It's just after ten o'clock.'

'And Sunday's dishes are still on the kitchen table.' Grandee marched into the hall, accusation in every line.

'I'll have them in the dishwasher in a minute.'

'Are we to get no apology for your lateness?'

Libby stopped looking for her apron in her holdall. 'There are no set hours for my presence here,' she remarked.

Philip Moorfield had followed his grandmother from the drawing-room. Libby thought she saw him hide a smile at her response to Grandee's challenge.

'My rooms have scarcely been touched while I was away,' Grandee said, shifting her ground.

'And I hear you took it upon yourself to dispose of my floral arrangements.'

'Quite right. The flowers seemed rather sad. As to the upstairs rooms, they've been given minimal attention while we remedied the damage done downstairs by the smoke.'

'Ah yes, I gather you felt it absolutely necessary to take up the carpets. The noise from walking on the parquet is quite unbearable to my daughter-in-law.' She turned to Rosanne, who was hovering behind her, clad in a beautiful Hungarian blouse and flounced skirt, but looking unhappy. 'Isn't that so, Rosanne?' She stepped aside so that Rosanne could play her part in the surprise attack.

'Er ... yes ... It does make an awful clatter, Libby.'

'The carpets will be back tomorrow.'

The wind was somewhat taken out of Grandee's sales by that response. She hesitated. Philip stepped in. 'Well done, then. I was going to recommend we all wore slippers if we had to walk on wood any longer.'

'And the curtains?' Grandee demanded, returning to the charge. 'Those you've put up are unsuitable. When will the tapestry curtains be back?'

'They are back already, Mrs Moorfield. I thought the substitutes were rather nice, with summer coming on—'

'You have no artistic taste! Those tawny shades look like army tents, and they're too lightweight for rooms with such high ceilings. I want the tapestry curtains put back.'

'Very well.'

Brenton appeared, coming in through the back door of the house. 'Well, hello there,' he cried with pleasure as he joined them. 'Prim was looking for you this morning – where did you get to?'

'I was taking Freddie to school. He's going on a field trip—'

'Freddie! Angela says Primmie never stopped talking about him all day yesterday,' Rosanne put in, with a hint of approval.

Libby smiled. 'Glad she enjoyed it.'

'Enjoyed what?' asked Grandee, looking from one to the other in irritation.

'Oh, great excitement! Prim went to a birthday party on Saturday, Grandee, wearing her first party frock.'

'A birthday party, Brent? I didn't know about this.' There was vexation in the words.

'Well, you were at your beauty spa. I didn't think you'd want to be kept up to date with Prim's outings.'

'And where was this party?' Grandee inquired, eyeing Libby with suspicion.

'At my flat. It was my little boy's seventh birthday,' Libby said.

The old lady stiffened. She gave Brenton the full power of her disapproving stare. 'And that is why you didn't inform me, Brent. You knew I would forbid it. It was quite inappropriate.'

'Oh, come on, Grandee, you wouldn't deny the kid a little bit of fun, surely,' Philip interposed.

'Not at all. But I should like it to be more suitable than a visit to the home of a servant.'

With that she turned and made her way across to the morning-room, closing the door behind her with unnecessary vigour.

'Oh, dear,' murmured Rosanne. 'Now she's undone all the good from her little rest at the Haven.'

Philip was shaking his head. He said to Libby, 'I'm afraid she'll never forgive you for taking her to task about Prim. Perhaps I was wrong to let that happen.'

'Prim was all lit up about the party on the way home on Saturday,' Brenton said. 'And, you know, I sort of get the impression she's still on a high.' He followed Libby into the kitchen. She thought he was probably in search of a mid-morning coffee.

'How's the studio?' she inquired, gathering up crockery from the littered table.

'Oh, brilliant! The only thing is, it's so well laid out now ... I can't find my way around it. But as I work, I'm getting the hang of it.'

'Did you lose much stuff when it all crashed?' She knew how awful that could be from experience with her office computer.

'Good lord, no. I save everything ... Besides, I sometimes have to take special things with me when I go abroad – to load into the venue's computer systems. It can be quite tricky, sometimes, with different systems ... you know?'

She nodded but she was busy loading the dishwasher. By the time she was standing up, Brenton was moving towards the door and looking, she thought, rather dashed. But she had things to get on with.

Angela drove up later, while Libby was up-stairs picking up bath towels and turning off dripping taps in the main bathroom. She put all the towels in the laundry basket and came out on to the landing. Angela came upstairs at the same moment.

It was clear that after delivering Prim to play group, she'd gone on to a hairdresser. Her hair had had a professional colour treatment and was now styled with gel so that it stood out around her head in little pale blue spikes.

'My tortoiseshell mirror is missing from my dressing table,' Angela said accusingly.

'I just saw it in the bathroom,' said Libby.

'Oh. Right.'

Libby set down the laundry basket and moved towards the suite of rooms belonging to Grandee.

'That party frock you made me buy for Prim is a total loss. She dripped chocolate ice-dream all down its front.'

Angela's manner was antagonistic, to say the least. Libby said soothingly, 'Well, that happens with little kids. A dry-cleaner will get it out.'

'That's just a waste of money. She's never going to go to another birthday party before she's completely grown out of it.'

'Oh! What a thing to say!' Libby was utterly taken aback.

'You think she's so popular her little friends are queuing up to invite her?' Her mouth twisted into a scornful smile. 'Since I've had charge of her, I've realized the mothers who collect the other kids scarcely know her name. So that's how much they talk about her.'

'She's ... Well, she's shy...'

'Huh! At boarding school, you learn pretty quickly not to be shy!'

'You went to boarding school?'

Angela threw out her arms in an all-embracing gesture. 'The combat zone where you get to know your worth. Everybody equal, nobody superior to anybody else. The first one I went to was free-expression, so we all wore casual clothes and got the same pocket money allowance and made our own decisions about what we wanted to learn. What *I* learnt was how to cope.'

Libby didn't know how to respond to this. It was a glimpse into Angela's childhood – unexpected, and distressing because of the bitterness of her tone. She was trying to think of a reply when Angela frowned and said, 'I suppose you think you know a lot about kids, but that party's really upset Prim. She keeps on about it, although as far as I can gather she hated the magician.'

'Oh, yes, she couldn't understand that it was all just fun – I'm sorry about that. But my little boy cheered her up.'

'Oh, the famous Freddie! I'm pretty sick of hearing about him and his stupid boat.'

Libby was affronted, and decided it was time to end the conversation. She took hold of the handle of the vacuum cleaner and went into Grandee's rooms.

Some hours later, when she was acquainting herself with the new little sleeping area in Brent's studio, she heard Prim come home from play group with Angela. She longed to speak to the toddler, to find out if everything was all right with her, but Angela took her straight to the morning room which had become accepted as Prim's play area. She thought it best not to speak to Prim while Angela was in her present mood.

When it was time to leave, she sought out Philip to explain to him about the reinstalling of the carpets next day. Among other things, she'd decided not to turn up at Ashgrove while the carpets were being dealt with – the longer she could stay out of Angela's way, the better. 'As it will mean a big disruption in the house, perhaps you and the rest of the family could arrange to stay out of the drawing-room and the dining room tomorrow?' she suggested.

'No problem. I'll pass the world along.'

'Jake Grover will be in charge of the carpeting, so he'll see to the rest of the housework tomorrow. I'll send another staff member with him to clean upstairs while he's overseeing the main rooms.'

'Er ... You mean you won't be here?' Philip asked in dismay. 'Did Grandee's remarks offend you?'

'Well, I can't say I enjoyed them. But the fact is, it's half-term. I'm taking my little boy out for the day.'

'Half-term. That's – what? A week?'

'Yes, but I'll be here as much as I can. And Jake and Amy are very responsible.'

'Half-term,' he murmured. 'I remember all that. Mama used to come and collect us to go to some ashram or something, wherever she was taking instruction or studying at the time. Kuan Yin, I seem to recall – that was the doctrine about mercy and tolerance where she wore a lot of Chinese robes.'

'She collected you?' She heard echoes of her earlier conversation. 'You went to boarding school too? Angela was talking about that this morning.'

'Yes, I went to three different ones in all.'

'Co-ed? Angela couldn't be with you – she'd be too young.'

'No, no, we all went to different places. Depended on what Mama's view of life was at the time.' He laughed. 'The one I hated most was where we were only allowed raw food. I think that was something to do with the Druids. Never had a cooked meal for almost six months. But I kicked up so much fuss that in the end Mama found me another place.'

Libby gazed at him with amazement. 'No wonder none of you have any idea how to wash dishes or cook a meal.'

'Yes, we're a hopeless lot, I'm afraid.' But he became serious. 'Angela came off worst, I think. She can be a bit weird.' He paused in thought. 'She really hates being saddled with Prim. And because of that, I'm afraid she resents you as much as Grandee does.'

She shrugged. She already knew that only too well.

'You mustn't mind the way Grandee gets snobbish. It's just that she ... Well, you know, she used to *be* somebody.'

'I understand.' She let the words signify that

she didn't want to stop and chat. This tête-à-tête was not enjoyable.

He was quick to take the hint. 'So ... er ... You won't be here tomorrow.'

'That's right. I want to spend as much time as I can with Freddie, so you'll see other members of my staff from time to time.' She chose to be official. 'But I assure you the housework won't suffer.'

'Well, that's good.'

'If that's settled, I must go. I have to collect Freddie...'

'Of course. That's fine.'

She was glad to get away. Although of all the family, Philip was the one who seemed to her the most approachable, she wasn't in the mood today to make contact.

Other families on Libby's client list had taken the opportunity of the half-term holiday to take their children abroad. Their homes needed no special care for that time, so there was some elasticity in the work schedules for a change. With some juggling she managed to keep Ashgrove up to standard – so long as Jake was also there, a female staff member could be persuaded to brave the lion's den.

At the end of the week's break, Libby resumed her normal routine with some reluctance, but she felt she must go back if only to see how Prim was faring. This sentiment was in contravention of her own rules, but she couldn't deny the fact that she had taken a personal interest in Prim.

The child came into the kitchen soon after her

arrival. She greeted Libby with a pouting welcome. 'Where did you go?' she demanded. 'You weren't here for *ages.*'

'There was a school holiday. I was looking after Freddie.'

Prim frowned. *'My* school didn't have a holiday!'

'Your school isn't quite the same. Freddie goes to a school for bigger children, you know.' She set breakfast dishes on the table. 'Now, what's it to be this morning? Brekkiflakes?'

The resentment in the child's manner was eventually soothed by suggestion of a different version of fruit salad to go with the cereal. And when later she joined Libby to do some dusting, she was entranced at being given a hog's-hair brush and invited to clean the wicker furniture in the morning room.

She knelt on the seat cushion of the first chair, earnestly poking the brush into all the crevices, delighted with herself.

Routine was thus re-established. The child spent her time in Libby's company at every opportunity. On two occasions she actually wept genuine tears when Angela took her off to play group, which did nothing to improve Angela's disposition.

On Thursday afternoon, as Libby was about to leave, Vivienne Moorfield came into the kitchen with an expression that didn't bode well. 'What has happened to the William de Morgan dish with the copper lustre decoration?'

'I beg your pardon?'

'The dish that stands on the walnut side table

in the drawing room.'

'I've no idea.'

'It appears to have been moved. Where did you put it?'

'I haven't touched it, Mrs Moorfield.'

'Well, that's a strange thing to say, since you presumably dust it regularly.'

'That's quite right, but of course things get moved. I wouldn't particularly notice if it wasn't in its usual place.' She tried to picture the item Vivienne Moorfield was talking about, but there were so many knick-knacks scattered about the old house that memory failed her.

Grandee gave her a hard stare. 'If you've moved it, I want it put back where it belongs.'

'Very well. When I come across it, I'll put it on the drawing-room table.'

She thought no more about it. On Tuesday of the following week, Grandee was waiting for her in the hall when she arrived at eight thirty. This was so unusual that it was a clear danger signal.

'Where is the silver cream jug by William Kingdom?'

The cream jug was kept in a glass-fronted cabinet in the dining room along with other small pieces of silver. Libby had no idea of the silversmith's name but supposed all the items in the cabinet were precious, since it was kept locked and she had to ask for the key when the silver was to be cleaned.

'I haven't seen it,' Libby replied. 'I don't pay much attention to the display cabinet.'

'I think you did on this occasion. The cream jug is gone. The de Morgan plate from the drawing-room has never been found.' Grandee pointed an accusing finger. 'You took them, and no doubt the tortoiseshell hand mirror that Angela reports missing from her room.'

Libby was dumbfounded. After a moment of utter silence she said, 'Are you saying I'm a thief?'

Grandee ignored the challenge. 'I have called the police,' was all she said.

Seven

The police sergeant in his uniform exuded solidity and calm. 'My name is Sergeant Grant,' he said, 'and that's WPC Waynforth.' He nodded at the uniformed figure just inside the door of the drawing-room. Rosanne had conducted them in there, and now huddled miserably in a chair, her plump features crumpled with distress. Grandee stood by the marble fireplace, one hand on the mantelpiece, a figure of authority.

'What items did you discover to be missing, Mrs Moorfield?' the sergeant asked, notebook at the ready.

'A silver cream jug by William Kingdom, made about 1810 and kept in the cabinet in the dining room. A lustre dish by William de Morgan – that disappeared about a week ago and has never yet turned up. My granddaughter mentioned to me some time ago that a hand mirror backed with tortoiseshell had disappeared from her room – not very valuable perhaps, but a collector's piece all the same. And my daughter-in-law – Rosanne, what was it you said had gone missing?'

'Well ... I don't know that it's gone, Grandee ... An ivory box with lotus blossoms carved on the lid. I bought it thirty years ago in India; I don't think it's worth much.'

'You've looked for these pieces, of course, madam?'

'Of course, Sergeant.'

'This dish by Morgan – that's china, is it?'

'It's a rare piece by William de Morgan from his Fulham pottery. He was a friend of William Morris and Burne-Jones. It's probably worth something like a thousand pounds.'

Sergeant Grant turned to Libby. 'I have to ask you, Mrs Fletcher. Did you take these things?'

'Certainly not.'

'Nothing disappeared from this house until *she* came here,' Grandee exclaimed, pointing a trembling finger at Libby. 'She took them! She smuggled them out in that holdall she brings with her.'

'I'd like to examine the holdall and your car, Mrs Fletcher.'

'Look where you like. I haven't taken anything from this house.'

'I want her arrested! She's been nothing but trouble since she first came and who knows what else she's filched...'

'The house does seem to have rather a lot of things lying about,' mused Sergeant Grant.

'Could someone simply have picked things up and put them elsewhere?'

'The silver cabinet is kept locked. No one could just "pick something up" from there.'

'And where is the key to it kept?'

'My grandson's office. And of course she cleans in there, so she could easily take the key from the drawer.'

Sergeant Grant sighed. It was clear he thought the security in Ashgrove left a lot to be desired. 'Could anyone else get access to the key?' he inquired. 'A friend perhaps, someone who called—'

'We had a fire here a little while ago,' Rosanne put in, brightening a little at what she clearly thought was a helpful suggestion. 'Firemen everywhere—'

'The firemen didn't come into the house,' Libby said. She didn't want anyone else falsely accused. 'They were in the studio – that's the glass-clad building at the side of the house. It used to be the conservatory but Brenton uses it as a studio and all his electronic equipment fused and caused horrible fumes. It's true we had workers in the house taking up carpets and so forth, but they were under supervision. They didn't go into Philip Moorfield's office.'

'Is Mr Moorfield available to speak to about the security of the key?'

'He is abroad. He works on finding locations for films. His brother, Brenton Moorfield, is abroad too – in Prague, I believe,' Libby said.

'Have you ever had access to the key to the silver cabinet, Mrs Fletcher?'

'Of course. I have to have it on silver-cleaning day.'

'And you have to ask for it?'

'No.' She sighed inwardly. 'It's just in a drawer in the desk.'

The sergeant looked serious. 'I'm afraid I'll have to ask you to accompany me to the station, madam.'

Rosanne cried, 'No, really?' and jumped up in consternation. Libby saw Grandee give a brief smile of triumph.

'Am I being arrested?' Libby asked, her thoughts flying at once to the problems that would ensue. Who would collect Freddie from school? Who would deal with office matters?

'No, not at present. It's just so that you can be questioned in more detail and perhaps you'd want to make a statement.'

It seemed to Libby that, as she was led out, there was some sympathy in the face of the woman constable. Then she was put into the police car and driven away.

At the police station she was left alone in a room for quite some time. Its walls were painted pale blue, and it contained a table, a few chairs, and some recording equipment. The windows were clad in Venetian blinds that looked as if they were some kind of security device.

By and by a plain-clothes detective came in with a clipboard. He introduced himself as DC Noonan, and he had what she felt was a comforting Northern Irish accent. 'I'm going to ask a few preliminary questions and we'll see how it goes.' He nodded at the recording equipment. 'Off the record, OK?'

'Yes.'

'Now, do we have your permission to search your home?'

She explained that she lived above her office in the town.

'Well, we'd like to take a look at your office too.'

'Very well.'

'Mrs Moorfield is having the house contents checked against the inventory put together for insurance, but that won't be until tomorrow. She's asked that you be detained until that's done, but the Super feels that's a bit ultra vires, so if we can have your cooperation we can perhaps clear this up today.'

'If by cooperation you mean am I going to admit to taking those things, forget it,' Libby said vehemently.

'But there's definitely a space in the silver cabinet where that cream jug ought to be. It's been taken out, and it's not lying about anywhere else on the premises so far as we can see.'

'Anyone in the house could have taken the key from Philip's office.'

Noonan gave her a look of surprised inquiry. 'But you're the only employee that has access to Ashgrove.'

'Why does it always have to be the cleaner that's the culprit?'

'You're not saying someone in the family stole these things?'

Libby came out with it before she could prevent it. 'It's my belief she took the things herself and hid them somewhere.'

'She? Who?'

'Grandee. The senior Mrs Moorfield. I think *she's* the thief.'

'She took them herself? Why on earth would she do that?' cried Noonan.

'So that she could accuse me. She's been trying to get rid of me ever since I began working there.'

There was a small silence. Then the detective said, 'Let's get this straight. You're suggesting that Mrs Moorfield, who employs you, wants to get rid of you but can't just give you the sack. So she plays this trick of stealing her own belongings and accuses you. Is that it?'

'More or less.'

'Come off it, Mrs Fletcher. That story isn't very likely.'

'If you doubt me, telephone Philip Moorfield. He'll tell you that the background I've given you is the truth. Mrs Moorfield Senior – Grandee – has ordered me out of the house twice, and each time Philip has managed to cancel the dismissal and put things back on track again.'

Noonan thought about this. 'Constable Waynforth did mention that she seemed a bit of a tartar,' he murmured. 'Why do you stay there, if the old lady is so unreasonable? Plenty of jobs for domestic staff, aren't there?'

Libby explained about the year's contract. 'I'd have to refund the money if I didn't fulfil the obligation, and I can't afford to do that. Let me tell you, Philip Moorfield doesn't want to see me leave. He's had staff from every agency in the district, and they've all walked out on him. I was stupid to let myself be trapped by my own contract.' She made a sound that was almost a groan. 'What a fool!'

'Well, look, Mrs Fletcher – it's a bit extreme, isn't it? Why has the old girl got such a down on you?'

'I stood up to her about...' She paused. 'I don't want to go into all that. Let's just say I spoke to her about a bit of a problem in the family and ... well ... she didn't like it.'

'And you're really saying you think she's capable of pulling this stunt?'

'Telephone Mr Philip Moorfield. He'll vouch for me, I think.'

'Ah, well, you say he's abroad, and the Super doesn't like expensive calls overseas.'

'Good heavens, I'll pay for the call myself!' Libby burst out.

DC Noonan smiled. 'I'll go and have a word.'

Time went by. WPC Waynforth arrived with a tray of lunch. 'Only cold stuff, I'm afraid. The canteen cook only prepares enough for staff.'

'I'm not hungry.'

'Drink the tea, then. I made it myself.'

Libby was glad of the tea. It was a long time since breakfast. But the idea of eating was unthinkable. She was sick with anxiety about Freddie. She kept reassuring herself: the police would have gone to her office, they would have explained their presence and made their search, so Libby's friends would know she was at the police station. Someone – Amy or Jake – would fetch Freddie from school.

119

A little before three o'clock DC Noonan reappeared. 'A bit of a delay,' he said. 'Couldn't quite get hold of Mr Moorfield at first – he seemed to be out somewhere on the docks at Calais. But he verified what you told me and gave it as his considered opinion that you wouldn't steal anything.'

She nodded wordlessly.

'Search of your holdall, your car and your premises produced nothing to support Mrs Moorfield's claim—'

'Of course not!'

'That being so, the Super says we can let you go. Although he'd like you to be around until this matter gets sorted.'

'I'm not going anywhere,' Libby said. She felt weak, irresolute, and close to tears. She made a big effort and pulled herself together. 'My car's still at Ashgrove?'

'Yes.'

'Can you get me a lift so that I can collect it? My little boy is probably still waiting for me at school.'

'I think we can manage that.'

Delivered to the drive at Ashgrove, she unlocked her car and delved for her mobile. A list of messages waited. Mostly from staff at Housecare, anxious about what was going on. One was from the head teacher at Freddie's school inquiring about her failure to collect him but the one after that was from Amy, saying she'd fetched him home.

When Libby put her key in the downstairs side door, she heard the clatter of footsteps on the stairs. As she came in, Freddie threw himself upon her. 'Mummy! They said you'd been *arrested*! I waited and waited and Miss Boxton said ... And then Auntie Amy came. Did they put you in a *cell*?'

Freddie had decided not to cry about a year ago. Crying was babyish, he said. But he was crying now, clutching her as if he might lose her for ever if he let go.

She held him close. How dare they? How dare they subject her to humiliation and apprehension and cause her little boy to weep? And how dared she? For Libby was convinced that Vivienne Moorfield had contrived this whole scheme. I'll never forgive her, she vowed to herself.

From the door leading from her office, members of her staff began to crowd into the downstairs passage. They engulfed her in hugs and eager greetings, bringing reassurance and causing Freddie to swallow his tears. Libby knew he'd hate anyone to know he'd cried.

They all went into the office. She gave a censored account of what had happened, because she didn't want her little boy to know how she'd been treated. Then they all felt they needed a drink so tea was made, a bottle of wine was brought down from the flat, and Freddie was allowed a can of 7-Up.

Jake managed to have a private word. 'Are you really saying that my starry lady laid a trap for you?'

'She certainly did, Jake. She's got a really mean streak.'

'Seems so.' He shook his head in disillusion.

121

'You won't be going back, eh?

'How right you are!'

'So I shan't be seeing her again, so makes no matter, does it.' He considered this. 'What about the little maidie?'

'Prim?'

'She's just going to comfort herself with the swing we made, poor little mite. That's a shame, but there you are.'

By and by the celebration began to simmer down. There were husbands and families waiting for them at home. They all hugged and kissed and said goodbye.

Freddie, too, was wilting. He'd had a frightening and exhausting day, and so made no protest at being offered early bed. He asked his mother to leave his bedroom door open. She did so, understanding that he wanted to stay in contact with her.

About nine o'clock, when Libby herself was thinking an early night would be the best thing, she heard the bell ring at the side door. She went downstairs.

'Who is it?' she called through the closed door.

'Philip Moorfield.'

'Go away!'

'I've come to apologize—'

'No. I don't want your apology, go away.'

'Please give me five minutes. I just want to say I'm sorry.'

'I accept that. Now please go away.'

'Libby, I've *got* to have the chance to speak to you. I need to see you, to make sure you're all right.'

There was so much real concern in his voice that she felt herself weakening. After all, it wasn't his fault. And there were things that needed to be said.

'All right,' she said. 'Five minutes.'

She unlocked the door and he came in uncertainly. She led the way into her office – she had no intention of letting him into her living quarters, where his voice might disturb her sleeping son.

The office had been tidied before the staff all trooped off home, but there were chairs grouped around her desk and the faint scent of wine in the air.

She sat down in her desk chair. Philip took one of the others, the one furthest away. She waited.

'I want you to accept that none of this would have happened if I had been at home,' he began.

'Very well.'

'When the police called, they did it through the London office. It took some time to patch me through from my position on the dockside. I told them at once it was all nonsense.'

'It seemed very real to me.'

'Of course. I can only imagine what you were feeling.' He hesitated. 'They told me what you'd suggested, that Grandee herself had taken those things and hidden them out of spite, and I ... Well, I could only agree.'

It occurred to her for the first time that this could hardly have been pleasant for him – to have to agree that his grandmother was a malicious old harpie. But she said nothing of that.

He went on. 'I dropped everything and made

straight for the train back to London. When I got to Ashgrove I found everybody in turmoil – it seems Grandee had telephoned the police to see what was happening and was furious that you'd been released. My poor mother was in floods of tears.'

Libby found herself saying, 'How about Angela? And Prim?'

'That I don't know. Mama had enough sense to tell Angela to take Prim out somewhere – I suppose to the nearest shopping mall, if I know Angela. No, the scene at home consisted of Grandee in one of her major tantrums and Mama trying to cope with her. When I arrived I got Grandee's version of what had happened.'

'Did you accuse her of taking the things herself?'

'Well ... yes, I did, and of course that made matters worse.'

'She denied it?'

'Vehemently! And now she's taken herself off to that beauty place – the Haven – to sulk and get over it.'

Libby had no response to this. She didn't care where Grandee had gone.

Philip hesitated, then said, 'Of course the contract between us is considered to be honoured in full. You won't want to come to Ashgrove any more.'

And suddenly she lost her temper. 'Never in a million years!' she cried. 'I never want to see you or any member of your stupid family again as long as I live! And I hope you enjoy living in the kind of mess that you produce, because

124

nobody else will ever put themselves in danger of the kind of treatment meted out to your *servants*!'

'Libby, I don't think I ever treated you like a servant. Please accept that if I had been at home, this idiotic fracas would never have happened—'

'It would have happened but you would have smoothed it over somehow for the sake of peace and quiet. It doesn't seem to occur to any of you that your freaky grandmother is doing damage – real damage – with her selfishness and lack of regard. Brenton doesn't seem to know how to communicate with the rest of society, your mother protects herself by living in a dream world, Angela is becoming a drunk, and Prim ... Prim...' Her voice broke.

Philip got up from his chair and made as if to move towards her. She gathered herself together and said fiercely, 'I want you to leave, please.'

'All right.' He headed for the office door. There he paused and said, 'Prim will miss you.'

'That can't be helped.' She rose and made a herding gesture with both hands to urge him out.

He nodded. She let him out of the front door and locked it behind him. Then she went back into her office, sat down in the desk chair, laid her head on the desk and allowed the tears to engulf her at last.

Eight

It was strange, the following day, to be free of having to face the trials of Ashgrove, Libby sat over breakfast with lazy enjoyment. Freddie, on the contrary, was in an odd mood. She understood that it was caused by the previous day's upsets, and begged him a day off school so as to get over it.

She let him dress himself in his favourite clothes – a T-shirt proclaiming his support of Manchester United, blue jeans, and trainers with flashing signals in the heels. She herself chose a dress that hadn't been out of the wardrobe since the previous summer, a floral print with strappy shoulders. She felt as if she'd come back into the ordinary world after being cooped up with cranks too long.

Libby took Freddie to a children's zoo. He hung about close to her at first, but soon the pleasures of stroking angora rabbits and feeding the pigs overcame his anxiety. She allowed him some treats by way of lunch. All in all it was a successful day.

She got back to routine work in her office after that. Things were very peaceful. She caught up with the backlog, and rejoiced in dealing with people who didn't complain or dither or ignore important matters.

A couple of days later she got a visit from WPC Wayncroft, who informed her that the complaint by Mrs Moorfield had been marked, 'No action'.

'Does that mean I haven't got a record?' Libby was able to ask with a smile.

'Stainless. And the Super's made a mental note to be a bit wary of Her Ladyship.' The constable was smiling too.

'Thank you,' Libby said, profoundly grateful that she could put the whole incident behind her.

That turned out not to be strictly correct.

On the Thursday of the following week Libby was shopping in town. She sauntered along the High Street in the June sunshine, pausing to note the week's bestseller in the window of the bookshop, considering the smoothie maker in the window of the kitchen shop, and at last turning down a little side street. She wanted to visit a shop that sold Italian specialities.

As she strolled along, she glanced in at the window of a bric-a-brac shop owned by an acquaintance. He sometimes sold her upholstering braid or brass-topped nails salvaged from old chairs. There, on a little wooden easel, gleamed the de Morgan plate from Ashgrove.

Libby stopped in her tracks. Was it another plate from the same pottery? Was it a replica?

No, for alongside the easel stood a little ivory box carved with lotus blossoms.

She stood in thought for a time, then she went in. The owner, Thomas Denton, came forward to greet her. 'Hello there. How nice and summery you look.' He gave her an approving survey. 'Nothing special in the way of upholstery items for you today. I hear you sold your chaise longue for a good price though!'

She smiled and nodded. 'Thomas, I want to speak to you about that plate in the window, the lustre plate on the easel.'

'Oh, the de Morgan? Didn't know you were interested in that kind of thing. If you want it, I can do you a special price, because I got it for a song.'

'How did you come by it?' she asked, holding her breath.

'The weirdest thing! This girl came in, had a few things in a plastic carrier, and asked me what I'd give her for them. The de Morgan was one of the things. I said, "What about a fiver for the plate?" and she ... well, she took my breath away, because she said, "OK".'

'Tommy,' Libby murmured in disbelief.

'True as I stand here! Of course I couldn't let her sell it for that – it would have been on my conscience. So I said, "It's worth at least a hundred," and she offered me the carrier bag and said. "You can have the lot for one-fifty."'

'And ... what was in the bag, Tommy?'

'An ivory box – that's in the window too, did you see it? Then there was a rather nice Edwardian hand mirror, and a silver cream jug. Now, the jug! I looked up the hallmarks – it turned out to be by William Kingdom! I asked her how she'd come by all this and she said her grandmother had left the things to her in her will.'

'And did you believe her?'

'Well...' His plump face creased into an apologetic grimace. 'She had rather good clothes and a very expensive hair job, and no drug tracks on her arms or anything, so I decided it was on the level. I paid her five hundred for the lot – that was pretty fair, don't you agree, Libby?'

She shrugged. 'I don't know. I'm not an expert on silver.'

'It was all perfectly pukka. I got her to sign a receipt for the money.' He stopped, beginning to look alarmed. 'What's your interest in all this?'

'Can I have a look at the signature?'

Now he was worried. 'Am I going to be in trouble?'

'Not from me. Please let me look at the receipt, Tommy.'

'Oh, very well.' He stomped off to a partition that served as an office, returning with a receipt book. He licked his finger to turn back a page or two and showed her the signature. 'Eleanor Rigby.'

'Oh, *Tommy!*'

'What's wrong?'

'Have you never listened to the Beatles?'

'Never intentionally. Why?'

'"Eleanor Rigby" is one of their famous songs.'

'Oh dear.' He looked very put out. But then he brightened. 'Doesn't mean she wasn't left the things by her grandmother, does it? Maybe it's just that she didn't want anyone to know she'd sold them.'

'Her grandmother is alive and kicking.'

'Libby, you *know* the girl who sold me the

129

items?'

'I think I do. Listen, can you just take the plate out of the window, and the ivory box, and put them out of sight for a bit?'

'And for why, may I ask?'

'I'd like to phone someone and get him to look at them.'

'Please don't say it's the rightful owner.'

'No. But I think he ought to see them.'

Tommy was very unwilling, but Libby let him see she intended to give him a lot of argument. He succumbed. 'Well, all right.'

She used her mobile to make the call to Ashgrove. Rosanne answered, and put the call through to Philip's office without query, apparently not recognizing the voice on the end of the line.

Philip Moorfield, on the contrary, recognized her immediately. 'Libby? Is something wrong?'

'Depends what you mean by wrong. Can you come to Denton Bric-a-Brac?'

'Where?'

'Denton Bric-a-brac. It's a shop in Shepherdess Walk.'

There was undisguised bewilderment in his voice when he replied. 'You mean now?'

'If it's convenient. And I think you should make it convenient.'

A faintly puzzled sound. Then he said, 'I'll be there in about twenty minutes.'

Tommy had made instant coffee for himself and Libby. 'Quite exciting, this,' he remarked. 'Just when I make a bargain buy and end up with a piece of really good silver, there's a mystery!

130

Is this about family heirlooms?'

She just shook her head at him.

Philip appeared rather later than he'd suggested, somewhat flushed with irritation. She thought he'd probably had trouble parking. She introduced him to Denton, with whom he shook hands rather gingerly.

'What's this about?'

'Mr Denton has some things to show you.'

Tommy Denton gave her a quizzical look but went to his office, and returned carrying the de Morgan plate with the other items balanced on it.

Philip gasped.

'Would you please tell Mr Moorfield how you acquired these articles, Tommy?' Libby invited.

Tommy cleared his throat. 'About ten days ago a young woman with a spiky blue hairdo sold them to me for five hundred pounds.'

Philip looked around the shop as if seeking help. His expression showed dismay, then unwilling acceptance. He said, 'Angela, of course.'

'So you know her, sir,' Tommy said with an anxious smile.

'Yes, alas.' Philip turned to Libby. 'How did you find all this?'

'I was walking past. The de Morgan plate was in the window.'

Philip seemed unable to summon up any words. At length he said, 'She didn't even have the sense to take them somewhere farther away!'

'Well, she probably thought *I'd* be suspected of bringing them here,' Libby pointed out.

'Yes, I suppose she did.' He stood thinking what to do next. She had never seen him so distressed, and felt an impulse of pity. It couldn't be much fun, having to handle the fact that Angela was a thief and a cheat.

Philip said, 'Mr Denton, would you sell me these articles?'

'All of them?'

'Yes, please.'

'What sort of price did you have in mind?'

'Just tell me how much you want for them.'

Tommy exchanged a glance with Libby. 'Shall we say ... seven hundred and fifty?' He waited rather nervously for her response but she said nothing. Fifty per cent profit. Well, Tommy could have sold the items separately and made a lot more. The silver jug alone was worth more.

'You'll take my credit card?' Philip inquired, producing it.

'Certainly, sir. I'll just get the thingamajig.'

Libby went outside while the transaction was completed. Philip emerged with the stolen articles in a brown cardboard box, each of them presumably treated with the respect they deserved and suitably wrapped.

'Thank you for not going straight to the police with this,' he said.

'All I wanted was to get things cleared up.'

Philip was shaking his head in self-reproach. 'We had the right motive but the wrong culprit. It was Angela who was out to get you, not Grandee.'

'I shouldn't have been so quick to blame your grandmother. I'm sorry about that.'

'I'm the one who has to apologize. I am very sorry, Libby. Is there anything I can do to make amends?

'Just don't ever ask me back to Ashgrove,' she said, and walked away.

Two days later she received a handwritten letter from Philip.

I enclose a typed statement of apology that you can produce at any time if the matter of the items missing from Ashgrove should arise.

To let you know what happened when I got the things home – I just put them back in the places where they used to sit. I haven't said anything to anyone, I just put them back.

Angela has said absolutely nothing about that. Grandee called me into her boudoir to ask if I knew how they came to be returned, and I said I'd been able to retrieve them and not to give it any more thought. She tried to pursue the matter but I just kept saying it wasn't to be discussed. So she got into one of her haughty moods and told me to go and that was that.

I remember you accused me of always just smoothing things over, but I honestly don't see what good it would do to bring Angela's behaviour into the open. I don't feel qualified to handle her. She needs to see a counsellor or something, but I tried that a while ago and she just won't go.

If you would like to make a claim for compensation for the treatment you received, please do so, but I would ask you to keep it a private matter between just the two of us.

With best wishes, Philip Moorfield.

This caused Libby some thought. For a few days

she sat trying to start a reply, but she realized she didn't want money – the apology was enough. As to Angela being brought to book ... Her own judgement had been at fault; she'd been so sure Grandee was the culprit. So she was in no position to ask for compensation after being so unjust herself.

In the end Libby just let the matter slip. She was enjoying the normality of life after Ashgrove. Summery weather was taking its hold; she and Freddie could go out for picnics and excursions. He was showing an interest in sketching outdoors, and today was taking swimming lessons at school. Everything was on an even keel.

Until one dull sultry morning in mid-June.

The telephone rang at about ten thirty. All her staff except Jake had gone to start their day's work. Libby was planning out the schedule for the coming week, and Jake was in the kitchenette making their morning coffee. Expecting the call to be from a client, she answered with the office salutation: 'Housecare Helpers'.

To her astonishment, it was the voice of Rosanne Moorfield that responded.

'Libby – is that you?'

'Yes, it is.' She hesitated for the merest moment. 'Mrs Moorfield, what's the matter?' For it was clear from the weeping inquiry that something bad had happened.

'Is Prim with you?' Rosanne asked.

'Prim?' Libby was seized by apprehension. 'No, why on earth should she be with me?'

'Because we can't find her, Libby!'

And with that the breath went out of her. She had to make a conscious effort to pull air into her lungs before she could reply. 'What do you mean, you can't find her?'

'She isn't in her room. I thought she might be in the morning-room but she isn't. I looked everywhere!' Rosanne's voice had none of its usual dreaminess. Although clearly close to tears, she was making an effort to speak with definition, and there was an undertone of panic.

'Everywhere? Did you look in Grandee's rooms?' It was of course forbidden for the little girl to enter there. All the same, that was a tempting area for a toddler.

Jake had been alerted by the sharpness in Libby's tone. He came back from his task to hover anxiously at her elbow. 'It's Prim,' she whispered to him.

Rosanne was babbling: 'Yes, everywhere, up-stairs, downstairs, in Brent's old bedroom. I even went to the studio and he let me look there, and then we went down to the cellars together to see if she had somehow unlocked ... But she wasn't there. She's not anywhere in the house, Libby.'

A million thoughts raced through her brain. 'Could she have got out?' This was unlikely, be-cause the doors locked by merely being pushed shut. And yet...

Rosanne's response confirmed her fears. 'Well ... I heard Angela come home in the early hours, barging about. You know she sometimes just sort of ... collapses in the hall...'

'You mean she could have left the front door

open.' She heard Jake give a groan at this ominous question.

'Well, it's possible...' Rosanne said.

'What does Angela say?'

'She's ... she hasn't surfaced yet.'

Which meant she was still in bed nursing a hangover. 'Get her up!' Libby commanded.

'Brent's trying to do that. And I've rung Philip on his mobile, and he's coming straight back – he was a few miles on his way to Southampton.' A pause. 'Libby, could you come? I mean ... you know Prim better than anyone really...'

The words contained a truth so appalling that the only reply had to be, 'Yes, I'll be there in fifteen minutes.' She put the phone down.

'I'll come too,' Jake said.

'No, why should—'

'The more hands the better.'

Luckily the traffic in town was having its mid-morning lull, and they got to Ashgrove in record time. Libby had not yet bothered to return the keys so she had them in her hand ready to unlock the front door, when it swept open to reveal Philip Moorfield.

'Thank God,' he breathed. He looked past her at Jake, and frowned in recollection. 'You're the odd-job man, aren't you?'

'That's me, sir,' Jake agreed. 'Clean the windows, mow the lawn, that's me.' They were in the hall now, where Rosanne was waiting with her hands clasped together as though in prayer.

'Well, we've looked everywhere,' Philip said heavily. He led the way into the drawing-room. Grandee and Angela were there, Grandee sitting stiff-backed in an oak chair, well turned out in a dress of black and white silk. Angela, half-lying on the sofa, was in a tracksuit and barefoot. She had one hand to her forehead, and the rest of her face looked wan.

'What's her room like?' Libby asked.

'It's ... well, it's normal, I suppose. A bit untidy,' said Philip.

'Can I go up and have a look?'

'Of course.'

Grandee, determined to be in charge, inquired in a steely voice, 'You're that man that does the garden?'

'I am, milady,' said Jake, standing tall so as to make a good impression.

'You woke me up yesterday morning. I looked out and saw you, on the mower.'

Libby, on her way out, paused to stare in surprise. Jake said in apology, 'Well, you know ... the grass ... it gets like a hay meadow if somebody just doesn't take a blade to it.' He gave her a weak smile. 'I just nipped round to give it a tidy, as a good deed.'

Idiot, she thought. He hoped to get a glimpse of Grandee, I suppose. She hurried out and went upstairs.

The little girl's room showed that little had been done to it since Libby ceased to attend to the house. There were toys scattered on the floor, clothes lying about on the chair and the window-seat, various mugs and beakers on the little dressing table.

Libby surveyed it in silence. After a moment she said, 'Where's Mitzi?'

'Who's Mitzi?' asked Philip, who had followed her upstairs.

'Mitzi is her favourite doll. Her mother sent it
to her from Tokyo.'

Philip was at a loss.

Libby opened the toy cupboard and then the
wardrobe. Next she examined the little row of
soft toys on a shelf. 'It's not here,' she said.

He stood looking at her, perplexed. 'What does
that mean?'

'It means...' She broke off. 'I don't know what
it means.' She hurried downstairs again, and
leaned over the sofa to look into Angela's face.
'Angela!'

'What?' groaned the girl.

'Does Prim still love Mitzi?'

'What?'

'It was her favourite toy. I don't see it upstairs.
What's happened to it?'

'How do I know?'

'Angela, if you don't pull yourself together
and speak properly, I'll take you into the kitchen
and put your head under the tap!'

Angela shrank back, but took her hand away
from her brow.

'Now, are you paying attention?'

'Yes.'

'Was Prim playing with Mitzi yesterday?'

A long silence. Then Angela said, 'Yes, she
had it at teatime.'

'Did you put her to bed last night?'

'No. I had a date.'

'I saw Prim to bed last night,' Rosanne volunteered with some trepidation.

138

'Did she have her doll with her?'

'Yes, I think she did. She ... she was cuddling it when I left her room, I think.'

Everybody was waiting and watching. Libby said, 'So where is it now?'

'What do you mean?'

'Prim is gone, and so is Mitzi.' She was putting herself in Prim's place, thinking the thoughts of the child she knew so well. 'She took her doll with her. I think that means she's wandered out somehow.'

There was a silence while this suggestion struck home.

In a surprisingly hard tone, Rosanne said, 'Angela!'

'What?'

'You stumbled about this morning when you came in. Did you leave the door open?'

Angela said nothing.

'Did you leave the door open?' Philip asked. And this time Angela knew better than to ignore the question.

'I ... I don't remember.'

'Was the front door open when you started looking for Prim?' Libby asked, turning to Rosanne.

'No, but then she might have closed it behind her. We've always made a point that the house doors must be kept closed. It's really to keep out stray cats. There are a lot...' Her words died away. She stood shaking her head in misgiving.

Philip went out into the hall. They heard him open the front door, and as if on command they all went after him. In the drive they paused and

139

looked around.

It was a circular drive lined with shrubs and one or two ash trees, all now in full leaf. At either end of the drive was the lane that connected them to the road which led to the town. There were fields and paddocks to the south, and some open grassland cared for by the town council to the north. Grey clouds hung over the scene.

Jake surveyed the terrain, giving it the long stare of the sailor accustomed to seeing out of the corner of his eye. Finding nothing there that seemed relevant, he went round the side of the house towards the gardens at the back.

Libby followed him. She found him standing at the top of the slope gazing around. From the cedar tree Prim's swing hung motionless in the sultry air.

Jake began to move down the edge of the lawn towards a patch of blue flowers that gleamed just beyond the garden, among the grass and weeds on the towpath. All at once he stopped, shading his eyes.

'Look!'

Down the slope of the newly mown lawn, gleaming with a heavy dew, a narrow trail had been made. Someone with very small feet had walked down the lawn when the dew was fresh, making a track to the gate.

The gate, always kept locked, was partly open.

And beyond the gate was the towpath, and the canal.

Nine

The waterway at the edge of Ashgrove's garden was not, strictly speaking, a canal. The River Wey wanders south from Liphook, taking many little turns and circulations until at Weybridge it joins the River Wey Navigation Canal.

Ashgrove stood near the bank of one of the side streams, quiet and almost dreamy in its rustic seclusion. Now and again a rowing boat would go by in summer, or a punt with a group of youngsters looking for a picnic spot. Sometimes a fisherman would try his luck from the bank, but that was rare: the fish in this little tributary weren't worth the trouble.

Now men in waist-high waders were slowly walking the course of the stream. On the tow path a uniformed police officer was taking a video record of the search. It was past midday, but the sun hadn't yet penetrated the cloud layer. The air was heavy. The searchers were perspiring though it was still early in the quest. No sign of a little body had been found.

Libby saw that the Moorfield family had unconsciously divided into two groups. One division was indoors: Grandee was sitting in the drawing-room awaiting the outcome with icy dignity. Angela was upstairs, sent there by Philip with orders to get herself together. Brent had taken refuge in his studio.

Philip and Rosanne were on the path by the water, mother and son close together for comfort, watching the men move warily about in the stream.

Libby and Jake were there too, anxious, silent, afraid to put their thoughts into words. Libby said at last, 'I can't understand how that gate wasn't locked, Jake.'

He hesitated. 'It's not unusual, me dear. When I was regular there in the garden tending to the shrubs and that, I sometimes saw it ajar.'

'You never mentioned it.'

'I never though to say. Mrs Moorfield would go out sometimes, to pick flowers on the outside of the hedge – wild roses she'd cut, and the other day, it was larkspur she was after.'

'Larkspur? That's that tall blue flower?'

'So 'tis.'

She said no more. There were sprays of larkspur in two of the vases in the drawing-room. Grandee must have been out on the path, gathering them for her flower arranging. The logical conclusion was that she had forgotten to lock the gate when she came back.

A set of circumstances caused by thoughtlessness had left the way open for Prim to be abroad when the rest of the house was asleep. Wakened by the sound of Angela's homecoming, perhaps the little girl had got up to speak to her. Useless to ask Angela if that had happened. Her memories of her early-morning entrance seemed to be blotted out.

So Libby was imagining Prim roused and awake. By four in the morning it was practically full daylight at this time of year. Used to getting herself up and dressed, perhaps she'd started her day, and gone out to play on the swing ... And then, somehow – for what reason Libby couldn't tell – Prim had gone down the lawn and out through the open gate on to the footpath.

At first everyone had been hoping that the child had wandered along the path. But searchers had been out for a long while now, looking for her in the pastures or among the trees and bushes that bordered the track, and so far without success.

At last the men came out of the shallow stream. 'Nothing there,' they reported. 'Only the usual – empty lager cans, bits of fishing line, old shoes, that kind of rubbish.'

A general conference was called in Philip's office.

'Can you suggest anywhere the child might have gone, sir?' the police inspector requested.

Philip shook his head. 'There are only a few places that Prim knows. The play group, but of course that was one of our first thoughts. And it was a long shot because she always goes there by car – she couldn't possibly find her way on foot. Then we thought of Mrs Fletcher's home – but she wasn't there. Otherwise, Prim only went perhaps once to a commercial play centre and once to a children's zoo.'

'We ought to contact those.'

'But she couldn't possibly go there. She wouldn't know how to get to them, Inspector.'

'Best to cover every angle. Do we have the telephone number of these places?'

Angela was summoned, and had recovered enough to remember the names of the organizations. But the telephone calls brought no helpful responses. No little girl answering Prim's description had been found on the premises.

'She's a quiet little maid,' Jake remarked. 'Has she ever talked about things she'd like to do? Go on a train, go to a funfair, anything of that sort?' He was directing the questions to Angela.

'Not that I can remember.' Angela was very pale and, for once, appeared to be concerned. Libby couldn't help feeling it was rather too late to be showing anxiety over Prim, but checked herself. Don't waste time on blaming people, she warned herself.

'Just have a chat with Constable Waynforth,' suggested the inspector, beckoning her forward. 'Something might come to mind.'

Libby began to feel she was of no use there. Time was getting on, and soon it would be time to fetch Freddie from school. And today, especially, she was anxious to be there when Freddie ran across the playground, anxious to gather her own child safely into her arms. She signalled to Jake and began to make their farewells.

'You're not leaving?' Philip said, taken aback. He was gaunt with anxiety. Her departure seemed to surprise and disappoint him.

'I have to. I've got to meet Freddie from school.'

'Oh! Of course. How selfish we've been...'

'Not at all. Of course I want to do anything I

144

can to help find Prim. But I can't suggest anything and I really feel I'd better get going.' She
found her voice was breaking. She wanted to be
gone before she began to cry.

Rosanne said, 'You've been so kind, both of
you.'

'I'll stay on, if that's all right with everybody.'
This was Jake, embarrassed at letting it be seen
that he was deeply worried.

'Of course,' Philip said. 'You were the one
who spied the footprints on the lawn. You're a
star.'

Jake went with Libby out to her car. 'I thought
I'd just hang about for a bit,' he said, 'and if
anything happens, I'll ring you.'

'Yes, thank you, Jake. I wish I could stay too,
but I don't want Freddie to be kept waiting for
me.'

'You go along, my maidie. You look worn out.'

Back home with Freddie, she made tea for
herself and set out apple juice and biscuits for
him. He had a school project for the weekend, so
he set about it with paper and his birthday pencils in his room.

Libby busied herself with catch-up work at her
desk. Her crew came in one by one to report on
the day's end and to be instructed for the next
day, which would be Saturday – always a light
day. When they dispersed she was about to make
the evening meal for her son when her phone
rang. She saw the call was from Jake and snatch-
ed it up.

'It's all right, me dear, she's been found!' he
announced at once.

'Oh, thank god!' Relief washed over her. For a moment she couldn't speak.

Jake went on, 'She's at New Haw—'

'What on earth is she doing there?'

'Dunno – everything's in a bit of a muddle but it's something to do with a narrow boat...'

'A narrow boat? How could it have anything to do with a narrow boat? That's on the canal!'

'Don't ask me. Her daddy's gone to fetch her home. I can tell you, maidie, the rest of this family's gone to pieces under the strain!'

'Is Angela getting things ready for her? It'll be past her bedtime by the time she's at Ashgrove.'

'Not she! *She* walked out the minute the news came through that the little moppet had been found.'

Once again Libby was left speechless. Then she said, 'So who's doing that? Seeing her bed's made, getting her a meal?'

'Nobody. Mrs Rosanne is weeping in the drawing-room and my princess lady has gone up to her room.' He was quiet for a moment then said, 'If you want my opinion, Libby, you're needed here. I don't think anybody's had anything to eat all day. I got meself a sandwich just after you left, and I made tea for the lot of 'em, but that's all they've had that I know of.'

'I'll be there as soon as I can,' she replied. 'I'll see about food.'

But what was she to do about Freddie? He should be having his dinner and then getting ready for bed. She couldn't leave him alone in the flat. If she were to ring around to her friends, it might take half an hour for a sitter to get to her.

She made up her mind.

'Freddie,' she said, 'get yourself a jacket. We're going out.'

'Out?' He was astounded. The only times he'd been out at this hour were when he'd been taken to a carol service or a pantomime at Christmas. She saw him light up with the excitement of the idea. 'Where we going?'

'To Prim's house.'

'Prim? That little kid that came to my party?'

'That's the one.'

While he got his jacket she rang the catering firm habitually used by the family at Ashgrove. She ordered hot food in large enough quantities to feed them all, herself, Freddie and Jake included.

When they reached Ashgrove, Philip Moorfield and Jake were waiting at the front door.

'Is Prim home?' Libby asked Philip.

'Not yet. Any minute now. Brent said he was going past Addlestone when he rang a few minutes ago.'

She nodded acceptance of this, then led the way into the drawing-room. Rosanne was there, her face crumpled with the effect of weeping, her hair loose from its usual ribbon bow. She struggled out of the sofa to engulf Libby in a hug.

'Oh, my dear girl,' she moaned. 'How good of you to come!'

Libby was astonished. It was the first time she'd had a greeting of warmth on entering Ashgrove. She returned the hug, but broke free to say, 'This is my little boy, Freddie. I couldn't

147

leave him at home alone. Freddie, this is Mrs Moorfield, and this is her son Philip Moorfield.'

Freddie had been taught to offer his hand on being introduced, but this encounter was too much for him. He edged nearer his mother. She felt his hand creep into hers.

'I ordered hot food,' she said to Rosanne. 'Jake told me you hadn't had anything to eat, so far as he could tell.'

'Oh, what a good idea! I should have thought of that.' She flapped her hands inadequately. 'Should I open some wine?'

'That might be welcome. And, Jake, put the kettle on for hot drinks.'

'Righty-o.'

'Would it be all right if I went up to see if Prim's room is OK?' she asked Rosanne.

'Of course, of course.' Rosanne's expression told her that she now saw she should have thought of that too.

'I'll be back in a minute,' she told Freddie. 'You go and help Jake in the kitchen.'

Prim's room was in the same state as when Libby had looked at it first thing in the morning. She opened the window to air it out and quickly made the bed.

She came downstairs a few minutes later. A car was entering the drive. The front door opened and Brenton came in, carrying his little girl. He set her down as his mother and brother rushed out of the drawing-room to greet them. Jake and Freddie hurried from the kitchen.

Pale and nervous, Prim looked at them all. It seemed that they scared her a little. Then she saw Libby. Like an arrow she flew into her arms, sobbing with delighted relief. For a while she was only a warm little presence against Libby's breast, her face hidden there as she cried. By and by she raised her head.

'You were g-gone such a long t-time, Libby!'

'I know. I'm sorry.'

'And'la said you were never c-coming back.'

'Never mind, never mind.' She wiped away some of the tears with her fingers. The little girl tried to smile in response. She drew in a big sobbing breath.

'And'la was *horrid* to me.'

'Don't bother about that now, sweetheart. Are you hungry?' Prim shook her head. 'What have you had to eat today?'

'I had ... I had c-crispies in a shop. But I didn't *like* them so then the lady gave me orange – in a b-box with a straw. It was funny.'

'Would you like a drink now?' A solemn nod. 'Let's get you tidied up, pettikins, and then we'll get you some milk.'

During this conversation, no one else had said a word. Now Freddie spoke up. 'Me and Jake have put the kettle on.'

Prim twisted her head round to look at him. 'Freddie?'

'Hello.'

Prim hid her face against Libby again. Into Libby's dress she muttered, 'Will Freddie get me a drink?'

'Yes, as soon as you're tidied up a bit. We'll go upstairs and just wipe your face and hands. And Freddie can make you some hot milk.'

'Thank you,' Prim sighed.

As Libby was helping her change into a sleep-ing-suit with bunnies on the front, she heard the van arrive with the food. She urged the little girl towards the door of her room but she stood still, holding up her arms to be carried.

Libby knew from experience that this depen-dency would soon pass. She'd been through that with her own little boy at one point. Once familiar things were around her, Prim would become more herself again. But the day's events had had a big effect on her.

Downstairs Jake had set out plates and cutlery around the dining table and was dishing out pasta somewhat haphazardly from the caterer's containers. Freddie was carrying wine glasses from the sideboard to the table, one at a time and very carefully. The Moorfields were taking their places at the table, somewhat confused at being restored to this weird normality – a meal in the dining room with Prim home safely.

Libby paused in the doorway with Prim in her arms. 'Would you like to sit with Daddy and Nana in here while you have your drink?'

Prim whispered her reply against Libby's cheek. 'Can Freddie and me go in the kitchen?'

'Of course, Primmie.' She beckoned to her son, who came at once, and they made their way to the kitchen. She set Prim on a chair by the familiar old pine table, and nodded to Freddie to take his place there too.

'Now,' she said. 'What are we going to have to eat? Toast? Banana sandwich? How about Puffi-pops?'

Banana sandwiches were at the moment Freddie's favourite food. He voted for that at once. Prim, watching him in admiration, nodded that she would have the same.

Luckily Rosanne Moorfield's store of vegetarian food provided the fruit and wholemeal bread. Soon both children were munching happily. Libby heated milk for Prim and got out fruit juice for Freddie. Soon it was obvious that both were growing heavy-eyed. It was past Prim's usual bedtime and almost time for Freddie's. And it had been an eventful day.

A little ice cream for dessert satisfied Prim's appetite. Freddie thought he'd like a second helping. While Libby was spooning it out of the container, Jake came in.

'Everybody's pleased with the grub, though Mrs Rosanne says she'd like a salad – she wouldn't have any of the meat sauce with the pasta.'

Libby sighed inwardly but got out a few ingredients. Jake gave Freddie a tap on the head. 'What you doin' out so late, young sir?'

'I missed Tracy Beaker,' Freddie said.

Prim's eyes were closing. Her head began to drop forward. Libby scooped her up. 'I'll take her up and put her to bed, poor little love. She's dead on her feet.'

'Okey-doke. I'll do the salad – you'll help me, eh, Fred?' Freddie looked undecided whether it was a good thing to make a salad, even with Jake as chef, but shrugged agreement.

Within ten minutes Prim was in her bed and fast asleep. Libby tiptoed out, leaving the door ajar. Downstairs in the dining room, the Moor-fields had finished their pasta and were sitting with the wine, in a state of thankful relief. They looked round in welcome as Libby came in.

'Sit down,' invited Philip. 'Have a drink. I bet you feel the need of it.'

'I won't, thank you.' Libby had had nothing to eat so far and didn't want to drink wine. 'I only came in to find out what had been happening to the child.' This was addressed to Brent, who nodded acceptance of her plea.

'It was the weirdest thing,' he began. 'She went out of the garden gate because she saw a narrow boat moored at the bank.'

'A narrow boat? In the side stream?'

'Yes, the poor guy – Jerry Rushton – he was going down the main channel in the dark and took a wrong angle and then, what d'you think, he ran aground. So he decided to wait till the morning to drag her off, and went to sleep. I get the feeling he had a beer or two in consolation. Anyway, Prim sees the boat when she goes wandering out at dawn, and decides to climb aboard.'

'What on earth for?'

'That's the mystery. When he found her hours later waking up among all the cushions and rugs on the bunk in the main cabin, she was talking about the Bahamas.'

'The Bahamas?'

'She was saying she wanted to sail to the Bahamas,' Brenton repeated. 'Don't ask me why.'

'My father is in the Bahamas,' Libby said.

'Freddie's grandfather. He works in a boat-fitting yard.'

'Perhaps that explains it.' He was only slightly interested in solving the mystery. 'Anyway, Rushton thought she was some kid who'd trotted aboard from the canal side at Wey Manor Road – by this time, I should have said, he'd managed to free his boat from the silt at our garden and had headed to New Haw to join the Basingstoke Canal. He tied up at New Haw to buy some fittings for his boat, Minerva.'

'So what then? That must have been earlier on – why didn't he have her sent home?' Libby demanded.

'Well, you see, he thought she belonged to some nearby family. So he just left her there on the towpath while he went off to buy his stuff. And it was only a lot later that he realized she was still there, all on her own and looking scared. So he took her into the tuck shop and bought her some food and asked the shopkeeper to ring around among the local people that she knew had kids.'

'Who of course knew nothing about her,' Philip said, shaking his head in dismay. 'Poor little mite ... And then it seems they did the sensible thing and asked her for her name and address. And you know, she can recite that.'

'So at last they called the police,' Brenton continued. 'There isn't a police station there, so they rang our lot, the station at Ashley Park, who realized who she was at once. And rang us to say she was found.'

'Thank heaven,' Rosanne said, clasping her

153

hands in gratitude.

Libby nodded agreement, thankful that Prim had not fallen into bad hands in stowing away on her boat to the Bahamas.

Now a glance around the table suggested to Libby that not everyone in the Moorfield family had eaten. 'Didn't Grandee have any supper?' she asked.

'No, she went up to her room once we knew Prim was safe. I went up and told her there was a meal ready but she just refused to listen,' murmured Rosanne.

Perhaps that was because she feared being challenged over leaving open the gate to the towpath, Libby thought. All the same, the old lady ought to eat.

'Perhaps you could take up a tray?' she suggested.

'Oh ... please ... not me. She's been in such a foul mood all day,' Rosanne moaned.

'I'll do it,' Philip volunteered, though without enthusiasm.

'Right. If you'll just give me five minutes I'll invent a sort of summery dish with what's left of the pasta and some of the salad Jake made.' Rather an inadequate effort, she thought, glancing at it – but then, Jake was used to catering for himself on a more manly basis. She tapped a wine bottle. 'And I daresay she'd like a glass of wine to go with it.'

Jake appeared. 'I'm making coffee. And Libby, that lad of yours is dead on his feet.'

'Yes, I'm just going to get a tray ready for Grandee and then I'll be taking off.'

Five minutes later Philip was on his way upstairs with the food. Libby found her son sitting where she'd left him at the kitchen table, his head supported on a hand which was not too steady. She was considering whether to wake him or gather him up and carry him out to the car, when a little figure came in at the kitchen door.

'Libby? I woke up 'cause Uncle Philip's talking to Grandee. And I can't find Mitzi. Where's Mitzi?'

Probably aboard the Minerva, thought Libby. 'Never mind, sweetie,' she said. 'We'll find her tomorrow.'

'But I always sleep with Mitzi,' the little girl whined.

'Just for tonight you'll have to give someone else a chance to sleep with you. Who do you like best after Mitzi?'

'I don't know. Sugarplum?'

Sugarplum was a ballerina doll. 'Let's tell Sugarplum she's allowed to sleep with you tonight. Shall we?'

This time Prim clambered slowly upstairs at her side. Waning daylight was still gleaming at the sides of the window blinds. Libby didn't raise them, for fear of wakening Prim too much. But in the dim light they couldn't find Sugarplum.

'I want Sugarplum,' wailed Prim.

'Ssh, now, Sugarplum's being naughty, she's hiding.' Normally she could have laid her hands on the doll, but it was some time since she'd last tidied the room. Almost nothing seemed to be in

155

its right place.

Prim's collection of toys wasn't extensive. She had some cloth animals from babyhood, building bricks, picture books, and three dolls – Mitzi, Sugarplum and Gloria. Gloria was a china doll in beautiful clothes, totally unsuitable as a bedtime companion. Libby chose the largest of the soft toys, a velvet elephant, but it was rejected with tears.

'I want Mitzi! Where's Mitzi?' Sleepy and overtired, she was heading for a long fit of crying.

Libby picked her up. 'Bedtime now, Primmie, time to go to sleep. Look, your pillow's all crumpled into a lump. Let's smooth it out, and...' She swayed the child gently to and fro. 'Let's put your sleepy head on it, and tomorrow, tomorrow we'll look for Mitzi and we'll find her and you can swing her on the swing...' She let her voice begin to die away as she put Prim into her bed.

'Tomorrow,' Prim repeated drowsily. 'Can I do dusting with you tomorrow?'

'Yes, love, we'll do dusting, and we'll tidy away your toys, and we'll make special fruit salad for breakfast...' She was gently moving towards the door.

'Don't go away!' Prim cried, getting up on an elbow. 'I don't want you to go, Libby.'

'All right, Prim, I'm here. But it's time to sleep. Shh now, go to sleep.'

She sat on a chair by the little dressing table so that Prim could see her. Slowly the child's eyes drooped shut. Her breathing became even and slow. She was asleep. Libby glanced at her watch. Should she creep out now?

There came a soft tap on the door. She went to it. Philip was outside. 'Quiet,' she warned, 'she's just dropped off again.'

'And so has your little boy. I came to tell you I've put him in the corner of the sofa. He's far off in dreamland.'

Libby stifled a groan. 'He ought to be in bed,' she said. 'But I feel I can't leave yet – Prim's very clingy, I don't know if you'd get her to sleep again if she woke and found me gone.'

'Why don't you stay then?' he suggested.

'What?'

'You could use Brent's old room. He never sleeps there any more. And you could put the little boy in there too. Just until the morning.'

'Oh, I don't know...'

Prim made a grumbling sound and twisted about in bed.

'Ssh...' soothed Libby. 'Ssh now, it's sleepy time...'

The restless motion stopped.

'Tell you what, I'll bring Freddie up and put him on Brent's bed. You can make up your mind what to do by and by.'

She decided somewhere around ten o'clock that it would be best not to rouse Freddie by carrying him out to the car. And besides, Prim kept coming half-awake, in the grip of some momentary nightmare. Brent's room was just across the passage. It would be easy to tiptoe across and settle her down again.

She went downstairs to speak to Jake, who had cleared away the dishes from the dining room, stacked the dishwasher, disposed of the caterer's containers, and had generally been making himself useful.

'Everything's more or less shipshape,' he reported. 'You're staying, I gather.'

'It seems best, Jake. But it looks like it might be a disturbed night.'

'OK then, don't you bother about getting to the office in the morning. I'll see the day gets started. In any case, Saturday's pretty easy. Can I use your car to get home then?'

'Of course.' She found her handbag and gave him the keys. 'Thanks a lot, pal. I don't know what I'd have done without you.'

'Goodnight, then. I'll come and fetch you in the morning.'

'Goodnight.'

She went out into the quiet night to see him drive away. Then she went back indoors, closed the door firmly behind her, and went upstairs to join her little boy in a strange bed.

And so it was goodbye forever to her rule about not getting involved with clients.

Ten

During a long and wakeful night, Prim's sleep was often disturbed by some momentary nightmare. Libby soothed her back to sleep each time, quietly moving back and forth between Brenton's room and Prim's.

Freddie slept through it all, stirring only slightly. Libby had taken off his shoes and socks then covered him lightly with a throw. She stretched out beside him, using only the pillow from the duvet set.

Around midnight she heard Angela come home. There was no disturbance in her entrance; she came quietly upstairs and went into her room. After that, silence.

Prim fell at last into a normal sleep when dawn had already come. But soon after, at about five o'clock, Libby heard sounds out in the passage. She tumbled off the bed and went to inquire.

It was Philip, with his shoes in his hands, trying to make a silent exit. He opened his mouth to speak. She put her finger to her lips. They crept downstairs one after the other, into the hall.

'I was trying not to wake anyone,' he whispered. 'I'm terribly sorry to go when the family is all at sixes and sevens like this, but I should have been in Southampton yesterday.'

'It's all right.'

'Was everything OK during the night?'

'She only slept in fits and starts. I don't know how she's going to be today.'

'Will you stay?' he appealed.

'I think I'll have to. I promised her we'd do dusting together.'

'Poor little thing ... Her idea of fun is to do the housework with you! Well, there may be something nice in store for her today. Brent's going to try to organize a two-way video link-up with Jackie. I was going to leave you a note about it.'

'Jackie?' For a moment she was at a loss. Then memory came back: 'Prim's mother – of course!'

'That was where Brent got to yesterday – in his studio, remember? He was trying to contact her, but she was out on a fashion shoot with a gang of models. He got her on the phone when it was around ten o'clock her time – Tokyo's eight hours ahead of us.'

'She must have been terribly worried...'

'Certainly was, from what I heard. But as soon as she knew Prim was safe home, she fell into bed. Now of course when it's getting on for noon where she is, Prim's still fast asleep.'

'What time is the video link going to be?'

'Brent can't be sure. He got all this marvellous new equipment after the fire, so he's pretty sure he can do it his end, but Jackie's got to get permission to use the firm's equipment, in their boardroom.'

'Oh dear.'

'Oh, they'll say yes when they hear it's to talk

to her kid after a day like yesterday. You know how the Japanese are about kids.'

She summoned a smile. 'I don't, actually. I know next to nothing about Japan.' A thought struck her. 'Prim will be able to ask for a new doll. Mitzi went missing somehow yesterday.'

'Oh, I think Jackie will send her a trunkful of Mitzis now.'

He glanced at his watch and moved towards the front door. He said apologetically, 'I really have got to go. Filming can't begin until I've okayed the site and made a contract with the site owner.'

'Of course.'

'You've got my mobile number?'

'Yes, thank you.'

He took her hand and pressed it between both of his. 'I'll keep in touch.'

When he was gone Libby debated whether it was worth going back to bed. But it was very early and she was feeling disoriented and woozy. She dragged herself upstairs again and tried to sleep.

At about eight o'clock, she heard Jake drive her own car up to the house. She tumbled off the bed and went down to greet him, warning him to be quiet with a wave of her hand.

'Morning,' he murmured, coming in holding a big carrier bag. 'How's tricks?' She made a so-so gesture. 'You look like the death of Nelson.'

'Oh, thanks.'

'I've brought you clean clothes. Amy came in early to pick them out for you.'

'Darling Jake, what would I do without you? I

feel as if I've been wearing these things for a hundred years.'

'What you need is a shower, a change of clothes, a good strong cup of tea, and a full English breakfast. So up you go, get yourself tidied up, and I'll do the cooking.'

'You'll be lucky if you can find the ingredients for a full English breakfast in this house,' she told him. 'Nobody's done any food shopping except Rosanne, as far as I can make out, and she's a vegetarian.'

She showered, and changed clothes in the main bathroom. A glance in at Prim and then Freddie told her they were both still asleep. A lovely aroma of toast was wafting up from the kitchen and she was suddenly aware that she was ravenously hungry.

Jake had a tea towel round his waist and was stirring something in a saucepan. 'Scrambled eggs,' he said. 'Lots.'

'Oh, gorgeous.'

He took his saucepan off the stove and began spooning the eggs on to toast. He gestured with the spoon. 'Tea's made.'

She poured herself a steaming mug of tea and sat down at the kitchen table.

While she was eating, Brenton came in. It was clear he expected to see her, for he gave her a welcoming smile. 'How's everybody this morning?' he inquired, heading for the teapot.

'Philip has gone to Southampton. Otherwise we're the only ones up.'

He sat down opposite with his tea. 'I sort of gathered your little boy stayed over.'

162

She nodded, finishing her meal.

'Prim seemed quite ... well, she seemed pleased he was here.'

'Oh yes, I think she's got a slight case of hero worship,' she acknowledged with a smile. 'She'll get over it.'

'Oh. Why should she? I mean, it would be quite nice, wouldn't it, if they were friends?'

Libby could have told him that seven-year-old boys didn't much want to be friends with girls, particularly girls as young as Prim. But she wanted to get upstairs again, before Freddie could wake up to find himself in a strange bed in a strange room. She got up, gathering her plate and mug to go in the dishwasher.

'I'm trying to set up a video link between here and Tokyo,' Brenton said quickly, as if to detain her.

'Yes, I heard that from Philip. Are you going to tell Prim? She'd love to hear from her mother.'

'Better not. It's a bit dodgy, trying to get everybody lined up Jackie's end, with the gear available. But if all goes well, we ought to be teleconferencing about ten o'clock this morning.'

'Right-o, we'll be ready. Where is this going to happen? Philip's office?'

'No, no, the studio. I'll give you the signal when it's ready to go.'

She made for the door. 'I have to get going. I expect one or other of the children will be waking soon.'

'See you later?' he called as she hurried out.

She didn't bother to reply. She thought she

163

could already hear the sound of someone stirring upstairs.

It turned out to be Prim, who came out of her bedroom rubbing her eyes and heading sleepily for the bathroom. Libby glanced in at Freddie, who was still sleeping. She waited outside the bathroom for Prim, who blinked herself awake to say, 'Hello, Libby.'

'Good morning.'

'Is it getting-up time?'

'Yes it is. Shall we turn on the shower and have a good scrub?'

The child obediently returned to the bathroom and at first submitted passively to being washed. But when Libby began to run the sponge round her ankles, telling her it was a kitten, she began to giggle. Water was splashed about in quantities. While her hair was washed, she tucked a nail brush in among the suds. 'That's a hedge-hob,' she announced. 'I put a hedgehob in my hair.'

Wrapped in a bath towel, she trotted into the bedroom. Libby made a great fuss of choosing what she should wear. 'Oh, that's blue. That's not a Saturday T-shirt. How can you wear a Tuesday T-shirt with Saturday shorts?' And so on, until the child was dressed and smiling at her reflection in the dressing-table mirror.

Freddie wandered in, looking puzzled. 'Are we still in Prim's house, Mum?'

'Yes, we are, and Jake brought your Saturday clothes so when you've had a shower and done your teeth, you can put them on.'

'I didn't know I had any Saturday clothes.'

Libby knew that what Amy had picked out were simply everyday items. But she said, 'Well, today's Saturday, so they must be your Saturday clothes, mustn't they?'

'I'm wearing my Saturday close,' Prim informed him importantly.

'All right then,' Freddie grunted.

When they were both ready she led them down to the kitchen. Brenton had gone, but Jake was still there, at ease with a fresh pot of tea. He greeted them with a mock salute. 'Morning, maties. What are we going to have for breakfast?'

'Toast?' Freddie was sniffing the air.

'Toast and scrambled eggs, that's the main menu today.'

'Lovely.'

Jake glanced at Prim, who had said nothing yet. 'What's your liking, little miss?'

'Strambled eggs,' she said.

It was the first time that Libby had ever known her to have a cooked breakfast.

They settled at the table with orange juice while Jake set about cooking. 'Are we going to do dusting after breakfast?' Prim asked.

'Dusting?' Freddie echoed, amazed.

'Not you, love. Just Prim and I.'

'How long's that going to take? I thought we were going to the farmers' market.' The farmers' market was one of his favourite venues – there were all sorts of goodies to be sampled there.

Libby hesitated. This was a problem she hadn't yet resolved. As a rule she spent as much time as she could with Freddie at weekends, yet she didn't want to leave Prim. She felt the little girl needed a quiet day at home, to feel safe again after yesterday's adventure – and she also felt she couldn't leave her to the tender mercies of Angela.

Jake caught her eye, and guessed her dilemma. 'What say you and me go to the market, eh, Fred? I think your mum's got a load of work to do here today.'

Freddie was pleased, then dubious. 'We're not staying tonight again, are we?'

'No, love, no, we'll be going home about tea-time. I tell you what,' she said, visited by an inspiration, 'it looks like being a lovely day. We can have a picnic tea in the garden before we leave – how about that?'

'We-ell ... OK.'

Prim, meanwhile, was beaming with pleasure. 'A picnic,' she repeated. 'Like in my picture book, with bunny rabbits sitting on the grass.'

'Just like that. And you can help me make the sandwiches.'

After breakfast Freddie drove off with Jake. Prim helped stack their dishes in the dishwasher and, under Libby's supervision, switched it on. Libby then sat down to write a shopping list, as food – except for vegetarian supplies – was almost non-existent in the larder and refrigerator. She marvelled at Rosanne's outlook: she shopped only for her own menus but forgot to order for the rest of the family. Or perhaps she hoped that by force majeure she could turn them all into vegetarians.

So that the little girl wouldn't become bored,

she asked her for suggestions for the list, including the makings of the picnic. They were still busy with it when Rosanne appeared, clad in silk Turkish trousers and a cotton top.

'Nana, are those your Saturday close? I'm wearing mine,' Prim announced.

'Are you, dear? That's fine. Good morning, Libby. Is that toast I can smell?'

'Freddie had scrambled eggs on toast. So did I. Jake had tea.'

'Oh, I think I'll make myself a tisane,' murmured Rosanne, brushing her hair away from her face and sighing. 'I feel the need of something to revive the inner self after a day like yesterday.'

Libby got up from her list-making. 'Come along, Prim,' she said. 'We'll telephone Darville's to deliver the supplies.' And out they went, leaving Rosanne with her tisane.

She used the drawing-room phone to make the call, with Prim standing at her side to prompt her. Delivery was promised for after lunch.

Next she had to plan what to do about cleaning the house. Some three weeks of neglect had left it in a mess. She was still scribbling directions to herself when she heard Angela coming down the stairs. It was noticeable to Libby that Prim at once leaned in closer.

Angela made for the kitchen, where her mother could be heard greeting her. Then there was a loud exclamation from Angela. 'You mean she's here now?'

An indistinct response, perhaps intended to be placatory.

'Good grief, haven't we had enough fuss and bother?' After that there was only the sound of normal conversation, although there came a clash when the kettle collided with the tap as it was filled.

Prim looked up at Libby, anxiety in her face.

'Let's go upstairs and start the dusting in your bedroom,' Libby suggested, understanding that the child was afraid Angela would come into the drawing-room next.

Thus the day's housework was started. Without her own holdall and its personal tools, she had to find polishes and mops and dusters in the hall cupboards. Prim proudly provided her own duster, saved from the first day she had used it.

Prim's room, Brenton's room, Philip's room and the main bathroom were rather quickly attended to. Then Libby happened upon Angela as she came out on to the landing.

'It's time for Prim to go to play group,' Angela announced.

'Ah ... She won't be going to play group today.'

'Oh? Nobody told *me*.'

'It's better for her to stay quietly at home for a day or two,' Libby said.

'Whose idea was this?'

Libby ignored the challenge. 'It's nice for you to have the weekend free, Angela, don't you think?'

The sulky expression relaxed. Aggression faded. The girl pursed her lips, shrugged a little, then said, 'I suppose I'm still expected to be here to put her to bed and all that, am I?'

'No, that's all right.'

'Well ... Can't be bad, can it? Then I'm off now.' She headed for the stairs. Over her shoulder she said, 'Don't wait up!' and chuckled as she disappeared from view.

Prim came out of her bedroom with her arms full of little garments for the washing machine. It was inevitable that she'd heard the exchange. She looked at Libby for a long moment then said, 'Are we going to do dusting in Angela's room?'

It was the first time Libby had ever heard her get Angela's name right. It might mean that the child had discarded some line of defence that the mispronounced name had provided. Or perhaps it merely meant that she'd grown up just a little more.

As predicted, there was a ring on the telephone in the drawing-room, which proved to be Brenton signalling that the video link was about to happen. Libby said to Prim, 'How would you like to speak to your mummy?'

'Mummy's in Tokyo,' said Prim.

'But you've spoken to her on the telephone before, haven't you?'

'Yes, and she told me she was sending me my watch.' Prim lifted a wrist, on which the Japanese watch showed bright. 'Daddy put it to the right time,' she added with some regret. 'It doesn't flash any more.'

'Daddy's arranged for you to speak to Mummy, and see her at the same time, Prim. Would you like that?'

'Really?'

'Yes, love.'

'When? When can I?'

'If we go to the studio, I think we'll find she's on a screen there.'

The little girl dropped her armful of clothes and rushed for the stairs. Libby swept her up and carried her down. Set free, Prim ran for the back door, which was open to air the house out. The door to the studio was only round the corner of the building. Her father was standing there, smiling and waving her forward. Prim darted in, and Brenton closed the door.

Sighing with satisfaction, Libby went back to her chores.

She had started on the dining room when Prim came skipping back from her father's studio. Libby came out to hear the news.

'I told my mummy about Mitzi getting lost, and she says Mitzi prob'ly wanted to visit her family in Tokyo so Mummy's going to find her and send her back to me.' This came out in a delighted rush.

Well done, thought Libby. Someone in the family understood how to be kind to a little girl.

Brenton had come over to ensure Prim was safely indoors. Libby asked, 'How did it go?'

'Oh, all right,' he said, drawing back into his shell a little. 'Jackie was a bit ... well, you know ... upset about what's been happening.' He patted Prim on the top of her head. 'Bye, love. Be good.'

And with that he returned to the haven of his studio, where machines would give him

170

undemanding friendship.

Rosanne had gone out to serve in the Saturday rush at her shop. The house was quiet. Libby and Prim went to the kitchen to see what they could find for lunch. The menu turned out to be baked potato with melted cheese and salad. Prim was delighted with melted cheese. It seemed she'd never seen it before.

Now they put the laundry from the bedrooms into the washing machine. Prim was allowed to switch it on. 'If we had a wash line we could pin the things up to dry outside,' Libby said.

'Like in my picture books!' Prim made flapping movements with her hands. 'The breeze would blow. That would be lovely.'

'We'll get Jake to put up a washing line for us one day.'

'Tomorrow?'

'Not tomorrow. Jake won't be here tomorrow.'

A little gasp of alarm. 'Will you be here, Libby?'

'Yes, pet, I'll be here. But not all day. Freddie and I are going out on a little adventure.'

'An adventure? Like the Bahamas?'

'No, not as far as the Bahamas. Just down the road a bit, that's all.'

That seemed to reassure Prim a little, but she seemed mournful. She screwed up her face in thought. 'Freddie doesn't see you on a video thing.'

'No, he sees me standing beside him. Like I'm standing beside *you* now.'

'Oh yes!' She brightened, then held up her arms to be picked up.

Libby obeyed the summons. How was this going to end, she asked herself. But, she supposed, if she was going to get herself involved with the Moorfields, she might as well do it whole-heartedly.

She took Prim up for a nap in her room then returned to the downstairs cleaning. She was dusting a side table in the drawing-room when she heard Grandee coming downstairs at last. She came out, cleaning cloth in hand, to inquire if she needed something to eat, for it was now past noon.

The head of the house paused in the hall, elegant in a soft dove-grey dress and a shady hat.

'Good morning,' Libby said. 'Can I get you anything? Tea, coffee?'

'No, thank you. I seldom eat until lunchtime.' She touched the brim of the summery hat. 'I telephoned my daughter-in-law at her shop to remind her of my plans for the day. She tells me you stayed here overnight with your little boy.'

'Yes.'

'So as to be on hand if Prim was restless.'

'Yes.'

'That seems somewhat overdramatic to me.'

'It was Philip who asked me to stay.'

Grandee made a little gesture with her hand, sweeping away the explanation. 'Let that go by. There will be no need for you to act nightwatchman again tonight. Angela will—'

'Angela has gone out and I believe intends to stay out late.'

'Gone out? Who took the child to her play group, then?'

'She didn't go to play group. She's been with me, helping to tidy the house.' Which greatly needs it, she added mentally.

'And where is she now, may I ask?'

'She's having her afternoon nap.'

'But when she wakes up, she'll seek your company again, I imagine.' There was disapproval in every word.

Before Grandee could say anything more, Libby launched into an explanation. 'It's about reassurance,' she said. 'For the past few weeks I imagine she's only had Angela for a companion here at home and she told me herself Angela had been unkind. Hence the intended voyage to the Bahamas—'

'And who on earth put that absurd idea into her head in the first place? I gather it came from some game at that birthday party—'

'Mrs Moorfield, Prim is a very anxious, unhappy little girl. I wish you'd acknowledge that fact. Today has been spent giving her comfort, making her feel part of the family instead of an unwanted nuisance...'

'I suppose using your customary psychological aids? Duster and broom?'

Libby clenched her teeth in an effort to stay calm. 'We're having a picnic in the garden this afternoon,' she said. 'When I suggested it, her face lit up. Do you realize she's never been on a picnic? That when the police asked yesterday about places she might go, the list consisted of only two or three ideas – the play groups and a couple of children's parks? No one ever takes her anywhere, spends any quality time with her—'

'That has only come about recently. Un-fortunately the last nanny we hired had to be discharged and so Angela has taken on the role...'

'And there couldn't be a worse stand-in! Philip asked me to stay last night, and I promised Prim I'd be here today, so we'll see how it goes.'

'Philip is probably under pressure because of business matters. I understand he had to go early this morning. I'll take it up with him when he comes back. But in the meantime I think my wishes come first in what is, after all, *my* house.'

'Don't ask me to leave,' Libby said, forced against her will to become a petitioner. 'I promised Prim a picnic with my little boy and I don't want to break my word.'

Grandee's expression was a mixture of vex-ation and acceptance. 'Of course I ... I wouldn't want the child to be disappointed in such a small thing.' A pause. 'I'm being taken by some friends to the summer show at the Royal Academy. It may be quite late when I come home. I sincerely hope you will have gone by that time, and will not reappear to carry on this absurd charade.'

'Whatever you say.' Libby recognized this instruction as punishment. And she guessed the reason for it: she was being punished for inter-fering in the family's affairs, for being better able to help Prim than anyone else in the house, but above all for knowing that it was Grandee who had left the gate open so that Prim could get lost.

A car drove up outside, and there was a faint toot on the horn. Grandee sailed past Libby, opening the door to reveal a handsome Lexus drawn up at the entrance. Someone leaned out from the back seat to call, 'Come along, Vivienne, or we'll lose our table at the Savoy!'

In a moment she was gone. Libby watched the car swish out of the drive and away. And now she and Prim were the only people left in the great old house.

Prim was already sitting up and looking around when Libby went up to rouse her from her nap. 'Is it time for my picnic?' she inquired.

'Not quite. We have to make the sandwiches first.' The supplies had been delivered from the shop, but were still in their cardboard box. Libby set it on the kitchen floor so that Prim could help unload it.

Next came the making of the picnic food. From Rosanne's plentiful store of fruit, Libby made a smoothie. Prim was entranced, was allowed to taste the mixture, and had the important task of carrying the jug to the refrigerator. She also helped to make the sandwiches. When Jake and Freddie came back, they found the picnic site ready, a trio of bright tea cloths spread on the grass near the cedar tree.

After their picnic meal, Freddie pushed Prim on her swing for a while. He tried out the swing himself but declared it 'too feeble'. Then he fetched a ball from the car and tried to play with the little girl, who totally failed to catch the ball. But she ran about eagerly, determined to do whatever might please her guest.

By and by a light rain began to fall. Gathering up the picnic equipment, the grown-ups led the way indoors. The children followed, after standing outside for a while with mouths open and heads tilted, to see who could catch the most raindrops. But Prim was beginning to droop. Bedtime was approaching.

Libby left Jake and Freddie watching television while she put the little girl to bed. She read to her from a picture book, the story scant but the tone of her voice low and reassuring, so that Prim's eyelids began to close. She was soon fast asleep.

'Are we going home now?' Freddie asked when she came downstairs.

'Not yet. Can't leave Prim alone in the house, duckie.'

'Oh, I s'pose not.' He returned to his television programme.

About half an hour later Rosanne returned to Ashgrove, having shut up shop for the weekend. Libby explained that Prim was asleep and that Angela was unlikely to be back to take care of her should she waken.

'You'll listen out for her?' she asked Rosanne.

'Of course. Yes, leave that to me, Libby.' Rosanne adopted a dependable expression.

In the car on the way home Freddie inquired, 'Will you make that smoothie again tomorrow, Mum?'

'You'll be lucky, chum. That one had mango and things in it. Haven't got any of those at home.'

He sighed. 'We should have bought some

mangoes at the market, Jake.'

'None of that foreign stuff there, me hearty! You'll have to make do with strawberry and apple.'

'We-ell ... That's not so bad, either.'

Next day's plan was a visit to a children's safari park – a few degrees up from a petting zoo, reported to have elephants and other foreign imports. Freddie was taking his coloured pencils and sketching book, in hopes of seeing something worth drawing. They were ready to go when Libby's office phone rang. She picked it up in the kitchen. It was Philip Moorfield.

'Libby? Listen, Libby, I just got back from Southampton to find Prim in floods of tears. She expected you to be here this morning.'

'Not possible,' she replied. 'Your grandmother warned me off yesterday.'

'What?'

'When she was about to go off to the Royal Academy show, she told me she didn't want me in the house.'

'Oh, for the love of Pete!' There was a pause while he conveyed this news to someone else.

Brenton came on the line. 'Libby, Prim's really in quite a state. You couldn't ... I mean, could you just drop in for a few minutes?'

'I'd rather not. I've had enough encounters with Grandee, thank you.'

Another off-line conversation, then Brenton said, 'Could I bring Prim to your place? Just for a visit?'

'I'm on my way out. Freddie and I are going to a safari park.'

'Oh, I see.'

There was another halt in the conversation then Philip Moorfield spoke. 'Listen, Libby, I know it's a lot to ask, but could you take Prim with you on this outing?'

'What, to a safari park? There are big animals there, Philip. I think it might scare her and I don't want to have to handle a crying child. I want Freddie to enjoy it.'

'Yes. Of course.'

'I'm really sorry' – and she was – 'but Freddie's been looking forward to this.'

'I understand. It was thoughtless of me to suggest it.'

'But Prim's making herself sick with crying, Libby,' Brenton said, apparently now on an extension line. 'And Mama's been sort of trying to settle her down but she's not having any success. What should we do?'

'I don't know,' Libby confessed.

Philip spoke again, in a hesitant tone. 'How about ... Listen, Brent ... How about if you take Prim to this place?'

'What?' This was Brenton, totally at a loss.

'To the safari park. You could meet Libby and her little boy there.'

'But that's...'

'You mean accidentally-on-purpose?' Libby put in.

'Something like that. What do you think?'

She thought it was like having an assignation with a lover. But it was a solution. She found it hard to bear the thought of Prim sobbing because she'd let her down.

178

She gave directions to the safari park, then debated whether to tell Freddie about the plan, and decided against it. Let it all happen as if by accident. Freddie, who had been in his room finding his drawing tools, was blissfully unaware of the plan. Libby set off, feeling a little guilty yet believing this was a good solution to the problem.

Prim and her father were already in the car park when she and Freddie drove in. Freddie saw Prim almost at once. 'Look, Mum, there's that little kid from that house yesterday.'

'So it is.'

The two parties joined up. Brenton was carrying Prim, which was a relief to Libby, for otherwise she thought the child might have rushed to her in tears. They sedately made their way to the ticket office and set off on their tour of the animals.

As Libby had expected, Prim wanted to stay a long way from the elephants and the camels, but was pleased with the deer and the llamas. By and by she was happy to be set on her feet and to trot along at Freddie's side. Freddie, who had several books about animals, gave her a lecture about llamas.

Free to converse, Brenton began a stumbling speech of gratitude. 'It's so good of you to be so sort of kind and understanding about Prim. I'm beginning to see that, you know, things aren't going too well with her.'

'That's certainly true, Brenton. The poor little thing is like a lost soul. You ought to *do* something about it, because this is a very important time in her life, you know.' Will he understand, she asked herself. Will he come out of his castles in the sky and deal with the real world?

'I want to do something about it, I really do. And you've been so sort of wonderful with her, and she thinks so much of you, that I was wondering...'

'What?'

'How would it be if you and I ... you know ... sort of ... well, I wondered if you'd like to get together.'

She stared. 'Get together how?'

'I've been thinking it would be, like, you know, a perfect fit if we got married...'

Eleven

It took a while for Libby to get her breath back. At last she managed to say, 'But you're already married, Brent!'

'Oh ... Well, that's not working, really, now is it? I'm here and Jackie's there, and ... you know ... It's a dud as far as marriages go, don't you think?'

'But ... but you must have been in love to begin with?'

'Oh, sure, we were the talk of the college, wrapped up in each other. Oh, yeah ... But then you know, we both copped out because we didn't think college was doing much for us, and got married, and then Prim came along.' He rubbed his stubbly chin, his expression rueful.

'And that should have made you closer, surely...'

'Libby, you've seen what it's like with us. I mean, at Ashgrove. It's not easy. Grandee ... Well, Grandee never liked Jackie. Thought she was "common". And of course, you know, Jackie *is* abrasive. So they didn't get on from the outset and then when the baby came...' He sighed. 'And Jackie of course wanted to go back to work. She was with Bremnitz – it's an advertising company.' He looked inquiringly at her but she had never heard of it. 'Specializes in fashion advertising.'

The two children, having watched the llamas for a while, were moving on to the next enclosure, where some ibex were drowsing on some rocks. She nudged Brenton to follow. He seemed surprised, as if he'd forgotten their existence.

'So was it a problem, Jackie going back to work?' she prompted. She really wanted to find out how it came about that Jackie had left for Tokyo.

'Oh, everything about Jackie was a problem to Grandee. Jackie wanted us to move out, but, you know ... I wasn't doing too well with my stage-effects business at first. And the studio ... I couldn't afford to rent a studio, so Jackie went back to working at Bremnitz, and Grandee hired a nanny for Prim.' He frowned in thought. 'I think that was Alma, the first one. Yes, a fully trained nanny, wore sort of a uniform ... She was awfully capable.'

'I've always felt that Prim had had a good start,' Libby acknowledged.

'Yes, well, Alma – if that's what her name was – she had a set-to with Grandee and walked out. So we got another one. That was Margaret, I think. Sweet sort of person. And so when Jackie got the offer of this job in Tokyo, she decided to go, try it out, see if she could do it, and there was no problem about Prim because she and Margaret were getting on fine.'

'And how old was Prim?'

'What? Oh, about eighteen months, I think. Maybe going on two years old.'

'So she's been without her mother for about a year and a half.'

'Yes.'

'And how many nursemaids since then?'

He shook his head. 'Two? I'm not really sure. Grandee hired them, you know. Except the last one, the one that went into the passage to have her secret ciggie – I engaged that one and I had to give her the push, and then you know we were sort of stuck, so Angela took over.'

'That's dreadful, Brent! That little girl has learned to like so many people and then they just disappear out of her life one after the other!'

'I know, and that's why I thought ... you know ... you and I...'

'No.' They were standing together but facing towards the animals, so she took one of his hands and turned him towards her. 'We scarcely know each other. And Freddie's only just met you. And I don't want to get married. And you're still married to Jackie and Jackie is Prim's

182

mother. Her *mother*, Brent. You can't just switch Jackie and me in the same way as you switched nursemaids.'

'Well, now, I didn't mean it like that, Libby,' he said, sounding hurt. 'I like you. I do, I like you a lot. There's something about you ... And I didn't mean we'd rush into it, not at all. We could be engaged, couldn't we, and people would get used to the idea—'

'Grandee? Grandee would get used to the idea of you being engaged to the cleaner?'

That gave him pause. Then he said, 'Well, we could find a place of our own. I don't know why I've let myself get bogged down at Ashgrove.'

'Because of the studio?' she suggested.

'Ah. Well. Yes, perhaps. But things are going pretty well with the Tyrants now – I could afford to find a new place and move the equipment...'

'That might be a good idea. But I don't think I should play any part in that, Brent. I understand how you feel...' She broke off. She didn't understand him at all. And she was quite sure she didn't want to marry him, or even be engaged to him. 'I've been getting along pretty well up to now and I don't want to change anything.'

He studied her face, and could see she meant what she said. He drew in a long breath and replied, 'That's a pity.' Then he turned his gaze back to the ibex on their rocks and murmured to himself. 'A great pity, that.'

The rest of the afternoon could have been embarrassing but luckily the children kept them occupied. They had a snack lunch in the cafeteria, which was a great adventure for Prim.

183

Another round of the enclosures, with long pauses at the animals they admired most, took up the rest of the afternoon. When it was time to head for home, Brenton delayed Libby for a moment, holding her back as the children ran towards their cars in the car park.

'Phil and I had a discussion after we spoke – you know, on the telephone this morning,' he informed her. 'Grandee's having some friends in for dinner tonight, so he sort of didn't want to upset her, but once they've gone he says he ... well, it's time to have a straight talk with her. He's going to, you know, more or less lay down the law, and tell her you're to have the freedom to come and go as you like because ... well, we need you at the house.'

'Oh...'

'Of course that's if you ... you know, want to. I can imagine you think we're the family from hell.' He broke off, nodding at his own words. 'I don't know what's the matter with us! We can't seem to organize ourselves – work together – maybe we lack something that other families have. But you know, Libby, you've made a world of difference to Prim. And so, because of her, Phil and I are asking you to disregard Grandee and come back to us.'

Libby saw the little girl pause and look back for her, anxiety in her face as she realized they were about to part. That look convinced her. 'Yes, I'll be there in the morning.'

Prim was hesitating by the cars, waiting for Libby to catch up.

'Come along then, everybody,' Libby urged.

'Time to go home. I'll see you in the morning, Prim.'

The child smiled in relief, going with her father without complaint, waving a cheerful goodbye as they drove off.

Libby didn't hurry to get to Ashgrove the next morning. When she arrived, Prim was already in the kitchen having breakfast, watched by her Uncle Philip. 'I chose Brekkiflakes this morning and Uncle Phil got the packet down for me,' she announced importantly. 'And I've got cranb'ries on them, see?'

'The red looks pretty with the brown, doesn't it? Well done.'

Philip nodded towards the door. She went out, and he joined her in the hall. In its dimness, he loomed over her. She braced herself, sturdy body ready for some complaint, some fault-finding. But there was nothing intimidating in his manner; on the contrary, she thought she glimpsed uncertainty on his narrow features. 'I had a word with my grandmother last night,' he said.

'Yes, Brent said you were going to.' She gave him a smile of sympathy. 'Was it outright war?'

'Let's say the skirmishing was quite lively. However, I had some good points in my favour, the main one being that it was getting on for midnight and Angela – Prim's nominated carer – hadn't yet come home. My mother had to see Prim into bed – and you know, Mama is a kind woman, but her memory doesn't seem to work very well. She forgot to read a story...'

'Oh! And of course Prim couldn't settle down.'

'Exactly. You know that, and I know that, and I expect even Angela knows that – but it had to be explained to Grandee about four times. In the end she understood that Prim needs someone who's good with children—'

'But listen, Philip, I'm not a nursemaid. I've no training—'

'I understand – believe me, we've been through all this half a dozen times with the trained nurses we've hired.' He waved away her objection. 'I'm not asking you to be Prim's nanny. It's just that, if you could be here, in the house, and let her trot around with you the way she seems to enjoy, and ... well, make her feel that everything's all right...'

'Will you speak to Angela about being on duty instead of out with her pals?'

'I'll try. She's still in bed, but when she surfaces I'll have it out with her.'

Libby felt an impulse of compassion for him. He was the only one who seemed to have any idea that there was something amiss in their family. The others seemed to wear blinkers that prevented them from seeing their problems.

'All right then,' she agreed. 'I'll consider myself as re-hired. But we have to have a different agreement about rates of pay and so forth.'

'You mean you think you ought to have danger money?' he asked, smiling.

'Something like that. Who else is up, besides you and Prim?'

'My mother went out early – she's expecting a delivery at the shop. Grandee hasn't appeared yet, but you know she seldom surfaces much before lunch. Brenton – I think he came in from the studio earlier to make himself some breakfast; there were signs of his being in the kitchen.'

Prim appeared in the kitchen doorway. 'I've finished my breakfast but I want another drink, please, Uncle Phil.' She trotted up to him, expecting immediate aid.

'Just coming, Primmie.' There was something touching about the tall figure bending over the tiny child. He straightened and said to Libby, 'I'll drop by your office this evening, if I may, to discuss a new arrangement.'

She nodded agreement, and he went to pour orange juice for Prim. She took out her mobile to call Amy, her chief assistant, whom she knew to be free this morning.

'I really need you, Amy,' she cajoled. 'There's two or three weeks' work that needs catching up with here. Just for today, come and lend a hand.' A short discussion persuaded Amy that to work at Ashgrove for one day wouldn't be too unpleasant. Relieved, Libby got her cleaning equipment out of her holdall and started her chores in the dining room.

By ten o'clock, when Prim should have been heading for play group, Angela still hadn't surfaced. Philip came in search of Libby. 'What shall we do?' he asked in vexation. 'I thought today things would be back to normal for the kid.'

Libby and Amy were finishing off in the dining room, with Prim carefully dusting the chair legs. Libby came to join Philip at the door

187

of the room. 'She ought to go,' she murmured. 'She ought to be with kids she knows, in a familiar atmosphere. Her daddy will have to take her.'

'Right. I'll go and roust him out of the studio.'

'And tell him that *he's* got to give Angela the chop,' she said, with a little surge of anger at Brenton's vacillation.

'What?'

'He's Prim's father; he's the one who's paying her for supposedly looking after the child. He gives her an ultimatum – either she really takes on the job, or he's not going to pay her whatever it is she's getting at the moment.'

'But ... do you think Brent can do it?' Philip was frowning, perhaps trying to picture his younger brother in a confrontation.

She shook her head at him. 'Isn't it time he faced up to his problems?'

'Well, it's true he doesn't seem to grasp that we nearly had a disaster last week ... So if he tells Angela he'll stop her salary, you think it'll make her sort herself out?'

'Does she have money otherwise? An allowance?'

'Ye-es. Mama gives her pocket money. But it isn't much, Libby. It comes out of the profit from Mama's shop – and as you can imagine, that's not much.'

'Good. She needs money if she's going to go out with that crowd every evening. Of course, she may still have some of the money from those things she stole and sold to Tommy...' She thought this over. 'But she's bought a lot of new

188

clothes – there can't be much left by now.'

He was dubious. 'She may promise to behave. But can she really change? If she gets the salary from Brent, she'll be tempted to go out and meet up with her friends instead of minding Prim.'

'She's *got* to change, Philip. I think she could become an alcoholic if she doesn't change her outlook pretty soon.'

He grimaced in shock at this prospect. 'But she's only seventeen, Libby...' He broke off, and she thought that perhaps he was having memories of his little sister in the throes of a hangover. He sighed. 'So what's Brent got to say? That she's to agree to stay at home and really look after Prim?'

Prim, having heard her name mentioned more than once, came toddling over to find out what was going on.

'We're just saying that Daddy will be taking you to play group today,' Philip told her.

'I didn't go yesterday. I went to the zoo instead.'

'But today it's play group,' he replied. 'Shall we go and tell Daddy to get his car out?'

She went obediently, leaving Libby sighing with relief.

It was back to routine – more or less. She rejoined Amy in the dining room.

'Are you often called into conference?' Amy asked.

'Oh, it was just about getting Prim to her nursery group.'

'But why is that anything to do with you?'

Libby felt herself colouring up. 'It's just that ...

189

I know more about raising a kid than anyone else in the house.'

'Humph,' said Amy with a rather cynical smile.

While they were having a lunch break in the kitchen, the doorbell rang. It was a cardboard carton from the retailer in north London who had provided the first Mitzi doll. Libby slit all the sticky tape so that the little girl would be able to unearth the doll quite easily and as she straightened from doing so, she met Amy's sceptical gaze.

'I thought the rule was don't get involved?'

Libby sighed, but made no reply.

Angela appeared as they were clearing up after their snack lunch. She was dressed in a rather haphazard way, in tracksuit trousers and an evening top, and looked really ill, Libby thought. She rather wished Philip hadn't gone out, so that he could see this verification of her fears for the girl.

Angela made no response to the automatic 'good morning' from the others, who quickly left her to her task of making some strong black coffee.

'Good Lord,' Amy said as they made their way upstairs to clean her room. 'Is that the girl who's supposed to be looking after the kid?'

'Yes.'

'Oh, well. Now I can see why you...' She let the words die. 'All the same, Libby, it's not a good idea to get too fond of her.'

'I know, Amy, I know.'

Soon after that, as they were busy repairing the

mess left by Angela in the main bathroom, they heard the door of Grandee's suite opening. Libby stayed where she was, but Amy tiptoed to the bathroom door to peer out after they heard her pass along the hall.

'She's all dressed up in a silk two-piece and matching shoes,' she reported in a whisper. 'Looks like a garden party, maybe.'

A moment later Libby heard the front door open and close. So at least for today, the lady of the house was steering clear of the servants.

When Brenton came in mid-afternoon carrying Prim piggyback, she crowed with delight on seeing the cardboard carton. 'It's Mitzi! Mummy's sent her home!'

True enough, inside was a replica doll, dressed exactly the same except that she had pale blue shoes. Libby had come down from finishing off in Grandee's suite to see how she took this change. 'She must have worn out her old ones,' she explained. 'Travelling is hard on shoes.'

'I like blue shoes. Oh, look, there's a message from Mummy!'

There was a photocopied handwritten note tucked in the box, provided by computer magic. 'Take good care of Mitzi, because she missed you while she was away. Love, Mummy.'

'I missed you too, Mitzi,' Prim exclaimed when this had been read out to her. She hugged the doll close. 'I think she'd like a swing,' she added, heading for the back door to the garden.

When she'd gone, Brenton looked at Libby. 'Where's Angela?'

'In the drawing-room, watching TV.'

191

He drew in a deep breath and went to speak to his sister. Libby was a little surprised. She had thought he might evade the issue. She always felt he was more comfortable in the world of stage effects than in the real one.

Soon it was time for Libby to leave. Amy had already gone.

The telephone in Philip's office began to ring. The door was open, so she heard the machine click on. A moment later she heard a woman's voice on its speaker. 'Hello, this is Jackie here. I just wanted to check whether Prim's doll arrived and ask her if she's happy.'

She knew it would be recorded, but she felt it would be better to answer and ask the caller to wait while she fetched Prim. She went in and picked up the phone.

'This is Libby Fletcher, the Housecare worker...'

'Oh ... Libby? Prim talked so much about you when we had the video link! It's nice to get a chance to speak to you.'

'Prim's in the garden. I'll fetch her if you can just hang on a bit...'

'Yes, thank you, but wait a minute – I'd really like to talk to you. Is that all right?'

The voice was light, the manner crisp and businesslike, and yet there was an undertone of anxiety. She had an idea what Jackie looked like from photographs, one in Prim's room and also one in the bedroom she used to use when she was living with Brenton at Ashgrove. She was a slight blonde girl, hair in a carefully careless style, and with very pretty clothes. Libby pictur-

ed her as she might be now in her Tokyo guise –
a businesswoman, and a highly regarded design
consultant. She was trying to get to know the
woman who figured largely in her little daughter's life although she was so far away.

'I can spare a few minutes, but I must start for
home soon – I have to collect my little boy from
his school.'

'You have a little boy?'

'Yes, he's just turned seven.'

'Oh, that makes sense. *That's* why you've
taken such an interest in Prim.'

'I suppose so.'

'When I was living at Ashgrove, Angela was
still at school. Now she's caring for my little girl,
and somehow I get the impression...' She seemed unable to put her fears into words.

'She's not very good at it, that's what you're
thinking,' Libby prompted. 'Well, it's true. And
Brent is at this moment with Angela in the drawing room telling her she's either got to shape up
or get out – at least, get out of the task of looking
after Prim.'

'And if she doesn't shape up?'

Libby sighed to herself. 'I don't know. It probably means trying to find yet another nanny.'

'And that will make about half a dozen she's
had.'

'Listen, Mrs Moorfield, can I be frank?'

'I wish you would. I feel so much at a loss here
on the other side of the world.'

'The fact is, Prim doesn't like Angela. She's a
little bit afraid of her—'

'Afraid of her? Does she mistreat her?' Jackie

cried.

'No, no, but she's in a permanent grouse about something or other. I get the feeling she just doesn't like children – or maybe it's just a phase she's going through. But whatever causes it, she's absolutely not the right person to be Prim's nanny.' She heard herself saying these judgemental things and added quickly and with some remorse, 'That's just my opinion, I suppose. Or no ... well ... Philip seems to agree with me. Look, I'll put it this way: I'd never let Angela take care of my boy.'

Jackie could be heard taking a long, slow breath. After a moment she said, 'Well, I suppose I knew that, really.'

'Look, I must go, Mrs Moorfield...'

'Of course. Could you get hold of Prim so I can speak to her?'

'Hold on.'

She hurried across the hall. Brenton was leaning against the mantelpiece and Angela was confronting him with a face of fury. 'What right have you got to read me the riot act?' she shouted as Libby came in.

'Excuse me...'

'You're never here half the time. You're off in Paris, or Oslo, or some other place, and even when you *are* here you're shut up in the studio—'

'Excuse me,' Libby said very loudly. 'Prim's mother is on the phone in Philip's office, and would like to speak to her. Could someone please go and get her in from the garden?'

Angela swung round on her. 'Why don't you

194

go and fetch her, Mrs Childcare Expert? You're so—'

'I'm going home. Brenton, you go and get your daughter. Goodbye for today.'

She went out trembling with anger. Another silly row in the Moorfield household. But that was all going to be taken care of, she told herself. She pulled herself together and got into her car to go and pick up Freddie.

Freddie was full of information about his school day. 'We had a lesson about islands. Did you know Britain has lots of islands? You can fly to some of them, but I'd rather go in a ship. We had a video about the Scilly Isles – isn't that a funny name?'

She listened and smiled at his jokes and nodded appreciation at all the geography. She had a momentary impulse to stop the car and hug him, but she knew he'd think that odd. He was so normal, so full of life and enthusiasm. Compared with him, the little girl at Ashgrove was almost a shadow.

Libby knew it didn't matter what Amy said; she couldn't just ignore the child. She had to do what she could for her, and if in speaking to Jackie she'd perhaps said too much, she wasn't going to regret it.

Her staff came wandering in at the end of the day to report on progress and get the next day's schedule. Libby was at her computer making printouts for those who had complicated tasks, and Amy came to sit next to her with her glass of wine.

'The kid was pleased with her doll, eh?'

'Oh, absolutely thrilled. Her mother telephoned just after you left.'

Amy smiled cool approval. 'Good thing. I was beginning to feel you thought *you* were her mother.'

'Come on, Amy!' She studied her old friend. Amy was in her fifties, but was determined to seem to be in her thirties. She was perhaps a bit self-centred, but she had a softer side, as Libby well knew. 'What would you like me to do – ignore the fact that the poor thing was being almost totally neglected?'

'Sweetie, you can do what you like so long as you realize that it might cost you something in the end.'

'Such as what?'

'Well, are you planning on going to Ashgrove every day of your life until you're ninety? No, of course you aren't. One day you won't be working there any more and you won't see the kid – and how will you feel then?'

'But, can't you see – it's the present that's got to be looked after, not the future.' She tried to find words to describe the problem. 'Prim's like a little tortoise, afraid to put her head out of her shell in case somebody snaps it off. If somebody doesn't do something now, she may *never* come out of her shell.'

'What are you two so serious about?' Jake inquired, ambling up with a glass of beer in his hand.

'Oh, Ashgrove,' said Amy with a turning down of her lips. 'My favourite venue.'

'You're joking, me dear. But I like Ashgrove.

It's got a very handsome princess living there in her ivory tower.'

Amy stared at him in disbelief. 'Don't tell me you fancy her? If you mean the senior Mrs Moorfield, she's an old tyrant. And don't think your Captain Fish-finger talk would win her over. She's above your station, me hearty.'

'Cruel, cruel,' Jake mourned. 'But you may be right. Listen, Libby, I thought I'd just ask – what about the financial set-up with that lot? I mean, you're still going, but weren't you thrown out...'

'Never mind about that, Jake. Philip Moorfield is coming this evening to discuss new terms.'

Others drew closer to get information and collect their printed schedules. Freddie pushed forward, complaining that he needed something to eat. The working day thus came to an end, she and her son had supper, and he headed for bed with loud yawns.

Soon after, Libby got a call from Philip Moorfield. 'Would it be all right if I dropped by in about ten minutes?'

'Good heavens – where are you?'

'I'm at a restaurant in the High Street.'

'In that case I can offer you after-dinner mints and coffee.'

He came bearing a bottle of wine from the restaurant. Libby led him up to her kitchen and let him open the bottle while she got out glasses. They sipped in a companionable silence at the kitchen table. He glanced around, inspecting the room. She felt it fell short of the grandeur of Ashgrove, but he was nodding approval.

'Cosy place in winter, I'd imagine.'

'A bit too cosy during the day in this summer weather. I'll put in air-conditioning one day, perhaps.'

'How long have you been here?'

'About four years.' A little silence fell. 'When I left,' she said, 'Jackie was on the phone from Tokyo...'

'Yes, she and Brent had a long session.' Philip gestured with both hands to indicate how long the talk had been. 'Brent was a bit gloomy afterwards. I think she was giving him a hard time about what had happened to Prim.'

'Yes.' She considered this for a moment. 'What's the result about Angela?'

'Oh, Lord ... Well, to give you just some idea, they were quarrelling off and on for hours—'

'For hours?'

'Then she marched off to get herself a drink in the dining room. I'd got home around five, so I was able to shore up Brent's courage at that point and he went after her. She seems to have burst into tears when he literally took her rum-and-Coke from her.'

'Oh, Philip!'

'Yes, well, it wasn't much fun. She was sobbing in the drawing room with her face buried in the sofa cushions. Mama arrived home from the shop and was close to tears herself. It ended with Angela agreeing to give the kid some real attention. So then she collected Prim from where she was playing in the morning-room, made her a snack in the kitchen then put her to bed – all with a good deal of public display to let us see her devotion to duty.'

'You sound unconvinced.'

'I thought it was ... ostentatious. But it may turn out all right.'

'Did Prim seem happy?'

'I don't know. She just seemed to go along with it.'

He seemed so perplexed and troubled that she put out a hand to cover one of his. 'It's a beginning. Give it time.'

He looked at her with an expression she couldn't read. It seemed to contain admiration, gratitude, and something more. He raised her hand to his lips and kissed it softly.

For a moment she was too surprised to move. Then came an impulse – only momentary – to lean towards him to be kissed on the mouth. Common sense intervened, however, and she drew back swiftly.

'Well now, we're here to talk business,' she said. 'I've got a weekly routine worked out for the future; it's down in my office. I'll just get it.'

And with that she escaped into the passage and went swiftly down the stairs.

Twelve

The atmosphere at Ashgrove seemed strained the next day. Rosanne explained, 'Angela has a dental appointment. She staged a bit of a tantrum yesterday, threw herself on a chair in the morning-room, and managed to chip a tooth.'

'Oh dear.'

'Grandee was out late last night so I expect she won't be up and about until lunchtime. Phil and Brent are off somewhere on business. I'll be taking Prim to play group and fetching her back.'

That day passed in peace. But the following day Libby sensed an atmosphere of tension, of suppressed excitement. Yesterday had been about a new regime becoming established; today was somehow full of uneasiness. Not until she was preparing to leave at the end of the day did she learn the cause.

Brenton came over to her as she was putting her gear in her car. 'I didn't want to tell you while you were going to be ... you know, doing your dusting thing with Prim, because I wanted it to be kept from her and I didn't know whether you'd agree to that...'

'I beg your pardon?' She had no idea what he meant.

'Well, you see, Mama thought it might over-excite her and when I thought about it, I agreed.'

'When you thought about what?' Libby asked, now beginning to be alarmed. Who could tell what strange notion might have occurred to this family?

'Jackie's coming on a visit.'

'What? But that's great! When is she arriving?'

'Tonight. When Prim gets up tomorrow morning, her mother will be here.'

Perhaps her telephone conversation with Jackie had prompted her to make the trip, Libby thought, pleased. Then anxiety crept in – was it a good idea not to tell the child about it? But true enough, she'd be so excited at the prospect that she'd never get to sleep tonight if she knew.

All the same, she felt that Prim would be in a state of almost delirious happiness the next day. She decided not to arrive at the house until late, to allow the excitement to die down.

She heard voices from the lawn at the back of the house as she came into the hall in the morning, and she went there to find a family scene. Jackie Moorfield proved to be a more fashionable version of her photograph. Tiny, a true blonde, she was clad in white slacks and a white knitted silk pullover – like a post-modern angel. Jackie was sitting in one of the wicker chairs from the morning-room, and Prim was sitting on her lap and holding one of her hands as if she intended never to let it go. Brenton hovered nearby – to Libby's amusement, he had got rid of the black bristle that had hitherto

201

masked his chin and mouth and was dressed with unexpected neatness.

A new doll was in place on the seat of the swing. Rosanne, red-eyed with recent tears but smiling, was gently moving it to and fro. No other member of the family seemed to be around. Grandee was probably still in her suite. Philip might have gone out on business. Angela might be nursing her dental work.

Libby was introduced, and Jackie was effusive in her greeting. 'There's such a lot I gotta thank you for!' she cried, springing up with Prim in one arm and holding out the other.

Libby let herself be embraced.

'I'm being squashed!' Prim giggled. 'But I don't mind 'cause Libby's my best friend. She lets me do dusting.'

'Yes, I hear my little girl's quite the expert at dusting.' Jackie spoke with a mixture of laughter and sadness. 'And she knows how to turn on the washing machine. That's always gonna be a useful talent.'

Libby was apologetic. 'It was the best I could do, Jackie.'

'Believe me, I know how difficult it musta been.'

There was a pause. No one knew what to say next.

'Well, I must get on,' Libby said finally, and made her escape.

She was busy in the upstairs rooms when she heard them all go out for lunch. Grandee hadn't yet come out of her suite. Libby listened at her door for a moment, but heard no sign of activity.

It was afternoon now, late even for Grandee. She tapped on her door intending to ask if she was all right.

'Mrs Moorfield?'

'Go away.'

'Can I get you anything?'

'Go *away!*'

Libby retreated. She knew that Grandee disapproved of Jackie. Had she stayed in her room so as to avoid being part of the welcoming committee?

It occurred to Libby that Rosanne, as a young bride and then a young widow in this household, must have found it difficult in her time to live with Grandee. Perhaps that was why she'd been away so often at retreats and ashrams. Perhaps that was also why the children had been sent off to boarding school – simply to get them out of Grandee's glacial domain.

She shook her head, mulling this over. It was to be hoped that no one would suggest sending Prim to boarding school. A child so shy and timid would never survive it. She busied herself in the housework, glad to be occupied and alone.

Philip came home late afternoon. She was finishing up in the hall as he opened the front door. 'Hello,' he said, heading past her for the drawing-room. 'Where's everybody?'

'Prim and her parents and grandma went out about lunch time, Grandee about an hour later. Don't know about Angela, she seems to have been out all day.'

'Jackie was dying to meet you. I expect you had a long talk...'

'No, I came rather late today, and they were all out in the garden when I arrived so I had to just say hello and then get on.'

His face changed at her words. A look of concern came across it. She sensed at once there was something unwelcome about to be said.

'She didn't tell you their plans?'

'No ... well, I didn't give her time to.'

He hesitated. 'She and Brent were up nearly all night discussing things. Jackie arrived with a suggestion already mapped out, something she thought would solve their problems.'

'Yes?'

'She's found a job for Brent in Tokyo.'

'Really? Oh, well, that's—'

'It's to do with a Japanese boy band, called Pati-Pati.'

'What does that mean?' she asked, smiling.

'You'll be amazed to hear it means "Party-Party". It seems the group is absolutely all the rage in Japan. And they want to extend their audience by going into *manga* – and now you're going to ask what that means, and as far as I understand it, it's a type of Japanese comic for grown-ups.'

'I understand. Comics for grown-ups. Those sort of highly coloured things full of big explosions signified by balloons saying "Ke-po-ow!" Freddie rather hankers after those.' She paused. 'But how does music from the band translate into a comic?'

'They're going to use the comic as a sort of graphic diary, I believe. A team of artists will go with them to their gigs and sketch what happens

204

both on-stage and in the audience. They expect the sales of the manga to be enormous, a weekly publication. And Jackie has persuaded them to hire Brent to do their stage effects. So that there will be something worth putting into the comic, you see.'

'Yes, I see. That sounds like a good idea, actually. So Brent likes it?'

'Enormously. He was working out how to get all his electronic gear shipped to Tokyo but Jackie's persuaded him not to bother. She says he can buy anything he needs in Tokyo, probably cheaper than the cost of flying it out.'

'That makes sense. She's thought it all out.'

'Yes, she has.'

He fell silent. Libby, taking in his news, had been kept busy with the unexpectedness of it all. Now her mind had accepted the scheme, and had gone on ahead. 'And Prim is going with them?' she asked.

'Yes.'

'Yes, of course.'

She felt strange. She dared not take a breath because she was sure it would cause her pain. Silent and unsteady, she stood looking down at the tiles of the hall floor.

She felt a hand on her shoulder. A voice came to her as if from far away. 'Are you all right?'

Victorian tiles. Very fine of their kind, arranged in a pattern of black, white and red. She'd admired them from the very first time she saw them. That had been some months ago. Not a long time, but it had seemed a large section of her life. And that was strange, because of course this was just another house, just another family needing help with the daily chores.

Philip Moorfield was speaking to her. She looked up.

'Let's go into the drawing-room and sit down.'

'What?'

'You've gone quite pale.'

'No. Have I? Well, that's nothing. I have to go in a minute. I have to get Freddie from school.'

'Just sit down on the bench, then. You need to relax for a minute.' He drew her to it. She sat down obediently.

'I'll get you a drink.'

'No!'

'But you need something...'

'I have to drive to the school...'

'I'll drive you. Sit there, be quiet, I'll get you a brandy...'

'No, no.' She struggled to her feet. For some reason she was close to tears. All at once she found Philip was holding her close and she was leaning against him. For a moment she felt the comfort of that embrace. Then she pulled herself away, blinked once or twice, and turned to gather up her holdall.

'I have to go.'

'Libby...'

'I'm sorry, I was a bit shaken for a minute but that was just silliness. I don't want to be late for Freddie.'

'But are you sure you're—?'

'I'm all right.' She made for the front door, then paused. 'When are they leaving for Tokyo?'

'Tomorrow night.' He understood the hidden

question. 'They're not going to tell Prim. Their flight leaves in the evening. The plan is to let Prim get to sleep and take her to the airport, then when she wakes it will be a lovely surprise – she'll be in Tokyo with Mummy and Daddy.'

She shook her head vehemently. 'That's not a good idea.'

'I thought perhaps it wasn't.'

'Suppose she wakes on the plane? She'd be terrified.'

'But that's what they think is best...'

'Explain it to them. She should be told tomorrow morning, so she has the whole day to get used to the idea. It's going to be a lovely adventure; she's going to Tokyo to meet Mitzi's family – something like that.'

'It would be better coming from you, Libby. Jackie thinks a lot of you.'

'Oh, I shan't be coming tomorrow.' Was it cowardly? No, this was a time when it was a really good idea not to be involved.

'Not coming?'

'No. I think that's best. After all, they are her parents ... I mustn't interfere ... And it would be terrible if there was a big row in the house just when they should be trying to make everything seem like going on a picnic...'

'I understand. So I'm to say that you recommend making it seem like an outing to the zoo or something?'

'Yes. And Jackie should be close to her all day, and Prim should help with the packing, and that kind of thing. It should all be sort of ordinary, like doing the dusting.'

'Right, I'll tell them.'

'I have to go,' she said, opening the front door.

'You won't be here tomorrow?'

'No.'

'Next day?'

'I expect so.'

And then she was in the drive, opening her car door, glancing at the clock and thinking she shouldn't let her mind wander to what she'd just heard as she drove to the school.

Freddie was so immersed in telling her about his school day that he didn't notice how absent she was. The end-of-day gathering and their evening meal went on as usual. Once she was by herself and not obliged to be sociable, she sat down in her living room with a glass of wine and the television. But the crises and dramas of the news bulletin passed her by. Her mind was elsewhere. She thought with regret about Amy's warning. She knew she should have paid it more heed.

Ironically the situation was somewhat reversed – it was Prim who was leaving, not Libby. And it was *good* that she was going. She would be with her mother and father. No one to scowl at her, to begrudge her time and attention. Instead a loving and concerned mother – perhaps over-eager to make up for her failings of the past, but Jackie had sense. She would understand that Prim would need plenty of reassurance in this new life in a new country, but that she had to be given room to grow.

These thoughts were her comfort all next day. They kept her steady, yet she was startled when her phone rang in the late evening. It was Philip Moorfield.

'I'm in your neighbourhood,' he said. 'May I drop in?'

'Oh ... no ... well...'

'I just want to make sure you're all right. You were so shaken this afternoon.'

'I'm quite all right.'

'And I thought you'd want to see the drawing Prim made for you.'

'She made me a...' Her voice failed her. She drew in a quick breath then said, 'I'd like to see that, of course. Where are you?'

'Parked in your backyard.'

'In that case ... Just a minute, I'll come down.'

She hurried down to the back door. He was waiting there with a big envelope in his hand. She took it, but knew the light would be too poor to see it well on the doorstep. With a gesture of invitation she turned and went back upstairs. Her living room was lit only by the fading evening sky. It was quite late, she supposed; she'd lost track of time.

Switching on the lamp by the sofa, she sat down and slid the drawing out of the envelope. A disorganized sort of little aeroplane was in the background. Near it stood a much larger stick figure clad in shorts and a T-shirt, waving a piece of brightly coloured cloth. Prim's duster.

She let the drawing fall to her lap. She put both hands up to her face. Tears trickled between her fingers. Her throat struggled to subdue a rising sob.

She felt Philip's arms come round her. She was

gently pulled towards him. She hid her face against his chest.

'Don't cry, sweetheart, don't cry. She'll always remember you...'

'No, no, she'll forget, and it's best that she should.'

'But you'll always be there, that special sense of someone who cared, her guardian angel. You were the most important thing in her life when she needed it most, Libby.'

She looked up to see how sincerely he meant it.

He bent his head, to kiss her on the lips.

Thirteen

Much later, she woke to find herself in his arms and in her bed. Outside, light from a street lamp sent out its faint ray. She turned her head. His face was touched here and there by the light, and she thought how strange it was – that she could imagine the features hidden in the darkness, could remember the smile that changed his grave expression. She relaxed against him, stifling a sigh of pleasure. But then she stiffened a little. She could hear sounds.

The television in her living room. They had left it without a thought as they made their way to her bedroom and the beginnings of their love.

She slipped out of bed. Her dressing-gown was

on a hook on the door. She drew it around her, opened the door only a little so that the sound of the television programme shouldn't disturb him.

Outside, she tiptoed first to her son's room. She peeped in at him. He was sleeping that deep, abandoned sleep of the child – his arms thrown out, the sheet kicked aside, off in dreamland sailing a phantom ship across a mythical sea.

In the living room the television was informing the public that things weren't going well with negotiations for peace in the Middle East. She found the remote, switched it off, then sank down on the sofa.

What was she doing? Had she embarked on an affair? And if so, why?

The reason presented itself at once. She had always felt an attraction towards Philip. He had seemed the nicest of the Moorfield family, the one who showed some concern for his little niece, who had championed Libby when she tried to help the child.

But nothing would have followed from that had he not come here this evening. She tried to think back, to remember what had happened. But it was hazy in her mind. All she knew was that he had put his arms around her, and that she had found it the most wonderful thing in the world.

She went back along the passage, silent on bare feet, and gently opened the bedroom door. She saw Philip rouse at her entrance. He sat up. 'What time is it?'

'A little after three.'

'I missed you,' he murmured as he took her

hand to pull her down beside him.

'I woke up and heard the television still chattering on.'

His arm was round her back. He drew her down to him so that she was lying across his body. The thin cotton of her dressing gown was eased aside. He began to kiss the nape of her neck and the beginning of her spine. Her face lay against his shoulder. She rubbed her cheek against it, and knew that they were on the threshold of renewed passion.

A chill seized her. She tried to straighten up. He held her fast, so that she had to say, 'No, no – let me go, Philip.'

But he held her close against him. She closed her eyes in a moment of surrender then put her hands either side of his head to push herself upright.

'We can't do this, Philip.'

'You know that's not true.' There was amusement in his voice.

'No, no, I mean it's not right. My little boy is asleep in the next room.'

'That didn't matter before.' Now he had let go of her so that she could move further away. He was trying to make out her expression in the dimness.

'That was because everything went out of my head...'

'Just let that happen now...'

'No, I'm serious, Philip. Freddie might wake up and come walking into my room any minute.'

'Let's lock the door then.' He was making light of it but the amusement now was less authentic.

'Philip! Talk sense. I can't, I just can't. He's never known a man to be in our home except as a casual visitor. He'd be so ... I don't know ... baffled, upset...'

If there had been a moment when they might have been swept away by longing, that had gone. When he spoke again, he was entirely serious.

'So this is the wrong place and, so it seems, the wrong time. But elsewhere, and on another day – or is this to be a one-off?'

'No, no! Oh, of course not – that's if you want us to – but this is such a ... a bolt from the blue that I don't know how to deal with it. I never thought that I ... well, I'd made a decision that I'd do without entanglements.'

'Oh, come here, you feather-head. Surely you know this isn't just an "entanglement".' He gathered her closer and kissed her. And, despite her misgivings, they made love with a passion equal to their first time.

By and by she regained her senses. She murmured, 'Really, Philip, you have to go. Look, it's getting light. And Freddie wakes early.'

'You mean you're turning me out without giving me breakfast?'

She sighed and shook her head at him.

'All right then, but I expect to see you at Ashgrove by and by.'

'Look, Lothario, when I'm at your house I'm there to do the housework...'

'We'll see.' She was still smiling over that when she waved goodbye to him at her door.

She got up late, and had to call on Jake to drive Freddie to school. She found herself unwilling to start her day, so when at last she arrived at Ashgrove it was past noon.

She found Rosanne in the kitchen, fussing around in the effort to make a midday snack from a store of rather tired vegetables. 'Oh, Libby, I'm so glad to see you! I'm afraid the dining room is in a terrible mess because we had a big farewell dinner last night.'

'No problem.'

'Grandee may be a bit difficult today. She seemed upset yesterday about Brent leaving, and went off to bed very early.'

Upset about Brent leaving? That was rather a surprise. She ventured, 'And Philip?'

'Oh...' Rosanne was flustered, averting her face and speaking with reluctance. 'He's gone to fetch Angela home.'

'Fetch her?'

'She went off in her car last night and ... you know how she is, so unpredictable. It seems she drove off more or less at random. Well, I don't quite understand the outcome, but it seems she's banged her car into a tree or something and doesn't know where she is.'

'Good gracious!'

'So she rang Phil from her mobile, and he's gone to get her.'

'The car is damaged? Why didn't she ring for roadside assistance?'

'Well, you see ... I don't think she'd have pass-ed a breath test if the accident had to be reported to the police.'

'Rosanne...'

'What?'

'Don't you think you ought to get help for Angela?'

Rosanne sighed, turning her head away. 'I've tried, dear. You know how difficult she can be.'

'But this accident – she could have hurt someone.'

'I know. And you know how that would have damaged her karma.' Putting the last of her salad ingredients on her plate, she made for the door. 'I think I'll eat this in the garden. It's such a nice day.' She wandered out. Libby made as if to stop her then drew back. What was the use?

She cleared the dining room table, loaded the dishwasher, tidied the drawing-room, then went upstairs. Angela's bed hadn't been slept in, of course. She looked in at Prim's room. Clothes and toys had been left everywhere after the rush of packing. She backed out and closed the door. She'd do that tomorrow. Today was too soon.

She whisked a duster around the other rooms, cleaned the bathroom, then listened at the door of Grandee's suite.

There were sounds of movement. Perhaps she was getting ready to go out. Libby was getting a bit bothered about Grandee's rooms. There seemed to be very scant opportunity to clean them properly because Grandee was so often locked up in there.

Well, no matter for the moment. Time was getting on, and though she'd done too little in the house, she'd have to leave soon to get Freddie. Without seeing Philip.

He rang her at home that evening. 'Desperately sorry not to be there when you came, angel.

Did Mama tell you what happened?'

'Yes, Angela had an accident.'

She heard him utter a muted groan. 'She'd no idea where she was...'

'No sat-nav?'

'Good heavens no, you've seen her car. It's held together with safety pins. It took me ages to find her, and then she was fast asleep – fast *asleep*! In a ditch. I had some rope and stuff in the boot so I managed to drag her car out and then I telephoned a garage and had it towed away.'

'And how is Angela?'

'A couple of bumps and bruises, and the devil of a hangover. Mama's fussing around her but all that does is make her truculent.'

'Shouldn't she see a doctor?'

'She refuses. I don't know what's to be done with her, honestly. But why should I unload all this on to you? I really rang to explain why I wasn't home today, and to say ... alas, I have to go to Berlin tomorrow.'

'Berlin?'

'Yes, location needs canals and such like – Berlin has some good sites.'

'How long will you be away?'

'Couple of days. Libby, you couldn't come and join me there?'

'Now be reasonable, love. You know I can't.'

'I suppose not. It's a shame; Berlin's an interesting place.'

'Some other time, Philip.'

'Yes.' There was a pause. 'I ought to go and pack.'

'Yes, that would be sensible.' But she had something to ask. 'Listen, before you go – is everything OK with Grandee?'

'Ah, did she give you a hard time or something?'

'No, quite the contrary. I never see her at all. She still hadn't come out of her room when I left around three.'

There was a short grunt of vexation. 'She's been having one of her tantrums this evening. You remember those things that went missing?'

'Only too well.'

'She was on about them again...'

'But you put them back, Philip.'

'She's got it into her head that it was *you* who put them back.'

'Oh, good Lord!'

'I tried to explain what really happened but she didn't seem to be listening. It seems she stayed in her room today because she knew you were in the house and didn't want to let you in, in case you stole something else.'

'Philip!'

'I know – but she's eccentric. Luckily her course of action now seems to be to stay away from you whenever you're around.' He waited for her to respond but she didn't know what to say. 'Libby, she's just a bit of a screwball, to some extent out of touch with things.'

'I know.'

'We'll talk about it when I get back.' He sighed. 'I don't really want to go, but a lot depends on getting permission to film in Berlin.'

'I understand. It's all right.'

She was sad at not being able to see him, yet a part of her was relieved. Philip seemed to see no problems in their relationship. But she had a seven-year-old son who had never even met him so far. What would Freddie make of him?

Rosanne was preparing to leave when she got to Ashgrove next day. 'How's Angela?' she inquired.

'Up and about. She's sorting out some clothes to take to a charity shop.'

Libby was surprised. It had never occurred to her that Angela would be charitable. 'And Grandee? Philip told me on the phone last night that she wasn't too good.'

The younger Mrs Moorfield sighed. 'Something's troubling her. She's always been rather touchy. But recently she seems to withdraw into herself a lot.'

'I find it difficult to get access to her suite...'

'Oh yes, I know what you mean.' Rosanne stood, pensive, trying to find a reason for her mother-in-law's attitude. 'What I think is this, Libby: although Grandee would deny it, her realm of inner calm was terribly disturbed by Prim's going missing.'

Could be, thought Libby. Grandee was probably to blame for that unlocked gate, but she'd never admit it to herself or anyone else. That might well disturb her inner calm.

'And now Prim's really gone away,' Rosanne went on. 'And I think she may feel guilty about that.'

'But why should she feel responsible? Prim's mother came and quite rightly took her into her care.'

'Well, it's difficult to explain, but you see, Grandee never liked Jackie. And Jackie came here and took Prim away – and Brent too. It was as if Jackie was punishing Grandee for her past rebuffs.' She made a prayerful gesture with both hands. 'It takes humility to admit you're in the wrong, and Grandee has never been humble.'

'I suppose.'

Rosanne smiled at having apparently accounted for Grandee's withdrawal. She nodded goodbye. When she'd gone, Libby got straight to work. There wasn't much to do in the downstairs rooms because the house had been more or less empty the day before. She went upstairs, firm in her intention to make a beginning on tidying Prim's room. It was quite a shock to find Angela in there, shoving Prim's clothes into old carrier bags.

'What on earth are you doing?'

'Sorting out stuff to go to Sizing Down.'

'What!' Sizing Down was a shop well-known to Libby. She'd bought many things for Freddie there. It acquired outgrown children's clothes and equipment of good quality, to resell at very reasonable prices.

When she'd got her breath back, Libby asked, 'Who gave you permission to do that?'

Angela made a face. 'Who should I ask?'

That was a good question. Libby paused.

'I bet you think I shouldn't touch any of the little angel's belongings,' Angela sneered. 'And her room too – you're going to make it a shrine, are you?'

219

There was so much venom in the words that Libby almost backed away.

The girl looked unwell, with a bruise turning yellow on her cheekbone. The hands holding the T-shirts were clenched like fists. Always unsociable, today she seemed as angry as a wounded bear.

Libby said, 'I was going to clean and tidy in here, and then ask your mother what she wanted done with Prim's things.'

'Oh, do ask! Mama's likely to burst into tears if you talk about Prim or Brent. And I've got a plan for this stuff, so get lost.'

'But you can't just sell it!'

'Why not? It may have slipped past you, but Brent won't be paying me anything now that I'm not acting nanny. And my allowance from Mama wouldn't go far at the shopping mall. I need the money.'

'Oh, for heaven's sake, Angela!'

'What? You don't like plain speaking?'

'Is that what you call it? Plain speaking?' Libby countered, too indignant to stop to think. 'All I ever hear in your voice is resentment.'

'You do? And that surprises you, does it?'

'What have you got to be so resentful about? You live rent-free in a lovely house, you get food and drink any time you want it, you don't have to lift a finger to clean your room, you have a car and can drive where you like, you don't go to classes or do any work – what's making you so bitter?'

Colour rose in Angela's face, suffusing her pale cheeks and turning the bruise darker. Anger

220

seemed to shake her physically. She threw down the clothes she was holding and with her open hands made a sweeping movement that took in the room.

'Look what she had! Everything – clothes, toys, books, pretty little furniture! D'you know what I had when I was her age? I wore dresses made out of awful cloth from Batavia or Rangoon or somewhere; I slept on a futon. And soon after that I was at boarding school. And if I was unhappy, did my Mama came sweeping down out of the sky to make it all better?'

The emotion she'd unleashed was almost frightening. Libby said with uncertainty, 'But it was the same for your brothers, wasn't it? They told me they'd had a hard time. But they've got themselves together—'

'What's their name?' Angela interrupted.

'What?'

'What's their name?'

'Er ... Brenton and Philip Moorfield.'

'What's my name?'

'Angela Moorfield.'

'And what's the difference?'

'What's the...? I've no idea.'

'Then I'll tell you. Philip and Brenton have their father's name. I've got my mother's name. And why? Because nobody knows my father's name, that's why.'

This was a revelation to Libby. Was this the root of all the rancour, the malice that seemed to hang over the girl like a dark cloud?

'But, Angela! Nobody bothers about that kind of thing these days.'

'Nobody calls you a bastard?' Angela's mouth was turned down in grim sarcasm. 'So if nobody says it out loud, that makes it all right? If you never get a birthday card from Daddy, it doesn't matter? You should try it, chum. In my life, he's just an empty space. Somebody who spent a night with my mother years ago, now long forgotten.'

'Now wait – you don't know your mother's forgotten him...'

'I've challenged her about it. She gets flustered and tearful and shuts up like a clam.'

Libby felt an impulse of pity. She could guess how difficult it was to have a vague, fuzzy-minded mother like Rosanne.

'Well ... well, perhaps it shouldn't be a challenge,' she ventured. 'Perhaps if you sat down with her and just chatted patiently with her...'

'I'm not the patient type. You must have noticed.'

'But if it's important to you ... It is important, isn't it, Angela? Would you really like to find out something about your father?'

'Oh, shut up!' she cried, making for the door, about to thrust Libby aside bodily.

Libby stood her ground. She was a sturdy woman, and years of physical work had given her muscles. She caught the girl with one arm as she collided with her, held her off for a moment, then turned her so that she had both arms around her.

'Don't run away, love,' she murmured. 'Things have changed in the family – perhaps now's the time...'

To her surprise, Angela buried her face in her shoulder and began to cry.

They stood like that for some minutes, an unlikely twosome, two people who had been less than friendly towards each other until now. Libby patted her on the back, making the kind of soothing noises she made to Freddie when he was hurt.

'You c-can't imagine what it was l-like,' Angela sobbed. 'At school ... other k-kids had p-parents at sports day. Even those whose mums and dads weren't married – they turned up, they cheered for their kid ... Mama would come sometimes, but her heart was never in it. She d-doesn't understand about winning a race...' A sob of misery. 'Or getting an A for arithmetic ... She thinks only spiritual values matter. And I've never been spiritual!'

Libby held the girl quietly, and when she spoke her voice was barely above a whisper. 'Never mind,' she said. 'Never mind, it's not too late to change things. It can be all right, Angela; it can change if you try.'

'No, nothing will change. And you see, Prim's mother came for her. And Brent was *here*, even if he didn't do very much. And you – *you* never let your kid down; you're there for him. You wouldn't ever send him away to boarding school. You know Mama doesn't care about *me* the way you care about Freddie.'

There was no denying the truth of that. Rosanne Moorfield was quite a different kind of personality altogether.

All the same, Libby felt that she must be

willing to try for an understanding with her difficult daughter if she could be made to realize how unhappy she was.

'Why don't you just try?' she coaxed. 'When she comes home, ask her to sit down with you. Tell her some of what you told me – but say it softly, Angela. Let her know you missed her when she wasn't there, that you miss her now when you're feeling so lost and unhappy.'

'I'm not lost!' Angela straightened up. There was indignation in her expression. She blinked away tears and sniffed to clear her throat. She caught a glimpse of herself in the little mirror on Prim's dressing table.

'My God, I look a wreck!'

'Yes you do. Go and wash your face and put on new make-up.'

'And that will sort everything out, will it?'

'No, but if you go to the shop and ask to talk to your mother, that might make a difference.'

'Go to the shop? Somebody might walk in while—'

'Hang up the closed sign.'

Angela summoned a choked little laugh. 'You're asking a lot.'

'Oh, well, don't do it then. But it seems a shame to have cried all over my working shirt for nothing.'

'Huh.'

But she went out, and a moment later Libby heard her in the bathroom running the tap and splashing her face with water. Next she was in her room, presumably re-doing her make-up.

Soon a taxi came to the house, and Angela

came out of her room. She paused at the door of Prim's room to speak to Libby. She was holding herself stiffly, full of resistance.

'I suppose your advice was right. But I just can't. I've tried before, and, well ... I suppose I'm just chicken. So I'm off to see my pals.'

With that she was gone. Libby shook her head but dismissed the matter. It was too late not to get involved with the Moorfields, she told herself, but at least she could stop adding further involvements to her list.

That was a short-lived resolution. Next morning, when she was clearing up in the kitchen, Angela came in. Although she'd spoken as if she were going clubbing yesterday, this morning she was quite clear-eyed and alert for a change.

'Libby...'

'Yes?'

'Look, I ... You must think I'm a real scaredy-cat, backing out the way I did yesterday. To tell the truth, I thought about what you said all the time I was out last night...'

'You did?'

'I don't know why I should be bothered about what you think of me.' She gave a rueful smile. 'I never liked you – you must know that. I bet you soon worked out that I was the one who took those things that went missing.'

'I'm afraid I did.'

'It was to get you in trouble, so that you'd have to leave. Didn't work, though, did it?'

'Well, it worked temporarily.'

'So now what I'm going to ask is ... Well, you'll think I've got a nerve, to even think you'd

225

help. But the thing is, Mama's here this morning.'

'Oh?'

'She's in the drawing-room, reading up on some floral product that she's thinking of buying for the shop. And I thought ... I thought perhaps you...'

'You're not asking me to talk to your mother about your missing father?' Libby said in amazement.

'No! Of course not! Good heavens, you must think I'm a total ninny. No, it's just ... I wondered if you'd come and sort of try to reassure Mama while I get started.'

'Oh, Angela, I really don't think—'

'Just for the first minute or two. To sort of soften the shock when I ask the first question. Because she always starts to cry and I can't ... It puts me right off; I don't know how to deal with it.'

'You just need to be firm...'

'That's easy to say! She'll start talking about her cosmic aura or something and I know I'll lose my temper.'

'Well...'

'Just for a minute or two. To back me up.'

'All right then.'

They went to the drawing-room. Rosanne was on the sofa reading, with advertising brochures spread out on the cushions and a thick textbook on her lap.

She greeted them with a smile. 'Now you've arrived at the crucial moment. Do you think that *Epilobium* is a good name for a floral body

226

lotion?'

'Mama,' said Angela.

'Yes, dear?'

'Can we have a serious talk?'

Libby saw Rosanne stiffen. She let the book slide to the floor. 'What, dear?' she asked cautiously.

Angela wavered, coming to a standstill a yard or two away. Libby felt this was certainly not the moment to falter. She sat down beside Rosanne on the sofa and took one of her hands. 'Angela wants to ask you something serious, Rosanne.'

'But ... but ... I'm busy.'

'Not too busy to listen to her when she's in misery, surely?'

'Misery?' There were tears already threatening at that word.

'Mama, I want to know my father's name,' Angela said suddenly.

'Oh, Angela ... The fact is ... the fact is...'

'What? Mama, what?'

'The fact is, I don't *know*!' And the tears began to fall.

Fourteen

The next twenty minutes were full of mild confusion. Angela backed away, hugging herself protectively. Rosanne continued to cry amid attempts to apologize and explain. Libby sat patting her hand while she nodded at Angela to come and hug her mother – without success.

In the end, Rosanne was calm enough to sip a weak brandy and soda, fetched by her daughter. Angela had taken a seat on the edge of an armchair opposite. Libby was to some extent trapped, for by this time Rosanne, instead of having her hand held, was gripping hers very tightly.

'So...' Angela began rather coldly. 'Can we talk about this now, Mama? Are you OK?'

'Well, I feel more able to ... You must realize, dear, this is very difficult for me...' She bent her head, and stared into the brandy glass. 'I'm so ashamed.'

Nobody said anything. A silence fell and seemed likely to go on forever. Then Libby said, 'Would you like me to leave, Rosanne?'

'No, no, Libby, please ... I feel that you might help me to explain – I think you might understand...'

'I'll try to understand too, Mama. I didn't ask

you about it so as to be beastly to you. I just want to *know*.'

'Of course. I should have had enough courage to ... But you see, I was so stupid. And I don't have the excuse of being a young girl caught up in the first glow of love. I ... you know, I was in my thirties, I'd had two children, and though I was lonely after Mervin died, that's no excuse, dear.'

There was a pause.

'Mervin,' Libby prompted. 'That was Philip and Brenton's father?'

'Yes, he died when they were little, in a climbing accident in the mountains of Kalimantan.'

Her listeners looked blank.

'It's part of Indonesia. He was cataloguing plants for a scientific survey and he fell.' She sighed. 'You know, the climate is so...' She released her grip on Libby to wave a hand in front of her face to indicate heat. 'They had to bury him there and Grandee took it terribly to heart.' She was looking far back into her past. 'More than I'd have thought, really. But an only son, you know ... It was a bad time. I felt I couldn't move out and leave her and so I stayed on here although Grandee had never really wanted us in the house. But Mervin had asked her to let us stay here, to be safe and happy while he was away.' She shook her head at the memory.

Angela moved impatiently, but Libby frowned her into silence.

At length Rosanne said, 'I did the best I could, although the atmosphere was often icy here. I ...

well ... It seemed best to send the children to boarding school. I found comfort in what had always been an interest, one I shared with Mervin – the search for a holistic way of living.'

'Indian head massage and astrology,' Angela snorted.

'I know you don't share my beliefs, dear,' Rosanne said placatingly. 'But they've been my support and my solace all these years. And so I went to a congress on the island of Rhodes that year, to study the tarot. I've come to think that was the wrong path for me, but at the time it was quite enthralling.' She made a wide gesture to suggest a far-reaching search. 'We were in a wing of a big modern hotel above a beach – it was beautiful. The sea is so all-embracing, isn't it, so great and raw and rich! And at the congress there was this young man.'

She paused. Angela drew in an audible breath.

'I just ... He was so handsome, so full of enthusiasm and zest for life. I found him fascinating. Of course he scarcely noticed me. There were several young girls there, and he spent his time with them, and who can blame him? But when the end of the congress came, we had a big farewell gathering with ceremonies of blessing and a feast of love—'

'A feast of love,' Angela echoed, looking down at the carpet.

'Yes, and when the dawn light was making the sea all rosy and warm, we ran into the waves, and we embraced each other in farewell, and then we went to our rooms to rest before we set out for our homes, and I ... I linked my arm with him ... And he was full of happiness and generosity and we spent those last few hours together.' She faced her daughter with a mixture of embarrassment and pride. 'And that was how you were conceived, my dear, in kindness and fellowship.'

Libby was wondering if she could possibly disengage herself and slip away. This was a story that no one else but mother and daughter should have shared. They needed to be alone to come to terms with it.

But Rosanne turned to her for agreement. 'You understand, I'm sure, Libby. You've had to live your life without your husband. You understand loneliness.'

'Yes, I do.'

Angela put out a beseeching hand towards her mother. 'But who *was* he, Mama? What was his name?'

'Well, you see, dear ... We were in Greece. We all took the names of characters from Greek legend. I was Lydia, he was Apollo.'

'What?'

'It added to the heightened state we wanted to attain. We were all from Olympus.'

'You never knew his real name?'

'Well, he was called Apollo because he was so handsome and also because his first name began with an A. I think ... I have a feeling his real name was Antoine.'

'He was French?'

'Oh yes. Didn't I mention that? Oh yes, we were a multicultural gathering and he ... he was so typically French, so full of their joie de vivre.'

'But his last name?'

'No, that I never knew. We never needed them. We gave each other these names from a list of Greek heroes and goddesses and so on, and we always used them.'

Libby cleared her throat. 'Did you try to get in touch with him afterwards?' she inquired.

'No, dear, I decided not to do that because, you see ... Well, I didn't know I was pregnant until some time later ... And I didn't know anything about him or how to contact him. And so, you know ... I turned to my spiritual advisers and was helped and guided.'

'Guided not to try to contact him?' Angela asked with angry incredulity.

'It was a time of learning, of coming to terms with my karma. I came to understand that I'd been given this great gift at a moment when we were all as one, after a gathering of the soul and the spirit.' She broke off, to look pleadingly at her daughter. 'It would have been greedy to ask for more. And although I see now that I failed you...' She faltered before going on. 'I wanted to bring you up in that same freedom of love and comradeship, my dear.'

'Oh, Mama,' Angela sighed, but there was no longer much anger in her voice.

Rosanne was sitting with her gaze on the trees beyond the window. Their branches were gently moving in the summer breeze. 'I wonder if I've lived a worthy life,' she said, tears beginning to well up again. 'How will it be recorded in the Great Book?' She got up and hurried out of the room, passing her daughter with her face averted.

Libby and Angela were left together in a moment of extreme awkwardness. Libby's impulse was to hurry out too, but Angela was frowning and rubbing her cheek, perplexed.

'Well, what about that!' she scoffed. 'Is *she* naive, or what?'

'Oh, well ... I think there was an era when her beliefs were really in vogue, Angela. The flower children, that kind of thing. And their influence still lingers on.'

'What, going on holiday and calling yourself after Greek gods and goddesses?'

'You'd prefer to go as – what? One of the Spice Girls? J-Lo?'

'As if! That's all a load of popcorn. And anyhow, I would know who everybody else was! I mean, if you've got all your marbles, you can't help finding out things about people.' She lifted her eyes heavenwards in despair. 'No wonder she never wanted to talk about it; she comes across as an utter dimwit.'

'Angela!'

'Oh, I should show more respect? How can you respect somebody who doesn't even bother to find out whose baby she's having!'

'I know it's hard for you. But you don't have to be as weak-willed about it as your mother, now do you?'

'What on earth do you mean by that?'

'Well, we've got the Internet now, haven't we? People find people all the time – they meet up with old school friends, families are reunited...'

'What, you think I should go on the net?'

'Why not?'

Angela looked flustered. 'But I don't *know* anything!'

'You know the conference was about the tarot and it was in a hotel on the island of Rhodes.'

'Oh, great.'

'It happened ... How old are you?'

'I'll be eighteen in November.'

'Right, it happened about nineteen years ago.'

'So what? I go online and ask, "Were you in Rhodes nineteen years ago"?'

'The conference must have been organized by some firm or other, Angela. Use your head! Find out who ran the thing—'

'And then what?'

'Find out the names of the people who attended and, if there's a Frenchman, try to contact him on one of the get-together services.'

'Good lord...' There was no enthusiasm for this project. 'It sounds like an awful slog.'

'And it's not worth it? You don't really want to find out who your father was?'

'Oh!' Angela went red. 'I didn't mean that...'

'It might be a bit of a slog, but just try. You might find you quite like having something difficult to do.'

'Oh, come off it! I don't need a lecture—'

'It's not a lecture, I mean it! You might enjoy doing something you can put your heart into. Up to now, you seem to be ... frittering your time away.'

'Thanks a lot.'

'Come on, kid! What have you been doing except meeting your pals and going shopping?'

234

She was watching the girl carefully, ready to draw back if she was being too harsh. She tried a coaxing tone next. 'A bit of research seems a good idea to me – unless you're scared?'

'Scared? Why should I be scared?' Now indignation was beginning to rise.

'Perhaps you think he's no good. Or a stupid old stick-in-the-mud. Or perhaps you're afraid that he won't want to know about you.'

'We-ell...' She frowned as she considered these alternatives. Then she said, with some justification, 'You know, he might be a very respectable type with a wife and family – that's quite possible, isn't it? How do we know he wants to be reminded of his carefree past?'

'Ah...' That was a point well worth considering. 'In that case, perhaps you'd only want to go as far as finding out his name? Would that do? You don't actually need to contact him.'

'I suppose. But what would be the point if I didn't get in touch?' She shook her head with sudden vehemence. 'No, I don't want to do it.'

And with that she marched out, all sulky defiance, banging the door. Libby surveyed the closed door. So much for that.

Antoine Somebody. A young and handsome Frenchman. It was rather a pleasing result. Better than finding out he was a fat old London stockbroker. She smiled to herself, not entirely dissatisfied, and feeling a great sense of relief. At least the conversation had taken place, the breakthrough had been accomplished.

She went back to her to tasks in the kitchen. When she got home that afternoon, she discovered that all this talk about fathers had made her realize she hadn't spoken to her own for over a month. It was always difficult to contact him in the Bahamas. His mobile didn't operate at certain spots among the islands, and when she rang his bungalow she often got the answering machine. But this time she was lucky.

They had a catching-up chat, and then Freddie demanded his turn. 'Grandad, I'm going on a ship in the school holidays!'

'Good gracious, whatever next! Where are you off to? The Antipodes?'

Freddie had no idea where that was. 'It's a steamship, it goes round the coast. Mum arranged it ages ago, you have to book early 'cause it's very popular – and Grandad, it calls in at ports all the way, and it calls in at the Clyde, and you know you told me, Grandad, that that was where all the great ships were built!'

'That sounds great. Send me postcards from every port of call!'

Freddie spent the interval before bedtime in his room, looking up his picture books about ships. While he was occupied, the phone rang and this time it was Philip, from Berlin.

'Had a good day?' Libby asked.

'Pretty good. The local council is quite willing about the film cameras but it's going to cost a bit. How was your day?'

Libby gave him a brief account of the interview between his mother and his sister. He listened in awestruck silence. 'You mean Mama actually went through it to the end? Because in the past, Angela's always complained that she

236

beats a quick retreat at some point.' She could hear real concern in his voice. 'How is she? Mama, I mean.'

'Oh, a bit shaken, I suppose. Lots of tears. But I'm sure you agree she is a bit emotional, Philip. However, the great thing is, when I was cleaning upstairs, I heard sounds from Angela's room.'

'Sounds?'

'Advertising jingles. She was on the Internet.'

'And you think...?'

'I'm guessing she was trying out the idea of looking for Papa Antoine. I suggested starting with the travel firm that organized the conference. I could be wrong, of course.'

'That's great! That's splendid!'

'Philip, it may end in nothing.'

'But at least she's grappling with it. Until now it's been her excuse for opting out of everything.'

'We'll see.'

'Well, from my side,' he began, clearly wanting to get on to more personal matters, 'the good news is that I hope to be back at Ashgrove in a day or two. And then I'm going to make sure I stay there for the rest of the summer, so that I can see you every day.'

'Ah.'

'Ah, what?'

'Philip, the school holidays are coming up. I'm not going to be at Ashgrove every day.'

'What?'

She stifled a laugh at his impracticality. 'What world do you live in, my friend? Six weeks, and I've got an active and impatient young man to keep happy.'

'So are you going away?' he cried in dismay. 'Where?'

'I'm not actually going far, because of course my staff all have their family holiday plans too. So I'm taking Freddie on a sort of coastal cruise on an old restored steamship – well, it's oil-fired now but it used to be a steamship. It's called the *Kincardine*. And for the first ten days of the holidays we'll be dodging up the coast from the Bristol Channel round to the Clyde.'

'Libby!'

'I'm sorry, love, but that's the way it is. I promised this trip to Freddie at Christmas and it's been booked ever since, so we're going, and that's that.'

'But it *is* only ten days?' He was anxious for reassurance.

'Yes, but then there's the other sixty-two days. You know? Theme parks and visits to museums – but there's a bit of relief because Freddie's going several times on a day camp—'

'What's a day camp?'

'Oh, it's where they go to a nature reserve or something, and learn things to do with wildlife – pond-dipping and photographing deer if they see any, that sort of thing.'

'And you don't go with him?'

'No.'

'Well, that raises my hopes. On a day like that could we ... have some time together somewhere?'

'I think that could be arranged. I'm leaving Jake in charge while I sail off to the Clyde so he could take over on occasional days—'

'Jake – the gardener? You leave him in charge?'

'Oh, don't be fooled by the "me-hearties" manner – he's not just an old sea-dog. He was first mate on merchant ships, so he knows a bit about management.'

'So he's taking over for six weeks?'

'No, no, I'll be at Ashgrove myself, intermittently, because the holiday schedule means I've only got temps to fill the spaces. And I couldn't send a temp to Ashgrove.'

'Why not? It seems to be less of a battlefield these days.'

'That's true, in a way. With Prim gone, Angela seems quite subdued. And if she really takes on this Internet search, perhaps things will be even calmer. But there's still your grandmother, Philip. She keeps herself locked up in that suite a lot of the time. It's ... it's disturbing.'

'But she's always been cranky, Libby.'

'You know that, and I know that, but some student earning a few pounds during the holidays would find her hard to deal with. So my plan is to run business as usual as much as I can, while somehow giving Freddie a proper holiday.'

'With occasional days off?'

'You mean you can't live without me?' she teased.

'Don't joke about it. I'd planned a lovely summer...' She heard him sigh. 'Libby, being in love with you is full of problems.'

'You mean, chiefly Freddie.'

'Well, you said it yourself. He's never had a man in the house.'

'There's no hurry, Philip,' she said gently. 'We don't have to deal with it all at once. Let's just see how it goes.'

'I suppose so.'

'And I'm not going away until the end of next week.'

'That's true...' He sounded more cheerful.

And with that they closed the subject for the time being.

They had opportunities to be together on only two occasions before the departure of the coastal cruise. Then Libby took Freddie – in a state of scarcely subdued excitement – to Bristol to board the old ship. She was anchored off a quay at a nearby resort, gleaming white and with bunting flying from lines between her two aerial masts. 'Isn't she *beautiful*?' sighed Freddie as they headed for her gangway.

But Libby had stopped dead. Standing at the ship's rail, alongside the purser, was none other than Philip Moorfield.

Fifteen

By the time they'd made their way up the gang-plank, Libby had got her breath back. She was able to show their tickets to the purser and then to smile at Philip.

'What a surprise to see you,' she said in a neutral tone. 'Freddie, this is Mr Moorfield, from Ashgrove – you know, the house where Prim lived?'

'How d'you do,' said Freddie, as he had been taught to. 'Is Prim your little girl? Is she here?'

'Prim went to Japan with her daddy,' Libby reminded him.

'Oh yes. She went on a plane, though.'

'Yes, she left one night and she was in Tokyo the next day,' Philip said. 'But you think a ship would have been better?'

'It would take longer. You would see places on the way. I think you pass India, when you sail to Japan. Of course planes can land in India at airports and things, and I suppose you could go for a walk and see things.' His attention was wandering, because seamen were beginning to catch ropes being thrown from the quayside and there was a quivering on the deck beneath their feet that meant that they would soon be under way.

241

Freddie moved along the ship's rail, and Libby went too. She was fairly sure he would prove to be well-behaved aboard, but until she'd monitored his reactions for at least a few hours, she was going to stay near at hand.

Philip followed. Seeing that her son's attention was engaged elsewhere, she asked in a low voice, 'How on earth did you get here? I thought they were fully booked.'

'Yes, quite right, but there's always someone that drops out. And as I knew the firm that owns the ship, I asked to be told the minute there was a vacancy.'

'You know the firm?'

'Yes, an advertising company did some filming on board a couple of years ago. And I did the leasing.'

'You never said!' she said accusingly.

'Well, I didn't know whether I was going to be on board or not. I thought it better to say nothing. But here I am. Say you're pleased.'

'Philip, won't you find it boring?'

'We'll see. Honestly, sweetheart, I want to get to know Freddie. I have to, don't I, if anything is going to come of this?'

'That's true.' She was secretly thrilled. If anything was going to come of it ... That seemed to mean he hoped they had a future.

They stayed among the crowd at the rail while the ship moved away from the tidy little resort, and its quay and its buildings began to grow smaller in the distance. Having surveyed the business of departure, Freddie now wanted to explore the ship.

This didn't take long. The vessel was small, and arranged now for day trips. There were no cabins: new passengers could come aboard each day, and passengers taking the ten-day voyage were provided with overnight accommodation in hotels at their ports of call. When they investigated, they found that Libby and Freddie were to stay at hotels different from those booked for Philip. The expression on Philip's narrow face became mournful.

Their tour of inspection took them to a large and rather handsome restaurant, some sitting arrangements below deck, a shop selling sweets and souvenirs, a games room, and then the area where only crew were admitted. Freddie led the tour, finding the way as if by radar. He paused often to take pictures with the camera he'd been given for Christmas, and stood longingly by the velvet rope that prevented access to the forbidden zone.

'I bet it's great up on the bridge,' he sighed.

'Well, perhaps you'll be allowed a look-see later.'

'I wish!'

Soon it was lunchtime, and then there was an anchorage off shore so that passengers could be ferried by dinghy for a visit to one of the seaside resorts that gleam along the coast of the Bristol Channel. Freddie was wild with delight at the anchors being run down, dinghies being lowered, the thrill of threading one's way through storage to a little opening in the ship's side into a rocking boat ... He ignored the fact that this could only be done on a very calm day and that not many others wanted to try the experience.

When evening approached the *Kincardine* eased itself into Swansea Bay, docked, its day-trippers departed and its round-trip passengers were taken by minibus to hotels in Swansea for the night. Philip was dropped off at a high-class establishment near the Law Courts, while Libby and Freddie were set down at a much more everyday place by the coach station. The only one who was quite content about this was Freddie.

It rained the next day. However, Philip scored a goal by arranging a trip to the engine room for Freddie. Libby watched them go with a rueful smile, and was left sitting in the passengers' lounge reading a book.

The days that followed were the same mixture of pleasant relaxation and boredom for the grown-ups, and great enjoyment for Freddie. The little boy was enthralled by everything that occurred on board – good weather, bad weather, beautiful seascapes, industrial docklands, all were full of interest for him.

And so it was with real regret that he said farewell to the *Kincardine* at Dunoon on the Firth of Clyde. For his mother and Philip there was a sense of relief, but of something more. Philip had become an accepted part of Freddie's daily life, and that was a source of great satisfaction.

For him it was an added thrill to go London by rail. Trains weren't as wonderful as ships, but they had their good points. He expected to say goodbye to Philip at Paddington, but there was yet another thrilling surprise in store: Philip had

244

arranged for a new-model Lexus to be waiting there, and it was in this very smart car that they were driven home.

'Are you driving to Ashgrove now?' Freddie asked when he and his mother were set down at the door of their flat.

'No, I'll be getting my own car – it's garaged with the firm that owns this one.'

'What kind of car have you got?'

'It's a recent-model Audi.'

'Oh, I've seen advertisements about them; they're supposed to be awfully good. Could I see it some time?'

'Why not? Call round some time with your mama.'

'Could I?' He found this unusual. His mother never let him accompany her to any of the places where her firm did housework. He'd been at Ashgrove once, but that had been at a time of crisis and he remembered almost nothing about it. He looked at Libby with pleading eyes. 'Could I, Mum?'

'We'll see.'

And with that he had to be satisfied.

Both the office and the flat seemed strange after the variety of hotel rooms they'd been in. Freddie rushed at once to check on his belongings, his books and ship models. Libby looked first to see if there were any urgent messages on her office line, then set about making a snack to keep them going until suppertime.

Jacob Grover rang as they were sipping tea and nibbling cheese crackers. 'How d'you like the life at sea, me boy?' he asked Freddie.

'It was marvellous, Jake!' He went on to list all the ports they'd visited, all the hotels they'd stayed in, and promised to let him have first viewing of all his snapshots.

'I'll look forward to that, then. And now can I talk to your Ma?'

Libby wanted to know how things had gone during her absence.

'No great snags. Amy took on the problem houses, and the temps held up well, though none of them seem to have polished a table until now.'

'You were never a student, Jake. Students never clean their digs until the end of term. Who took on Ashgrove?'

'Amy did the housework, I did the garden – roses needed dead-heading and I mowed the lawn.' He gave a little sigh. 'I got many a glimpse of my beauty, but she sails past me with her head in the air...'

Normally she would have passed this off with some teasing remark, but he sounded truly downhearted. 'You know she's used to artistic types, Jake. If you keep turning up in overalls, she's never going to get the right impression of you.'

'I can't very well ride the lawnmower in a suit, Libby!'

'No, but couldn't you perhaps turn up at some place where she'd see you outside the "work-man" role?'

'Where, for instance?'

That of course was the question. 'She goes to London a lot. She meets friends in art galleries. They have lectures and outings and go to first nights and stuff like that.'

'Ha! And does any of that sound like me?'

'We-ell...'

She heard him give a rueful chuckle. Then he said, businesslike, 'I left a possible work schedule for tomorrow – have you seen it?'

'Yes, seen it, but I haven't thought about it yet.'

'Still all at sea, are you?'

'Oh, very funny. See you tomorrow.'

And so it was back into the work routine. Freddie was to spend the day at the house of a school friend. She couldn't deliver him there until a reasonable hour in the morning, so it was rather later than usual when she arrived at Ashgrove on the Wednesday morning.

Angela came dashing downstairs the moment she heard her enter the house. 'Libby! I've been hanging about waiting to get your opinion. You know that Internet search and everything?' She was brimming with enthusiasm, a sight never seen before by Libby.

'Yes?'

'Well, I didn't get far with looking for the firm that ran the New Age travel thing. So what I did was, I joined some chat rooms – you know, the kind interested in psychic stuff and spiritual renewal and so on. And I think I may have ... well, it may be a connection.'

'Well, that's great—'

'But I don't know what to do next.'

They went into the kitchen to sit down and talk about the problem. 'I worked my way through quite a lot of groups, and now I've found one where the idea of a group of Greek gods and goddesses has rung a bell. So what I want to ask is ... Do you think I should mention Rhodes? Be definite about the place and the time?'

'Why not?'

'Well ... it seems such a big step. *He* might respond.'

'But that's what you want, isn't it?'

'But then I'd have to explain why I wanted to contact the group.'

They discussed it at length. Libby felt that she ought to be getting on with the housework, but also that she ought to pay attention to Angela. She had a sense that things were changing for her. She seemed so different already – non-aggressive, her sulkiness gone.

In the end it was decided that she should ask if anyone recalled a conference about the tarot held in a hotel in Rhodes. There really seemed good sense in going that much further. They had reached this satisfactory moment when Grandee walked in.

This was a surprise to Libby, because Grandee had been something of a recluse recently. And it was a surprise to Grandee too, for she stopped dead on seeing Libby.

'What are you doing here?' she cried.

Libby rose from her chair because she could sense hostility and wanted to be on her feet to meet it. 'I've come to clean the house,' she said.

'But you had left! Other people have been doing the housework.'

'That was only for ten days...'

'That young woman – Amy, Annie, whatever

her name was – she said you'd gone away.'

'I went away on holiday with my little boy, that's all.'

Angela intervened. 'Grandee, I told you that Libby was on holiday—'

'Oh, I never believe a word *you* say! You live in a world of videos and shopping malls...'

That was enough to bring back the old Angela, in fighting mood. 'Thanks a lot!' she riposted. 'And you're such a realist, are you? Traipsing about with your has-been art experts and judging at amateur exhibitions! You don't know anything about what's really going on—'

'And what *is* going on?' asked a voice from the doorway. Philip had come out of his office down the hall. He stood taking in the scene, aware that something bad was happening.

'I want that woman dismissed!' exclaimed his grandmother, pointing a trembling finger at Libby. 'I thought she'd gone from the house but of course she's never going to go until she gets what she wants!'

'Grandee! Calm down! You'll make yourself ill.'

'There's nothing wrong with me! I told you before, that woman is a thief and I don't want her in my house!'

'She's not a thief, Grandee, she—'

'She stole things and when I called the police she put them all back, but I know what she's really after...'

'Grandee,' said Angela loudly. 'Libby didn't steal those things. That was me.'

'What?'

'I took the silver jug and Mama's ivory box.'

'That's nonsense. Why should you...?'

'You see? You don't know anything about anything! I *expected* Libby to get the blame. I hated her for getting me into trouble over Prim. I sold the things to a shop in Weybridge.'

'And I bought them back and put them where they belonged,' Philip said in a tone that tried to bring good manners back into the conversation. 'I didn't want any more trouble but perhaps that was a mistake.'

Grandee was silenced for a long moment. She stood with her head up, as if trying to sense some silent message. Then she smiled. 'I know what she's really after. She wants something a lot more valuable than a few knick-knacks. But she's never going to get it no matter how she schemes and plots and takes you in!'

'Grandee, what on earth are you talking about?' Angela demanded, as if she were now Libby's defender.

'She's after the furniture that Dennis designed for me. I've seen her looking at it when she pretends to clean it! She wants it, but I'll never let her get her hands on it!'

'Grandee, be serious. What furniture? What are you on about?'

'Oh, you're just an ignorant child – you know nothing; nobody can expect you to have heard of Dennis Aggerton, but he was a great artist, he could have been as great as Picasso but he missed the way and now nobody recognizes his genius! But I have the things he made for me – he made them especially for *me* and nobody is

250

ever going to take them from me!'

This tidal wave of words seemed to rouse her to physical action, for she wheeled round and hurried from the kitchen. Philip went after her, catching up with her halfway up the staircase. They heard his voice trying to soothe her, and hers, much louder, in protest.

As for Libby and Angela, they stood aghast at what had happened.

'She's going totally round the bend,' breathed Angela.

'She's suffering from some kind of anxiety condition,' Libby said.

'That's just another way of saying she's crazy.'

'Angela, don't be so unkind! She's an old lady who's in some sort of ... I don't know ... it's an illness.'

'Oh, you don't really know her! She plays this game any time she wants to get her own way.'

'But there's more to it. She thinks I'm trying to steal—'

'What, that awful furniture! Who'd want it? You don't want to pay any attention to that.'

But Libby had gathered up her holdall and was heading towards the kitchen door.

'You're leaving?' Angela asked in alarm.

'I can't stay, Angela. Just suppose she came downstairs again and found me still here. She might have a heart attack or something.'

'No, no, that's all an act.'

'I'm going, Angela. And it's too late in the day to find someone on the staff to send in my place, I'm afraid.' By now she was out in the hall, and Angela was at her heels, trying to think of some way of preventing her exit.

'But Mama had guests last night. There's all the dishes and stuff on the dining-room table—'

'Put them in the dishwasher and switch it on. It's not hard.'

'Oh ... well, I suppose...' She dithered, then said awkwardly, 'Is there anything else I could do?'

Libby was astonished but managed not to show it. 'You could tidy up in the family bathroom.'

'Er ... how do you do that?'

'Make sure all the taps are turned off, wipe round the bath and the shower with a cloth – you could use one of the wet towels for that. Then you take the towels and put them in the wash basket.' Angela was looking at a loss, so she added, 'That's the wickerwork basket by the washbasin. And to replace them you need towels from the linen cupboard.'

'Where's the linen cupboard?'

'It's the door next to the bathroom.'

Angela gave a giggle. 'I always thought that was an ancient secret staircase to a dungeon. I was scared to death of it when I was a kid.'

Libby managed a smile. She hadn't been enjoying the recent events. 'I think you're going through what's called a learning process, Angela. I'll leave you to it.'

'It's true things have been different this last week or so. D'you know, I've only been out clubbing once since I had it out with Mama? And I haven't missed it, really.'

'Good for you.' Libby's attention was on

getting out of the house.

'And you know what else?' She touched Libby's arm and suddenly looked shy. 'I'm thinking of enrolling in classes to help me get some A-levels.'

Now Libby was stopped in her tracks. She couldn't just walk away from a conversation like this. 'Well, that's marvellous. What brought that on?'

'Dunno. Perhaps it was hearing Mama say that my father was so bright and good-looking. I began to think ... what if I actually got in touch with him, and he thought I was an idiot?'

Libby took her hand off the handle of the outside door. 'What subjects are you going to take?'

'I thought perhaps English and French. I was quite good at those. I actually took some GCSEs at the last school I was at, but I walked out before A-levels.' She hesitated, then added, 'And if ... you know ... I ever speak to him or send him an e-mail ... Well, he's French. My father, I mean.'

'That's true. That's a really good plan, Angela.'

'You really think so?' Delight lit up her face. 'I have to ask Mama if she'll pay for the classes. Or I could ask Phil. What do you think?'

'Why don't you talk it over with both of them?'

'Mama's an easier touch than Phil.'

'Why don't you think about getting a part-time job? You wouldn't be going to classes full-time, would you?'

'Oh. I never thought of that.'

253

'It's an idea, isn't it? When do the classes begin?'

'I think it's September. I haven't gone into it very far.' She was screwing up her face, trying to come to grips with this great scheme now that she'd put it into words.

'Well, think it over. Look in the small ads for job vacancies. Do a bit of planning.'

'It could work. I'll give it a go.'

'That sounds great, kiddo. Keep it up. And now I've really got to go.'

'Yes, I'm sorry to keep bothering you...'

'No, no, that's fine. But we'll talk more some other time. Bye for now.' She opened the door and slipped out into the drive, breathing a deep sigh of relief.

To take her mind off the encounter with Grandee, and since she had this unexpected freedom, she went shopping for fresh food supplies. She took her time over it, enjoying the feeling of leisure although she couldn't really escape anxiety about the situation at Ashgrove. It seemed to her that Grandee had been in the grip of something other than just a tantrum. And, moreover, she thought now that it had been coming on for some time.

She had lunch at a sandwich bar. When she got home, Philip Moorfield's car was parked outside her office. Philip himself was inside, being entertained by Jake Grover.

'So I think the plan was to go there next year,' Jake was saying as Libby came in. He got up from behind her desk to explain. 'I was just telling Mr Moorfield about Freddie and his longing

to sail to the Bahamas.'

'Ah yes. That's a project that depends on a lot of factors.' She nodded a greeting to Philip and sat down at her desk, which Jake rightly took as a hint to remove himself further. He went off to the back premises to stack newly arrived supplies.

'How are things at Ashgrove?' she asked, as of course she must out of mere politeness.

'Pretty awful. Grandee's locked herself in her rooms and keeps telling everybody to leave her alone. She sent Mama into a flood of tears when she tried to talk to her through the door.'

'You know, Philip...'

'Yes?'

'I think she ought to see a doctor.'

'I tried that,' he said. 'She threatened to turn me out of the house if I so much as mentioned it again.'

She gave an ironic smile at the words, and shook her head. 'Of course you could never leave her in that great old place on her own, and she knows it.'

'Yes, she does. In her way, Grandee is a great politician. She knows the real facts but as they don't suit her she ignores them.' He picked up a pencil from her desk and began to scribble patterns on her notepad.

'She has no income of her own?'

'As far as I've ever been able to find out, there's not a penny left of Grandfather's money – and that was a lot, you know. But it all came from investments in British car firms, and that's gone a long way downhill since his day. And

255

Grandee spent pretty lavishly.' In embarrassment at these disclosures he was now making dollar signs on her pad. 'Ever since we left university Brenton and I have provided all the running costs of the house, which does of course belong to her. We're both in careers that brought in a lot so she's never lacked for anything – but whether she grasps the real situation I'm never quite sure.'

'And now Brenton's gone and what he earned has gone with him, right?'

'That doesn't matter too much. But the fact is that no one else in the family is bringing in a reasonable income. Mama's little shop scarcely makes enough to be worthwhile – what she lives on is the insurance that Papa took out. The thing is, she and I live in Grandee's house and Grandee is a sort of control freak. Yet we can't leave her because she's ... well...' He paused. 'I'm very sorry for the stupid things she said this morning, Libby. Perhaps tomorrow things will be better.'

'What does that mean?'

'Well, by tomorrow she'll probably unlock her door and come out into the real world again. I hope she'll behave – but I don't think you should expect an apology.'

Libby gave him a cool and steady look. 'You're not expecting me to turn up at Ashgrove, are you?'

'Well, yes ... You know she came round last time.'

She was shaking her head. 'I'll send a replacement. I just don't feel inclined to go through anything like that again.'

'Libby...'

'No.' Her tone made him throw down his pencil and look at her in anxiety. 'I've got my own family to think about. I've got a little boy who wants to enjoy his school holiday and have his mum around enjoying it with him. If I have to keep facing uproar at your house, I don't think I'd be very full of the joys of life.'

'But we can sort this out—'

'I don't see how we can, Philip. It seems to be a sort of Catch-22 situation. I think it would be a good thing if we didn't see each other for a while.'

Sixteen

For the next two days, Libby and her son enjoyed themselves in their own way. They went on the train to Brighton, Freddie washed the car and to a large extent himself, Libby caught up with the daily routine of Housecare Helpers. Her place at Ashgrove was taken, although with some protest, by Amy.

'I just got finished with doing their chores! I don't want to go back.'

'Oh, come on, things aren't so bad there now that Angela isn't grumpy about the little girl...'

'That's what you think! I couldn't get her out of her room to clean it; she was practically stuck to her computer.'

'Amy, you know I can't send one of the temps. Please do it for a day or two until I sort something out.'

But nothing had been sorted out when on Saturday morning Libby's office phone rang. And it was Amy, sounding very anxious.

'Listen, Libby, things are in a real pickle here! That awful old lady hasn't been out of her room in days, and now Mr Moorfield's very bothered about it. Apparently he got back from a business trip last night and this morning he hit the roof!'

'What?'

'Her that they call Grandee – it seems she's never reappeared since that row she had with you, and that was on *Wednesday* – Wednesday, Libby! So those rooms of hers have never been cleaned since I did them on Tuesday and that can't be right, now can it?'

'But she must at least have been downstairs to get something to eat, Amy.'

'They say not after Wednesday, she hasn't. When I got here on Thursday morning there was a mug and a plate to wash up, so it looked as if she'd come down in the middle of the night and had a piece of cake and a cup of cocoa. But those two, the young Mrs Moorfield and that daughter of hers, haven't seen her since then. They say she's locked herself in and won't come out.'

'Locked herself in?'

'Young Mrs Moorfield, that's Rosanne, she's in floods of tears, and the girl is upset and angry...'

'And Philip Moorfield – where is he?'

'He's upstairs trying to coax her to unlock her

door and come out, but she just keeps telling him to go away, or so I gather.'

'Oh, Lord!'

'Listen, Libby, it's a really bad scene here, and I don't want to be involved if anything worse is going to happen.'

'What do you mean by that?'

'I mean, I'm coming back to the office! You know these people better than I do; it's up to you to sort it out.'

'Hold on...' But it was too late. Amy had rung off.

Libby glanced about the office. No one was left to send as a replacement – and in any case she knew she was going to have to go herself.

Jake Grover was somewhere out the back, sorting out tools for a job scheduled for later. 'Jake!' she called. 'Could you take Freddie for an hour or two? There's a crisis at Ashgrove.'

'And where else would it be?' he responded as he wandered up to her desk.

'Can you look after Freddie?'

'Where is he?'

'Still upstairs getting dressed. I'll just let him know the change of plan.'

'No problem.'

She nodded her thanks and hurried off to explain to Freddie, who complained, but not much, since Jake was a pal of his.

Fifteen minutes later Libby was turning in to the drive at Ashgrove. Angela must have heard the car, for she had the door open as soon as Libby approached. Her expression was a strange mixture of anger and alarm.

259

'Thank goodness you're here! That other woman just took off.'

'What's happening?'

'Oh, Mama's in the drawing-room trying to calm her aura or something,' she reported with scorn. 'Phil's upstairs trying to persuade Grandee to be sensible.'

'She's really been upstairs since Wednesday?'

'Yep. Talk about grandstanding!'

'No, no, this is more than just a tantrum, Angela—'

'Oh, come on, she's always staging scenes like this.'

'She's an old lady and if she's not come downstairs in nearly three days, she must be nearly starving by now.'

'She's just kidding us it's a hunger strike or something, but she's got that tray to make tea or coffee and a Venetian glass jar full of biscuits, so it's all a scam.'

'Angela, how can you be so...?' She broke off, then changed tack. 'Listen, she's an old lady. Tea and biscuits for three days is *not* a good thing.'

'We-ell...'

'And in any case, what's her reason for going on a hunger strike?'

'She's protesting.'

'Against what?'

'Who knows?' Angela cried. 'She just wants to get us in a tizzy. She's a control freak.'

'Where's Philip?'

'Upstairs trying to get her door open.'

Libby ran upstairs. Philip was in his shirt-sleeves, toolbox at his side, and on his knees trying to insert a chisel between the doorjamb and the door of Grandee's room. He stopped as she came up.

'How did you get here?'

'Amy rang me. What's happening?'

'I'm trying to force the door, but these great old Victorian things are so well made I can't get anything in there. And if I did, I think it would bend, rather than open the door.'

'You need something stronger – something like a tyre iron, perhaps?'

'That's not got a fine enough edge. I've been down to the garage, but there's nothing but gardening tools, trowels and pruning shears, things like that.'

Libby tapped on the door. 'Mrs Moorfield?'

No answer.

'Mrs Moorfield, open the door.'

'Go away!' The head of the house spoke in a voice that lacked something of its usual power.

'Mrs Moorfield, come on now, you're making your family very anxious. Open the door.'

'G-go away!'

'Grandee, please open the door,' begged Philip.

No reply.

'Mrs Moorfield, you're being very selfish and unkind. Now come on, this is just childish. Unlock the door.'

A pause. Then a trembling voice said, 'I ... I can't.'

'What?' said Philip, leaning closer to the door. 'What do you mean, you can't? Are you ill?'

'I've tried to open the door. The lock won't work.'

'Of course it will. Turn the key and open the door, Grandee.'

'The key won't turn.'

'What?'

'It got stuck the other night. I ... I thought it needed some oil.'

'Yes?'

'So I put some of my bath oil on a cotton bud and tried to push that in beside the key. But it broke off...'

'And then what, Grandee?'

'It just won't work. The k-key is *in* the lock and it won't turn, I've tried and tried.'

Philip gave a muffled groan. 'It's jammed,' he said quietly to Libby. 'The lock's as old as the house – I think the tumblers must have packed up.'

They were silent for a moment as this sank in. Then he turned back to the prisoner within the room. 'Why didn't you say so before?'

'I ... I didn't want to look a f-fool.'

And, amazingly, Grandee could be heard starting to cry.

'I think I'd better find a locksmith in the Yellow Pages...'

'I'll ask Jake,' Libby said, and got out her mobile.

Jake was just about to leave the office with Freddie. 'What, my princess is locked in a tower?' he said with a mixture of amusement and alarm.

'Philip hasn't got the right tools to force the door, Jake, and Mrs Moorfield has been locked in her room for nearly three days now.'

'Good heavens! Well now, tell Philip just to leave the lock, and instead undo the door hinges—'

'But, Jake, the hinges are the other side, *inside* the bedroom!'

'Of course they are,' he agreed at once, recalling the great mahogany doors of the old house. 'Well, look, I'll come and see what I can do, but what about the boy?'

'Amy should be there in a few minutes,' she said. 'She rang me to say she was heading back to the office. Ask her to take on Freddie just for a couple of hours.'

'Right. Expect me in a little while.'

On arrival he came storming up the staircase holding up his toolbox. 'Let's have a look-see.' But a minute or two of inspection told him what Philip had already learned – there was no way to get in from the outside short of breaking through the panels of the sturdy old door with something like an axe.

'And we don't want to inflict something like that on her after all she's been through, do we?' he remarked, looking concerned.

'Well, then, a locksmith would have the tools to get at the lock mechanism from outside, wouldn't he?' Philip said. 'Long-nosed pliers or something?'

Jake gave his chin a thoughtful rub. 'Tell you what the quickest thing is ... I'll just nip to the garage and get the ladders.'

'What good will that do?'

'I know the windows of this house – I've washed them every two or three weeks since the spring. I can nip up the ladder and be inside the lady's room in a jiffy, and then I'll take the door off the hinges from the inside.'

'But the windows will be *fastened* from the inside, Jake,' Libby reminded him.

'Oh, never you trouble your head about that, my lamb. I'll fiddle one of them old catches with something, or if worst comes to worst I'll break one of the panes and reach inside.'

'It'd scare her to death—'

'No, no, you explain to her that I'm coming.' He picked up his toolbox and hurried off, Philip at his heels.

When they'd gone, Libby tapped again at the door. 'Mrs Moorfield? Mrs Moorfield?'

No reply.

'Mrs Moorfield – Grandee – can you hear me? Jake is going to come and get in through your window'

There was a sound from within, bed springs perhaps, as someone rose from the bed. There was a slight pause before Grandee spoke. 'Who's that?'

'It's Libby. Libby Fletcher, you know? How are you, Grandee?'

'I'm ... I'm a bit tired.' Tears trembled in her voice. 'I don't feel very well.'

'You should make yourself some tea or coffee and put lots of sugar in—'

'There isn't any sugar. I don't take sugar.' A stifled sob. 'There's no milk left for tea. Oh, I'm so tired of all this...'

'Jake is going to come through one of your windows so he can—'

'I really want the door to open but it won't.'

'Yes, I understand, but Jake is going to get it open—'

'Oh! Oh, something's at my window! Oh, what's that?'

'It's a ladder, Grandee. Someone's coming up to—'

'A *man*! At my window!'

'Yes, don't be scared, it's Jake – you remember Jake, he looks after the garden for you...'

'What's he doing? Oh, my!' Grandee was crying again.

Angela came pounding up the stairs. 'What's going on? There's banging and noises at the back—'

'Jake's trying to get in at the window to—'

'Jake? Who's Jake?'

'The handyman.'

From the other side of the door came the screeching of an old sash window being opened, and the loud comforting tones of Jake Grover.

'Now don't you worry, me dove, everything's going to be all right. I'll get your door open in a jiffy. Don't be afraid, you know me, don't you?'

'Go away! Go away!'

'Angela,' said Libby, 'go downstairs and heat up some soup—'

'Soup? We haven't got any soup.'

'Good lord, there's tins in the larder! Put some in a jug and heat it up in the microwave so Grandee can have something simple to eat.'

'Oh.' Light dawned. Angela nodded and hurried off.

From inside the bedroom came Jake's voice

265

again. 'Just sit you down then, me treasure, and take your ease. There now, that's better. Everything's going to be sorted in a minute or two.' Grandee was crying loudly, like a frightened child. 'Come on now, my princess, this is no way to go on. You've had a bad time but it's all better now. There, there.'

Philip spoke from just inside the room. 'Libby, you still there?'

'Yes, of course.'

'I'm just going to try to get at the hinges.'

'Where's Jake?'

'I came up behind him on the ladder. He's comforting Grandee.'

'Comforting her?'

'Sitting beside her on the bed with his arms around her.' There was the gritting sound of a screwdriver being applied to metal. 'These things are as tough as the door – a hundred per cent Victorian workmanship. Ouch!' But then came a mutter of triumph. It's giving way...'

The next few minutes were very strange. Jake Grover could be heard soothing Grandee, and Grandee could be heard crying and stammering excuses for being in tears, while Philip worked at the ancient hinges and at last detached one. Then he started on the other, uttering groans of exasperation.

Angela came up with a tray holding a big bowl of soup and a plate of toast. She hovered anxiously beside Libby.

The old door tilted to one side, creaking as it pulled itself away from the grip of the lock. A gap appeared. She edged through as soon as there was enough room to pass.

She drew up short at the sight of the senior Mrs Moorfield in the arms of a man. Libby nudged her in the back. 'Go on,' she urged.

'I've brought you something to eat, Grandee,' she announced. 'I'll put it on the table in the boudoir.' And off she went, anxious not to witness Grandee in this state.

Libby stepped into the bedroom. Philip was urging the door further open from inside. The lock gave way at last. He leaned the door against the wall. 'There, Grandee! Free at last!' he remarked, trying to lighten the moment.

She attempted to stand, but tottered. Jake was at her side. 'There now, my pretty, lean on me. That's right, and now off we go, we'll sit down and have a bite to eat and then we'll go downstairs, shall we, and find out what the world is like outside this weary old room, eh?'

Philip and Libby watched his tyrannical grandmother being led like a child into the next room. The man supporting her had his head bent close as he murmured words of encouragement. Angela came out of the boudoir as they entered. She joined Philip and Libby by the door.

'We-ell,' she breathed. 'What do you make of *that*?'

Seventeen

It took an hour or two for the household at Ashgrove to recover from these events. Grandee emerged from her seclusion, her suite was cleaned and tidied, and a carpenter and a locksmith were called. The lock was taken away for repair, a temporary catch was installed, the door was restored to its place by midday – and Grandee refused to re-enter the suite. She was firm. But she was not herself. There was no hauteur, no air of command.

'I don't want to go back in there,' she said in a low voice.

The solution was suggested by Libby, who was still at Ashgrove attempting to restore something like order. 'Why not use Brenton's old room?'

Grandee nodded agreement. So Libby got the room ready and Grandee went in. She sat down on the chair in front of the dressing table and looked at herself in the mirror.

'I need my face cream and my eye make-up.'

Libby fetched them.

'My hairbrush.'

Libby brought it.

'I want to get out of this dressing-gown. I think I'd like my grey dress with the flowers.'

Off went Libby to find it.

That seemed to be all for the moment, so Libby went in search of Philip. 'She ought to see a doctor,' she said. 'She's not herself.'

'I suggested that. She says she's all right.'

'But she's not.'

Grandee came downstairs wearing her grey dress and with a little make-up applied. She made her way into the dining room, where a meal was waiting for everyone, including Libby and, to Libby's surprise, Jake. Grandee had asked that he be included.

Rosanne was hovering to serve the first course – a vegetarian meal, naturally, of courgettes and green beans in a mild cheese sauce with brown rice. Jake, sat next to Libby at the table, murmured, 'She needs something more tempting than this, Libby.'

Libby nodded silent agreement.

Angela had opened a bottle of wine. When her glass was filled, Grandee raised it with a rather shaky hand and said, 'I'd like to say a thank you to Mr ... er ... Mr Grover.'

'Oh, you call me Jake, me dear. Everybody does.'

'Then, Jake, thank you for coming to my rescue.'

'Pleasure.'

'Is there anything I can do to express my appreciation?'

He hesitated. ''Twould be nice if ... say ... you'd come out for a meal with me?'

'Oh!'

'Never mind, then,' he said.

'No, I'm sorry ... I didn't mean...' Grandee was

crying again.

Everyone except Jake stared at her in consternation. He, as if by instinct, got to his feet and went to her. 'Come now, my bird,' he said, helping her out of her chair. 'You're not fit for all this. Come on, now, let's find a cosy place, eh? And we'll sit down just quiet-like, the two of us, and you can tell me how you feel and we'll look out on the garden and see the grass and the flowers, and mebbe we'll gather a few for you to do one of your arrangements, eh?'

She went with him without a word. He knew enough about the house to lead her to the morning-room, and they heard the door close.

Nobody around the dining table said anything for a long moment. Then finally Philip said, 'I think we ought to take some food in there in a minute or two. And – no offence, Mama – but I think it ought to be something more appealing than rice and vegetables.'

Angela nodded vigorous agreement. 'Could we order something decent from Angelo's?'

Rosanne looked hurt, but said nothing.

Philip went to the phone. Libby rose too, but hardly knew what to do until Rosanne, pink with embarrassment, began to gather up the dishes. Libby followed suit. By and by the dining room was cleared, the food suitable to be frozen was stored away, and Rosanne had retired to her room upstairs.

Angela hovered about in the kitchen, trying to be helpful. 'I shouldn't have said that about the food, should I?' she muttered.

'Well, perhaps not, but it was what we were all

thinking. Your mama isn't a good cook, Angela.'

'No.' A long hesitation. 'I'd go up and apologize, but ... you know ... I don't know what to say.'

'It'll come to you.'

'You think so?'

'Well, try, anyhow.'

With a heavy sigh Angela departed on this errand. By and by a ring at the back door announced the arrival of the food from the caterer. Libby set places round the kitchen table, arranged a tray for the pair in the morning-room, and announced that lunch was ready. The special containers held *gazpacho* as a starter, sole *mornay*, and a simple apple tart as dessert.

When she took the tray to the morning-room, she found Grandee sitting in the wickerwork settee protected by many cushions, playing cards with Jake on the space between them. She turned her head at Libby's entrance, looking a little confused at being caught playing something as simple as Rummy.

Jake grinned. 'Ah,' he welcomed Libby. 'Now that's better. Do you feel up to a mouthful or two, my jewel?' He watched the first course being set out on the table, then nodded at Libby to make herself scarce.

She was happy to obey. Here at last was someone who seemed to know how to handle Grandee.

When it came time to leave, Libby went to find Jake. By now he was in the garden with Grandee, picking flowers while she gave orders from one of the chairs from the morning-room.

'Are you coming, Jake?'

He interrupted his task to join her at the French windows. 'I'll hang on a bit.'

'All right then. But I've got to get back for Freddie.'

'So you have, maidie. But I'm just getting Vivienne to tell me a few things about herself.'

'Vivienne!'

'That's her name, you know.' He was smiling to himself.

'You staged that dramatic ascent through her window just to get to know her, you rascal!'

'No I didn't. But I'm glad I did it.' He glanced back at Grandee, who was arranging roses into a bouquet in her hand. 'It's worth doing.'

'Well, tomorrow's Sunday, no work on a Sunday. Will you be coming back?'

'That's yet to be seen,' he replied, but he seemed confident.

Libby rang Amy to say she was on her way. 'What happened in the end?' Amy asked. 'Did you get the old girl out of her rooms?'

'Mrs Moorfield is sitting in the garden at this moment with Jake and he won't be pleased if you refer to her as "the old girl".'

'What does that mean?

'I'm not quite sure. So how's Freddie getting on?'

'We're at the park and Freddie's swinging on a swing. What do you want me to do? Shall we come back to the office?'

'Might as well. Day's about to end, isn't it, and staff that have been out at work will be coming in to report. See you there.'

'Right. I'll just round up the lad.'

'Thank you, Amy.'

'Don't mention it.'

The few staff who had had Saturday employment began to come back to the office soon after Libby arrived. Two temporary workers were paid up to date, and one agreed to stay on. Libby gave Amy some account of the events at Ashgrove but without going into details. She herself wasn't quite sure how matters stood.

One thing seemed certain, however: Grandee could never rule over her family as she had done before. Something had changed – Grandee herself, perhaps, but certainly their view of her. Her armour had been pierced – perhaps even discarded.

Philip rang later. 'Thank you for all you did for us today.'

'I didn't do much. It was Jake who turned out to be the hero of the hour.'

'Yes, didn't he! He left a few minutes ago, but he's promised to come back tomorrow.'

'Promised? To Grandee?'

'Yes, it seems she ... I don't know ... She feels she needs him.' He gave a little chuckle. 'First time I've ever known Grandee to "need" anyone. The extraordinary thing is, he's persuaded her to see Dr Staffham.'

'Well done Jake!'

'Yes, it's amazing. Staffham is more or less the family doctor but Grandee's always seemed to get by with just a ten-minute check-up. I rang and asked for an appointment for her and it's fixed for Monday.'

'That's good. She must be suffering after-effects of not having any proper food for those days she was shut in, and perhaps she's ... well, you know ... suffering a bit from depression or something.' She hesitated, then added, 'Listen, I know it's not really any of my business, but how often does she really sit down and have a proper meal in the dining room?'

'Only occasionally, when she invites guests. In general she gets herself a snack except when she goes out to eat in a restaurant with friends.'

'What would you think about having a cook come in and do some of the meals? It seemed clear to me today that neither you nor Angela are really keen on your mother's cooking.'

'Well ... You know we've never been able to keep one! We've evolved this method of having food sent in for big occasions and otherwise we do the best we can.'

'I think I could find somebody who'd take it on, Philip. During the summer vacation period, a lot of students are looking for jobs, and I've got one on my books who is a foodie. She's done some cooking for another family. I think I could get her to make a midday meal for you. And as things at Ashgrove aren't as difficult as they used to be, she perhaps would stay until at least she has to go back to uni. What do you say?'

'That would be great.'

'I'll see if I can get hold of her for Monday.'

'Will you be coming?' he asked, sounding hopeful.

'No, no, don't forget, we're still in the school holidays. I'm taking Freddie to a motor car museum tomorrow. Monday isn't planned yet.'

A pause. 'Could I join you tomorrow?'

'Well ... That wasn't in the plan. But...'

'But?'

'How about if you drop round later – in about an hour, before Freddie has to go to bed, and we'll see how he feels about having you with us.'

Freddie was perfectly amiable when it came up in the conversation. Libby was at her desk, still clearing up accounts on her computer. Freddie had been showing off the photographs he'd taken on the coastal steamer trip to Amy, so now he wanted to show them to Philip. Then of course he wanted to enthuse about the motor car museum. It seemed quite natural to include Philip when he seemed keen. He left his mother and Philip still chatting when he went to get ready for bed.

Libby heaved a sigh of relief. It was such a blessing that they seemed to get on together. No matter whether this was a long-term thing or only a summer affair, it was pleasing that Freddie showed no animosity. Then, with an inward smile, she admitted to herself that Philip's offer to drive them in his new Audi A4 had probably had something to do with it.

This proved to be the main topic of conversation during their journey the next day. Freddie was allowed to sit in the front passenger seat for the first few miles, safely belted in and with his booster seat. He was enthralled by the new driver information system, even though, if he was honest, he didn't entirely understand all of

275

its merits.

The day seemed to go very fast. Even Freddie grew weary of vintage sports cars and Tin Lizzies. When Philip delivered them to their door, it was clear the little boy was fading fast.

'Would you ... would you like to come in?' Libby invited, knowing full well that if he did, they would be in each other's arms the moment Freddie had fallen asleep.

And so it was. They spent the night recalling the heaven of their first love-making, reawakening the passion that had been kept at bay so long, and with a new understanding of each other.

'Shall I see you later?' he asked as he kissed her when it was time for him to go.

'No, Freddie's pal rang this morning so tomorrow we're going with him and his family on a picnic.'

'Ah.'

'I'm sorry. The school holidays still have another two weeks to go, my love. I *have* to spend time with him because I'm not always there for him during term time.'

'Of course. I understand. What about later in the week?'

'Well, Freddie's going away on another day camp on Wednesday. We could spend the whole day together.'

'But *I* have to be in Belfast to inspect locations for a documentary film.'

'Oh, what a shame! Well, how about Friday – will you be back?'

'Not until Saturday.'

'Umm, there's a gala day on the Wey at Guildford. Could you come to that?'

And so, by means of occasional days of good luck, they were able to meet even if sometimes it was only to be together in a crowd. The holidays came to an end; Freddie went, not unwillingly, back to school. Libby felt that a new phase of their relationship might be about to begin, and in any case it was time for her to return to Ashgrove.

Amy had been replaced by another member of staff, Britta, who could only work mornings. The part-time student cook was Celia, who was available to make a midday meal three days a week.

Jake, often at the house these days, had kept an eye on things. 'Everything's going fairly well, but it has a sort of makeshift feel to it. The rooms need more attention than they're getting. The young Mrs Moorfield isn't around much. I think she's feeling put out because Celia's food has been quite a hit. But apart from that, things seem to have settled down.'

'And Grandee? How is she doing?'

'Seems much more herself.' He paused. 'There's still something bothering her. She's never set foot in that suite of rooms, you know.'

'Really? Well, I suppose it's understandable. She might be remembering it as a prison, or something like that. Does she talk about it to you?'

'Never a word.' He frowned at Libby. 'You mustn't think that because she sees me as more

277

like a friend now, that she's going to tell me all her heart's troubles. No, no, my dove, things are never as easy as that.'

'She kept the appointment with the doctor?'

'Oh yes. It seems she went like a lamb.'

'And what did Dr Staffham have to say? Did she tell you?'

'I gather she got some medication to help lift her spirits a bit, and some advice about going out more.'

'But she goes out a lot, Jake.'

'Yes, but only with these arty types and only to exhibitions and stuff like that. The doc seems to have told her to go and see a happy musical.'

'A happy musical!'

'Yes, something not highbrow. *Mama Mia* or something like that. So far she hasn't done it.'

'And do you think she will?'

'It could happen. We rented the video of *Sleepless in Seattle* and watched it together the other day, and she loved it.'

Libby laughed. 'Had you seen it before?'

He smiled at her reaction. 'No, I asked the girl in the shop to recommend something and that's what she gave me. Turned out to be just the thing.'

'Well, well ... What do you think will come of all this, Jake?'

'No idea, except that Vivienne's looking a bit better and seems to be looking outside herself more.'

'And that's thanks to you, isn't it? No one else knew what to do and you somehow just walked in and did it.'

278

'That's me,' he said with a mock bow. 'Mr Fix-it.'

Her first day back found Libby going through the house to see what had been neglected. All the family members seemed to be out, and Britta led her through the premises. In a way, the situation wasn't too bad. Nothing had been done to Grandee's suite except to dust around it. Angela had taken to tidying her own room, which was an unexpected bonus. Rosanne's room needed attention. 'It's such a clutter with joss sticks in jars and little statuettes, and clothes spilling out of her wardrobe,' Britta complained. She admitted she had ignored it.

The downstairs rooms were passable, Libby felt. Yet there was a subtle change in them. At first she couldn't identify what it was, and then she realized that Grandee's belongings were dotted about – an art magazine left on an occasional table, a silk scarf thrown over a chair, a sales receipt on a mantelpiece. It meant that Grandee had been spending time downstairs, in the main body of the house.

Grandee herself came home mid-morning, when Libby was helping Britta bring down the cleaning equipment from the bedrooms. She paused in the hall, elegant in a silk two-piece suit and shady hat, watching as they came down.

'Good morning,' she said.

'Good morning, Mrs Moorfield.'

'Mrs Fletcher – Libby – could I have a word with you when you have a moment?'

Libby, halfway down the staircase and a little startled, took a firmer hold on the vacuum cleaner she was carrying. 'Certainly, Mrs Moorfield.'

'I'm just going to take off my hat and see to my hair. Then I'll make myself a cup of coffee and take it into the morning-room. Perhaps you'd join me there?'

'Of course.'

They were about to huddle together to allow Grandee to pass on her way to her bedroom, but to Libby's surprise Grandee hung her hat on the hall stand, glancing in its mirror to brush at her hair. Then she made her way towards the kitchen.

Britta exchanged a glance with her. 'If she's going to complain to you that I left her bedroom window open all Friday, I already apologized for that.'

'Was she very cross?'

'Well, no, she just said she didn't want insects in her room.'

They put away their cleaning tools in the broom cupboard. By the time that was done, Grandee was walking from the kitchen towards the morning-room carrying a steaming mug – a sight Libby had never before witnessed. There really had been a change at Ashgrove.

She felt as if she were a school child who had been sent to the headmistress for rebuke as she followed the old lady into the sunny morning-room.

'Ah,' said Grandee as she came in, 'I thought this would be a good place to have our chat. Sit down.'

'Our chat'? What would they be chatting

about? Libby sat down in one of the wickerwork armchairs.

Grandee cleared her throat. Then she took a sip of coffee. 'I've been thinking about ... my suite of rooms.' There was a pause.

'Yes?' Libby encouraged.

The old lady took a deep breath. When she spoke her voice was grave. 'I've decided to sell all the special furniture and décor by Dennis Aggerton.'

Eighteen

To Mrs Moorfield Senior, this was clearly a momentous announcement.

Libby didn't know how to react. She sat like a polite visitor, looking attentive, waiting for the next remark.

'I thought,' said Grandee, 'that as you've always been so interested in it, I'd give you first refusal.'

Another pause. This time clearly it was Libby's turn to speak but she didn't know what to say. 'I ... er ... don't quite see what you mean by ... first refusal?'

There was a touch of something like the old asperity now. 'I mean I'm selling it all, and you can suggest what you would pay for it.'

'But – Grandee! That suite of furniture is

281

unique! Absolutely unique! It must be worth a fortune.'

'I thought probably it might bring in something rather good.' Grandee smiled to herself. 'Of course, it had occurred to me that you wouldn't have the funds yourself. A house-cleaner isn't likely to ... But you could probably raise it somehow – arrange for someone in the trade to lend you the money and then pay them back by selling the items – item by item, if you thought that the best way to get a good price.'

'Mrs Moorfield!' Libby was too astonished to find any further words.

Grandee waited, eyebrows raised. 'Well?'

'I ... I don't know what you've been imagining, but I'm not a ... a furniture dealer—'

'Oh, not professionally, I suppose, but I'm sure you do know something about furniture because you knew those pieces, and the other parts of the decor, the curtains and pelmets and all that, you *knew* they were something special.'

Libby got her breath back. 'Yes, I knew the approach was very unusual. I recognized it as Fifties style, one step on from World War Two Utility, unique because it was attempting to brighten things up in the grim post-war era. But that's because I'm a furniture restorer.'

'Er ... excuse me, you're a domestic worker.'

Libby was acutely aware that she was clad in worn jeans and an old loose smock from her days of pregnancy. The outfit wasn't high-class, but it was her work clothes. 'I do house-cleaning only so as to make some sort of an income and look after my little boy. I studied Applied Arts at university. One day I want to start out as a furniture restorer. I've done a few things already but I can't branch out on my own until I've saved enough to get suitable premises.'

Grandee stared at her in consternation. 'You went to university?'

'Yes, I did.'

'Then why are you cleaning my house?'

'Because I can make a steady income at it until I'm ready to do what I really want to do.'

Clearly this was so incomprehensible to Grandee that she was utterly silenced. They sat looking at each other. Libby was dreading what would happen next. She had put a damper on what had clearly been a great plan.

Grandee at last managed an attempt at a smile. 'I seem to have got quite the wrong end of the stick. But then, I think I've done that more than once in the past months.'

'Don't bother about that...'

'I suppose I owe you an apology. I believe I've been rather ... overbearing towards you. I'm beginning to look back and see that I ... that on the whole my manners...' Tears began to gather in her eyes. She blinked them away with annoyance. 'Well, that's the past. And the fact is, you are still doing housework, and I daresay you'd like to make a ... well, it might be a tidy sum. What do you say?'

'I've just explained that I'm not in the furniture-dealing business.'

'Well, that's a pity, because I do so want to get rid of it all!' Once more tears sparkled. She bit her lip then stared past Libby's head to regain her control.

Libby could understand that the old suite of rooms and its contents were a burden to Grandee now. The rooms that housed them held frightening memories for her. The former tyrant of the family was having trouble ridding herself of the past and taking the steps towards a new way of life.

'We-ell,' she said, her mind racing, 'I certainly can't handle the stuff myself, but I believe I could find someone who would know a buyer.'

'Really?'

'I went to a weekend seminar earlier this year, and the man who organized it has all kinds of contacts. Would you like me to...?'

'I thought *you* might be the right buyer because you ... it seems to me that you ... well, you've proved yourself to be reliable. So this person ... is he, you know, reliable?'

'Very. He gives talks on television, that kind of thing.'

'Would I know his name?'

'It's quite likely. Perry Lermontis?'

'Mmm. It does seem to strike a chord. Is he the kind of man who would know the name of Dennis Aggerton?'

'I'm pretty sure he would have heard of him, or at least it would strike a chord.' Libby smiled, and Grandee responded with a little nod of appreciation.

'Well then, could you contact him?'

'I certainly could. I've got his number somewhere.'

'When could you do it?'

'Oh, any time.' Grandee gave her an expectant gaze. 'You'd like me to do it now?'

'If you would.'

'I'd have to look in my planner. Just let me go out to my car to get it.'

Off she went, more than a little startled at what had just happened. Leaning against her car in the late summer sunshine, she pressed the buttons on her mobile to contact Lermontis.

A dealer in antique furniture, a lecturer and something of an entrepreneur, he wasn't immediately available. Libby gave her name and number to his secretary, saying, 'Would you tell him I'm offering a large suite of furniture by the Fifties artist Dennis Aggerton, a one-off design and in very good condition?'

That done, she went back to the morning-room to report to Mrs Moorfield. She took her mobile with her, and was not surprised that it rang while she was still discussing the probabilities with her.

'Mrs Fletcher? Libby, isn't it? You had that very pretty chaise longue at the seminar a few months ago.'

'That's me. Mr Lermontis, would it interest you to look at this furniture collection by Aggerton? I think there are nine pieces, together with curtains for two sets of windows, some cushions, and the bedclothes. All specially designed for the original owner, who is now prepared to part with them.'

'Ahem. I took just a moment to look up Aggerton, my dear. He seems to have had rather a short career, yet one or two of his paintings have recently fetched very good prices.'

'I don't know his paintings. And so far as I can gather, this is the only piece of interior design he ever did.'

'You say he did this for the present owner?'

'Yes.'

'May I know who that is?'

'Mrs Vivienne Moorfield.'

A faint whistle of amazement. 'The sitter for David Jacobson's *Lady with Lilacs*?'

'Yes.' This was a guess – she didn't really know it for sure.

'I saw that recently, in Moriowski's New York office. Well, now, of course I'm interested. That whole group is coming into fashion again. I begin to be very interested in this furniture collection. When could I see it?'

'Just a moment.' She turned to Grandee. 'Mr Lermontis would like to view the furniture. When could he come?'

'Let me speak to him.'

She handed over her mobile. Grandee introduced herself, and there followed a dialogue in which it became clear that Lermontis was asking about her days as a model and she was being coy but rather boastful. Libby quietly withdrew.

She was in the kitchen stacking the dishwasher when Grandee came in to return the mobile. 'He's coming tomorrow morning. He seems very interested. He says he has a Russian billionaire who's furnishing a house in some grand place on the Black Sea, and thinks my Aggerton suite might be just the thing for him.'

'Splendid. I'll give the stuff a little brush-up to

286

make it look its best.'

'Polish the metal bits.'

'No can do. That's what makes the pieces so interesting, Grandee – Jake thinks that metal is just chromium plating on something like steel and the surface is getting very fragile now – it can probably be restored but it's going to cost a bit. Because, you see, I should think almost nobody would know how to do it. I think only Dennis Aggerton has ever done it. At least, I've never seen anything like it before.'

'Really? I'm glad you told me. I'll be able to pass that on to Mr Lermontis and he can tell his Russian friend and maybe push the price up.'

Libby laughed. 'Good idea.' This practical and optimistic style was an improvement on the Grandee of earlier. 'Come upstairs and watch me polish up the wood.'

But Grandee hadn't quite recovered enough to go into that suite of rooms. She shrank back at the suggestion. 'I don't think so,' she murmured.

Before leaving that afternoon, Libby left a note for Philip, who was in London but was expected home that night. 'Try to be available to show Perry Lermontis around Grandee's suite tomorrow. She's putting the furnishings in it up for sale but she doesn't want to go into the rooms to show him round. She'll explain who he is, etc.'

As she drove to Freddie's school and then home, she thought it over. She was sure this was a major turning point in Grandee's life, but exactly what would come of it, she couldn't guess. She reported the events to Jake, who liked to hear any news about 'his lady', as he called her.

'She never mentioned anything to me about selling the stuff,' was his rather hurt response.

'She didn't know whether it could be done, Jake. She used to have a lot of pals in the art world, but I think the antique furniture business is new to her.'

'But that stuff isn't antique, Libby. It probably isn't worth much.'

'It's rare, *exceptional*, one of its kind. I think it *may* fetch an exceptional price.'

'That's good, because you know, m'dear, I don't think Vivienne really has much money of her own. Seems to me that when she has to pay for anything – like when she goes to that spa of hers – she pays for it with a credit card that Philip provides.'

'You may be right. Lermontis may be going to bring her quite a useful little windfall.'

Mr Lermontis arrived at Ashgrove the next morning in a shining new BMW and carrying a video camera. 'You won't mind, my dear, if I film the collection?' he asked Libby as she showed him in. 'My client is in Moscow, you see, and it would be difficult for him to get away to view the pieces.'

'You must ask Mr Moorfield, Mr Lermontis.'

Philip joined them in the hall, to be introduced and murmur words of welcome. He led the visitor into the drawing-room where Grandee, in soft floral silks and pearls, greeted him graciously. Libby went off to attend to the day's work.

Later Philip and his grandmother took Lermontis out to lunch at a very prestigious restau-

288

rant. As Libby was preparing to leave mid-afternoon, the two returned looking pleased. 'He's gone back to London and he'll transmit the pix to the guy in Moscow. He's going to let us know.'

'Do you think it's going to be a sale?'

'Well, I got the impression that if this Russian doesn't take it, he's got a couple of other possibles.'

'Billionaires?' she teased.

'At least very rich, Libby. Honestly, I gathered that these bits of furniture are going to bring in quite a lot.'

This important matter was superseded by even more important news, at least to Angela Moorfield. She emerged from her bedroom one afternoon about a week later, to grab Libby by the arm as she went by with a load of laundry for the linen cupboard.

'I think I've found my dad!' she announced in a whisper.

Angela staggered as she spoke, so that Libby had to steady her. 'What's happened?' she asked.

'Come and look.'

She went with the girl into the room where the computer screen was showing a handsomely coloured logo heading a display of two or three photographs and some text.

'It's ... I think it's his website.'

A name in capital letters danced across the screen. Behind it three pictures of a house were displayed, a quite handsome two-storey building with balconies at the upper floor and standing in what seemed to be a snowy garden. Printed on its roof were the words *Ma Maison*. The name danced across the screen again and this time Libby was able to read it.

Antoine Nermoneau.

The text of the website proved to be in French. Angela began to read it aloud, pausing to try for a translation. 'If you are interested in ... I don't know what that means but the next thing is skiing ... climbing ... the poems of ... who? Oh, Du Bellay – never heard of him ... Sixteenth-century literature...' She broke off in dismay. 'Good lord!'

Libby was trying to make out the rest. 'He seems to be a professor. Teaches French literature but he's trying to explain that he's a bit of an outdoors man too, that's why he's put in the skiing and climbing. Scroll on a bit, Angela, let's see what else. Look – more about *Ma Maison*.'

'*Elle se trouve* – it's situated – oh! Oh, good heavens! Montreal? Montreal? In Canada?'

The text was quite lengthy so it took them more than thirty minutes to get through it, pausing to consult each other about their translation. Their schoolgirl French fell somewhat short, but they were able to make out that Antoine Nermoneau was an intelligent, good-humoured man who, they thought, lived alone 'but often has friends at his home for an evening of wine and conversation'.

There was a photograph, but only head and shoulders, showing the head covered with a bright red-and-white knitted cap while the face was largely obscured by snow goggles. Clearly Antoine Nermoneau was no fool; he wanted to be friendly but didn't want to disclose too much of himself on first acquaintance.

There were links to other pages. Click 'Skiing' if you want to know more about that; click *'Nouvel Age'* if that is your interest.

'Well, that's the end of that,' sighed Angela. 'I don't ski, I know nothing about French literature, and if he is my dad, I can't talk to him because my French isn't good enough.'

'But, Angela, he's Canadian. He must be able to speak English, don't you think?'

'Oh, but Montreal – that's the pro-French part, isn't it? I bet he doesn't speak anything but French.'

'But if he *is* the man from the Rhodes group, surely he must speak English. Well, you know, your mother never mentioned anything about language differences.'

'Oh, it's probably not him anyway.'

'How did you get the link to this web page?'

'I was in a chat room all about life-coaching and chakras and the Golden Way and stuff, and I'd asked if anyone had ever been under the nickname Apollo. And this guy came in with an answer that he'd used it once, and gave the website. And then you know, *Nouvel Age* – that means New Age and all that hoo-ha.' She clicked back to the opening page, where the name danced across the screen. 'Antoine,' she mused. 'It's the right name.'

'Why don't you ask your mother if *her* Antoine spoke English?'

'Oh, I ... I don't like to.'

'But you're getting on better with her now,

aren't you? At least, I thought you were.'

'Yes, I've sort of got to understand her a bit more, I suppose.'

'Ask her.'

'And if he speaks English, what good will that do? I can't talk to him about his karma or anything like that.'

'But you don't want to talk about his karma. You want to talk about a seminar on a Greek island nineteen years ago.'

'Yes, that's true...'

'Ask her, and if that takes you one step further, try the next.'

'You mean, click one of the links? And try giving a message in English? You mean like, "I've never learned to ski but were you at this stupid conference about the tarot?"'

'Now, now, don't get angry about it. He's interested enough in New Age matters to be in the chat room but he doesn't make a big thing of it.'

But Angela was in retreat now. 'No, I've had years of that with Mama. I don't think I want to go any further, Libby, and then find he's got a beard and wears sandals.'

She blanked out the screen. Libby took that as dismissal, and left. Later it occurred to her that for all her protestations, Angela had switched off only the screen. She hadn't switched off the computer. Well, Angela will come to her own decisions, she said to herself.

Libby didn't come regularly to Ashgrove these days. Fewer occupants meant less clearing-up, which Britta had learned to deal with. Jake was there often enough to correct any mistakes she might make. But there was to be a video link on Saturday from Tokyo.

Philip said, 'I know you'll want to hear the news. Are you planning on being at the house?'

'Well, no, I was going to do something with Freddie...'

'What, exactly?'

'Oh, I don't know – there's a football match he's rather interested in—'

'Are you interested in football, sweetheart?'

'No, I'm afraid not.'

'Then let me suggest something else. Why don't you bring Freddie to Ashgrove?'

'But he's not interested in Brenton or Prim–'

'No, no, I wasn't planning on dragging him into the link-up. I thought he might like to inspect the family cars.'

'The family cars!' She giggled.

'You can laugh, but we do have several. There's mine, which he's keen on, and there's Mama's which has been painted up, you know, with some Eastern symbols and things. And there's Angela's, which I admit is an old clunker, and then there's Brent's abandoned pick-up.'

'But you couldn't just let him loose...'

'I thought perhaps Jake could keep an eye on him, talk to him about the vehicles. He's been a driver for a good many years, probably knows a bit about the various models.'

'But it's a lot to ask, giving up his Saturday...'

Philip grinned. There was a touch of kind-hearted mischief in his expression. 'Well now ...

293

Grandee wants to try to get to know Jackie a bit better so she wants to be in my office when the link is opened up. I think Jake could be tempted by the offer of a glass or two of wine with us all afterwards.'

She shook her head at him in some vexation. 'Do you think you should be encouraging that?'

'Why not?'

'Because there's no future in it! Grandee may feel like leaning on him for the present, but do you really think she wants him as a long-term friend?'

She was voicing a concern that had been growing in the last few weeks, and he quickly changed his manner. He met her reproach with the seriousness it deserved. 'Libby, I don't claim to know how Grandee's mind works. She's been an enigma to all of us for years. But that was when she was all locked up in her obsession to remain an artistic icon. Don't you feel that she's changed?'

'We-ell...'

'This plan to sell the Aggerton furnishings – the old Grandee who used to want to cling on to her former glory would never even have thought of that.'

'I suppose that's true...'

'And if Jake is prepared to take things as they happen...'

'But I don't want him hurt! I don't think you understand – to him she's his fairy-tale princess.'

He gave a little frown. 'He's been around in the world a lot longer than you have, Libby. He doesn't need protecting.'

'Oh. You mean I'm interfering?'

'No, I think you're perfect,' he said, and the moment of discord passed.

Jake was delighted to take on the role of guide around the Ashgrove garage. Freddie was in seventh heaven at the idea of seeing more of the Audi, and perhaps being allowed to sit in its driving seat and in the driving seat of other cars, under the watchful eye of his old friend.

The video link took place at ten o'clock in the evening Tokyo time, early afternoon in Surrey. Philip's office seemed crowded. Libby stood just inside the room; the others were seated for the best view of the computer screen.

A family group came into view. Prim was there sitting on her mother's lap but so sleepy that her eyelids were drooping shut. Jackie said, 'She told me she wanted to send love to everybody. Didn't you, Primmie?'

'Yes,' came the drowsy murmur.

'We recorded a bit from Prim earlier and we'll send that later,' Brenton said. He seemed changed by his new career and perhaps by the start of a real family life. He was alert, head up, in a shirt and tie and with a good haircut.

There were questions and answers about settling in Tokyo. It was a great change – they were living in a flat not far from the business centre, no garden, no lawn, no swing hanging from a cedar tree. But the connection with the pop group was proving successful, contracts had been signed, the first issue of the *manga* publication was due to be come out in six weeks' time. 'It's so challenging!' Brenton reported with an enthusiasm that rang in his voice like a bell.

'Prim's going to a nursery school for children of foreign business executives,' Jackie said, then added rather boastfully, 'She's picking up Japanese ever so easily.'

It seemed to be over very quickly although everybody had had a list of questions ready to ask – even Grandee, whose presence at first took Brenton and his wife by surprise. Libby knew Philip had been keeping his brother informed of the events at Ashgrove, yet to have Grandee speaking to them without disdain was probably a new experience.

Libby never had a chance to ask any questions. But the sight of the toddler happily asleep in the arms of her mother was all she needed. She might still regret losing contact with the child, but she knew she needn't worry about her. The ties of affection that for a time had bound her to Prim were loosening.

Later, they assembled in the dining room for wine and canapés. Libby was intrigued to note that nothing had been ordered from caterers; the temporary cook Celia had prepared it all yesterday evening. Freddie found them too spicy but was comforted with a large helping of ice cream.

Somewhere around five, when the gathering was about to disperse, Angela drew Libby aside.

'I did what you suggested – you know? About speaking to Mama so as to find out if Antoine Nermoneau ... if he spoke English. Goodness, I don't know why I made such a song and dance about it. She was quite OK when I brought it up.'

'And he does speak English?'

'Of course he does! And I've been having chats with him by instant messaging. And ... and ... Libby, I've got his phone number in Montreal and *I'm going to call him*!'

Nineteen

Now that the holiday season was ending, staff were returning to Housecare Helpers. Students who had been temporary employees began to think they should be looking for digs for the coming year, and said goodbye. Families who had spent the summer abroad were now telephoning to say they'd be back in a week and could Housecare please open up their houses and make sure they were aired and ready?

The football season was in full swing. Philip took Libby and her son to a local match and was invited in for supper when they got back to her flat. After Freddie had gone to bed, they had a chance to talk – a thing impossible in the hubbub of the local team's supporters.

Philip had been abroad in the preceding week. Libby had been busy organizing the work schedules so had not been at Ashgrove for some days. There was catching up to do.

297

'So what do you think has happened?' he began.

'About what?'

'Grandee's furniture. Your pal Lermontis arranged a very profitable sale of that Aggerton stuff.'

'Good work. How profitable?'

'Have a guess.'

'Ah...' She had really no idea. 'Fifteen hundred? A couple of thousand?'

'More,' he urged, hiding a smile.

'Well then, twenty-five hundred?'

'Put another nought on the end of that.'

'What?'

'The Russian tycoon paid twenty-five thousand for it.'

'You're joking!'

'No, I mean it. He got into a duel with some other money man and seems to have been determined not to be a loser. Of course Lermontis has to get his commission, but it's a very handy sum.'

'I should say so!' Libby was truly astonished. 'Do you think it's worth that much?'

'I've no idea. But Grandee is quite shaken by the result.'

'Shaken? In what way?'

'In a good way. She's turned quite talkative and seems to be making plans. For instance, she had Angela empty her wardrobe and dressing table so the furniture could be taken away. Asked Angela, it's unheard of! Did you know?'

'No, I haven't been to Ashgrove for about ten days, Philip.'

'Well, she's selling her clothes...'

'What?'

'Most of them are pretty out of date, I suppose. But they were made by great dressmakers so Angela's helping her to sell them on the Internet and it seems to be going great guns. She had herself driven into London last Thursday – I saw a programme for a fashion show lying about. So it looks like a new outlook on life, and a new wardrobe.'

Libby was laughing at the news, but she felt an unexpected sympathy with Grandee. 'That's great, isn't it? She's not so young any more yet she's ... I don't know ... it's as if she's making a new start.'

'Looks like it. I'll tell you something, the whole house seems different these days. There's quite an atmosphere of enthusiasm. Look at the idea of Angela actually helping Grandee to do something on the Internet – that would never have happened a few months ago.'

'Oh, well, Angela has a project of her own that keeps her involved, I think.'

'Could be. She's certainly not the moody lazy-bones she used to be. Mind you, Grandee's paying her for her help but that's only fair.'

'And your mother? Is she sharing in all the activities?'

He grinned. 'In her own way, I suppose she is. She's consulting the I Ching quite a lot these days but she always has a tendency to do that when she's puzzled by the world around her.'

After a time they let the changes at Ashgrove slip from their minds, and turned instead to their own feelings. Libby had long ago admitted to herself that she was deeply in love. When she was in her lover's arms she felt that she needed nothing more. Yet when, in the early hours, Philip was preparing to leave, she felt a little pang of misery. How long must they go on snatching precious hours in secret?

There were two obstacles. The first seemed to be crumbling: perhaps Grandee no longer looked down on her as a lowly handmaid. Yet there was always her son to think of. She had no idea whether he would be happy if there was a permanent partner in her life. She was afraid to broach the subject with Freddie, and was ashamed of herself for being such a coward.

The office held her attention for the next couple of days. The new schedules were working well so she caught up with her paperwork. At the end of the month the pay cheques went out, thus lifting her staff and giving her a sense of satisfaction.

A satisfaction soon to be disturbed.

Jake lingered on after the usual Friday get-together at the end of the day's work.

'There's something I'd like to tell you, Libby dear.'

'Yes?' She studied him. His usually cheerful manner seemed somewhat dimmed.

'I ... er ... want to hand in my notice.'

She simply stared at him.

'A month's notice, maidie, as per contract.'

'Jake!'

'So I'll be leaving end of October.'

'No, no! Jake, why? Have I offended you in

some way?'

'Of course not, Libby. You and I are good friends and always will be.'

'Then, why? You're not retiring, are you?'

'Never. No, while there's life in me body, there'll be living to do.' He was smiling now, so that she understood there was no breakdown in their relationship. She drew in a breath, waiting for his explanation. 'The fact is, my jewel, I'm going round the world.'

That made sense. Footloose and fancy free – he had always been his own master.

'You're going back to sea?'

'Well, for the first part of the trip, yes, I'll be on a ship. To New York. Then, you know, we'll stay a while and then think what we want to do next.'

'We?'

'Vivienne and me.'

For a second time she was too taken aback to speak. Jake was smiling broadly now, delighted at having given her such a surprise. 'Yes,' he said, 'me and my princess. We're going off to see the world.'

'Good Lord.'

'Vivienne got all this money for the furniture, you see, and it's brought her her freedom. She's been dependent on her sons for her upkeep for quite a few years now – she admits it was her own fault, that she threw away all the money her husband left her. But now she's got a bit of her own, and we've decided to put together what we've got and take off.'

'But that's ... It's brave but quite risky, Jake.

301

How long are you going to be away?'

'Who knows? Might be a year. We'll see how it goes. Don't you worry about us, me dove; I'm a jack of all trades. I can always earn us a bob or two if the funds run out. And if we get tired of wandering, we can always come home.'

'Well, this is ... I don't know what to say ... Of course I wish you all the best, Jake, you know that. It's just such a ... such a shock. What shall I do without you?'

'No problem. It's still a month to go – I'll find you a replacement in that time.'

She wanted to cry out, 'I don't want a replacement!' But that would be childish. She had to accept that Jake, although she thought of him as practically one of her family, was a single man with his own ambitions and desires. 'Has Grandee told the family?' she asked instead.

'Not yet. She's taking them out to dinner this evening to tell them the news.'

It seemed to her that a restaurant wasn't the right place for earth-shattering news like this, but once again, she had no right to criticize. 'So it's off into the wide blue yonder, then. When do you actually sail?'

'Soon.' Jake rubbed his hands together. 'I must say, it's kind of nice being partners to a woman like Viv. She's full of surprises.'

'Surprises? So was it her idea to go off gallivanting round the world?'

'Absolutely. Mind you, I backed it up the minute she mentioned it. That's what she needs – to get away from everything that reminds her of cooping herself up so long like a hermit.'

They chatted for a while longer then it was time for Libby to think of preparing supper for Freddie. Jake took his leave. As she peeled vegetables and got out saucepans, Libby found herself smiling. She was wondering if Jake called Grandee 'Viv' when they were face to face – and if so, how Grandee reacted.

Just as Libby was preparing for bed, Philip rang. 'I gather you've heard the news,' he remarked.

'Yes, at about seven o'clock. I wonder all the clocks in Surrey didn't stop for a second or two at the announcement.'

'Amazing.' She heard him sigh. 'It's great, really. I have to keep telling myself that. She's not travelled for years and years – she used to be invited here and there, to give little talks, stuff like that. But for some reason she gave that up, and I can hardly remember her away from home for more than a day or two – and then it was generally to some spa or beauty clinic in a stately home not too far off.'

'Jake told me you were being taken out to dinner. How did it go?'

'Oh, I bet you can guess how my mother reacted.'

'She burst into tears?'

'Right. Angela took it as some sort of joke at first but after a bit she ... well, she surprised me; she was quite supportive.'

'But you've all accepted the fact, I take it. She's really going away.'

'It's what she wants to do, and if she wants to go with Jake, well, that's the way it is.'

'What is she doing about the house?'

'Nothing. When I brought it up she just said that Angela and Mama and I could live here as usual. She's not thinking of selling it or anything like that, she says. So I suppose she envisages living here again at some point.'

'What, with Jake?'

'Who knows?'

'She might change her mind about going,' Libby ventured. 'After all, it's still a month away.'

'I don't think so. Grandee has never been one to change her mind once it's made up. And besides, they've booked their passage and paid for it – some slight reduction in the fare if you book in advance...' He gave a muted chuckle. 'That's Jake's influence. I don't think Grandee has ever thought about getting a reduced rate for anything, until now.'

They talked it over for some time but the conclusion seemed to be that Grandee and Jake really were going to set off together on a leisurely trip round the world.

'You sound exhausted, love,' she said as they made their farewells.

'I've had more relaxing evenings,' he agreed. 'What I'd like most in the world at this moment is just to be with you, but honestly I think I'd fall asleep at the wheel if I tried to drive.'

'So goodnight, and sleep well.'

'Goodnight.'

The staff of Housecare Helpers were as astonished as Libby when they heard the news. At first

304

they found it almost impossible to get used to, and then after a few days there was a tendency to tease Jake. He, however, accepted it all with his usual good humour, so that in the end it became a matter of fact. And their chief anxiety was about the replacement for Jake: it must be someone who had his abilities and friendly outlook.

Now that Ashgrove was no longer regarded as a sort of punishment area, Libby had been sending various members of her staff, going only about once a week to check that the work was being done well. On one of her visits she found Angela sitting on the drawing-room sofa, as so often before, and with her iPod in action.

As Libby came in, she took out the earpieces. 'Hello, haven't seen you for a while. What do you think of the great adventure?'

'You mean Grandee and Jake?'

'What else? My word, you should have seen us when she gave us the news! Everybody else in that restaurant thought we'd gone crazy.'

'I imagine it was a tremendous shock...'

'Poor old Mama! I had to take her off to the cloakroom in the end, so she could splash cold water on her face and calm down.'

Libby smiled and shook her head. 'It's hard to know why she was so upset. Grandee's never been exactly kind to her, as far as I recall.'

'True, true. But then you see Mama thought we were going to be turned out of house and home, and that shop of hers doesn't bring in much so renting somewhere in this area could have been really dreary.'

'But that wasn't the plan, it seems. You're

being left in your usual quarters.'

Angela shrugged. 'Well, you never know,' she said, and picked up her headset.

From the little gadgets was coming, not loud music by some heavy metal band as Libby had thought, but a voice speaking rather quietly. Seeing her surprise, Angela coloured a little and muttered: 'French conversation lessons,' she explained.

'Aha!'

'It's not so "aha"; I'm not as good as I thought I'd be.'

'But this is so you can chat to your father?'

'So far we have to stick to English. I feel such a numbskull. There he is, messaging in chatty English to me, and I'm still having trouble understanding what's on this tape.' She held one of the earpieces towards Libby.

From it emerged words that sounded like a couple of lines from a poem. Libby remembered them from her school days, about a grasshopper and ant. She smiled. 'Stick at it, chum. Soon you'll be speaking the language like a native. At least using email you can have a think before you reply.' She paused. 'You said a while ago that you had his number. Do you speak on the telephone often?'

'No,' said Angela after a hesitation, 'because, you see, the time difference makes it difficult.'

'But that time when you told me you'd got his number – how did it go?'

'Er ... we talked a bit. But he was sort of guarded, and I felt a fool.'

Libby understood at once that Angela hadn't

been able to broach the fateful subject. *I think you're my father*. It was a hurdle too high for her.

'So, how do matters actually stand? You mentioned to him about your mother being at the discussion group?'

'I sort of did. I mentioned ... I asked if he remembered Lydia.'

'And did he?'

'Yes, but...'

'What?'

'He thought I was Lydia.'

Libby was speechless.

'Right. You think I'm an idiot,' Angela groaned. 'And I am. I should have said at once that I was Lydia's daughter. But I ... I couldn't get the words out.'

So that was why Angela had made no more telephone calls. How could she have responded if, by any chance, he began to speak about the night he and her mother had spent together?

Understandably, she was reluctant to telephone and embark on this awkward explanation. And it was something she probably felt she couldn't deal with in an email.

Libby sat down beside her on the sofa. For a long moment there was silence between them. Then she said, 'Angela, you *do* think he's your father?'

'Yes, I do. And Mama says she thinks he really is her Antoine.'

'Do you want to sort it out and let him know?'

'I do,' Angela sighed. 'Even if it scares him off, even if we never exchange another word on the phone or by email, I want him to know I'm his daughter.'

'Do you know what I would do in your place?' Libby ventured.

'What?'

'I'd write him a letter.'

'But I've only got his phone number, Libby. I haven't got his address.'

'Ring the nearest big library and ask if they've got a phone book for Montreal. Then go and look him up.'

'What? Trawl through pages and pages looking for the number to find out where he lives?'

'Angela! You've got his *name*.'

'Oh. Oh! Of course! Honestly, I think my brain's turned to mush with all that's been going on.' Excitement made her eyes sparkle. But then her expression changed to uncertainty. 'What if he's got an unlisted number?'

'He's a professor of philosophy. When I was at university my tutor was in the phone book, so that any of us could ring him if we needed help with our work. But if Antoine *is* unlisted, you could try writing to him at the university.'

Angela threw her arms around her. 'You are really bright,' she cried.

'Yeah, yeah,' Libby said, disentangling herself. 'You'll get his address, and you'll write to him – agreed?'

'Well, yes, I will.'

'A handwritten letter,' commanded Libby.

'What? My handwriting's terrible.'

'Practise,' Libby commanded, and got to her feet.

'OK, teacher,' Angela said with a giggle.

It was great to see this once listless, unambitious girl setting her mind to something. She went off to inspect the upstairs rooms smiling to herself.

All too soon the day came when Grandee and Jake were to set sail for New York. The rest of the family went to Southampton to see them off, but although Philip invited her, Libby decided not to go. She had a feeling that Grandee would think it intrusive. She had made this explanation to Jake and said her goodbyes the previous evening.

'Ah, you misjudge her, me dear,' he said. 'She's put all those petty ways behind her now.'

'I'm sure you're right. But just in case it would somehow jar on her...'

'Then this is our leave-taking, eh? Well then!' And he took her in a bear-like hug and kissed her. '"It's farewell and adieu to you", as the song goes, and I must tell you, my jewel, that in all my life, I never had a better boss than you, Libby Fletcher.'

She was too close to tears to say much. 'Don't forget to send postcards,' she murmured. And then he was gone, a mainstay of her business and of her life for the past four years.

'The departure was a weird experience,' Philip told her the next day. 'But I must say they looked a happy couple and ... I don't know ... completely ready for this big change in their lives.'

'How did it go with Angela and your mother?'

'No tears, thank heaven.'

Libby pushed some papers about on her desk,

bending her head so as not to let him see she was miserable at losing Jake.

They were in her office. It was mid-morning, and Philip was sitting across from her in the chair generally used by someone being interviewed for a job.

She heard him get up. Next moment he was pulling her to her feet and holding her close. 'Poor love,' he soothed. 'I know he was important to you – and Freddie too.'

She began to cry. 'Freddie's heartbroken,' she mourned. 'This morning he didn't want to go to school. He said ... he said he wished he could have sailed away with Jake.'

'But he didn't really mean it, sweetheart. He'll get over it. Don't be unhappy, Libby. Everything's going to be all right.

And so she found some comfort, in the shelter of his arms.

Twenty

Before she knew it half-term had come around. It seemed to Libby that the children had only been back at school ten minutes, yet now once again there was the problem of being free to keep Freddie active and happy.

To her astonishment, Philip suggested a solution for at least one day. 'How about if I take him to Portsmouth to see the *Mary Rose*?'

This surprised her, and she hesitated.

Philip tried to persuade her. 'He's dead keen on anything to do with the sea and ships, and although I agree there's not much of the *Mary Rose* to look at, there's a lot of history attached.'

'But – but – you're not much interested in ships, are you? Would you enjoy doing that?'

'Absolutely. We could go in the Audi – he'd like that. And we could take some of the minor roads and perhaps stop off somewhere for lunch – chicken in a basket, that kind of thing.'

He'd clearly given it some thought. Libby was extraordinarily pleased. It remained to be seen whether Freddie would agree to it, however, but after a moment's bafflement at the offer, enthusiasm flared up.

'I've wanted to go there for a long time. Do you know that the ship was built for King Henry VIII? The horrid one with all the wives?'

'You never mentioned you wanted to go there,' his mother objected.

'Well, it's not so easy if you were to take me because you always have to have your mobile on in case anything goes wrong with one of the house-cleaning jobs.' He gave her a fierce frown. 'Remember the time we had to come back from Guildford Fair because Amy had fused somebody's electric lights?'

She tried to look suitably apologetic. 'Sorry, sorry. OK then, you think you'd like to go to see this smashed up old ship?'

'It's a famous ship! And it's only smashed up because the waves had been rolling her about for years and years after she was sunk in battle.'

'But she's worth seeing, all the same?'

'Yes, she is!' Freddie looked in entreaty at Philip. 'Tell her it's a good idea, Phil.'

'It's a good idea, Libby. Word of honour.'

'All right then, I agree. But Freddie has to promise he won't ask for two helpings of desserts when you have lunch.'

When the two returned from their outing, there wasn't a doubt it had been a successful day. When her son was delivered back home to her, he was wearing a *Mary Rose* T-shirt and beaming with delight.

'I've got a pop-up book, Mum – look, you pull the tabs and you see the *Mary Rose* as she was when she was launched.'

'Oh, that looks fragile. You'd better put it somewhere safe, love.'

'I'll make a space for it on my bookshelf. Don't you dust it!' he warned. 'You might damage it.'

'I promise.' When he'd raced out of the office with the precious paper model held open in both hands, Libby thanked Philip for the outing.

'We were going to go there ourselves some day,' she sighed. 'But you know how it is, I kept putting it off.'

'Perhaps there are other places we could go, together,' he suggested. 'We ought to look at our calendars and see what we can plan.'

'But it seems a lot to ... Did you really find it enjoyable?'

'Certainly did. He's a great lad. Oh, and by the way – he doesn't want to be called Freddie any more. He feels it's too childish now he's seven.'

'I beg your pardon?'

'He says he'd prefer Fred. What do you think?'

She was taken aback. 'He never mentioned any of this to me!' she protested. 'How come you're the first to hear of it?'

'Well, he didn't want to hurt your feelings. So I'm designated as the messenger. He says if you don't like Fred, he'd put up with Frederick, but he thinks that sounds bossy.'

Libby found herself beginning to grin. 'Frederick? That's his name, but you know – I've never used it.'

'I wanted to change my name at one point,' said Philip. 'I think I was about fourteen. There was a South African rugby player I admired, so I wanted to be called Aaron.'

'That didn't catch on, it seems.'

'No, but Fred isn't bad. I've been using it since lunch.'

'So I suppose I ought to try Fred.' She tried it over. '"Fred, do your homework".' She went to the office door and called upstairs, 'Fred, your supper will be ready in half an hour.'

There was a silence, and then a scampering on the stairs as the new-styled Fred came down. 'You don't mind, then?' he asked nervously.

'We'll give it a try. Mind you, I might decide I'd like to be called Mary Poppins.'

Amid laughter Philip said his farewells. Later, when the newly named Fred was sitting down to his evening meal, he announced, 'I'm going to save up and give Phil a present.'

'You are? Why's that?'

'Just as a thank-you for today. It was really

313

great, Mum. I think I'll buy him a magazine. You know he goes all over, looking at places to do filming, so I thought a magazine about scenery or something.'

'A travel magazine.'

'Are they expensive?'

'We'll have a look next time we're in town.'

When she thought it over, she was deeply pleased. Perhaps something might come of all this.

On Saturday she went to take a look at Ashgrove, to plan for some changes as winter approached. The central heating ought to be checked and heavier curtains needed to be hung. She took Fred with her. If Jake had still been on her staff, she could have counted on him to take charge of her son, but the replacement, Norman, was still too much of an unknown quantity.

Her idea had been that the boy could play in the garden, but it was a dull, drizzly day so he had to stay indoors. Having watched some television and looked at some of the old books in the bookcases, he became restless.

'Could I use the computer in Phil's office, Mum?'

'Certainly not.'

'Well, can I use your laptop?'

'You know quite well that I can't let you use that, pickle.'

'Well, what *can* I do?'

She was wondering if she could introduce him to the marvels of dusting, which had worked so well for Prim, but then had a better idea. 'I have to go up to the attic to look for some winter curtains,' she said. 'There's lots of old trunks and boxes up there. How would you like to take a look at what's in them?'

At first this was too much of a puzzle to him. All his short life he'd lived in a flat, so he was unacquainted with the idea of attics. But he went upstairs with her and followed her into the dim light of the old store room. There he paused and gazed around in awe.

'Gee! What a great place!' He hurried to a big old-fashioned leather trunk with a hooped lid, like an illustration for a treasure trove. 'Can I open this?'

'Yes, but if it's clothes or linen, don't pull things out. There are boxes and crates full of stuff but I don't know what's in them – and some things might have moth balls and things, and there might be heirlooms and delicate stuff such as lace. So take care.'

He tried the lid of the trunk, expecting it to be locked, but it opened. 'Toys!' he cried. Cautiously he lifted out a wooden model of a Ford motorcar, painted red and gold but worn and somewhat battered. 'Can I play with this, Mum?'

'How do you mean? It hasn't got a battery or anything, Fred.'

'No, just run it along – see if the wheels work. And look, there's a tram. Can I set them out, Mum? Please?'

'All right. But no rough stuff. And you'll have to put everything back where you found it.'

She watched him for a few minutes as he brought out three old-fashioned painted models of transport from the Twenties. Satisfied that he would do them no damage, she set to work to find suitable curtains for all the windows at Ashgrove.

It took some time, since lengths varied from window to window. As she laid the last set aside to be carried downstairs, she was aware that her son had become very quiet. This was always a sign that she needed to investigate. She looked around.

In the far corner of the attic, Fred was astride an old dappled rocking-horse and was gently swaying back and forth in blissful rhythm.

She made her way through the boxes to stand close by and watch. After a few moments he became aware of her. He smiled. Taking one hand from the horse's mane, he exclaimed, 'Isn't he great? I think he's called Trojan. He was prob'ly ridden by a guardsman in the Queen's coronation. I'm riding to Greenwich to see the *Cutty Sark* and then he'll need a rest and some hay.' He paused. 'Or does he have oats?' He leaned forward to speak into the ear of the rocking-horse. 'Do you eat hay, Trojan? I expect you like apples; I've fed apples to ponies and donkeys at the children's zoo.'

'He's lovely,' Libby agreed. 'I think he's very old. Perhaps as old as a hundred.'

'A hundred?'

'He might have been made about 1900. His mane is real horsehair and the reins look something special, perhaps adopted from a style from abroad – you see the embossed decoration?'

'That's because he's a special horse. I expect

he belonged to Phil's grandfather or somebody.'

'Could be – although I don't think Philip's family would have lived here when Trojan was made. He probably just came with the house.'

'He shouldn't be stuck in an attic, Mum. Can we take him downstairs?'

'No, no, I'm afraid not. You see, he's not our property.'

'But you're taking the curtains down...'

'That's different. The curtains are needed. Trojan's a toy, and you've got plenty of toys of your own, love.'

'But he's my horse! I found him hidden away under a dust sheet. Finders keepers!'

'Not in this case, Freddie. He belongs in this house and that has to be an end of it.'

'Don't call me Freddie!' her son exclaimed, and stamped his way out of the attic and down the stairs.

Libby was startled by his vehemence. Her first impulse was to hurry after him, but she'd come up for the curtains, so she picked up the pile before making her way down to the hall.

She was a little surprised to find that Freddie wasn't there. When she put her head round the door of the drawing-room and then the dining room, there was no sign of him. Worried now, she made a quick tour of the house but her son was nowhere to be seen.

She began to panic. The episode with Prim came back into her mind. But no ... Freddie wasn't likely to take himself off as a stowaway on someone's narrow boat. Besides, there had been very little traffic on this side branch of the canal for days now that winter was coming.

A last thought made her look in the garage. And there she found her son, standing on a stool he'd dragged from the work bench and about to prise open the locked glass cabinet on the wall which held the keys of the old cars.

'Freddie!'

He turned, his shoulders hunched, his head down, recognizing the tone of her voice. He stood like a penitent on the stool, a screwdriver in one hand, awaiting her wrath.

'Get down this minute. What do you think you're up to?'

He muttered something.

'What did you say?'

He lifted his head a little and said tearfully, 'I wasn't going to drive it. I was just going to sit in it.'

'And who gave you permission to do any such thing?'

The screwdriver fell from his hand. He frowned to prevent his tears from spilling over. He tried for a defiant tone. 'Well it's boring just being here doing nothing and you won't let me do the interesting things—'

'Oh, so you need to be kept entertained? It isn't enough that you have a whole attic full of boxes and trunks to explore, you want to take over someone else's belongings?' She made herself sound indignant, and indeed she was vexed at his behaviour. But perhaps that was because she felt she should have handled the situation with more sympathy in the first place.

'How would you like it if someone went into

318

your room and began to take charge of your things? Got your model ship out of its box and played with it?'

'That's different...'

'How, exactly?'

'Well, my ship is just a little thing—'

'So if you want to play about with something that doesn't belong to you, that's all right, so long as it's big and important?'

'N-no, I didn't mean that...'

'I want you to get down off that stool and come back into the house where I can keep an eye on you.'

He jumped down obediently.

'Pick up the screwdriver and put it back where you found it.'

He obeyed. Tears were beginning to spill down his cheeks. 'I'm sorry,' he blurted. 'I didn't mean it, Mum!' He ran to her, clutching at her apron and hiding his face in it.

She took him into her arms. 'There, there, Freddie – I mean Fred. It's all right. It's all right, now don't cry.' She rocked him to and fro, sorry to have reduced him to tears.

'I'm not crying.'

'I see that. A Fred would never cry.' He peered up at her from waist level and she saw a little smile struggling to emerge.

'N-neither would a Frederick,' he managed to say.

She laughed a little 'You won't remember, but when you were very little I used to call you Freddikins sometimes.'

'No you didn't!' he declared, repentance giving way to indignation. He pulled himself a little away from her so as to deny such a claim.

'Freddikins. And sometimes Freddibubbles.'

'That's *awful*!'

'Yes it is, but nobody was there to hear me – except you, and you didn't seem to mind at the time.'

'I bet I did! I bet you only did it when I was asleep!'

She offered him a tissue from her apron pocket. He wiped his eyes, took her hand, and was led in peace back into the house.

As they came in through the back door, Philip was just driving up at the front of the house. He came into the hall as they reached it, pausing in surprise at the sight of them.

'Hello there, young man! The last time you were here, you had to stay overnight – remember?'

'What? Oh, yes, Prim...' Fred suddenly made the connection between his running off without explanation and his mother's anxiety over the lost little girl.

They were still holding hands. He squeezed hers, looking up in contrition. She smiled back.

'What have you been up to today, then?' Philip asked.

'Oh, just checking things, getting winter curtains down, that kind of stuff,' Libby said.

'Sounds a bit dull. Just let me have a cup of tea and I'll unlock one of the cars for you, Fred.'

'No thank you,' Fred replied, looking down.

'What? Lost your interest in old cars?'

'N-no, but that's not for today,' Fred muttered,

perplexed at how to manage his repentance.

'There must be something we could offer you,' Philip said. 'What about the computer in my office? I haven't got any games but you could get on one of the travel networks—'

'No thanks,' Fred replied.

'Well, come and let's make some tea or something, and we'll probably find some cake in the larder.'

Fred looked at his mother for permission to accept this kindness when he knew he was still in some disgrace. They all went into the kitchen, where Libby made the tea and some orange juice for Fred, while Philip found the cake.

Libby knew he could sense something was wrong. He put himself out to chat to her son, describing little events during his drive home from Durham. By and by it seemed Fred had to mention what was foremost in his mind.

'That's a great rocking-horse upstairs in your attic,' he ventured.

'What? Oh, Pegasus? Good heavens, is he still there? I haven't thought of him in years.'

'His name's Pegasus? I called him Trojan.'

'Why was that? Oh, because he's made of wood – that's rather neat! So how is he, old Peggy?'

'He's ... he's fine, he loves having somebody to ride him.' The little boy hesitated. 'You can't call him Peggy! That's a *girl's* name.'

'Fred!' Libby warned.

'Sorry. I didn't mean that. He's great; he's big and strong even though he's old.'

'You should have brought him down,' Philip

suggested.

'Mum said not to.'

'Oh, well, I don't see why not...'

'He needs a good clean and he's full of worm-holes,' Libby said.

'I suppose he is. Poor old thing. Well, why don't we bring him down and keep him some-where ... the morning-room perhaps?'

'Your mother likes to use that quite often.'

'Well then, the garage? No, I've got it – Brent's old studio! And listen, Libby, you've trained as a furniture restorer, why don't I hire you to restore old Peggy – I mean Pegasus – and when you come to see to his treatment, you can bring Fred and he can have a go on him?'

'Oh!' Fred sighed.

Libby hardly knew what to say. It was as if her little boy were being rewarded for his earlier tantrum. Yet he was so enchanted by Philip's offer, and it was such a good opportunity to get her son acquainted with the house and its inhabitants – and, after all, he had apologized.

So she agreed to the proposition. The idea of restoring the rocking-horse pleased her. She didn't get enough opportunities to practise her chosen craft. If the chance ever occurred that she could actually take up the business of furniture restoration, she needed to keep her hand in.

Fred was determined to get the rocking-horse out of the attic as soon as possible. He persuaded Philip to come upstairs with him and bring it down. It was then carried in something like a procession to Brenton's old studio, where Libby left them cleaning off the dust with a moistened cloth.

She had carried replacement curtains to the separate rooms where they were to be hung on Monday, when she heard Rosanne Moorfield's car drive in and go round to the garage. She came out into the hall as they came in at the back door because she needed to explain about the curtains. She found Rosanne struggling with arms full of fruit and vegetables, with Angela behind her carrying a cardboard folder.

'Hello!' Angela carolled at the sight of her. 'Just the person we want to see!'

Libby paused, holding back her housekeeping information. There was an air of buoyancy and brightness about the two women that let her know something important was in the air.

Rosanne led the way into the kitchen. There she laid her purchases on the table, pulled out a chair, and sat down. She faced Libby with her head slightly thrown back as if to make a serious declaration – but smiling.

'Angela and I have something important to tell you,' she began.

'Yes, and we feel that as you had so much to do with what happened, you deserve to be told even before we break the news to Phil,' Angela interrupted.

'So I was going to telephone you, but it's lovely that you actually happen to be here—'

'Because, what do you know! Mama's selling up the shop!'

This was unexpected, but it scarcely seemed to warrant the glee with which Angela announced it.

'Angela dear,' said her mother, 'that's not important—'

'Yes, it is, but there's more, Libby – a lot more!'

'Angela,' Mrs Moorfield reproved, 'you're not making sense. Let me tell it.'

But Angela wasn't to be stopped. 'The fact is,' she announced, 'we're going to Canada!'

Twenty-One

The folder Angela was carrying landed with a thump on the kitchen table. 'We've been at a travel agent this afternoon, getting brochures and things. We're still doing research on the net for cheap flights. We're hoping to go early in the New Year because of course there's lots of folks wanting to fly around Christmas.' This was announced at breakneck speed, as if in fear of challenge.

'Christmas,' Libby echoed faintly.

'There, sweetheart, you see you've absolutely baffled her,' Rosanne chided. 'Let me explain. We've been talking to Antoine quite a lot over the past couple of months, and things have moved on.'

'They certainly have!' cried her daughter in triumph.

'I wrote to Antoine—'

'You know you told me to write?' Angela interrupted. 'I just couldn't seem to get it right, so in the end I asked Mama for help, and she took over the letter-writing.'

Rosanne blushed. 'It wasn't easy,' she murmured. 'Angela got off on the wrong foot when she telephoned so I had to explain all that. And introduce myself, of course.'

'And what ... what did Antoine say?'

'He was really rather sweet about it. Surprised, of course – he hadn't quite understood why Angie was asking questions about that old seminar.'

'But he took it well,' Angela continued. 'And we've been chatting back and forth both online and on the phone, and the long and the short of it is, he's asked us to go to Montreal and stay with him for a bit.'

'Stay with him? In the house that's on his website?'

'Yes, that's the place.'

'And ... what about Antoine? Has he got a family? What do they think about it?'

'He's divorced,' Angela said. 'He jokes about it but *I* think his wife caught him out with another woman. Anyhow, he's on his own, and he's got a son but he went with his mother so he doesn't see him very often, and he says he's thrilled to find he's got another family to "comfort him in his old age" as he put it.' She laughed. 'He's really quite a lad, isn't he, Mama?'

Rosanne looked uncomfortable at this assessment. 'Well, he's ... he teaches philosophy but he's not at all grave and pompous.'

'So we're going to Montreal and we're thinking of staying about a year or so—'

'A year! What about the formalities – visas, that sort of thing?'

'Antoine is arranging for a student visa for me.'

'Oh-ho! And what are you going to study, if I may ask?' Libby inquired, laughing.

'Catering and the hotel industry,' Angela riposted. 'I think I might try for a job in one of the ski resorts if I get my qualification.'

'My word! You mean, you'll stay on?'

'Why not?'

'That's all rather speculative,' her mother hastened to say. 'But the main point is that we've been invited to stay with her father for as long as we like, and once the travel arrangements are sorted out, we'll be off.'

'And you're selling the shop?'

'In a way. You know I've had part-time assistants from time to time and one of them, Beatrice Holden, has said she'd like to buy me out and keep the shop going.' She sighed and seemed a little reluctant. 'I'd have hated to see it taken over for something horrid, like one of those boutiques selling little glittery things...' Her voice died away. Clearly Rosanne wasn't quite as enthusiastic about this great adventure as her daughter. It seemed a sense of duty had made her decide to go with her, in case it all turned out badly.

But Angela was bubbling over with excitement and pleasure. She went on to recount what Antoine had told them about the house in Montreal, and the cafés, cinemas and bars in the area where they would be living. Libby heard it out with sympathy but felt she ought to leave as soon as she could. Philip, off in Brenton's studio with her son, had no idea of what was looming in his family.

She went to the studio to collect Fred, and said to Philip, 'Your mother and Angela have come home with some news. I think you ought to go and hear it.'

From her tone, he guessed something unusual was in the air. 'What's up?'

'Let's say it's something more important than cleaning up Pegasus.' She beckoned Fred. 'Come along, chick, it's time we were on our way.'

He was a bit unwilling, but set aside his cleaning rag. 'Philip says we can come back tomorrow and do some more work on him.' This was uttered in a questioning tone, asking her approval.

'We'll see.' She took his hand and urged him towards the door. Over her shoulder she said to Philip, 'Ring me if you feel like it.'

'What?'

But she had gone. She had no idea how he was going to take the news and felt the sooner he heard it, the better.

When he rang, late in the evening, he was angry with her. 'You knew about all this?' he challenged.

'Some of it.'

'Why didn't you tell me?'

She waited a moment before replying. 'In the

first place, I didn't know how far things had gone. It was a big surprise to me when I heard this afternoon. In the second place ... Well, if they'd wanted you to know, they'd have told you themselves.'

'I don't understand it! Why did it have to be a secret?'

'I'm not sure. Perhaps because it might be difficult ... I mean to say, Philip, don't you think it's an embarrassing thing to have to explain to your son: "I'm helping Angela to get in touch with the man who was my lover years ago"?'

'No, why should it be? Well, even if it's embarrassing – good lord, I had to be told in the end, so why not bring it out in the open from the start?'

'Because your mother always cries when things get difficult.'

A long pause.

'Did she cry while she was telling you this afternoon?' Libby went on.

'Well...'

'She's always seemed to me very thin-skinned. She has a different way of looking at life, Philip. You must know that yourself, from the way she tried to bring you up – you and Brenton and Angela – trying to start you off in alternative ways of living, trying to avoid the harsher side—'

'And a total mess she made of it,' he broke in. 'Brent made a wreck of his marriage, Angela nearly turned into a drunk, and I couldn't make a go of any relationship until you came along.'

He sounded so dejected that her heart went out

to him completely. 'Sweetheart,' she murmured, 'why are we miles away at the end of a phone line? Why don't you come here and we'll talk?'

But they didn't talk; they found ways to share their feelings without words.

Although Rosanne and her daughter had made decisions, they couldn't be carried out immediately. There was legal business about transferring the shop. Angela took up intensive French lessons with a local tutor. Rosanne had to face the fact that her Eastern garb wouldn't be suitable for Montreal in winter so went shopping for new clothes.

When coming to supervise work at Ashgrove, Libby often found little labels attached to items in their bedrooms, as the two tried to decide what they should take with them. Would they need their own mobiles? Their laptops? Was it worth packing hair-dryers? She smiled as she noticed the labels varied from week to week, especially in Rosanne's room.

'It's such a big decision,' Rosanne confided. 'Antoine has murmured once or twice that we might ... you know ... think of staying on.'

'You mean permanently?'

'Perhaps. I certainly think that Angie ... Well, for her there could be ... if she really takes the catering course, she could get a job and qualify for citizenship.'

'Do you think she wants to do that?'

'Ye-es. At least, I think she wants to make a permanent change of some kind. She was saying a few weeks ago that she feels that she's come to a turning point.'

'And you? Would you stay on?'

'It wouldn't be so easy for me. I haven't any skills to offer, there's no reason why I should get permission to stay.'

'It's not an immediate decision,' Libby soothed, hearing a tremble in Rosanne's voice. 'You can see how things go once you're there.'

Rosanne sighed. 'What I always wanted...'

'Yes?'

'Was to go back to India. There was a guru there whose teachings meant a lot to me.' She paused a moment, recalling those days that had been so formative for her. 'And now that Angie seems to be more on an even keel, I feel that I could, you know, follow my own path again one day.'

'Perhaps you will,' Libby said. She added, with some hesitation, 'Have you talked to Philip about it?'

She shook her head. 'It's all too indefinite in my mind as yet. And, you know, Libby, he was really quite hurt when we told him about Antoine and our plans. I don't want to cause any more upset.'

Libby thought, not for the first time, that she'd never come across a set of people who communicated so little. For years they'd lived together in Ashgrove, but each in their separate compartments – Grandee in her suite with its decor from her days of glory, Brenton in his studio with his electronics and scenic effects, Angela in her world of clubs and bars, and Rosanne seeking nirvana in esoteric religions. Even

330

Philip, she realized, was always out and abroad in the film industry, trying not to notice that his home was a collection of strangers.

There had been no ties of affection between them. When she looked back, she felt she had shown more concern for them than they had themselves.

Christmas was approaching. She couldn't help thinking that it would be a doleful affair at Ashgrove, with only three of them left in the great old house and two of those about to leave soon after the festivities.

When she asked Philip about the family's plans, he shrugged. 'We've never made much of things like that, Libby. Our main effort only amounts to a tree in the hall.'

'How would it be if I brought Fred on Christmas Day to have turkey and mince pies and all that?'

He was delighted. 'What a great idea! We could put presents for him under the tree – unless you'd have done that already at home?'

'Oh yes, but in our flat the tree can only be about two foot high. He'd love to have a second lot of presents under a big tree.'

'And he could have a go on Pegasus. How's the restoration going, by the way?'

'Not very well. I really haven't had all that much time to deal with him. But Fred loves him even with the wormholes and the faded paint.'

Philip's dark features were suddenly lit up by a smile of inspiration. 'Do you think he would like to see some reindeer?'

'Reindeer?'

'In the Highlands. A couple of years ago I found an estate in the mountains where they have reindeer, for an advertising film. We could drive north on Boxing Day, staying overnight somewhere en route. Then when we get to Aviemore, there are good hotels, and he could see real reindeer grazing on the mountainside.'

'That sounds marvellous, Philip. But do you want to be away from home when your mother and Angela will be leaving so soon?'

'Oh, why not! It's not as if we're going to weep tears of grief when we part.'

'Philip!'

He was taken aback at the reproof in her voice. He frowned at her. 'It's no use pretending we're bound by strong ties. We've never been like that, as a family.'

'But you'd want to spend some time together before they go?'

'Would I? They made their plans and they're going – it's got nothing to do with me, has it?'

'Yes it has. Come on now, you'd regret it if you didn't give them a farewell party and a hug and a kiss at the airport.'

He shook his head at her. 'We don't do things like that.'

'Well, you should. You really should, Philip.'

Because he was still frowning, she said no more. She gave her attention to the preparations for Christmas Day, which turned out to be a raging success. There were presents for everyone under the tree, among them the travel magazine that Fred had bought for Philip, rolled and then wrapped in holly-printed paper.

'My word, that's exactly what I needed,' Philip said when he unwrapped it.

'Really? It's about the Bahamas, where my grandad lives.'

'Well, funnily enough, I was thinking of going there one day.'

'I'll show you the best picture,' Fred declared, taking the magazine from its recipient and riffling through it, while his mother hid a smile. 'Look, you see all those little sails in the distance? Well, those are yachts heading into the harbour where Grandad works. Isn't that super?'

'Absolutely.' They sat down together on the sofa, so that Fred could instruct Philip about all the wonders he'd already noticed in the magazine. But the little boy was soon tempted away to try on his knight's outfit.

Rosanne sighed with pleasure as he racketed around the drawing-room wearing a set of plastic armour and waving a plastic sword.

'It's so lovely to have a child in the house again,' she murmured. 'Last year, of course, Prim was still here. But she was never as lively as Fred.'

'Have you heard from Prim?' Libby inquired.

'Oh yes, we saw photographs on the Internet. And we spoke on the telephone. Lots of lovely toys, she said. I sent her a model of Muffin the Mule – do you see that nowadays at all? We used to watch that together on some nostalgia channel and she used to love it...' Her eyes grew misty with tears.

Angela departed from her world of cool, to fight a mock duel with Fred, using a walking stick as a weapon. Libby watched them with amusement, and saw Philip was watching too. She crossed the room to sit beside him.

'She would never have done that a year ago,' she remarked.

'No ... She's changed.'

'It's the idea of having a dad that makes the difference.'

He gave her a silent glance, his expression uncertain.

'You don't think so?'

'I don't know. I'm just beginning to realize that I never really got to know Angela.' He was shaking his head at his memories. 'When she was born, I was at boarding school, studying for A-levels, determined to get into university. I was a bit ... well, I don't quite know how to express it. Offended, I think.'

'That your mother was having a baby?'

'Yes, and that there was no father around. But then I'd have hated it if there had been a father around.' He stifled a sigh. 'I think I was a crazy mixed-up kid.'

'Can't argue with that.'

'Oh, thanks a lot.'

'But you're not a kid now, Philip.'

'Meaning I should start to feel brotherly love? That's not going to happen.'

'Well, she'll be gone in a few weeks.' She touched him on the arm. 'So will your mother.' She didn't add that it was likely Rosanne might go off to lose herself in some ashram in the Himalayas.

'Hmm,' was all he said.

But it was time for Christmas cake and tea. Then it was home and bedtime for an exhausted little boy. All the same, he was up at six the next morning, eager to start the journey towards the reindeer – in which he only partly believed.

The five-day trip to the Scottish Highlands was an extraordinary contrast to the Christmas fever they left behind them. The shoulders of the mountains wore capes of snow, and the pine trees seemed almost black against them until the sun touched their branches. Led by a friendly guide, they found the reindeer herd quite easily.

'Oh gee,' whispered Fred when he saw the grey-brown creatures moving gently among the tussocks of frosty grass. 'Oh, wait till I do show-and-tell about *this*!'

His digital camera was always at the ready. Libby thought he'd taken enough pictures to fill a dozen albums.

She too had had a magical time. To be with Philip in these surroundings was like something out of a dream. And, what was more, a bond was growing between her son and the man she loved. Fred turned to Philip naturally when he needed help steadying his camera; he expected him to know the answers to any of his questions about the mountains, the streams, the stones that told of houses long since abandoned, the history of the land.

The funicular railway was one of his greatest delights. He asked to board the bright blue rail carriage each day of their stay. Gazing out of the window as the track took them up by an eight-mile route into the mountains, he watched skiers making the most of the light, early snow. 'Can we do that?' he begged.

'You have to take lessons, I'm afraid. And we're not going to be here long enough for lessons.'

'Well, let's stay longer.'

Philip looked to Libby for help. She said, 'We have to get back for Oliver's party, remember?'

'Oh, that...'

'You've bought the present you're taking and he's looking forward to that. You can't let him down, Fred.'

'I suppose not.' He sounded quite reluctant.

'And I've got work waiting for me, you know,' Philip added. 'Can't spend all my time herding reindeer or gallivanting up mountain railways.'

Fred frowned, but clearly saw he ought not to argue. And of course, there was always the pleasure of being driven in the Audi on the long trip home. He was taking pictures and saving up stories to make all his classmates jealous.

The office of Housecare Helpers seemed small and constricted after the great spaces of the mountains. Libby expected dozens of tasks to await her after the festive season, and found them – accidents with wine or food at parties, dirt tracked in during days of winter rain, and a fallen tree in the garden of one of her clients. She had only a small workforce available until January came, but they were already hard at work making houses ready for New Year celebrations.

Philip had gone on a location trip to Barcelona. In the aftermath of New Year, Fred was handed over to the care of other parents for children's parties, visits to pantomimes and excursions to exciting places such as the Natural History Museum and the site of the Battle of Hastings. Then it was back to school.

The day came for Angela and Rosanne's departure. Libby was at the house to help them finish packing and wait for their taxi. She found that Philip was nowhere to be seen – he was still in Spain, having trouble with a local authority over filming schedules, or at least so he said. She sighed inwardly. Resentment was keeping him from saying goodbye, and she felt it was something he would come to regret.

'He's busy,' Rosanne sighed. 'Business before pleasure, you know.' But her voice trembled as she said it.

The taxi arrived. Libby helped bring their suitcases out to the drive for the driver to load them. It was a late morning of dull, grey weather, and Angela was shivering in an unsuitably flimsy dress. She saw Libby's worried glance and said with a grin, 'It's OK, I've got a big quilted jacket in my travel bag.' And with that, to Libby's surprise, she gave her a hearty hug.

Rosanne, too, embraced her, though with more gentleness. 'Goodbye, dear. Give my love to your little boy.'

'I will. Please telephone when you have time, just to let me know ... if things are all right.'

'We will, of course, yes, we will. Goodbye, goodbye.'

And then they were gone.

Libby tidied the empty house before she left to fetch Fred from school. He was too occupied with tales of 'scientific experiments' with colouring water to notice that she was sad. They had a comfortable evening together with one or two of her house-cleaning staff and then he was off to bed.

Shortly after he went to bed Libby heard the downstairs doorbell. She went down to find out who was there and heard Philip's voice.

He came in looking troubled and rather anxious. 'Is it all right to drop in like this?'

'Of course, love. Any time.' She led the way upstairs. Over her shoulder she said, 'I thought you were in Spain?'

'I wanted to tell you...'

'Wait till we get to the living room. Come on, sit down. You look all in.'

She drew him down beside her on the couch. He looked down then said, 'I knew you disapproved of the way I reacted to Mama's going away. I was a real grouch about it, wasn't I?'

'We-ell...'

'I was determined not to be decent to them about it, not to wish them good luck when they went.'

'So you arranged to be abroad,' she suggested.

'Yes.'

'But here you are back again. You just missed them, Philip.'

'No.' He met her anxious gaze. 'No, I ... Last night I suddenly knew that I was being stupid, so I got an early-morning flight to Heathrow and then I went to the long-distance terminal and waited there for them.'

'Philip!'

'Idiotic, isn't it? Shows I haven't really grown up yet.'

'And did it turn out all right? Did you see them?'

'Yes, queuing up to go through security, loaded with baggage.' At last the faintest of smiles began to dawn on his face. 'So I queued up with them until they had to go through the departure gates. And we sort of talked.'

'Sort of?'

'I said I was sorry.'

'Oh, sweetheart,' she said, and took him in her arms.

Twenty-Two

Libby had asked Amy to meet her at Ashgrove to assess what needed to be done there, after the departure of Mrs Moorfield and her daughter. Philip came out of his office to greet them, although if truth be told, he'd parted with Libby only five hours earlier.

'Sounds empty, doesn't it?' he remarked. 'I suppose the sensible thing would be to put dust sheets over the stuff in the rooms that won't be used, and sort of forget about them.'

'And how many would that be?' inquired Amy, who wasn't entirely clued up about what had been happening.

'Well, everything upstairs except my room and

the bathroom.'

'Good lord! What a waste. Why don't you...?' She broke off.

'What?'

Amy was embarrassed. 'I was going to say, why don't you sell the place? But it's none of my business.'

He shrugged. 'I don't own the house. It belongs to my grandmother.'

'But I understood she'd left?' She didn't say, 'With Jake, our handyman,' but the words hung in the air.

'But could be back.' Philip glanced at Libby. 'Mrs Moorfield Senior isn't noted for her firmness of purpose.'

Libby understood what he meant only too well. Jake had felt confident he could deal with the temperamental outlook of his 'princess', but there was always the chance that she might quarrel with him and come flying home.

'Let's just tidy up and see how things look,' Libby suggested. 'We don't need to make big decisions here and now.' She led the way to the hall cupboard where the cleaning tools were kept. Philip went back into his office, and Amy made for the kitchen as a starting point.

In the aftermath of Angela and Rosanne's departure, the place was in a mess. Libby had cleared up behind them to some extent, but Angela had changed her mind about what to take several times, so her discarded clothes were over chair backs, on the hall stand, on the kitchen table, and on her bed. Rosanne had clearly had a plan to be helpful, so had collected all her knick-knacks in a woven reed basket, which she had then for some strange reason left in the larder.

'What's going to happen to all this stuff?' Amy demanded with irritation.

'My instructions were to take Angela's old clothes to a charity shop, and to sell this bric-a-brac of Mrs Moorfield's and give the proceeds to a Buddhist temple.'

'What a nerve! Why couldn't they do their own sorting out?'

'Well, you know they always were a difficult household...'

'And now they're all gone and left the only sensible one to cope with this great old barn of a place.'

'Let's get on,' Libby said. She wasn't eager to gossip about the situation.

As usual, Libby left in time to collect Fred from school. Amy was left to carry on with the chores. She reported the results at the usual Friday evening gathering in the office of House-care Helpers. 'I told Mr Moorfield that the best thing is to let out some of the rooms. The place needs to be lived in. We've all seen how leaving rooms empty leads to damp getting in unless you keep the heating on, and I just said to him, think of the expense – it would make more sense to have tenants even if it's only students.'

'Being your usual bossy self,' someone murmured. There was a general spurt of laughter.

'Well, somebody had to say it to him!' Amy retorted.

'But it would be difficult to organize the house so that it would work with tenants,' Britta said.

341

'What do you think, Libby?'

'I'm more interested in sorting out who's going to travel out to Hazeldene on Monday and clean up there—'

'Oh, the builders won't have finished. They never are!'

And to Libby's relief, the talk was diverted to problems other than those at Ashgrove.

On Saturday Libby had to take Fred to football practice. He had recently been chosen as centre half for Sutterley Junior School football team, an honour which now seemed to be the reason for his existence. Mothers and fathers were expected to support the team by turning up and cheering, even at practice, although Libby knew so little about the rules that she only cheered when the others did.

This took up all of Saturday morning, and then they went to buy new shoes for Fred. On Sunday she proposed they should go to Ashgrove so that she could do some work on the rocking-horse.

'Oh, I thought I'd go and play with Oliver. His dad has put up goalposts in their garden.'

'More football?'

'It's good,' he said. 'The more you play, the better you get.'

'But is it OK with Oliver's mum and dad?'

'Oh yes, his dad plays too; he said he'd give us a few pointers.' He nodded at the telephone. 'He said if you just give him a ring to say I'm coming, that'll be fine.'

She carried out this suggestion and was assured that Oliver's father was pleased to have Fred for the afternoon. She dropped him there on her way to Ashgrove. She longed to see Philip again, to be with him in the empty house so as to ease the sense of loneliness.

But she found the place deserted; his car was gone. Had he been summoned away by the needs of some film company? She was sighing over the fact that he hadn't been in touch to let her know when her mobile rang.

'I'm in Guildford,' he said. 'Where are you?'

'I'm at Ashgrove.'

'What are you doing there?'

'I was going to work a bit more on the rocking-horse.'

'Is Fred with you?'

'No, he's at a friend's house for the morning.'

'Come and join me in the town, treasure. We'll have a lovely long lunch somewhere.'

'What a good idea! Where exactly are you?'

'I'll be outside the Guildhall.'

'See you soon.'

She found him studying the window of a nearby bookshop. He turned at her voice and engulfed her in a bear hug. 'It's so good to see you,' he breathed.

She kissed him and drew back to study him. 'Something wrong?'

'The house was like a graveyard,' he confessed. 'I got up about six this morning and just tumbled into the car and went driving. I couldn't bear it.'

'You miss them?'

'No, of course not. I seldom saw much of them. Mama was often away on one of her enlightenment classes and as for Angela...' He

343

broke off. 'Yet the house seems lifeless without them.'

'Have you heard how they're getting on in Montreal?'

'There was a message on the machine – just to say everything was fine.'

'Why don't you ring them back, have a chat?'

He began to lead the way along the pavement. 'Let's find a place to eat. There's a good old restaurant somewhere around Bridge Street – how about that?'

The morning was cold but bright. The short walk to the restaurant was invigorating and they found they were hungry, so they took their time ordering the food.

'You know,' Libby began, 'Amy was talking about the house when we had our usual Friday evening session, and she said she advised you to let out some of the rooms.'

'So she did,' he agreed, with a somewhat rueful smile. 'Very forceful, isn't she?'

'You wouldn't want to do that?'

'It's not very appealing.'

'I suppose not.'

'I had what I thought was a better idea.'

'Oh yes?'

'I wondered if you would like to move in.'

'*What*?'

He threw up his hands in a gesture of appeal. 'I mean, with Fred, of course. Plenty of rooms to choose from. You could even have Grandee's suite, if you like.'

'No thank you. Grandee will come home from her travels one day, and what would she say to finding me in her domain?'

'I don't think she'll be back any time soon. She and Jake seem to be meandering through the southern United States. And from her latest message, they seem to be thinking of Peru next.'

'Peru?'

'To look at the Inca ruins.'

Laughing, Libby shook her head. 'That's Jake. He's got an old friend, a former shipmate, who runs an export business from Lima. He once sent Fred a model of the boats they use on some great big lake there because Jake had mentioned that Fred was interested.'

'So you do see that Grandee might be travelling for quite a long time yet. I mean, once they're in Peru, they might fancy a trip all across South America.'

'Just the same, I don't think she'd like it if I took over her rooms. So, no, thank you.'

'No thank you to the suite, or to the whole idea?'

She frowned at him. 'I can't do it, Philip. I've got a business to run.'

'You could run it just as well from Ashgrove.'

'Really? Do you think you'd enjoy having my work force coming and going, especially on Fridays when we do our planning sessions?'

'You could keep on your site in town...'

'Philip, be practical. Think of the expense of paying for two places—'

'Oh, I wasn't thinking of charging you anything—'

She sat back, in some indignation. 'I couldn't do that.'

'I don't see why not. People move in together and they don't charge each other rent, from what I gather.'

Now she couldn't help but smile. 'But this would be different...'

'How would it be different?'

'You said I could run the business from ... You mean you want me to ... What do you want?'

'I want us to live together.'

'Oh.'

'There are a lot of advantages,' he went on, in a manner that mixed seriousness and humour. 'I think Fred would like the house. He could get rides on the rocking-horse any time he wanted.'

'I think the rocking-horse has got a bit left behind. It's football now.'

'Plenty of room to play football on our lawn. He could invite the whole team.'

'But ... but ... I've never talked about anything like this with him.'

'You might try that before we take it any further, I suppose. But be sure to tell him about the space to play football.'

'That would be bribery.'

'Oh, I'm not high-minded. In fact, there was something else I was going to say, which I think is probably bribery too.'

'Such as what?'

'Well, aren't you the girl that said she really wanted a career in furniture restoring?'

'Ye-es. And?'

'I thought you could use Brent's studio. We could scrape all the black paint off the glass so that you'd have good daylight to work with, and

346

there's plenty of room. And if you look at it one way, you've already started with Pegasus.'

'But Pegasus isn't going to go on sale to the public.'

'No, that's true, but I was thinking, you know, you could use the big front drawing-room as a display area for the stuff you've restored, and you must admit that it would be a good address to put in your advertisements.'

She said nothing.

'Think about it.'

'I *am* thinking about it. I must admit it sounds great. But ... but if I were trying to build up a business doing restoration, I don't know how I could keep up with the work at Housecare Helpers.'

'You could put in a manager once you get the furniture repair thing going.'

'What?'

'Bossy Amy springs to mind.'

Their food arrived at this moment, so they fell silent as the waiter set dishes before them. 'Is there anything else you would like?' he inquired. She felt like saying, 'Yes, some advice on how to deal with this new idea!'

When they were alone again she studied Philip, half shaking her head in perplexity. 'You've really been thinking about this.'

'Yes. All night, practically.'

'You think I should offer Amy the job as manager?'

'She seems very capable,' he said with a faint grin, recalling the quick list of suggestions she'd offered for his empty house.

'Yes, she's excellent, as a matter of fact, except that she gets rather impatient with the clients sometimes.'

'You could keep an eye on her. You could be executive director and she could be manager. With a big raise in salary, of course. And that would work because once you get your own business going, you could take only a token salary from the house-cleaning.'

'But whether any of this happens depends on Fred.'

He let a long moment go by then said, 'Choose the right moment to tell him the idea. There's no hurry.' He added with a sigh, 'Although of course I really would like it if you came to live with me soon, Libby. And I think you would like it too.'

'Well, I must admit ... No, no, it would be too much of an upset in his life.'

'But you have a life too, Libby.'

'That's true. But ... Oh, don't let's talk about it any more. Let me just think about it for a while.'

'Think about it seriously,' he said, reaching across the table for her hand.

With the warmth of his clasp to urge his cause, she found herself nodding. 'I will, love. I will.'

Philip's plan never totally left her mind in the following days. It was always there, like some background music that quietly enforced its worth. She loved him. She wanted to be with him. She wanted to spend the rest of her life with him. That much was certain.

But could any of that outweigh her son's

happiness?

Fred had chosen the new shorter version of his name because he felt he was heading towards being a grown-up. Did that mean he was grown-up enough to accept a surrogate father?

He had seemed totally at ease with Philip during their trip to the Highlands. But day after day? In a new home?

She hesitated. A week went by. Saturday came, and Fred was going to football practice with the school junior team against the eleven-year-olds, known of course as Sutterley Seniors. Libby had to go with him and cheer them on.

'I'll come too,' Philip offered.

She stared. 'What? To a school football match?'

'Might be fun,' he said.

Fred was thrilled when he found Philip waiting outside their door with his splendid car on Saturday. He scrambled in ahead of his mother, allowed himself to be buckled in, and began an interrogation about the Audi's performance since the Highland holiday. How many miles now, what was the fuel consumption, was that the latest sat-nav system, and when would it next go for a test?

'Oh, I'll probably have replaced it by then.'

'What?'

'Every two years. I do a lot of driving, you see – all over the UK, looking at places where filming could be done.'

'But you don't take it when you go abroad, do you?'

'No, I generally have a car supplied by the

company.'

'What kind of car? Have you ever driven a Cadillac?'

'Yes, two or three times.'

'That's brilliant.' The mere idea caused him to fall silent.

Libby leaned forward. She said quietly into Philip's ear, 'This is enticement.'

He concentrated on his driving. She sat back, smiling.

The football game had its minor dramas. One boy had to have his knee bandaged, another was sent off for aggressive behaviour, but in the end the coach declared himself pleased with them and the two teams trotted off looking weary but delighted.

As he delivered Libby and her son to their door again, Philip said to Fred, 'How would you like to come over to my house tomorrow?'

Fred looked surprised. 'Your house? That's yours? *That* big old place where the little girl lives.'

'Prim – yes – she went to Tokyo.'

'Oh, Mum mentioned that.'

'You could bring your football. There's a big lawn at the back of the house.'

'Oh yes. But isn't there a canal too?'

'No danger of kicking the ball into the water – it's a pretty big lawn. And besides, the canal isn't very deep. We could fish the ball out if you landed a great big kick.'

Fred was looking at his mother for her opinion. 'You might take a look at the rocking-horse too,' she suggested. 'Or have you lost interest in that?'

'Oh yes ... Trojan ... No, you said his name was something funny.' He looked at Philip for a reminder.

'Pegasus – Peggy. But Trojan is better. Your mum has been doing some work on him; he's looking pretty good.'

'Would you like to go?' Libby asked.

'Well, I've got homework,' he sighed. 'I've got to find a specimen of shepherd's purse and take it to school for botany. But apart from that I haven't got anything special I was going to do.'

'I should think there would be plenty of shepherd's purse growing along the towpath at Ashgrove.'

Fred hesitated. 'Do you know what it looks like?'

'Sure. A little tough plant with a bunch of little white flowers. Grows in poor soil. My mama was keen on looking at everything that lived and grew in our surroundings.'

Fred was impressed. After another glance at his mother, who seemed to be saying nothing against it, he murmured, 'All right then, I'd like that, Phil.'

'Come in time for lunch.'

'OK.'

They said their goodbyes and Philip drove off. Fred said in a serious tone, 'He wants to be friends with us.'

'I think you're right.'

They went indoors, Fred bouncing the football on each of the treads on the way upstairs. 'Do you think he knows about football?' he asked.

'I'm afraid I don't know.'

'I bet he doesn't know as much as Oliver's dad. He knows everything.'

They went into the living room. It was a dull day. She switched on a lamp or two. A good smell of food was drifting from the kitchen. 'What would you like to drink with lunch? A hot drink or fruit juice?'

'Could I have tea please?'

'Run and wash your hands first.'

'OK.' He made for the door, then paused. 'Oliver's father is really a stepfather,' he said carefully. 'But he's nice, really.'

'Yes, he is.' She'd met him only once.

'I thought stepfathers were supposed to be horrible?'

'What makes you think that?'

'Well, in the stories – Snow White and Cinderella, you know – the stepmother's always horrible. You'd think stepfathers'd be the same.'

Libby sat down on the sofa and began to take off her outdoor shoes, as if they were having only a casual conversation. But she heard echoes of other conversations with her son, troubled about things he heard from school friends. And she sensed that he knew there was a relationship growing between his mother and Philip Moorfield. A potential stepfather.

She managed to smile at him, although she was shaken at the importance of his remark. 'Well, I wouldn't give too much importance to fairy stories. I mean, have you ever heard of anyone going to live with seven dwarves? Or driving to a ball in a coach drawn by mice?'

352

'We-ell ... No.'

'You can't depend on stories when it comes to real life. You know, in olden times, people in Greece used to think that when it thundered, it was somebody called Zeus throwing thunder-bolts from the skies. And now we know thunder is caused by...?'

'Static electricity in the clouds,' he repeated dutifully. There had been a time when Fred was scared by thunder and lightning.

'So you see, you shouldn't believe everything in the old tales. You have to use your own judgement.'

'I see.' He gave it a moment's thought. 'Judge-ment. Is that to do with being a judge?'

'Yes, but ordinary people have to make judge-ments all the time. Whether to wear a sweater or just a T-shirt. Even whether to have tea or orange juice.'

He laughed. 'Oh, that was easy!' He came back into the room to stand close at her side. 'You *are* funny, Mum. But I like that, you know.' He threw his arms around her, gave her a hug, and ran off.

She sat back in the sofa, feeling somehow drained and yet relieved. A difficult moment had passed. A question had been asked and answer-ed. What might come next, she didn't know.

The following day Fred put some necessities in his backpack to take with him on this outing – his football, his camera to photograph shep-herd's purse in its habitat, and a notebook to write down anything else he might glean about plants from Philip.

'Botany's very important,' he told his mother. 'Mr Watson says knowing about growing things will help us to grow food where there are a lot of people.'

'But I don't think many people eat shepherd's purse,' Libby said.

He grinned. 'Ha!'

At Ashgrove, Libby was touched to find plant pots on either side of the door, bright with early tulips. It had been her initial thought on seeing the house for the first time that it would look a hundred times more welcoming with something colourful growing there.

Fred looked around in uncertainty when they went in. He had been here in daylight quite recently but she thought he had vague memories of being there overnight when Prim went missing.

'Why don't you have a look around?' Philip invited. 'If you go through to the back, there's a door leading out to the garden and the garages.'

He looked to his mother for permission. 'Go ahead,' she said, with a little nod and a frown, meaning, 'No tampering with keys to the cars.'

Off he went. Philip said, 'I ordered food from the caterers. It'll be here any time now. Does Fred like stewed steak?'

'Oh, I thought I would be doing the cooking...'

'No, no, you're a guest today.' He surveyed her. She was wearing her best jeans and a blue silk shirt. 'You look lovely. No aprons to spoil it, please.'

He led her into the drawing-room. Music was playing softly from the sound system. There were fresh flowers in all the vases. The fire was burning brightly in the great old tiled fireplace. There was welcome in every aspect of the room.

'Oh, it looks lovely,' she exclaimed.

'Think you could live with it?'

'Now, sweetheart, please...'

'All right.'

Fred came racing in, breathing hard. 'I went down to the hedge to look at the canal. *A boat went by!*'

'Oh yes. That happens occasionally. It isn't a main stream, of course, just an off-shoot.'

'*You* could have a boat!'

'What, you mean a narrow boat? No, no, that's too big a project, I'm afraid. I'm away a lot; I wouldn't have time to look after it.'

Fred looked as if he was on the verge of saying, 'I could look after it.' But he managed to check the words.

'Of course,' Philip went on, 'a skiff, now that would be an easier thing to deal with.'

'A skiff? What's a skiff?'

'It's a little shallow thing I used to row for my college at university.'

'Did you?' Fred was tremendously impressed. He waited for more.

'Yes, you see, it was the only thing I was good at. Because I went to various different schools, and some of them didn't agree with team games like football or rugby. So I was a bit of a dead loss except at things you could do on your own.'

'Like rowing a skiff. So that's for only one, then.'

'But a rowing-boat would be better. You could

355

have two or more people in a rowing-boat.'

'Oh yes. Much better.'

'It might be worth thinking about. There's a firm at New Haw that sells them, I believe.'

'It would be good in summer,' Fred suggested. 'You could go for picnics in it.'

'So you could. I must take a look one day at what's available.'

The conversation was interrupted by the bell at the back door. The food had arrived, and not a moment too soon, in Libby's opinion, for her son had been on the verge of asking to go with Philip to look at boats.

Philip had made good choices to suit a hungry boy – asparagus rolled in ham to start with, which Fred immediately christened 'snails in blankets', followed by the hearty stew. They ate in the kitchen; Libby guessed that Philip had seen the old dining room as a little too overwhelming for a boy of seven.

The pudding had to be ice cream, naturally. Fred inspected the contents of the Ashgrove freezer and opted for one scoop of walnut and one of chocolate. 'Did you buy this from the special shop in the High Street?' he inquired as he tucked into it.

'No, I send in an order to a firm that delivers to the house. I don't do much shopping. I'm away a lot, you see.'

'Ah.' There was disappointment in his voice but he soon brightened. 'Perhaps you could tell Mum which firm it was so she could buy it?'

'Now that's enough of that,' scolded Libby. 'We've already got four different flavours in our freezer.'

'Yes, of course, sorry.'

Libby was busy making coffee for her and Philip. She hid a smile, for it was easy to see that Fred was finding Ashgrove very attractive.

After lunch came football. 'I'm not really completely sure of the rules,' Philip explained as Fred urged him out to the lawn. 'You'll have to explain them to me.'

'Oh, that's all right,' came the tolerant reply.

And his mother found it hard not to chuckle out loud. What could be more gratifying to a small boy than to teach a grown-up?

The day went well. As they drove home in the twilight, Fred chatted eagerly about what had happened. Libby listened, throwing in occasional cautions. For instance, there was no guarantee that Philip would take Fred with him when he went looking at rowing-boats.

Philip telephoned after Fred had gone to bed. 'Do you think it went OK?'

'You don't need to ask!'

'He's a great kid. You've done well with him, angel.'

She was silent.

'You're wondering if it will be a lot more difficult when we're together.'

'N-no...'

'Of course you are.'

'I can't help being ... sort of nervous. But I've always felt that Fred needs a father – or would feel the lack of one, when he gets a little bit older. So of course I want ... I'm hoping that...'

Her voice failed her. She felt a sob rising in her

357

throat.

'Don't be anxious, love. Let things take their course and we'll see what comes of it.'

'Yes.'

'So, goodnight. I have to be up at crack of dawn to fly to Egypt.'

'Egypt!'

'Nearby desert and dry climate – the company wants to film in what's supposed to be the middle of the desert, to advertise skin moisturizer. I'll be back by Thursday, I think.'

They said goodbye. She went to bed in a strange mood, comforted that she had been speaking to him but feeling at a loss because he was going away.

There was a big problem on Monday morning when Norman, the outdoors-man, failed to turn up. He was supposed to go to a tennis club to help get the courts ready for a set of charity matches. Amy shrugged in irritation but solved the problem herself.

'I'll get my nephew to go,' she announced.

'Your nephew? Isn't he still at college?'

'No, he's back with my sister for a few days – he's been given some time to do some special reading, but he'd be glad of the money. So shall I ring him?'

'Does he know anything about tennis courts?'

'Well, he can sweep the leaves off and put up nets, I'm pretty sure of that.'

'Right-o then, let's see what he says.'

The nephew was quite pleased to come to their rescue. 'That was great, Amy,' Libby told her.

And then, after a pause, 'Have you ever thought you'd like to take the work a bit further?'

'Further? Where to, for goodness' sake?'

'Well, have you ever thought you'd like to take charge of some of it?'

'What, here?'

'Yes.'

'Take charge of what?'

'Umm ... Sort out the work schedules, do some of the office stuff.'

'Paperwork? Accounts? No thank you.'

'But you're good at organizing.'

'But not forms and bills. I'm no good at arithmetic.'

'It's not all forms and bills. You have to talk to clients, keep the advertising up to date, order supplies, and of course handle the staff.'

Amy's pencilled eyebrows drew together. 'What's all this?' she demanded. 'Are you thinking of giving up?'

'No. At least, not in the near future. But I *am* thinking of ... Well, you know I always wanted to make a career in restoring furniture?'

'Oh yes. That lovely *chaise longue* – I remember you did well with that.'

'There could be a chance to do that on a bigger scale. So I wouldn't be able to give my whole attention to Housecare Helpers, and it seems to me that you'd be an ideal person to take over some of the work. But only if you feel you'd like it.'

Amy gave this some thought. 'What would I be? The staff organizer? Supervisor?'

'Well, I thought manager.'

'Manager of the whole shebang?'

'Most of it. Not the accounting, if you don't want to.' She paused. 'We could think about it, and see what might work.'

Amy stood with a perplexed expression. 'Well, I ... I'm surprised. I never imagined you'd suggest a thing like that.'

'Would you give it some consideration?'

'I suppose so. But ... wait a bit. You couldn't hardly do furniture restoration on a proper business basis up in your flat?'

'No,' Libby said, with an inward smile. 'But I have a place in mind.'

On Tuesday afternoon, Fred had a request to make. 'Instead of going straight home, could we please go to the bookshop in the town?'

'Of course, love. Is it something to do with school?' She knew study books might be too expensive for him to buy with his pocket money.

'No, it's for Phil. I want to buy a book about the rules of football. Will you lend me the money? I've seen a copy that Mr Maloney uses, and it costs one pound fifty.'

Mr Maloney was the teacher who looked after sports. Libby was delighted at what she'd just heard, but she thought she ought to sound money-wise and motherly. 'Was it a recent book? Because it may have gone up.'

Fred of course had no idea of the publication date. 'But I don't think it can be very expensive, Mum. It's a paperback, and not very thick.'

'All right, let's see if the shop has it in stock.' This turned out to be a simple task. The shop had various versions of the subject, some with pictures and therefore expensive, and some with rules and diagrams. Fred lingered over those with pictures. 'I wish these weren't so expensive. I'd like to give Phil something nice.'

'I don't think he'd know who some of those players are, Fred, if he doesn't know much about football.'

'Oh. That's true. So it would be all right to give him the plain book?'

'I think he'd be very pleased.'

When she thought it over, it seemed to her a very good omen. Little boys don't generally want to buy presents for people they don't care about.

Philip arrived home at Ashgrove on Thursday afternoon when Libby was there with Britta helping with a reduction of the larder's contents. Hearing voices, he came to announce himself. 'What are you doing?' he asked in surprise.

'Philip, don't you ever check the dates on packets? Those' – she nodded at the contents of a cardboard carton – 'are well past their sell-by date.'

'Really? There's a date on the packet?'

She and Britta exchanged a tolerant glance. Britta shrugged and went out with the out-of-date goods to the dustbins.

'Libby, if you're just going off to collect Fred, could you wait a minute while I get something out of the boot of my car? I brought him a present from Egypt.'

'Oh, how nice of you. Well...' She broke off in thought. 'It would really be better if you came to the flat later. Come to tea.'

'I'd love to.' He gave her a quick kiss on the cheek then retired to his office to catch up with his messages. She had no chance to speak to him by the time she left for Fred's school.

Libby brought a home-made cake out of its tin as soon as she and Fred got home. 'Oh, goody! Can I have a piece?' he cried.

'Yes, you can, because Philip is coming to tea.'

'No! Well, that's great, because I can give him the rule book!' He was elated at the idea. He dashed to his room to get the book, then was heard calling from the living room that he wanted a piece of nice wrapping paper for it.

The exchange of presents was a great occasion. Philip had brought a model of a felucca, a Nile boat of ancient design, handmade and bought in a market in Alexandria. Fred could hardly bear to handle it; it was so delicately constructed, with three slender masts.

'Oh, that's great! What a lovely colour on the hull – and look at the sails!' He gently pulled a thread. One of the sails grew up into a sharp triangle. 'Look, look – that's a jib sail! It works just like real life.'

Philip was just as pleased with his book, although he had to hide a smile when it was first unwrapped. 'Just what I need,' he enthused. 'I'll take it with me for plane journeys and things.'

'Next time you come to my practice match, you'll know about offside,' Fred suggested.

'Yes, I'll make sure to read it up.'

When it was time for bed, the little boy went out of the room holding his boat in careful hands. Libby went in a little later to say good-night, and saw it given pride of place on the window-sill with the rest of his collection.

'Goodnight, sweet dreams,' Libby said, with her usual kiss on the cheek.

'Goodnight, Mum. Say goodnight to Phil for me.'

'I will.'

'He's nice,' he said sleepily, turning on his side so he could see his boats first thing in the morning when he woke.

Libby went out quietly. Philip had put their dishes in the dishwasher and was sweeping crumbs off the table into his hand. 'Where do I put these?'

She took his hand, emptied the crumbs into her own, and dropped them into the sink without letting go of his.

He used it to draw her towards him. 'That went well, do you think?'

'It was marvellous. Stop worrying about it, Philip. He's getting very fond of you.'

He held her close. 'So ... Do you think things are going to work out for us?'

'I think they might, sweetheart,' she said, leaning against him so that her cheek was touching his. 'I really think they might.'

Some day. Let it be soon, she thought. And let it last a long time ... All our lives, perhaps.